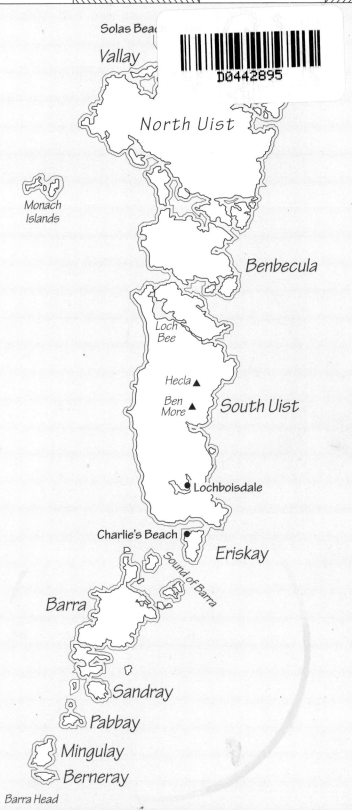

Solas Beach

Vallay

North Uist

Monach
Islands

Benbecula

Loch
Bee

Hecla ▲

Ben
More ▲

South Uist

● Lochboisdale

Charlie's Beach ●

Eriskay

Sound of Barra

Barra

Sandray

Pabbay

Mingulay

Berneray

Barra Head

# THE
# CHESS
# MEN

Also by Peter May

*The Blackhouse*
*The Lewis Man*

# PETER MAY
## THE
# CHESS
# MEN

Quercus

First published in Great Britain in 2013 by

Quercus
55 Baker Street
7th Floor, South Block
London
W1U 8EW

A CIP catalogue reference for this book is available
from the British Library

ISBN 978 0 85738 223 8 (HB)
ISBN 978 0 85738 224 5 (TPB)
ISBN 978 0 85738 218 4 (EBOOK)

10 9 8 7 6 5 4 3

Typeset by Ellipsis Digital Limited, Glasgow

Printed and bound in Great Britain by Clays Ltd, St Ives plc

In loving memory of wee Jennifer

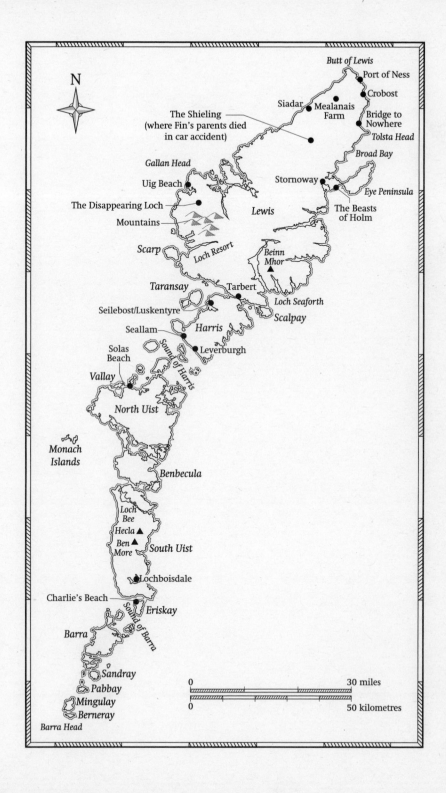

'Tis all a Chequer-board of Nights and Days
Where Destiny with Men for Pieces plays:
Hither and thither moves, and mates, and slays,
And one by one back in the Closet lays.

– *The Rubaiyat of Omar Khayyam*, xlix

# PROLOGUE

*He sits at his desk, grey with fear and the weight of this momentous step which, once taken, cannot be taken back. Like time and death.*

*The pen trembles in his hand as he writes.*

This has been on my mind for some time. I know most people will not understand why, especially those who love me, and whom I also love. All I can say is that no one knows the hell I have lived through. And these last weeks it has become, simply, unbearable. It is time for me to go. I am so sorry.

*He signs his name. The usual flamboyant scrawl. Illegible. And folds the note, as if in hiding the words he can somehow make them go away. Like a bad dream. Like the step he is about to take into darkness.*

*He rises now, and looks around his room for the last time, wondering if he really has the courage to go through with it. Should he leave the note or should he not? Will it really make any difference? He glances at it, fallen open now, and propped against the computer screen where he hopes it will be obvious. The pain of* regret fills his heart as his eye follows the looping letters he learned to write all those years before when his whole life still lay ahead of him. A bittersweet recollection of innocence and youth. The smell of chalk dust and warm school milk.

How pointless it all has been!

# CHAPTER ONE

When Fin opened his eyes the interior of the ancient stone dwelling which had sheltered them from the storm was suffused with a strange pink light. Smoke drifted lazily into the still air from the almost dead fire and Whistler was gone.

Fin raised himself up on to his elbows and saw that the stone at the entrance had been rolled aside. Beyond it he could see the rose-tinted mist of dawn that hung over the mountains. The storm had passed. Its rain had fallen, and it had left in its wake an unnatural stillness.

Painfully, Fin unravelled himself from his blankets and crawled past the fire to where his clothes were spread out across the stone. There was a touch of damp in them still, but they were dry enough to put on again, and he lay on his back and wriggled into his trousers before sitting up to button his shirt and drag his jumper over his head. He pulled on his socks and pushed his feet into his boots, then crawled out on to the mountainside without bothering to lace them up.

The sight that greeted him was almost supernatural. The mountains of south-west Lewis rose up steeply all around, disappearing into an obscurity of low clouds. The valley below seemed wider than it had by the lightning of the night before. The giant shards of rock that littered its floor grew like spectres out of a mist that rolled up from the east, where a not yet visible sun cast an unnaturally red glow. It felt like the dawn of time.

Whistler stood silhouetted against the light beyond the collection of broken shelters they called beehives, on a ridge that looked out over the valley, and Fin stumbled over sodden ground with shaking legs to join him.

Whistler neither turned nor acknowledged him. He just stood like a statue frozen in space and time. Fin was shocked by his face, drained as it was of all colour. His beard looked like black and silver paint scraped on to white canvas. His eyes dark and impenetrable, lost in shadow.

'What is it, Whistler?'

But Whistler said nothing, and Fin turned to see what he was staring at. At first, the sight that greeted him in the valley simply filled him with confusion. He understood all that he saw, and yet it made no sense. He turned and looked back beyond the beehives to the jumble of rock above them, and the scree slope that rose up to the shoulder of the mountain where he had stood the night before and seen lightning reflected on the loch below.

Then he turned back to the valley. But there was no loch. Just a big empty hole. Its outline was clearly visible where, over eons, it had eaten away at the peat and the rock. Judging by the depression it had left in the land, it had been perhaps a mile long, half a mile across, and fifty or sixty feet deep.

Its bed was a thick slurry of peat and slime peppered by boulders large and small. At its east end, where the valley fell away into the dawn mist, a wide brown channel, forty or fifty feet across, was smeared through the peat, like the trail left by some giant slug.

Fin glanced at Whistler. 'What happened to the loch?'

But Whistler just shrugged and shook his head. 'It's gone.'

'How can a loch just disappear?'

For a long time Whistler continued to stare out over the empty loch like a man in a trance. Until suddenly, as if Fin had only now spoken, he said, 'Something like it happened a long time ago, Fin. Before you or I were born. Sometime back in the fifties. Over at Morsgail.'

'I don't understand. What do you mean?' Fin was filled with confusion.

'Same thing. Postie used to pass a loch on the track between Morsgail and Kinlochresort every morning. Way out in the middle of bloody nowhere, it was. Loch nan Learga. So one morning, he's coming down the track as usual, and there's no loch. Just a big hole where it used to be. I've passed it many times myself. Caused a hell of a stir back then, though. The newspaper and television people came all the way up from London. And the things they speculated on . . . well, they seem crazy now, but they filled the airwaves and the column inches of the papers at the time. The favourite was that the loch had been hit by a meteor and evaporated.'

'And what *had* happened?'

Whistler lifted his shoulders then dropped them again. 'Best theory is that it was a bog burst.'

'Which is what?'

Whistler made a moue with his lips, his eyes still drawn to the slime-filled basin of the disappeared loch. 'Well . . . it can happen when you get a long spell without rain. Not very common here.' He nearly smiled. 'The surface peat dries up and cracks. And as any peat-cutter knows, once it's dry the peat becomes impervious to water.' He nodded towards where the giant slug trail led off into the mist. 'There's another loch down there, lower in the valley. If I had any money, I'd put it on this one having drained down into the other.'

'How?'

'Most of these lochs sit on peat lying over Lewisian gneiss. Quite often they're separated by ridges of something less stable, like amphibolite. When the dry spell is followed by heavy rain, like last night, the rainwater runs through the cracks in the peat creating a layer of sludge above the bedrock. Chances are that what happened here is that the peat between the lochs simply slid away on the sludge, the weight of the water in the upper loch burst through the amphibolite, and the whole bloody lot drained down the valley.'

There was a stirring of air as the sun edged a little higher, and the mist lifted just a touch. Enough to reveal something white and red catching the light at what must have been the deepest part of the loch.

'What the hell's that?' Fin said, and when Whistler made no reply, 'Do you have binoculars?'

'In my rucksack.' Whistler's voice was little more than a breath.

Fin hurried back to their beehive and crawled inside to find Whistler's binoculars. When he got out to the ridge again, Whistler hadn't moved. He continued to stare impassively at the hole where the loch had once been. Fin raised the binoculars to his eyes and adjusted the lenses until the red-and-white object came clearly into focus. 'Jesus!' he heard himself whisper, quite involuntarily.

It was a small, single-engined aircraft, cradled among a cluster of boulders, and lying at a slight angle. It appeared to be pretty much intact. The windows of the cockpit were opaque with mud and slime, but the red and white of the fuselage was clearly visible. As were the black-painted letters of its call-sign.

G-RUAI.

Fin felt every hair on the back of his neck stand up. RUAI, short for Ruairidh, the Gaelic for Roderick. A call-sign which had been in every newspaper for weeks seventeen years before, when the plane went missing, and Roddy Mackenzie with it.

Mist lifted off the mountains like smoke, tinted by the dawn. It was perfectly still. Not a sound broke the silence. Not even a birdcall. Fin lowered Whistler's binoculars. 'You know whose plane that is?'

Whistler nodded.

'What the hell's it doing here, Whistler? They said he filed a flight plan for Mull and disappeared somewhere out at sea.'

Whistler shrugged, but made no comment.

Fin said, 'I'm going down to take a look.'

Whistler caught his arm. There was an odd look in his eyes. If Fin hadn't known better he would have said it was fear. 'We shouldn't.'

'Why?'

'Because it's none of our business, Fin.' He sighed. A long, grim breath of resignation. 'I suppose we'll have to report it, but we shouldn't get involved.'

Fin looked at him hard and long, but decided not to ask. He pulled his arm free of Whistler's grasp and said again, 'I'm going down to take a look. You can come with me or not.' He thrust the binoculars back into Whistler's hands and started off down the hill towards the empty basin.

The descent was steep and difficult, over broken rock and hardened peat made slick by grasses washed flat by the rain. Boulders lined the banks of what had once been the loch, and Fin slithered over them, struggling to keep his feet and his balance, using his arms to stop himself falling. Down, down into the bowels of the one-time loch, wading through mud and slime, up to his knees at times, between rocks he used like stepping stones to cross the vast depression.

He had almost reached the plane before he turned to look back and see Whistler following just a few yards behind. Whistler stopped, breathing heavily, and the two men stood looking at each other for almost a full minute. Then Fin glanced beyond him, up through layers of peat and stone like the contour lines on an ordnance survey map, towards what just twelve hours before had been the shoreline. Had the loch still been there, the two men would have been fifty feet underwater by now. He turned to cover the remaining yards to the plane.

It was canted at the slightest of angles amid the shambles of rock and stone at the bottom of the loch, almost as if it had been placed there by the delicate hand of God. Fin was aware of Whistler's breathing at his side. He said, 'You know what's weird?'

'What?' Whistler didn't really sound as if he wanted to know.

'I can't see any damage.'

'So?'

'Well, if the plane had crashed into the loch it would be pretty smashed up, right?'

Whistler made no comment.

'I mean look at it. There's barely a dent on it. All the windows are intact. The windscreen's not even broken.'

Fin clambered over the last few rocks and pulled himself, slithering, up on to the nearest wing. 'Not much rust in evidence either. I guess it must be mostly aluminium.' He didn't trust himself to stand on the treacherously slippery surface of the wing, and crawled on his hands and knees towards the nearside cockpit door. The window was thick with green slime and it was impossible to see inside. He grasped the handle and tried to pull it open. It wouldn't budge.

'Leave it, Fin,' Whistler called to him from down below.

But Fin was determined. 'Come up here and give me a hand.'

Whistler didn't move.

'For Christ's sake, man, it's Roddy in there!'

'I don't want to see him, Fin. It would be like desecrating a grave.'

Fin shook his head and turned back to the door, bracing his feet against the fuselage on either side and pulling with all his strength. Suddenly it gave, with a loud rending like the sound of tearing metal, and Fin fell backwards on to the wing. Daylight flooded the interior of the cockpit for the first time in seventeen years. Fin scrambled back to his knees and grabbed the frame of the door to pull himself up to see inside. He heard Whistler hoisting himself on to the wing behind him, but didn't turn. The sight that greeted him was shocking, his olfactory senses assailed by a stink like rotting fish.

The fascia below the windscreen arched across the cockpit, a mass of gauges and dials, glass smeared and muddied, interior faces discoloured by water and algae. The passenger or co-pilot's seat, at the nearside, was empty. The red, black and blue knobs of the throttle controls between the seats were still visible, drawn back to their idle position. The remains of a man were strapped into the pilot's seat at the far side. Time and water and bacteria had eaten away all the flesh, and the only thing holding the skeleton together were the blanched remains of tendons and tough ligaments that had not decayed in the cold-water temperatures. His leather jacket was more or less intact. His jeans, though bleached of colour, had also survived. His trainers, too, although Fin could see that the rubber was swollen, distending the shoes around what was left of the feet.

The larynx, ears and nose had all lost their structure, and the skull was plainly visible, a few strands of hair clinging to the remnants of soft tissue.

All of which was shocking enough to the two old friends who remembered the young, talented, restless Roddy with his shock of fair curly hair. But what disturbed them most was the terrible damage inflicted to the right side of the face and rear of the skull. Half the jaw appeared to be missing, exposing a row of yellowed broken teeth. The cheekbone and upper part of the skull were smashed beyond recognition.

'Jesus Christ.' Whistler's voice came to Fin in a blasphemous breath.

It had only taken a moment to absorb the scene exposed by the opening of the door, and Fin recoiled involuntarily almost at once, banging the back of his head against Whistler's shoulder. He slammed the door shut and turned around to slide down into a sitting position against it. Whistler crouched on his hunkers looking at him with wide eyes.

'You're right,' Fin said. 'We shouldn't have opened it.' He looked at Whistler's face, so pale that pockmarks Fin had never before noticed were visible now, the result perhaps of some bout of childhood chickenpox. 'But not because we're desecrating a grave, Whistler.'

Whistler frowned. 'Why then?'

'Because we're disturbing a crime scene.'

Whistler gazed at him for several long moments, dark eyes obscured by confusion, before he turned to slither down off the wing and make his way back towards the shoreline, climbing steadily out of the crater and back up towards the beehives.

'Whistler!' Fin called after him, but the big man didn't even break stride and never looked back.

# CHAPTER TWO

Fin sat in Gunn's office, looking at the shambles of paper-work gathered like drifting snow on the detective sergeant's desk. The occasional car rumbled past outside in Church Street, and even from this distance he could hear the gulls circling the trawlers in the harbour. Bleak, harled houses with steeply pitched roofs filled the view from the window, and he stood up and crossed to it to widen his field of vision. Macleod & Macleod the butcher, no relative. The Blythswood Care charity shop on the corner, with its handwritten notice in the window, *We do not accept any left over goods from sales of work*. The Bangla Spice Indian restaurant, and the Thai Café. Folk a long way from home.

Life went on for others as if nothing had happened. And yet for Fin, the discovery of Roddy's remains in the aeroplane at the bottom of the loch had turned all of his memories on their head, altering for ever his recollection of history, and the way things had been.

'A bog burst seems about right. Your friend Whistler knows his stuff.'

Fin turned as Gunn walked in clutching a sheaf of papers. His round face was shaven to a shine below a dark widow's peak, pink skin splashed with an astringent and powerfully perfumed aftershave. Fin said, 'There's not much that Whistler doesn't know.' And he wondered what it was Whistler knew that he wasn't telling.

'There's the disappearing loch down at Morsgail right enough. And apparently there were a couple of large bog bursts in the early nineties on steep north-facing slopes on Barra and Vatersay. So it's not unknown.' He dropped his papers on to his desk, like a further snowfall, and sighed. 'Not much luck with the deceased's family, though.'

Fin wasn't quite sure why, but the reference to Roddy as *the deceased* was almost painful. And yet he had been dead for seventeen years. The most talented and successful Celtic rock star of his generation, cut down in his prime.

'Father died five years ago, his mother last year in a geriatric unit in Inverness. No brothers or sisters. I suppose there must be distant relatives somewhere, because it seems the house at Uig was sold off by the estate. Might take a while to track them down.' Gunn ran a hand back through his darkly oiled hair, then unconsciously wiped it on the leg of his trousers. 'Your pal Professor Wilson is boarding a flight from Edinburgh as we speak.'

'Angus?'

Gunn nodded. He had unhappy memories of his one encounter with the acerbic pathologist. 'He's going to want to examine the body *in situ*, and we'll get the whole scene photographed.' He rubbed his chin thoughtfully. 'It's going to be in all the papers, Mr Macleod. Bloody press'll be flying in like vultures. Aye, and the brass, too. From Inverness. Wouldn't surprise me if it was the high heid yins themselves. They just love to stand in front of the cameras and see their well-fed faces on the telly.' He paused, then, before turning to push the door shut. 'Tell me, Mr Macleod. What makes you think that Roddy Mackenzie was murdered?'

'I'd rather not say, George. I don't want to prejudice your interpretation of the scene. I think it's an assessment you should make for yourself.'

'Fair enough.' Gunn dropped into his chair and swivelled around so that he was facing Fin. 'What the hell were you and Whistler Macaskill doing up in the mountains in a storm anyway, Mr Macleod?'

'It's a long story, George.'

Gun raised his arms to interlock his fingers behind his head. 'Well, we've got time to kill before the pathologist's plane arrives . . .' He let his sentence hang. Fin's cue. And Fin realized it was only a couple of days since he and Whistler had been reunited for the first time in half a lifetime. Already it seemed like an eternity.

# CHAPTER THREE

## I

It had been an Indian summer, the long, hot dry spell stretching well into September, a rare phenomenon on this most northerly island of the Outer Hebrides. The furthest north and west you could go in Europe, the Isle of Lewis was burned brown by months of summer sun and unaccustomed weeks without rain. And still the weather was holding.

It had taken Fin nearly two hours to drive from Ness down the west coast to Uig that day. From as far north as Siadar, Fin had seen the mountains rising out of the south-west towards Harris, a dark brooding purple cut against the palest of blue skies. It was the only point on any horizon where the clouds still lingered. Not threatening but just there, drifting among the peaks. The yellow bloom of wild tormentil grew among the bracken, lending a hint of gold to a landscape in which even the heather was bleached of colour. The tiny petals dipped and bowed in the stiffening breeze that blew in off the ocean, carrying with it the smell of the sea and a distant whiff of winter.

On this first day of his new life, Fin reflected on just how much it had changed in little more than eighteen months. Back then he had been married, with a son, a life in Edinburgh, a job as a detective in 'A' Division CID. Now he had none of those things. He had come back to the womb, the island of his birth, but he wasn't sure why. In search of who he had once been, perhaps. The only thing he knew for certain was that the change was irrevocable, and had begun the day a driver took the life of his little boy in an Edinburgh street and failed to stop.

As he rounded the head of Loch Ròg Beag, Fin turned his mud-spattered Suzuki four-by-four off the single-track road on to a broken metalled path without passing places. Past a clutch of Highland cattle with their long, curling horns and shaggy brown coats, to follow the river upstream towards a puddle of a loch where, unusually, trees grew in the shelter of a fold of hills, and Suaineabhal Lodge stood in the shadow of their protection.

It was a long while since Fin had seen Kenny John Maclean. Big Kenny had left the island with the rest of them. But his life had taken an altogether different course. He lived now in an old crofthouse that had been extended and modernized, and sat on the far side of the path opposite the lodge. A rabble of dogs came barking out of a tin-roofed barn as Fin pulled up in the parking area. The lodge itself was based upon an old farmhouse, and when Sir John Wooldridge had first bought the Red River Estate he had built out side and back, and appended a conservatory at the front that looked out over the loch. Unlike Cracabhal Lodge at the head of

Loch Tamnabhaigh, which could accommodate more than twenty during the shooting and fishing seasons, Suaineabhal had only a handful of bedrooms and was reserved exclusively for fishermen. But it had a public bar, and at this time of year was filled every night with fishermen and ghillies, and locals out for a pint and a dram.

This morning there was not a soul around, until Kenny came striding up to the gate from the loch side and shouted the dogs to silent obedience. Cowed by the reprimand of their pack leader, they contented themselves with snuffling about Fin in quiet curiosity, breathing in his strange scents, sunlight falling around them in dappled patches like rain. Kenny wore green Hunter wellies over khaki breeks, and a multi-pocketed waistcoat over a military green woollen jumper with shoulder and elbow patches. As he approached, he whipped off his flat cap to reveal a cropped fuzz of ginger hair that was losing its colour, and held out a big callused hand to shake Fin's warmly.

'It's been a helluva long time, Fin.' Although most of his day would be conducted in English, with Fin he reverted to Gaelic without thinking. It was the language of their childhood, the first language that would spring naturally to both their tongues.

'It's good to see you, Kenny,' Fin said, and meant it.

They stood looking at each other for a moment, assessing the changes that the years had wrought. The two-inch scar that followed the line of Kenny's left cheekbone, the result of some childhood accident which had nearly taken his eye, had faded with time. Kenny had always been a big lad, bigger than Fin. Now he was enormous, filled out in every direction. He appeared older than Fin, too. But, then, he had always been an old-fashioned boy, rough-hewn from country stock and not very sophisticated. Bright enough, though, to go to agricultural college in Inverness and return to the island eventually to manage the estate on which he had grown up.

Fin, although not a small man, had retained his boyish figure, and his tightly curled fair hair still grew abundantly, green eyes fixing on the hidden wariness he saw in the darker gaze of his old schoolfriend.

'I hear you're back with Marsaili. Living with her, I'm told.'

Fin nodded. 'At least until I finish restoring my parents' crofthouse.'

'And her boy's yours they say, not Artair's.'

'Do they?'

'It's what I hear.'

'You hear a lot, it seems.'

Kenny grinned. 'I keep my ear to the ground.'

Fin returned the smile. 'Be careful, Kenny. You might get mud in it. Then maybe you wouldn't hear so good.'

Kenny snorted. 'You always were a smart bugger, Macleod.' He hesitated for a moment as his smile washed away, like sunshine passing behind a cloud. 'I hear you lost a son, too.'

The colour rose very slightly around Fin's eyes, darkening them. 'You heard right.' Followed by a long pause in which it was clear he was not about to elucidate.

The end of this personal nature of their exchange was signalled by the replacement of Kenny's cap, which he pulled down low over his brow. Even his tone of voice changed. 'I'll need to brief you on your duties. I imagine Jamie will have covered the bullet points. But like most landowners, he doesn't know much about the land.'

Fin didn't miss the point. Jamie might be his boss, but Kenny considered himself his superior. And now he was Fin's boss, and their brief exchange as equals was over.

'I'm not sure I would have taken you on as head of security myself. No offence, Fin. I'm sure you were a good cop, but not so sure that it qualifies you to catch poachers. Still . . . ours not to reason why, eh?'

Fin said, 'Maybe you could do a better job of it yourself.'

'No "could" about it, Fin. But managing an estate of more than fifty thousand acres, with extensive salmon, brown trout and sea trout fishing, as well as stalking and shooting, takes up all my time as it is.' He sounded like a brochure for the estate. 'And it's no small problem we have.'

## II

Kenny's Range Rover bounced and rattled over the potholed track, following the course of the river, the ground rising up ever more steeply around them. Bare, rugged hills peppered with rock and slashed by gullies rose up into mountainous peaks lost in cloud. Boulders clung to the hillsides, great chunks of gneiss four billion years old. Kenny glanced at Fin and followed his eyes. 'Oldest rock in the world,' he said. 'Those slabs of it have been lying around these hills since the last ice age.' He pointed up into the shadow of the mountain on their left. 'You see those watercourses running through the rock? Originally cracks in the face of it, they were. And when the water in them froze the ice expanded till the rock exploded, and threw these massive big fucking lumps of it all over the valley. Must have been quite a show. But I'm glad I wasn't around for it.'

Ahead of them a small loch reflected the cut-glass blue of the sky overhead, its surface ridged by the wind, and Kenny drew in beside a green-painted corrugated-iron shed that he called a lunch hut. A place where fishermen and their ghillies could shelter from the weather to eat their sandwiches. The vehicle track ended here. A footpath led down to the water while another wound its way up over the hill, climbing steeply through clusters of rock and fording clear-watered streams that would normally be in spate at this time of year. After weeks of drought most had been reduced to a mere trickle.

Kenny was fit for such a big man, and Fin fought to keep up with him as he strode quickly along the rising path. The track snaked between the cleft of the hills, hugging the south side of a sheer rock face to their right, before Kenny stepped off it and over the bed of an almost dry creek. Then he struck off through long grass and heather, heading for a hilltop to their left. Long strides that took him upwards to the peak a good few minutes ahead of Fin.

It wasn't until he reached him that Fin realized how high they had climbed, first in the Range Rover, and then on foot. He felt the wind fill his jacket and then his mouth, stealing his breath as the ground fell away beneath them to reveal a startling panorama of sun-washed land and water. Browns, pale blues, greens and purples faded into a shimmering distance at their feet.

'Loch Suaineabhal,' Kenny said. He turned, grinning, towards Fin. 'You feel like a god up here.' Something caught his eye high out over the loch. 'Or an eagle.' Fin followed his gaze. 'We have twenty-two nesting pairs of them between here and the North Harris estate. Highest density of golden eagles anywhere in Europe.'

They watched the bird riding the thermals, almost on a level with them, a wingspan of more than seven feet, feathers spread at their tips, and fanned out at the tail, like fingers, manipulating every movement of the air. Suddenly it dropped, like an arrow fired from the sky, vanishing briefly among the patchwork colours of the land below, before rising unexpectedly into view again, a small animal hanging from its undercarriage, gripped by lethal talons and dead already.

'Look down there towards the head of the loch. You'll see a collection of stone buildings with tin roofs. A shieling and a couple of barns. Two of our watchers live there. No way to get to them by vehicle. Only by boat or on foot. And it's a full day if you're walking it. You'll need to make yourself known to them.'

'Who are they?'

'Students. Making a bit of money during the holidays. It's a hard bloody life, let me tell you. No running water, no electricity. I should know, I did it myself when I was at the

AC.' He turned to the west, then, and pointed towards the four peaks that delineated the far side of the valley, Mealaisbhal standing head and shoulders above the others, the highest peak on Lewis. 'We had watchers over the other side in an old shieling at Loch Sanndabhan. You'll find it on the Landranger map. But they're gone. Beaten up three nights ago when they came across poachers laying nets at the mouth of Abhainn Bhreanais. And I can't get anyone to replace them.'

'I suppose you reported it to the police?'

Kenny laughed, his chest puffed out with genuine amusement. 'Of course. But as you very well know, a fat lot of good that does!' His bonhomie vanished in an instant, as if a switch had been thrown. 'These bastards mean business. Big money in it, you see. The price of wild salmon on the mainland, or in Europe or the Far East for that matter, is astronomical, Fin. I've heard that some of it's being smoked before being shipped out. Fetches even more. They're netting the mouths of the rivers and taking hundreds of bloody fish. Stocks are down and it's ruining our business. There's consortiums of businessmen who'll pay thousands for a beat on one of our rivers. But not if there's no fucking fish in them!'

He strode south to the edge of the slope, and in the far distance, beyond the shoulder of Cracabhal, they could see the big lodge on the shores of Loch Tamnabhaigh. He spoke over his shoulder. 'We manage the rivers and the lochs, making sure the fish get upstream to lay their eggs, conserving numbers. These bastards are taking indiscriminately. In ten years there'll be nothing left.' He turned towards Fin, a dark determination in his eyes. 'They have to be stopped.'

'Have you any idea who's behind it?'

Kenny shook his head grimly. 'If I did, there'd be a few broken fucking legs around the island. We need to catch them at it. Jamie took over the running of the estate after his father's stroke in the spring, and he's prepared to go to pretty much any lengths to put a stop to it. Which is the reason you're here.' The disapproval in the glance he flicked towards Fin was clear. 'But you might want to ease yourself in gently. Start with a soft target.'

Fin frowned. 'What do you mean?'

Kenny's smile almost returned. 'Whistler,' he said.

'John Angus?'

Fin's consternation made Kenny chuckle. 'Aye. Big idiot that he is!'

Fin had not set eyes on Whistler since leaving the island. He had been the smartest boy of his year at the Nicolson, perhaps of any year. With an IQ so far off the scale it was almost impossible to measure, Whistler could have had the pick of any university he chose. And yet, of all of them, he was the only one who had chosen to stay.

'Whistler's involved with the poachers?'

Kenny's chuckle turned to a laugh. 'Good God, no, man! Whistler Macaskill's not interested in money. He's been poaching for years. Well, you know that. Deer, mountain hare, salmon, trout. But just for the pot. Personally, I've always turned a blind eye to it. But Jamie . . . well, Jamie has other ideas.'

Fin shook his head. 'Sounds like a waste of time to me.'

'Aye, maybe so. But the daft bastard's got Jamie all riled up.'

'What happened?'

'Jamie comes across him a few weeks ago, fishing out of Loch Rangabhat. Broad daylight, bold as you like. And when Jamie asks him what he thinks he's doing, gets a mouthful of abuse for his trouble, and a kick up the arse when he tries to put a stop to it.' Kenny grinned. 'Wouldn't have minded seeing that for myself.' But the grin faded. 'The bad bit is that Jamie's his landlord, too, and looking for any excuse to shoehorn him off his croft.'

'I think he might find that Whistler's protected by the Crofters Act.'

'Not if he doesn't pay his rent. And he hasn't done that for years. Old Sir John might not have bothered, but it gives Jamie the perfect excuse. And since he also rents Whistler his house . . .' Kenny pulled a gob of phlegm into his mouth and spat it into the wind. 'The truth is, Fin, he's just a bloody distraction. You and he were always tight. It might be an idea if you were to have a quiet word with him. Then we could get on with the real job.'

## III

Whistler's croft sat up off the road, not far from the cemetery at Ardroil, a steep strip of land rising to a restored blackhouse with views out over the dunes and the vast expanse of Uig beach beyond. There were a handful of sheep grazing on the lower slope, and nearer the house itself old lazy beds had been reactivated to grow potatoes, rows of turned earth fertilized by layers of seaweed cut from the rocks and dragged up the hill.

Fin had been here often in his teens, sitting on the hill with Whistler, avoiding Mr Macaskill, smoking and talking about girls, and taking the view absolutely for granted. It was only his years of living in the city which had taught Fin how privileged they had been then.

But the place had changed. Gone was the old rusted tin roof, to be replaced by what looked like home-made thatch incongruously set with solar panels on the south-facing pitch. The whole was secured against the gales that blew in off the Atlantic by fishermen's netting stretched over the roof and weighed down by boulders dangling on lengths of stout rope. It was like stepping back in time.

The cannibalized remains of three or four rusted old vehicles, a tractor among them, lay around like the carcasses of long-dead animals. A beautifully herringboned stack of drying peats had been built a few feet from the west gable, and rising fifteen feet above it were the fast-turning blades of two home-crafted wind turbines.

Fin left his car at the side of the road and walked up the hill. There was no vehicle parked at the house. Fin knocked on the door, and when there was no answer, lifted the latch and pushed it open. It was dark inside, traditionally small windows letting in a minimum of light. As his eyes grew accustomed to it, Fin saw that the place was a shambles.

An old settee and armchairs, filthy and worn, horsehair pushing through holes torn in their covers. A table littered with scattered tools, and wood shavings that spilled on to the floor. Bizarrely, carved wooden effigies of Lewis chessmen stood in serried ranks along one wall; some of them eight or ten times the size of the originals.

The remains of a fire smouldered in the grate where a chimney had been built against the far gable, and the distinctively toasty scent of warm peat smoke filled the house. Stepping into it was like falling down the rabbit hole.

Fin turned at a sound that came from behind him. The figure of a large man stood silhouetted in the doorway, very nearly filling it. There was a momentary stand-off until he stepped into the light of the window and Fin saw his face for the first time. A large, broad face, black-whiskered by a week's growth. Long dark hair, shot through with what looked like strands of silver fusewire, was swept back from a deeply lined forehead. He wore patched and faded blue jeans, frayed around the ankles, and a thick woollen charcoal jumper beneath a waxed waterproof jacket. His boots were wet and caked with peat. Fin could smell him from where he stood.

'Well, Jesus wept and shrank his waistcoat! If it isn't that bloody Niseach, Fin Macleod.' His voice filled the crofthouse. And to Fin's embarrassment he took two strides towards him and gave him a hug that nearly squeezed all the breath from his lungs. His big whiskery face scratched against Fin's. Then he stood back and gazed at him, holding his shoulders at arm's length, liquid brown eyes wide and full of pleasure at seeing his old friend. 'Hell, man! Hell and damnation! Where in God's name have you been all these years?'

'Away.'

Whistler grinned. 'Aye, well, I think I'd figured that out by now.' He gazed speculatively at him. 'Doing what?'

Fin shrugged. 'Nothing much.'

Whistler stabbed a finger like an iron rod into Fin's chest. 'You were in the fucking polis. Think I didn't know?'

'Well why are you asking?'

'Because I wanted to hear it from the horse's mouth. What on earth possessed you, man?'

'I've no idea, Whistler. I took a wrong turning somewhere.'

'Aye, you did. Clever you were, Fin Macleod. Could have made something of your life, so you could.'

Fin looked pointedly around. 'Not as much as you could have made of yours. School dux. Smartest boy of your gener-ation, they said. You could have been anything you wanted to be, Whistler. Why are you living like this?'

There was a time when the Whistler of old might have taken offence, cursed vituperatively, even got violent. But instead he just laughed. 'I'm exactly who I want to be. And there's not many can say that.' He unslung a canvas satchel from his shoulder and threw it on the couch. 'A man's home is his castle. And I'm a king among kings. You saw those solar panels on the roof?' He didn't wait for an answer. 'Made them myself. And the wind turbines. Generate all the electricity I need. King of the sun and the wind, I am. And the water. Got my own freshwater spring. And fire too, begod. The peat's as free as the rest. All it costs is your labour. Look at this . . .'

He strode to the door and stepped outside into the wind. Fin followed.

'Grow my own food, too, or raise it on the hoof.'

'Or poach it from the estate.'

Whistler threw Fin an ugly look, but the darkness in it vanished in a moment. 'As we always did. A man's entitled to take from the land that the Lord gave us. And He gave it to us all, Fin. You cannae take it with you when you die, so how can anyone think they own it while they're living?'

'The estate spends money and time and manpower managing the fish and the deer, Whistler. And it was man who introduced the rabbits and the mountain hares for hunting.'

'And if I take a fish here or a deer there it does no harm at all. When the fish spawn there's more of them in the river. When the deer rut there's aye one on the hill. And the rabbits?' He grinned. 'Well, they breed like fucking rabbits, don't they?' His smile faded. 'I steal from no man, Fin. I take what God gives. And I owe nothing to no one.'

Fin looked at him carefully. 'What about your rent?' And he saw a shadow cross the big man's face.

'It's in hand,' he said, and turned back into the house, bumping carelessly past Fin's shoulder as if he weren't there. Fin turned, too, and leaned against the door jamb looking into the darkness of the house.

'What do you do for money, Whistler?'

Whistler still had his back turned to him, but Fin could hear his confidence wavering. 'I earn what I need to get by.'

'How?'

His old friend spun around and glared at him. 'None of your fucking business!' And there he was. The Whistler Fin had always known. Prickly and quick-tempered. But he relented almost immediately, and Fin saw the tension slip from his shoulders like a jacket removed at the end of the day. 'I pick up driftwood from the beach, if you must know. Fine, dry, bleached wood. And I make carvings of the Lewis chessmen for the tourists.'

He flicked his head towards the giant chessmen lined up against the wall. And then he laughed again.

'Remember, Fin, how they taught us at school that when Malcolm Macleod found the wee warriors hidden in that cove just down there at the head of Uig beach, he thought they were sprites or elves and was scared shitless. Scared enough to take them to the minister at Baile na Cille. Imagine how scared he'd have been of these big bastards!' And he hefted a bishop up on to the table.

Fin stepped in to take a closer look. Whistler, apparently, had unexpected talents. It was a beautifully sculpted figure, a minutely accurate replica, down to the smallest detail. The folds in the bishop's cloak, the fine lines combed through the hair beneath his mitre. The originals were between three and four inches tall. These were anything from two and a half to three feet. No doubt Whistler could have found employment in the Viking workshops in Trondheim where the actual pieces were thought to have been carved out of walrus ivory and whales' teeth in the twelfth century. But, Fin thought, he probably wouldn't have liked the hours. He ran his eyes along all the pieces lined up against the wall. 'You don't seem to be selling many.'

'These were commissioned,' Whistler said. 'Sir John Wooldridge wants them for the chessmen gala day. You know about that?'

Fin nodded. 'I've heard they're bringing them home. All seventy-eight pieces.'

'Aye, for one day! They should be in Uig year round. A special exhibition. Not stuck in museums in Edinburgh and London. Then maybe folk would come to see them and we could generate some income here.' He dropped into one of his armchairs and cupped his hand around his face to run it over bristled cheeks. 'Anyway, Sir John wanted these for some kind of giant chess game on the beach. The estate's helping fund the gala day. I suppose he must reckon it'll be good publicity.'

Fin found his eye drawn by the band of gold on Whistler's wedding finger. 'I didn't know you were married, Whistler.'

He was momentarily discomposed, then took his hand from his face and looked at his wedding ring. An odd melancholy washed over him. 'Aye. Was. Past tense.' Fin waited for more. 'Seonag Maclennan. You probably knew her at school. Left me for Big Kenny Maclean. Remember him? He's the bloody manager now on the Red River Estate.' Fin nodded. 'Took my wee girl with her, too. Wee Anna.' He was silent for a moment. Then, 'Anyway, the bastard didn't profit for long. Seonag got herself breast cancer and went and died on him.'

He sneaked a glance in Fin's direction, and then quickly away again, as if he was afraid that Fin might see some emotion in it.

'Trouble is, that makes him Anna's legal guardian. *My* daughter. No harm to Kenny. He's all right. But she's my kid and she should be with me. We're fighting it out in the Sheriff Court.'

'And what are your chances?'

Whistler's grin was touched by sadness. 'Just about zero. I mean, look around you.' He shrugged. 'Sure, I could clean up my act, and maybe that would hold some sway. But there's a bigger problem.'

'What's that?'

'Anna. The lassie hates me. And there's not much I can do about that.'

Fin saw pain in his eyes, and in the tightness of his jaw, but he was quick to laugh it off, pushing himself suddenly out of his chair, unexpected mischief in his grin.

'But I've carved out my own secret revenge.' He replaced the bishop among the chessmen along the wall and selected another which he lifted on to the table. 'The Berserker. You know what that is?'

Fin shook his head.

'The Berserkers were Norse warriors who whipped themselves up into a trance-like state, so that they could fight without fear or pain. The fiercest of the Viking warriors. Well, those old twelfth-century craftsmen made the rook in the likeness of a Berserker. Crazy bulging eyes, the mad bastard biting the top of his shield.' Whistler grinned with delight as he turned his carving around to the light. 'I've taken a few liberties with my version. Have a look.'

Fin rounded the piece to better catch the light and realized suddenly that Whistler had made his Berserker in the likeness of Big Kenny. There was no mistaking it. The same flat-faced features and broad skull. The scar on the left cheek. An irresistible smile crept across his face. 'You clever bastard.'

Whistler's laughter filled the room. 'Of course, no one will ever know. But I will. And now you will, too. And maybe when the gala's by, I'll present it to him as a gift.' He looked at Fin with sudden curiosity. 'You got any kids, Fin?'

'I've got a son by Marsaili Macdonald that I never knew I had till a year ago. Fionnlagh, she called him.'

Whistler glanced at Fin's left hand. 'Never married, then?'

Fin nodded. 'I was. For about sixteen years.'

Whistler's eyes searched Fin's, sensing concealment. 'And no kids?'

Fin found it hard ever to speak about it without pain. He sighed. 'We had a wee boy. He died.'

Whistler held him in his gaze for a long time, and Fin almost found himself wishing he would hug him again. If only just to share the pain, and maybe halve it. But neither man moved, then Whistler lifted his Berserker back on to the floor. 'So what brings you down to Uig, man? Not just to see me, surely?'

'I've got myself a new job, Whistler.' He hesitated just for a moment. 'Head of security on the estate.'

And Whistler flashed him a look so filled with betrayal that Fin very nearly winced. But it passed in a moment. 'So you're here to warn me off, then.'

'Seems you really pissed off the landlord.'

'That wee shit Jamie Wooldridge is not his father, let me tell you that. I remember him when his dad used to bring him here as a kid. Snotty wee bastard he was then, too.'

'Well, that snotty wee bastard's running the estate now, Whistler. Seems his father had a stroke in the spring.'

This appeared to come as news to Whistler, and his eyes flickered momentarily towards the chessmen.

'He's got bigger poaching problems than you. But you've made it personal. And he's your landlord, remember. You don't want to lose your castle.' Fin drew a deep breath. 'And I don't want to be the one to catch you poaching.'

To Fin's surprise, Whistler threw back his head and peals of laughter filled with genuine amusement issued from his whiskered face. 'Catch me, Fin? You?' He laughed again. 'Not in a million fucking years!'

# CHAPTER FOUR

The jetty at the fish-processing plant at Miabhaig passed below in a blur, smudges of red that were the Seatrek inflatable powerboats anchored in the bay. And although the waters of Loch Ròg penetrated only a short way along the deep cleft in the land that was Glen Bhaltos, the single-track road followed it in a straight line, flanked by green and pink and brown, broken only by the lichen grey of the gneiss that burst through it.

Fin saw the shadowed shape of their helicopter sweeping across the land beneath them, vanishing among the cloud shadows that chased and overtook it. The roar of its rotors in his ears was deafening. Ahead lay the golden sands of Uig beach, and the shimmering turquoise of the incoming tide, deceptive in its allure. For even after a long hot summer the waters of the North Atlantic retained their chill.

To the south, the mountains rose up, dark and ominous, casting their shadows on the land, dominating the horizon even from the air.

Fin and Gunn sat squeezed together in the back, while Professor Wilson sat up front wearing headphones and chatting to the pilot. As they swept across the beach he removed them and handed them back to Fin, shouting, 'He wants to know where to go!'

Fin guided the pilot the only way he knew, by following the road below. They overflew Ardroil and the gravel pits, banking left to pass above the huddled buildings of the Red River Distillery, and picked up the track that led south towards Cracabhal Lodge. They saw a convoy of three vehicles bumping its way among the potholes between the rise of the mountains. A police Land Rover, a white van, an ambulance. The recovery team making its way as close as it could get to the last resting place of Roddy's aircraft. They would have a long trek on foot up the valley.

Everything looked so different from the air. Fin saw Loch Raonasgail in the shadow of Tathabhal and Tarain, and identified Mealaisbhal to the west of it. He pointed, then, leaning forward. 'Up there, through the valley.'

The pilot banked steeply to the right and dropped height, and they saw the sprawl of house-sized rock that littered the valley floor, the spoil of primeval ice explosions sitting in water now where the inferior loch had burst its banks and flooded the lower reaches. Above that, beyond the giant slug trail through the peat, lay the simmering black hole left by the empty loch. It looked even more unnatural from the air, like the cavity left by a dental extraction.

The plane at the bottom of it, starkly visible in its final resting place among the rocks, seemed unreasonably small.

The pilot circled the valley looking for a place to set the chopper down, before finally deciding on the relatively flat and stable shelf above the loch where Whistler and Fin had sheltered from the storm. It was a soft landing among the high grasses, the broken mounds of ancient beehive dwellings all around, and when the rotors finally came to a stop, they all jumped down to look out over the gaping hollow of the valley below.

It was late afternoon by now. The sun was well up in the sky and tipping gently to the west, creating a subtle change in the angle and direction of the shadows in the valley. They had come equipped with boots and waders and stout sticks, and Fin led them down the same way that he and Whistler had gone that morning, carefully picking their way over rocks that had dried in the warmth of the sun, the surface of the peat at the bottom of the loch already starting to crust and crack.

There was not a breath of wind down here, and the midges clustered around them, getting into their hair and their clothes, biting, biting, biting, like myriad needles piercing their skin, not painful exactly, but irritating almost beyond endurance.

'For Christ's sake, did no one think to bring any bloody repellent?' Professor Wilson glared at Gunn as if it were his fault. His face was red with irritation and exertion, his unruly copper beard exploding from it like wire bursting through its cable sheathing. A frizzy halo of ginger grew around a head that was otherwise bald across the top, white and splattered with big brown freckles. He slapped at it with open hands. 'Jesus fucking Christ!'

But by the time Fin had given him a hand up on to the nearside wing, he had forgotten about the midge clouds, and was absorbed by the scene that confronted them. His eyes darted about, taking in every visible detail of the plane, before he slipped on a pair of latex gloves and pulled open the door to the cockpit. Even he, used as he was to the multifarious perfumes of post-mortem, recoiled from the smell that struck them almost like a physical blow. In the enclosed space of the cockpit, baking as it had been for hours now in the sun, the rate of decomposition had accelerated, catching up on seventeen lost years. The smell was much worse than when Fin and Whistler had opened it up that morning.

'We're going to need to get him back to Stornoway double quick, or we're going to lose what's left of him,' the professor said. 'Let's make this as fast as we can.' He clambered carefully over the roof of the cockpit to the far wing and tried to open the door at the pilot's side. It was stuck fast. Fin and Gunn scrambled over after him, and between them managed to prise it open. They moved back, then, to give the pathologist access to the corpse.

It was a grim sight, the mostly decayed body still fully dressed, the natural fibres of the clothes having survived better in the cold water than the flesh of the dead man.

Professor Wilson opened up the jacket to reveal a white T-shirt beneath it bearing a Grateful Dead logo. 'Dead he certainly is, but I doubt if he's very grateful.' He pulled up the T-shirt to expose the cheesy white tissue still clinging to the fatty areas of the torso. He explored the mush with fingers that simply disappeared into it. 'Adipocere,' he said, apparently undisturbed. 'There'll be more of that around his thighs and buttocks, but the internal organs'll be long gone I think.'

He moved the head very carefully to one side, revealing the bones of the spinal column at the neck. Just a few remnants of grey-white tissue were left holding the skeleton together. The pathologist removed a long, pointed instrument from his breast pocket and gently poked about among the bones. 'Pretty porous and brittle. These are going to break very easily, and the remaining tissue's not going to hold them when we start moving him. Best leave him in these clothes for transporting him. They're about the only thing that's keeping him in one piece. If this water had been any warmer, all we'd have found here would be a pile of bones.'

He turned his attention, then, to the skull.

'Massive trauma,' he said. 'Half his jaw's gone. His brain on this side would have been pulverized.'

'Is that what killed him?' Fin asked.

'Impossible to say, Fin. The injury could have been inflicted after death for all we know. All the same, it might be a good guess.'

'Any idea what could have done it?'

'Something blunt. Big. The size of a baseball bat, though flatter I'd say. But the force that was used to inflict an injury like this . . .' He shook his head.

'Not the result of a plane crash then,' Gunn said.

The professor threw him a look. 'Does this plane look to you like it's crashed, Detective Sergeant?'

Gunn glanced at Fin. 'No, sir, it doesn't.'

'No, it fucking does not! I'm no expert, but I'd say this plane didn't crash into the loch. It landed on it and sank. And one thing's for sure, this fella wasn't flying it.' He eased open the jaw with his metal probe. 'And all this damage to the jaw and the teeth means we'll not be able to make a positive ID from any dental records that might exist.'

'What about DNA?' Fin said.

'We can extract some from the bones, for sure. And there is a little hair left. But what do we have to compare it to?'

Gunn said, 'His parents are dead. No brothers or sisters.'

'So no immediate familial match possible. And I don't suppose he'll be in the database. What about personal items? Comb, hairbrush, shaver? Anything that might have remnants of his DNA.'

Gunn shook his head. 'I don't think so, sir. The parental home would have been cleared out for sale after their death. And who knows what happened to Mr Mackenzie's personal items from Glasgow?'

Professor Wilson scowled at him. 'Not much bloody use are you, Detective Sergeant?' Then he turned back to the corpse and slipped two fingers very carefully into the inside pocket of the leather jacket. By gentle increments, he eased out a bleached leather wallet. 'We might just have to rely on this.' He opened it up. If there had been paper money in it once, it was long gone. There was a handful of coins, and three credit cards all in the name of Roderick Mackenzie. From an inside flap the pathologist drew out a plasticized card with Roddy's photograph on it. Membership of a Glasgow fitness club. He looked back at Fin. 'You knew him?'

Fin nodded.

'I guess that's him, then?'

'It is.' Fin found himself staring at the faded face of the once handsome young man, with his head of blond curls and slightly lopsided smile. And, as before, when Gunn had referred to him as *the deceased*, he felt an odd sense of grief.

'So . . .' Professor Wilson turned towards Gunn. 'What do you think, Detective Sergeant?'

'I think he was murdered, sir.'

The pathologist shrugged, for once finding himself in accord with the policeman. 'Not conclusive, of course, but I'd say there was a damned good chance of it. What do you think, Fin?'

'It's what I thought the moment I opened the door of the cockpit, Angus. And I've not seen anything to change my mind.'

The professor nodded. 'Right, then. We want that recovery team up here as quickly as possible. Photograph the body, then get it back to Stornoway, and we'll see if there's anything else we can divine on the autopsy table.'

As the pathologist slithered down off the wing, Gunn caught Fin's arm. 'So he was up here poaching was he, Mr Macleod? Your pal Whistler.'

'He was.'

'In a storm?'

Fin nodded, but knew that Gunn could sense he was being evasive.

'Not that simple, George.'

Where Whistler was concerned, nothing was ever simple. And Fin turned his thoughts back to the events of two days before, wondering how he could ever have been so foolish as to have taken the bait.

# CHAPTER FIVE

## I

As he drove home the night after that first encounter with Whistler, Fin's thoughts had been dominated by him. The way he lived, the imminent eviction from his home.

The sun cast lengthening shadows among the dried grasses on the rise as he passed the turn-off to the Crobost Free Church. He cast a glance towards the manse standing on the hill above it, and the Reverend Murray's car parked at the foot of the steps. Although they had never seen eye to eye on God and faith, Fin felt enormous empathy for his childhood friend, and each time he passed the church shared something of Donald's hurt. Along with anger that people could so lack understanding.

The collection of houses and crofts that made up the village of Crobost, treeless and exposed to the wind, was strung along half a mile of clifftop above the beach at Port of Ness, the most northerly port on the island. But the harbour was storm-damaged and these days used only by the odd crabber. From here Fin could see a few small boats dragged up on to the sand, or bobbing in the shelter of the harbour wall, tugging gently on creaking ropes.

A good hundred yards or so closer to Port of Ness than Fin's parents' croft stood Marsaili's bungalow, just below the road. It had belonged to Artair's parents. But both they and Artair were gone now, and Marsaili lived there with her son. Who was Fin's son, too.

The old crofthouse up the road where he had lived until the death of his parents was only partially restored. Fin had stripped it back to its stone walls. He had put a new roof on it. But it wasn't yet habitable, and he had moved in with Marsaili. A temporary arrangement, they had both agreed. He was to have had Artair's mother's old room. But in no time he had found himself in Marsaili's bed. As if all the years which had passed since the summer of love they had shared before leaving for university had never been. The people they had become in between, the separate lives they had led, seemed unreal now. Like phantoms in a bad dream. And yet, Fin knew, there was something missing. Whether it was something in him, or in Marsaili, or something in the way they had never quite been able to recreate the magic of that lost summer, he could not have said. But whatever it was, it troubled him.

Marsaili's car stood on the gravel at the top of the path down to the bungalow, its tailgate raised. Fin drew in behind it. He crossed the grass to the path and felt it almost brittle underfoot, the peaty soil beneath it hard after so long without rain. The kitchen door stood open and he could hear Marsaili's voice calling from somewhere deeper in the house. 'And don't forget that knitted jumper. It's warm now, but it'll be cold in no time, and you'll need it.'

As he stepped into the kitchen he heard Fionnlagh's shouted response from the bedroom upstairs. 'There's not enough room in the case.' Fin smiled. Knitted jumpers were not exactly fashionable, and Fionnlagh was nothing if not a young man of his times.

'I'll come up if you want!'

'No, no, it's all right. I'll get it in somehow.'

Fin was quite sure that Marsaili would find that knitted jumper at the bottom of a drawer in days to come. She came into the kitchen sighing her exasperation. 'Boys!' The word exploded from her, and she threw a dangerous look in the direction of Fin's laughter. It was a look he loved. Full of the spirit of the Marsaili of old, auburn hair swept back from a fine face with smiling lips, and cornflower-blue eyes filled with the fire of ice. 'What's so funny?'

'You.'

'Thank you.' She gave him an ironic little smile without humour and returned to a worktop where she was in the process of preparing sandwiches for the ferry trip. 'So how does it feel to have a real job again?'

Fin leaned against the fridge. 'Doesn't feel like a real job. No office, no telephones, no one counting my hours.'

'When they're not counting them it usually means you're working far more than you should.'

Fin smiled and nodded. 'I probably will be.' Then he said, 'I met an old schoolfriend today.'

'Yes?' Marsaili was still focused on her sandwiches, and he sensed that she wasn't really interested.

'John Angus Macaskill. Everyone knew him as Whistler.'

'Oh, yes. Played the flute with – what were they called then – Sòlas?'

'That's him.'

'Good-looking big lad. But not right in the head, I think.'

Fin grinned at her description of him. 'Too clever for his own good, he was. Still is.'

'I never really knew him. We didn't mix in the same circles at school.' She began wrapping the sandwiches in tinfoil.

'No, you were too busy with Artair in those days.'

There was an almost imperceptible pause in the wrapping of the sandwiches, but she didn't turn. 'What's he doing now?'

'Living like a tramp in a tip of a croft down in Uig.'

She turned, holding the wrapped sandwiches in her hands, a glint of curiosity in her eyes. 'Like a tramp?'

Fionnlagh dragged an enormous brown suitcase into the kitchen. He was as tall as Fin. Perhaps taller. With his tight blonde curls gelled into points, and his mother's blue eyes. He nodded acknowledgement to his father as Fin expanded on his description of Whistler for Marsaili. 'He's sort of dropped out. Self-sufficient. Poaching, of course. And locked in some kind of custody battle for his daughter.'

'With his wife?'

'No, she's dead. Kenny John Maclean's her legal guardian.'

Fionnlagh broke in. 'Are we talking about Anna Bheag?'

Fin looked at him, surprised. 'You know her?'

'Anna Macaskill, from Uig?'

'That would be her.'

Fionnlagh nodded. 'She's trouble that one. In third year at the Nicolson. Never seen so many tattoos to the square inch on a lassie in my life. A good-looking girl, too, but wears her hair cropped, like a boy's, and got a face-full of metal.'

Fin was taken aback. It wasn't the image conjured up by Whistler's 'wee Anna'. 'What age is she?'

Fionnlagh shrugged. 'About fifteen, maybe. But no virgin, that's for sure. Hangs about with a druggie crowd. So God knows what she's on. Shame. Smart kid. But brains are wasted on her.' He glanced at his mother. 'Will I just take this out to the car?'

'On you go,' Marsaili said. 'I'll put the sandwiches in your rucksack.'

Fionnlagh started heaving his case out of the door. 'I don't need sandwiches. I can buy something on the boat.'

Marsaili headed for the living room and threw her riposte over her shoulder. 'Money doesn't grow on trees, Fionnlagh. You'll find that out soon enough when you're trying to live on a budget down in Glasgow.'

Fifteen minutes later they all walked up to the road with the last of Fionnlagh's stuff as Donald's car pulled in ahead of them and he helped Donna out with her case. Every time Fin saw Donald these days it appeared he had lost more weight. Gone were his boyish good looks, and more of his fine sandy hair. And Fin was struck, as he always was, by how young Donna looked. Hardly old enough to be the mother of Fin's granddaughter. Seventeen going on twelve. In spite of the long, hot summer, she had a winter pallor about her, as if she had never been over the door. And he wondered how much of himself there was in Fionnlagh, and whether his relationship with Donna would survive the years at university. At least, he thought, they had the glue of a child to hold them together. Unlike Fin and Marsaili. Maybe things would have been different had Fin known back then that Marsaili was carrying his child.

They transferred Donna's case to Marsaili's car. She was driving them to the ferry in Stornoway. Then they all stood around for an awkward moment, none of them wanting to initiate the goodbyes, and yet they would have to be said. Eventually, they went through the ritual hugs and kisses, and before she slipped behind the wheel Marsaili said to Donald, 'Tell Catriona I'll pick up Eilidh in the morning.' It was the last night the baby would spend at the Murrays'. Marsaili had agreed to look after her granddaughter during Fionnlagh and Donna's university years. An unwanted second motherhood, crushing the desire she had expressed only a few months before to resume her own studies, and go in search of the young woman whose potential she had wasted. She was sacrificing her second chance at life in order to give them their first.

Fin and Donald stood watching the car as it rounded the bend where the single-track road dipped down towards the Crobost Stores and the main road that would take them to Stornoway. This time tomorrow night their children would be in Glasgow, embarking on new lives, leaving their parents behind to come to terms with the mess they'd made of theirs.

Fin glanced up at the sun sinking now towards the west. The days were long still, and there were perhaps another several hours of daylight remaining. But soon those days would start shrinking fast, and the islanders would take badly to the onset of another long, bleak winter in the aftermath of the best summer in living memory.

The striking of a match turned Fin's head and he saw with something like shock that Donald was lighting a cigarette, hands cupped around a flickering flame. It seemed discordant, out of keeping with the black cotton and the dog collar, which themselves struck an odd note with his jeans and trainers. His face became thinner as he sucked on his cigarette. The last time Fin had seen Donald smoking would have been nearly eighteen years before, at which time it would almost certainly have been a joint.

'When did you start smoking again?'

Donald drew more smoke into his lungs. 'When I stopped caring.'

'About what?'

'Myself.' He blew smoke into the wind. 'Oh, don't worry, Fin. I'm not wallowing in self-pity just yet.' He glanced at him. 'Let's walk on the beach. I need to ask you a favour.'

The tide was on its way in again. Creamy foam rushing over compacted virgin sand broken only by the tracks of seagulls where they had foraged for creatures just below the surface. Fin and Donald left their own trail of erratic footprints in their wake, breaking frequently up the slope to avoid the incoming wash. Gulls wheeled and cawed overhead, enjoying the last of the sunshine that caught the gable ends of houses all along the road above the harbour. The wind was stronger now, but still soft in their faces.

They had walked some way in silence before Donald said, 'I heard the other day that they might ask me to quit the manse.'

Fin was astonished. 'What happened to innocent until proven guilty? You're only suspended, for God's sake!'

'It's for the Church's sake, Fin, not God's.' Donald kept his eyes focused on some distant point far ahead of them. 'Apparently some of the elders feel that the minister they have sent to preach in my stead should also have my house.'

'The same elders who've brought the charges against you, no doubt.'

The merest smile played about Donald's lips for a second. 'Of course.' Then it vanished almost as quickly. 'I think Catriona might be going to leave me.'

Fin stopped dead in the sand, and Donald had taken several more steps before he realized it and stopped too. He turned. Fin said, 'Why?'

Donald shrugged. 'Because I'm not the man she married, she says.'

'You're the man who saved her daughter's life.'

'By killing another man.'

'The fiscal himself said there wasn't a jury of your peers who would have convicted you for killing to save innocent lives. You did nothing wrong.'

'In the eyes of the law perhaps.'

'You had no choice.'

'There's always a choice.'

'And you chose the lesser of two evils.'

'God is clear, Fin. Thou shalt not kill. It wasn't a request, it was a command.' He drew a deep breath. 'At any rate, that's what my accusers will argue. And that's what I wanted to ask you about.'

'The sixth commandment?'

Which drew a chuckle. 'No, Fin. I think I am familiar enough with your views on the subject of anything to do with God and the Church.'

'What, then?'

Donald's smile evaporated. 'The Presbytery has decided to take the matter to a disciplinary court. Effectively a trial. Under Church law. If I want to keep my job I will have to defend myself. And they want to call witnesses. They want to call you, Fin.' Now, for the first time, he appeared to be uncertain of himself. 'Will you testify?'

And Fin remembered all those moments from childhood when Donald had stood up for him, even when it had meant putting himself at risk. He felt emotion rising in him like a river in flood. For a moment he could barely trust himself to speak. Then at last he found his voice. 'Donald, how could you ever imagine I wouldn't?'

## II

It was the following day that Fin had had his first meeting with Jamie in the landlord's private office. Fin and Kenny stood looking over the No. 13 Ordnance Survey Landranger map of West Lewis and North Harris spread across the desk, while Jamie used an orange felt-tipped marker to outline the various water systems that made up the Red River Estate.

It had been clear that Big Kenny was bored. He knew the estate and its water systems probably better than any other living soul, but Jamie was his boss, and Jamie wanted to brief Fin personally.

Jamie's office was cluttered, a large desk very nearly filling it. Glass cases of stuffed fish and fishing flies lined the walls, an imperious-looking stag's head mounted on a plaque above the door.

Fin remembered Jamie from teenage years spent in Uig with Whistler. Sir John Wooldridge had brought his son up to the island from boarding school somewhere in the south of England every Christmas, Easter and summer holiday to learn about the estate. He was a couple of years older than the rest of them, but even as a teenager had already acquired the subliminally patronizing attitude of the landowner. It had not really been that long since the whole of Lewis had belonged to a single landowner, and those of its people who rented crofts and worked the land were treated little better than serfs. When it had been decided, back then, that grazing sheep was a more profitable use of the land than crofting, many tenants had been forcibly evicted and shipped off on boats to Canada and America, with not much more control of their lives than the slaves taken there from Africa.

Memories were long, stories of the land clearances spanned generations, and landowners were still regarded with suspicion and a little fear. And although their powers these days were restricted by Act of Parliament, and crofters had security of tenure on the land, a landowner continued to be seen in a strange, reluctant way as being superior. A regard landowners also had of themselves.

Jamie was lean and tanned, but losing his hair, and since his father's stroke had brought his wife and two children to live with him full-time at Cracabhal Lodge. He had a creamy, languid, southern accent, although to Fin's surprise demonstrated a remarkably good grasp of Gaelic. His speaking of it was close to unintelligible, but his understanding was impressive. He wore moleskin trousers, knee-length boots and a Barbour jacket.

'We have five water systems on the estate, Fin, rivers that feed in and out of the various lochs. There is salmon, sea trout and brown trout fishing throughout. In fact, we have more than a hundred lochs for brown trout fishing, though it's not the brown trout that the poachers are after.'

He moved his marker across a landscape broken by myriad patches of blue to circle a long body of water that arced from the south to the north, and from west to east. 'Loch Langabhat. Old Norse for the long loch. It's about eight miles long. The largest freshwater loch in the Hebrides.' And there it was, in that single imparting of information, the condescending assumption that he was telling Fin something he wouldn't know – although it was Fin who had grown up on the island, and not Jamie. 'We share the fishing rights with another five estates. With proper management we've been increasing our average catch there year on year, doubling the take in the last five. These bloody poachers are going to wipe them out. Not just in Langabhat, but across all our water systems. And if they put us out of business, a lot of local people are going to lose their jobs.'

He straightened up and regarded Fin with speculative brown eyes.

'I'm relying on you, Fin, to find these people and put a stop to it. You'll have whatever resources you need.'

To Fin it seemed like a fairly straightforward police investigation. The poaching was not the work of outsiders. These were local people who knew their way around. Someone must know who they were. And it wasn't just a matter of catching the fish. Others were smoking it. Someone was buying it. There was a supply line leading away from the island to destinations in Europe or further afield, and since freshness was an issue where fish was concerned, it would be leaving by plane rather than boat.

'Well, I don't see why we can't wrap this up within a month or two, Mr Wooldridge.'

'Jamie,' Jamie corrected him.

Fin nodded. 'Jamie.' He didn't feel comfortable addressing him by his first name. Years in the force had conditioned him to refer to everyone, other than junior ranks, by their surname, or as 'sir' or 'madam'.

'Well, that's good to hear, Fin. I hope you're right.'

The sound of a vehicle pulling up outside drew the attention of an already distracted Kenny, and he crossed to the window of Jamie's study to look down into the yard below. There were a number of cars already parked outside Suaineabhal Lodge, customers in the bar downstairs, but the new arrival drew up opposite the lodge, at the gate to Kenny's house. 'That's my daughter home from school,' he said. 'I'll be back in a few minutes.' And he hurried out.

Jamie seemed annoyed by Kenny's sudden departure, as if he felt that his estate manager ought to have asked permission to leave the room. He folded up the map and handed it to Fin. 'Make yourself familiar with this. You'll need to get to know every square inch.' He rounded his desk and walked towards the door. 'Folk think it should be easy enough to catch poachers on an island.' He opened the door, but hesitated with his hand still on the handle. 'But the truth is, Fin, this estate encompasses one of the biggest inaccessible areas of wilderness in Scotland. There are large tracts of it you simply can't reach by road. It's like stepping back in time. The only way to get around it is on foot, or by boat.' He drew a breath. 'I'll be back in a minute. Then I'll buy you a drink in the bar and you can meet some of our ghillies.'

He disappeared off down the hall, and Fin found himself gravitating towards the window, drawn by curiosity, and Fionnlagh's description of Anna Macaskill, hoping to catch sight of the girl with the tattoos and the face full of metal.

The sky was overcast, and the light was beginning to go, but he saw her clearly enough standing beneath the trees on the far side of the path. The car which had delivered her to the gate was heading off, back along the narrow track to the main road, and Kenny was striding across the yard to speak to her.

In spite of Fionnlagh's vivid depiction of the girl, her appearance still came as a shock. Her neck and what was visible of her arms were covered in dark-blue tattoos. Impossible at this distance to tell what they were. Her hair was unnaturally black, and cropped as Fionnlagh had said, but dyed pink along one side, above an ear crusted with a dozen or more rings through the cartilage of the scapha. The opposite eyebrow was punctured by five or six studs, and several rings disfigured her lower lip. In addition she had a nose stud, and although Fin couldn't see it, he imagined her tongue was probably also pierced.

She wore a short black skirt over black leggings, and a charcoal-grey hoodie over a low-cut black T-shirt. A tan leather bag was slung high over her shoulder.

Oddly, in spite of it all, she had a pretty face, and something about her black-lined eyes told Fin that she couldn't be anyone other than Whistler's daughter.

But it was her stepfather who crossed below to greet her. Although larger than life in isolation, she shrank next to Kenny, who looked like a giant beside her, and Fin realized just how impossibly small she was. Hence the name that Fionnlagh had used for her – Anna Bheag. Wee Anna. He watched their body language. Anna appeared guarded, but not hostile. She didn't move away from the big hand that laid itself tenderly on her cheek, a fleeting gesture of warmth and fondness that belied the image of gruff masculinity that Kenny liked to project. They stood talking for some moments, easily and without rancour, and it was clear to Fin that their relationship was not afflicted by the antagonism that characterized so many relationships between father and teenage daughter. There was something almost touching in the way they were together.

And then he became aware of her eyes on him, and he could see a change not only in her expression, but in the way she held her whole body, turning in his direction, suddenly erect, hostile and provocative at the same time. She said something and Kenny turned, raising his eyes towards the window of Jamie's study. Fin must have been as plain as day to them, standing there in the window, watching.

She raised the middle finger of her right hand and thrust it in his direction. And even through the double-glazing he heard her shout, 'Why don't you take a picture? It'll last longer!' He felt shock, almost like a physical blow, and knew that the colour had risen on his cheeks.

Kenny said something to her, but she turned without another word and marched away up the path to the door of the house. Kenny looked back towards Fin, eyebrows raised, a tiny smile of embarrassment on his lips, and the smallest shrug of his shoulders signalled an apology.

## III

The bar was crowded, windows steaming up as the temperature outside began to fall. Half a dozen men were gathered around a pool table in an alcove, others had drawn in chairs at circular wooden tables. But most of them were standing, three or four deep along the bar, drinking pints, voices raised to make themselves heard above the hubbub. Somewhere in the background Fin could make out the distant thump, thump of music pumping through a sound system.

Bodies parted, like the Red Sea making way for Moses, as Jamie cleaved a route to the bar followed by Fin and Kenny. As they reached it Kenny moved his mouth close to Fin's ear and said in a low voice, 'Sorry about the lassie. She's at a difficult age.' And for a moment Fin wondered how on earth he succeeded in managing the estate and bringing up a teenage daughter at the same time. Then he remembered that Anna was away from home five days a week at student accommodation in Stornoway. Just as he had been. So, really, it was more like a part-time job. But you would never have guessed from looking at him that Kenny was a man who'd had to deal with the tragic death of his wife, and was single-handedly bringing up another man's daughter. His lover's daughter. The only part of herself she had left him.

Jamie ordered them pints without asking what they'd like, and the barman set up three glasses of fizzing amber that ran with condensation and foam on to a counter already shiny with beer. He lifted his own pint and raised it. 'To success,' he said. Fin and Kenny raised their glasses, too, and sipped silently on their beers. Then Jamie signalled to a group of men across the room, and shouted, 'Ewan. Peter. Come and meet Fin Macleod.'

A number of heads turned in their direction, and Ewan and Peter started pushing their way towards the group.

'Gamekeeper and water bailiff,' Jamie said. 'Good men, both.'

Ewan was a man in his fifties, with a deeply creased face weathered brown by all the hours he spent outdoors. Peter was younger, but a monster of a man with a full beard, like horsehair bursting out of a mattress. They all shook hands.

'Fin is our new head of security,' Jamie said. 'He's going to catch our poachers.' Both men cast sceptical looks in Fin's direction but kept their counsel.

Fin said, 'It might be an idea if we didn't advertise it, Mr Wooldridge. We don't want to go showing our hand even before we've played a card.'

Kenny laughed. 'You can't keep a secret here for five minutes, Fin. You should know that. The poachers probably knew all about you from the minute you set foot on the estate.'

Fin was barely aware of the door opening, the rush of cooler air around their legs, but the sudden lull in the sound of voices from all around the bar immediately caught his attention. He turned to see Whistler standing in the doorway, and the noise around them fell away to silence, save for the continued pulsing beat of the sound system.

Whistler looked like a wild man straight off the hills. His hair was blown and tangled by the wind. Another day's growth on his face made him seem even more unkempt, patches of silver mirroring the streaks of it in his hair. His eyes were black, without pupils or highlight. He scanned the faces all turned in his direction, and Fin detected the merest trace of a smile in the set of his lips. There was no doubt he enjoyed being the centre of attention, and his appearance in the bar at Suaineabhal Lodge was a first.

'What's wrong? Seen a crowd?' His voice bellowed out across the pub and everyone was suddenly self-conscious, but locked into a communal stare, and a silence that no one wanted to be the first to break. Whistler pushed his way to the bar. 'Pint of lemonade.' The barman seemed transfixed. His frightened rabbit's eyes darted from Whistler to Jamie and back again. 'Don't worry about how I'll pay for it.' Whistler appeared to be trying to assuage his doubts. 'My credit's good here. The Wooldridges owe me a fortune.'

'I think you have that wrong, John Angus.' Jamie's outward appearance of unruffled calm was betrayed by the faintest tremor in his voice.

Whistler swung his head in Jamie's direction. 'Oh? And how's that, Mister Wooldridge?'

'You're the one who owes us. More than ten years in back rent. So there's a good chance I'll be sending in the bailiffs to have you removed. From the croft, and the house. Unless you've come to settle up tonight.'

'I'd be happy to, if you'd just cough up what you owe me.'

Someone had turned off the music, and the silence was broken now only by the sound of the wind whistling around the door and windows.

'We owe you nothing.'

'Your father does.'

'How so?'

Whistler swung the rucksack off his back and thumped it down on the bar, unzipping it to reveal one of his carved chessmen inside. 'A full set he commissioned me to do for the gala day. Job done. Come and get them any time you like.'

Jamie returned his stare, unwavering. 'You can show me a contract, I suppose.'

And Fin saw doubt creep into Whistler's eyes for the first time. 'There was no contract. Your father trusted me, as I trust him.'

'Well,' Jamie smiled, knowing now that he had the upper hand, 'we only have your word for that. And since my father is still in a nursing home following his stroke, that won't be easily verified.' He paused. 'And I can assure you, there will be no money forthcoming until it is.' He lifted his pint glass from the bar to take a sip, supremely confident now that he had prevailed in the exchange. 'So if you don't pay up within the next week, you can expect that visit from the bailiffs.'

The glass never reached his lips. Whistler flew at him. A feral growl like the war cry of a wild animal issued from

a mouth baring yellowed teeth. Jamie's pint glass went flying, drenching several of the nearest bystanders, the sound
of breaking glass accompanying the crash of the two men
as they landed on the floor. The noise of the air being
forcibly expelled from Jamie's lungs was painful. Whistler's
full weight had come down on top of him. A big fist swung
through the air and caught the young landowner high on
the cheekbone. Another sank itself into his gut. Jamie
gasped in pain, but didn't have enough air in his lungs to
cry out.

Umpteen pairs of hands pulled Whistler away, Fin's and
Kenny's among them. And in the confusion of thoughts
flashing through his head, Fin remembered that it wasn't
the first time that he had helped drag Whistler off some
helpless soul. But Whistler was not about to be subdued
easily. He swung his arms wildly, breaking free of the hands
that grasped him, turning, eyes blazing and filled with the
highlights they had earlier lacked. His fist flew through the
air again, catching Fin squarely on the jaw, sending him
sprawling back through the crowd to hit the floor like a
dead weight, lights flashing in his head.

More than a few of the men there that night knew of the
history between Fin and Whistler, of their almost unbreak-
able teenage bond. It made the fact that Whistler had struck
him all the more remarkable. Voices which had arisen out
of the earlier silence to bay for blood subsided once again.
Feet shuffled backwards, and a space cleared around them.
Kenny helped Jamie to his feet, and Whistler just stood there,
breathing hard, glaring at Fin lying on the floor. 'Never

took you for a landlord's lackey,' he shouted, as if trying to find an excuse for what he'd done.

Fin pulled himself up on to one elbow and put a hand to his face to check if his jaw was broken. It came away with blood on the fingers where his lip had cut itself on his teeth. Hands reached down to help him up. He stared back at Whistler, and the hush which had descended became one of anticipation. But Fin had no intention of getting involved in a brawl. His hurt went deeper than any external injury. He shook his head. 'Never took you for anything but a friend.'

Whistler's remorse was apparent in moist eyes, and in the tightness of his lips, but it wrestled for ascendancy with the anger that still gripped him. 'I've no quarrel with you.'

'You just hit me!'

'And you've taken sides against me with him.' He turned and almost growled at Jamie, who flinched involuntarily.

'I've taken sides with no one, Whistler. I'm on the side of the law. And you're breaking it.'

'Sometimes being on the side of the law's being on the wrong side, Fin.'

'I don't think so.' But no sooner were the words out of his lips than he thought of Donald.

Whistler snorted, like a horse impatient to be off at a canter. 'Well, let's see. It's a full moon the morn's night. A great night to be out and about at Loch Tathabhal. Fish'll be biting, for sure. Maybe you'll see me there, and maybe you won't. But if you do . . . well, maybe then we'll see who's right and who's wrong.'

It was clear to every man there that Whistler was issuing a challenge. Catch me if you can. He turned and pushed his way roughly to the door and vanished out into the night.

'Call the police, Kenny,' Jamie said. He was white with anger, shaking and still trying to recover his breath.

'No.' Fin stopped Kenny in his tracks.

'He assaulted both of us, in full view of every man here.' Jamie could barely control his fury.

'Men fight,' Fin said. 'That's a matter between them. Not for the police. You told the man you were going to take away his home. His family home for generations. How did you think he would take it?'

'He's ten years behind on his rent!'

'And what's that to you? A few hundred pounds. You owe him for the chessmen.'

'Says who?'

'I've seen them. The full set. He didn't do that for fun. I suggest you check with your father.'

Jamie took two steps towards him, lowering his voice, a threat in it now. 'You get him, Macleod. You get him, or I'll bring in people who can.' Fin noticed how the friendly 'Fin' had been dropped now in favour of his surname.

'Oh, I'll deal with him,' Fin said, green eyes fixed on Jamie's. 'But for his sake, not yours.'

It was nearly twenty minutes later that Fin came out into the twilight. The wind had dropped, moonlight washing already across the hills, falling in silvered daubs through the leaves of the trees around the lodge. Stars were only just visible in a dark, azure sky, and the midges were biting, their season extended by the long, hot, dry spell. Clouds of the tiny flies, masked by the fading light, filled the night. Unseen but certainly felt.

The hubbub in the bar fading behind him, Fin saw the shadows of two figures beneath the trees across the yard, and he realized with a shock that it was Whistler and Anna. He could hear their voices raised in anger, but not what they were saying. They hadn't noticed him, and he stood still, watching from a distance, listening to their argument rising in pitch. Until suddenly she slapped her father with such force that he actually stepped back. The sound of it rang out across the night. Such a powerful strike from such a small person. Anna Bheag. Wee Anna. Dominating the big man who was her father. She turned immediately and hurried up the path towards the house, and Fin was sure he heard a sob catching in her throat.

Both men stood without moving for what seemed like an age, Whistler still unaware of Fin's presence, until Fin cleared his throat and the big man's head snapped round. They stood for several moments more, staring at each other through the late evening gloom. Then Whistler turned abruptly and walked away into the night without a backward glance.

# CHAPTER SIX

Fin and Gunn stood by the helicopter watching the recovery team at work below. It had taken another hour for them to get there, and the day was starting to fade. Professor Wilson had been amazed to discover that he could actually get a signal for his mobile phone if he stood up above them on the shoulder of the mountain. He was talking animatedly to someone back in Edinburgh.

Gunn was gazing into the valley in reflective silence. He turned suddenly towards Fin. 'I got a letter from the Presbytery yesterday, Mr Macleod. Calling me to give evidence at Donald Murray's trial, or whatever it is they're calling it.'

Fin nodded. No doubt his would be waiting for him at home. And he wondered what he would say to those people who wanted to throw Donald Murray out of their Church. He closed his eyes and recalled the horror of that night in Eriskay when two men from Edinburgh had faced them with guns and the promise of death. And Donald had arrived like an avenging angel to take the life of one of them and save all the others. A man motivated by the threat to the lives of his daughter and granddaughter, his progeny, the only reason, perhaps, that God had put him on this earth.

If you believed in God, that is.

'I don't *have* to go,' Gunn said. 'I mean, it's not a legal summons.'

Fin nodded. 'No.' Then frowned. 'But why wouldn't you?'

'Because I'm afraid I might do him more harm than good, Mr Macleod.' Fin had long since given up trying to get Gunn to call him by his first name. While still in the force Fin had been a Detective Inspector, superior in rank, and George was nothing if not a stickler for protocol. Even though Fin had long since quit the police.

'Why would telling the truth do him any harm?'

'Because after these bloody gangsters snatched Donna and the baby from Crobost, and went south looking for you and the others, all Donald Murray had to do was lift a phone and call the police. But he was so hell-bent on dealing with it himself. If he had just called us, things might have turned out differently.'

'Aye.' Fin nodded gravely. 'We'd all have been dead. A couple of unarmed island policemen would have been no match for two armed thugs from the mainland, George. You know that.'

Gunn shrugged reluctant acquiescence. 'Maybe.'

'Why else would the Crown have dropped the manslaughter charges?'

'Because they knew they wouldn't get a conviction in a court of law, Mr Macleod.' He scratched his head. 'But a court of the Free Church of Scotland . . . that's another matter altogether.'

Fin sighed and nodded acknowledgement, and was swamped by concern for a friend he felt powerless to help.

Gunn watched him for a moment, then turned back to the plane in the valley below. 'I don't know how we get that thing out of there. But I suppose they'll want it back in Stornoway for examination. There might be a hangar at the airport that we could use to store it. Or maybe the old Clansman mill in town. I think that's still empty. But then, we'd never get it through the streets. No, the airport would be best.'

He turned, looking for Fin's approval. But Fin was barely listening. He said, 'George, is there any chance I might be able to attend the post-mortem?'

'Not a hope in hell, sir. No offence. You were a good cop, Mr Macleod. And I've no doubt you would bring some useful experience to the PM. But you're not a police officer any more, just a material witness to the discovery of the plane. You and John Angus Macaskill.' He shuffled awkwardly. 'I had a call before we left. There's an inquiry team on its way. And if I let you anywhere near that autopsy room, the chances are I'd be the next one on the table being cut open to establish cause of death.' His smile was touched by embarrassment before fading. 'How come Whistler Macaskill didn't come with you to report the find?'

Fin hesitated. He remembered how strangely Whistler had reacted to the discovery of the plane. By the time Fin had climbed back up to the beehives Whistler and all his stuff had gone. And on the long walk back to retrieve his Suzuki, Fin had caught not a single sight of him. He glanced awkwardly at Gunn and shrugged. 'I guess he thought it wouldn't be necessary.'

Gunn gave him a long, hard look. 'Is there something you're not telling me, Mr Macleod?'

'Nothing, George.'

Gunn sighed. 'Well, I don't have time to go looking for him myself right now. But when you see him, you can tell him to present himself at the police station in Stornoway first chance he gets. I'll need a statement.'

# CHAPTER SEVEN

It was less than an hour later that Fin turned off the road and drove up the pebble track to park at the door of Whistler's blackhouse, even though all his instincts told him that Whistler would not be here. Tall grasses growing all around it bowed in the wind. He stepped down from the Suzuki and looked out over the sands. From this elevated position he could see across the bay beyond the vast expanse of beach to the islands of Tolm and Triassamol, which were almost lost in the oblique evening light.

The door to the house stood ajar, a door of unpainted weathered wood, grey and grainy. The latch and lock were rust-red, brown-staining the wood in streaks below them. Fin was certain that even if a key existed for the lock it would not turn in it. No one locked their doors on the island, and anyway, who would steal from a man with nothing?

Fin placed the flat of his hand on the door and pushed it into the gloom. It creaked loudly in the silence within, and as he stepped inside, the thickness of the walls immediately diminished the howling of the wind on the hill outside.

'Who the fuck are you?' The voice came from beyond the veiled sunlight that slanted in from the west through one of the tiny windows at the back of the house. It was shrill and demanding, but with a hint of alarm in it. Fin stepped to one side so that he had a view deeper into the house, and saw Anna Bheag, perched on the edge of an armchair by the ashes of a dead fire. Her hands were pressed flat on each arm, and she was tensed, ready to move in an instant, like a cat. But an ill-fed cat, skinny and mean, with eyes blazing resentment. The pink side of her head caught the light from the window and glowed in the gloom like neon.

'Fin Macleod. I'm a friend of your father's.'

'My father doesn't have friends.' She spat the words back at him.

'He used to.'

She was still on her guard and tipped her head to one side, squinting at him through the dust that hung in motes in the still light from the windows. 'You're that creepy guy that was watching us from the window at Suaineabhal day before yesterday.'

Fin smiled. 'I'm that guy, yes. But it's the first time any-one's called me creepy.'

'What were you looking at, then?'

'You.'

She seemed surprised by his directness. 'Why?'

'I wanted to see what the daughter of my old friend looked like.'

'I told you, the fucker doesn't have any friends.'

Fin took a couple of cautious steps further into the house and saw her tense. 'I was at school with him.'

'I never heard him talk about you.'

'I've been away from the island for a long time.'

'Why would you come back to a shit-hole like this?'

Fin shrugged and wondered why himself. 'Because it's home. And because I have a son here I didn't know I had for nearly eighteen years.'

For the first time he saw curiosity in her eyes. 'Here in Uig?'

'No, in Ness. He's just left for university.'

'He must have been at the Nicolson, then. Maybe I know him.'

'Maybe you do. Fionnlagh Macinnes.'

And now she relaxed a little. 'You're Fionnlagh's dad?'

Fin nodded.

'All the girls had a crush on Fionnlagh.'

And Fin remembered Marsaili saying the same thing about him. 'You, too?'

The appearance of something like a smile brought a little light to her face and she offered a noncommittal, 'Maybe.' Then it clouded again. 'You said your name was Macleod.'

'It's a long story, Anna. He and I thought he was someone else's boy for most of his life.'

'So where were you all these years?'

'On the mainland. Glasgow, then Edinburgh.'

'Married?'

He nodded.

'So what did your wife think when she found out you'd had a kid by someone else?'

'She didn't come with me.'

'Why not?'

He had dealt patiently with her relentless questions, but now she was delving into a dark corner of his life where his soul was still exposed and raw. He hesitated.

'You left her?'

Fin pulled up a chair at the table. The sound of its legs scraping across the wooden boards felt inordinately loud. He sat down. 'Not that simple.'

'Well either you left her or she left you.'

Fin gazed at his hands in front of him. Is that how it had been? He didn't think so. A loveless marriage of sixteen years had simply dissolved when the only thing which had held it together was taken away. He shook his head slowly. 'We had a son. Robbie. He was barely eight years old.' He couldn't bring himself to raise his eyes to meet hers, but detected the change in her voice immediately. There was a kind of hush in it. Intelligent anticipation.

'What happened?'

For a moment he couldn't trust himself to speak. Why was it so difficult for him to tell this girl that he didn't even know? 'He was killed in a hit-and-run accident in Edinburgh.' And if he closed his eyes he could see the police photographs of the street, kept still in a folder he couldn't bring himself to throw away.

There was a long silence, then, in the old blackhouse, before finally he raised his head and met her eye. There was a mix of emotions in her face. Sympathy, confusion, fear. But not of him. She took evasive action. 'So you were at school with my dad?'

'Yes.'

'Was he as big an arsehole back then as he is now?'

And Fin couldn't stop his lips from parting in a smile, or the laugh that came in a breath. 'Yes, he was.'

And she laughed, too, and was transformed in a moment from an ugly teenage Goth into a pretty young girl with lights in her eyes. The change was almost shocking. But while the image might have changed, the mouth was just as foul. 'So how the fuck did you become his friend?'

'You've heard of the *Iolaire*?'

She shook her head, and Fin wondered at how quickly history got lost. But he shouldn't have been surprised. He had known nothing about it himself until that day out at Holm Point.

# CHAPTER EIGHT

I first met Whistler Macaskill when I left Crobost school in Ness to go into third year at the Nicolson Institute in Stornoway. We had a certain swagger, us Ness boys. Thought we were a bit special. Until we arrived at the Nicolson and found that everyone else had a swagger, too. The Uig crowd, the boys from Lochs, the wild westers from Carloway. But the big city soon knocked it out of us.

I can laugh now, but that's what Stornoway felt like then. It was the only town on the island, with all its shops and cafes and restaurants, and its inner and outer harbour. It was home to the Hebridean fishing fleet and a population of eleven thousand. Sadly, there was no cinema in those days, since the Church had forced the Playhouse to close down following a showing of *Jesus Christ, Superstar*. At least, that was what they said, but it was before my time, so I don't know if it's true. The old cinema became the Royal British Legion Club, and still is.

The Church dominated life then, and in many ways still does. In all its various incarnations. But it was the presbyterian Church of Scotland and the breakaway Free Church that prevailed. They wouldn't allow flights or ferries on the

Sabbath when I was a boy, and there was not a single shop, cafe, newsagent or chippie open. You read your Sunday newspapers on Monday, and if you forgot to buy your cigarettes on a Saturday you would have an even more miserable Sunday than usual.

But that particular year, there *was* something special about the kids from Uig. They arrived with their own band. Six kids who'd been playing music together since primary school. Sòlas, they called themselves, the Gaelic equivalent of *solace* or *comfort*, and they had already developed their own unique mix of traditional Celtic music and rock. An eclectic fusion that in a few years would make them the most commercially successful Celtic rock band of their generation.

I wasn't really aware of them at first. I was too busy adapting to life away from home in the student lodgings at the Gibson Hostel in Ripley Place. We came down from Ness in a bus on the Monday morning, and back again on the Friday night. Not that I missed my life at Crobost. My folks had been dead for years by then, and existence with my aunt was spartan. My friend Artair had gone to the Lews Castle College because his grades hadn't been good enough to get him into the Nicolson. They wouldn't do that to kids these days in case it gave them low self-esteem. But it wasn't a consideration back then. Relations with my primary school sweetheart, Marsaili Macdonald, were in temporary abeyance. So in those first few months I was busy trying to forget her and make myself new friends.

The first time I came across Sòlas was when it was

announced there was to be a ceilidh at the school. I'd heard that a group of kids from Uig was going to be playing at it and someone said they were rehearsing in one of the annexes, so I went along to see if it would be worth going to the ceilidh or not. It was a decision that changed the course of my life.

There were six in the band.

Roddy Mackenzie was the keyboard player and leader. What he said went. He had a synthesizer. A Yamaha DX-9. And I'd never heard anything like it. Strings, brass, grand piano, human voices. It could make any sound at all, apparently, and convince you it was the real thing. He was a good-looking boy, Roddy. A little under six foot, with a shock of blonde curls that tumbled around his head and a smile that, annoyingly, could charm you even when you didn't want to be charmed.

The drummer, Murdo 'Skins' Mackinnon, had a high-hat and a snare drum when he arrived at the Nicolson. He used a packing case for a bass drum and biscuit tins for tom-toms. By the time he left he had a full Ludwig kit.

The guitarist, Uilleam Campbell, was a short, intense boy that everyone called Strings. Most people on the island had a nickname, because so many of the Christian names and surnames were the same. If you had sent a postcard from Australia to *Strings, Isle of Lewis, Scotland*, it would have reached him, no problem.

Iain MacCuish was the bass player. They called him Rambo, because anyone less like Sylvester Stallone would be hard to imagine.

And then there was Whistler. So-called because he played the Celtic flute as if he'd been born with it at his lips. Pure, haunting liquid music it was that poured from that flute of his. Sounds that swooped and soared with a flick of his finger, or a curl of his mouth. Strange somehow, coming from such a big brute of a boy whose temper and black moods would become so familiar to me. A boy so clever that while I spent untold hours studying for end-of-term exams, Whistler was off trapping rabbits, or pulling trout from the Red River, and still got the best grades in the school. I didn't know what autistic was in those days. But if you were to ask me now, I'd say that's what Whistler Macaskill was. Or something close to it.

And then there was Mairead Morrison, who played the fiddle and sang. She had the voice of an angel, a body that would arouse any teenage boy's passion, and a smile that would break your heart. Long dark hair falling around square shoulders, and startling Celtic blue eyes. I fell in love with her the first moment I saw her. Me and every other boy in the school.

I was standing in the annexe as the band started to pack up at the end of their rehearsal, drooling like an idiot as Mairead put away her violin, and didn't realize at first that the voice shouting 'Hey!' was being directed at me. It was a big, ginger-haired boy with a livid two-inch scar on his left cheek. He stood at the far side of the classroom. I looked at him. 'What's your name?' he said.

'Fin. Fin Macleod.'

'Where are you from, Fin?'

'Crobost.'

'Aw hell, another Niseach!' It was the Gaelic name for someone from the district of Ness, which was in the far north-west corner of the island where I lived. It drew a laugh from the members of the band. I saw Mairead looking at me and blushed. 'Well, I suppose you'll have to do,' carrot-top said. 'I'm Kenny John, but everyone calls me Kenny Mòr.' Which was Big Kenny. 'I'll need a hand to shift all this stuff over to the hall.'

'What do you need a hand for? You've always managed before.' Whistler was addressing himself to Kenny, but glaring at me.

'There's the new PA, Whistler, and Roddy's stack. I can't handle that on my own.'

'Crap! We've got enough hangers-on as it is!' Whistler stomped out of the classroom.

Kenny grinned. 'Ignore him. He's just pissed off because he saw you ogling Mairead.'

I blushed again, this time to the roots of my hair, and saw Mairead grinning in my direction. I had no idea then how Whistler's obsession with Mairead would shape his future. Kenny chucked me a cardboard box. 'Cables go in there. All neatly wound and tied off.'

I crossed the classroom and lowered my voice. 'Are Whistler and Mairead . . . you know . . . ?'

Kenny laughed. 'He wishes.' And under his breath, 'Like the rest of us.' He glanced towards the keyboard player. 'She's Roddy's property.' Then he looked at me again. 'Are you going to give me a hand or not?'

I nodded.

Which is how I came to be a gear humpher for Sòlas for the rest of my time at the Nicolson.

It is also how I came to be a member of the motorcycle group. I would say 'gang', but that has connotations which wouldn't be right. We were just a group of kids who wanted motor-driven wheels beneath us as soon as we turned sixteen. Roddy was the first, which was not surprising, since his parents were better off than anyone else's. He got a bright red shiny moped, and used to ride around town with Mairead sitting on the luggage rack at the back, her arms around him, and we all imagined what it must feel like to have her pressing herself up against you like that. I'm not sure how legal it was – having a passenger on the back, I mean – but the cops never stopped them.

I suppose that's what started the ambition in most of us. And one by one, those of us who could afford it got ourselves little 50cc mopeds, which in reality were not much more than motorized bicycles. The only money I had was whatever I earned humphing gear for Sòlas. By fifth year they were playing at dances and ceilidhs and pubs all over Lewis, and even down in Harris, and I was sharing a little in their success. But by the time I was able to afford a clapped-out old moped for myself, Roddy had already turned seventeen and graduated to a 125cc Vespa T5 Mk1. Classic blue. Second-hand, of course. It was only a scooter, and would have been scorned by real motorbike enthusiasts, but we thought it was solid gold.

There had always been a rivalry in the band between Roddy and Strings. They were the two major creative forces behind the original music that Sòlas was starting to produce. But that rivalry spilled over into the bike group, too, and it wasn't long before Strings appeared with his own 125cc machine. I can't remember the make of it now, but I'll never forget the colour. It was bright yellow. The same colour as the tormentil that grew among the coastal bracken in summer. You always saw Strings coming.

I spent most of my spare time working on my moped just to keep it on the road. It was a Puch. A Dakota VZ50. It had a 50cc fan-cooled motor with a three-speed gearbox, and was on its last legs. I never took it back to Ness, not just because my aunt would have disapproved, but because I seriously doubted if it would ever have got me there.

On fine spring afternoons, after school, we used to motor out on our bikes, past Engie's and Kenneth Mackenzie's mill, over Oliver's Brae towards the airport and the turnoff to Holm Point. This was a finger of land that extended out into the bay just before the narrow neck of beach and causeway that led to the Eye Peninsula. The fields around us were fallow and shimmered yellow, full of dandelions. There was a cluster of buildings at Holm Farm, but we stayed away from there, and congregated just beyond the road end looking out over the rocks that were known as the Beasts of Holm.

The oil-rig construction yard at Arnish was visible on the far side of the bay, as was the little squat lighthouse there on the rocks, and we had a splendid view back across the whole of Stornoway, sitting low and catching the sunlight in the shelter of the trees that climbed the castle hill behind it. You could hear the sounds of the town carried on the breeze, busy and distant, and dwarfed by the rush of the sea and the oystercatchers and wagtails that dipped and dived around us.

We didn't do much there. Just loafed around in the sunshine, smoking, drinking beer if we had any, flirting with the girls who had ridden out on the back of the bikes.

I suppose if any of us had been aware of the weathered granite obelisk that stood behind its rectangular wrought-iron fence right out on the point, we might have thought it was a war monument of some sort. But I don't think any of us ever paid it any attention. Until the day the old man shouted at us for disrespecting the dead.

It was a Friday afternoon. Some of us had free periods at the end of the day and had ridden out to Holm to profit from the spring sunshine before getting the bus home. We didn't notice him at first, out there at the point, standing by the rusted railing, among the grass and weeds growing all around it. A solitary, stooped figure in black, thin white hair whipped up around his head by the wind.

I had clocked him when we were parking up, but quickly forgot about him when trouble broke out between Whistler and Big Kenny. I'm not sure how it began. I was busy trying to chat up a pretty little girl called Seonag, who had ridden out to Holm Point on the back of my bike. There was a lot of laughter, and some of the boys had cans of beer in their saddlebags. But it was the tone of the voices raised above the rabble that caught my attention. There was real anger in them. And menace. I turned to see Whistler shove Kenny in the chest with both hands. There was enough force in that push to send Kenny staggering several steps backwards, and Whistler was gathering his brows like an imminent storm.

'I've fucking had it with you, Coinneach!'

I knew it was serious when Whistler used Kenny's Gaelic name. Kenny gathered the remnants of his dignity about him and puffed out his chest. 'You're seriously off your head, Macaskill, you know that?'

The jibe was like a red rag to a bull, and Whistler went for him, fists flying. Kenny took one to the head, another to his midriff, before the two of them landed with a thud in the grass, one on top of the other. Kenny's knee came up, trying to hit the sweet spot between Whistler's legs, but just missed, and we saw blood burst from his mouth as Whistler's big fist connected with his lips.

There were three or four of us on top of them in a moment. Hands grasping at the shoulders and arms of the big flute player, dragging him off the gasping Kenny. But Whistler was in a rage, one of those tantrums in which he lost all control. And he turned his fury on us. Unfortunately I was the nearest, and the first to make contact with knuckles like ball bearings. They struck me on the side of the head and knocked me to the ground, lights flashing in my eyes, in just the same way as they did all those years later.

By the time I had recovered my senses, Whistler had already turned back to Kenny and was advancing towards him with something like a growl rising in his throat. No one there was any match for him, least of all me. But that thrawn part of me which had always got me into trouble burned down my back like molten wax, propelling me into battle without thought or fear. Whistler and I, it seemed, were destined always to resolve our conflicts by the fist.

I dived, shoulder first, as I had been taught on the rugby pitch, and took him just above the knees. He went down like a sack of rocks, face-first into the ground, his own weight expelling all the air from his lungs, like the sound of the sea sucking at the cliffs. If it hadn't been for the voice that rose above the shrieks and cries of alarm and encouragement, I think he might have killed me when he recovered his breath.

None of us had been aware of the old man's approach. But his voice cut through the clamour, sharp and high, like a rapier.

'What do you think you're doing! Behaving like idiots in the presence of the dead. Have you no respect?' Had he spoken in English perhaps his words would have had less impact. But the Gaelic somehow carried more weight.

Silence fell upon us like a shroud, Whistler and I still lying gasping on the ground. Everyone looked towards the old man. He wore a shabby black suit, and I could see food stains on his grey pullover beneath it. The cap he had clutched in his hand out at the monument was pulled firmly down now over his head. His eyes were part shadowed, but they were dark eyes full of anger. His face hung

PETER MAY | 85

loose on a bony skull, his flesh goose-white and stained brown in places by age. He raised the hand in which he held his stick and pointed a finger deformed by bulbous joints in my direction.

'You should be ashamed of yourself, young Finlay Macleod.' I was startled to hear my name. I had no idea who he was. As I struggled to my feet, he turned towards Whistler. 'And you, John Angus Macaskill.' I could see Whistler's surprise, too. 'Both of you should know better. Neither of you would be here today if John Macleod hadn't made it ashore with his line.'

He swivelled his gaze, then, in the direction of Big Kenny, and his eyes lingered for a moment on the blood around his mouth. 'And you should be grateful, Coinneach Iain Maclean, that your grandfather was born during a home leave in 1916, or you'd not have been around either.'

No one knew what to say. And in the silence that followed we could hear the distant rumble of traffic along South Beach, and I don't know why, but my eye fell upon the lines of headstones in Sanndabhaig Cemetery, sentinels standing in silent reproach for a misdemeanour we didn't know we'd committed.

The old man bowed his head and walked through us towards the road end, supporting himself on his stick. And we watched him recede into the distance, making his slow, determined way in the direction of the main road.

'What the hell was that all about?' someone said. But I had lost interest in the group, focused now on the monument out on the point. The old man had aroused my curiosity, unsettling me, as if he had just walked over my grave. I forgot all about my fight with Whistler and left the group, their animated discussion carried away on the wind, and walked out to the point for the first time. The monument itself was a sad affair, weather-stained and neglected, the black engraved letters on it barely legible. Whoever had raised it there was long gone, and the reason they had done so long forgotten.

The world around me faded into some distant dimension as I crouched down to wipe my hand across the text, and only the words and the images they conjured had any presence in my consciousness.

*Erected by the people of Lewis and friends in grateful memory of the men of the Royal Navy who lost their lives in the* Iolaire *disaster at the Beasts of Holm on the 1st January 1919. Of the 205 persons lost, 175 were natives of the island and for them and their comrades Lewis still mourns. With gratitude for their service and in sorrow for their loss.*

I heard the sound of bikes starting up, and shouted goodbyes, as the group revved their engines and accelerated across the grass for the road home. I stood up, only to become immediately aware of a shadow at my shoulder. It was Whistler, a strange, bewildered look on his face. And beyond him, standing by his bike and staring out towards us, Big Kenny. Almost as if he were frightened to come and see for himself. All three of us had forgotten our fight by now, and the reasons for it. I searched Whistler's eyes for some sign of understanding, and when I saw none, asked, 'What's the *Iolaire*?'

He shrugged. 'No idea.'

There was a strange quality in the light that night. And when the bus passed the shieling with the green roof out on the Barvas moor, I felt a shiver run through me. And sensed, perhaps more than ever before, the presence of my mother and father at this spot where they had lost their lives.

By the time I got home the sky was an odd purple colour, streaked with grey, and all yellow along the horizon where the sun laid down its liquid gold from behind cloud you couldn't even see. Across the Minch, the mountains of Sutherland were as clear as I had ever seen them. Which meant there was bad weather on the way.

I couldn't get the old man out of my mind, and I suppose I must have been unusually quiet, for it was unlike my aunt to ask me what was wrong. She was a peculiarly disinterested woman, my aunt, self-contained and rarely given to shows of emotion. She never treated me badly, but I always sensed her resentment at having been burdened with the care of her little sister's boy. As if somehow I had stolen her life from her. A life, it appeared to me, that was already over, and passing in sad isolation in the big white house overlooking the jetty beyond the village.

She sat at the dinner table in one of her colourful chiffon wraps, candles burning already along the mantle, the smell of incense and cigarette smoke heavy in the air, like some melancholy memory of another life in a sixties world of youth and hope.

'Come on,' she said. 'Spit it out, Finlay.' She never spoke to me in Gaelic. And she never called me Fin. Just about the only person in the world not to.

'What was the *Iolaire*?' I asked her.

She cast me a curious look. 'Why do you ask about that?'

'I saw the monument out at Holm Point today.' I don't know why, but I didn't want to tell her about the old man.

Her eyes glazed over, gazing off into some distant past. She shook her head. 'It's something folk never really talked about. And today, I suppose, it's all but forgotten.'

'What happened?'

'They say it was very nearly the worst maritime disaster in British peacetime history. Second only to the *Titanic*.'

'And it happened here on Lewis?' I was incredulous. Why had I never heard of it before?

'On a black New Year's morning on the rocks at the Beasts of Holm. Within sight of the lights of Stornoway harbour, and with hundreds of folk waiting at the pier.' She was lost in silent thought for some minutes, and I didn't dare speak in case she wouldn't tell me any more. Finally she said, 'It was 1919, the Great War had just ended, and God knows, enough of our menfolk had died already in that senseless conflict. But the rest were on their way home. Survivors all. Desperate to put their feet back on the island of their birth, and feel the arms of mothers and wives, sons and daughters around them.'

She liked a single glass of wine with her meal, my aunt.

But that night she pulled the bottle towards her and poured a second.

'They were Royal Navy Reservists,' she said. 'From Lewis and Harris. Dumped by the Ministry on to the pier at Kyle of Lochalsh off trains from Inverness. The rear admiral requisitioned an old tub of a steam-yacht called the *Iolaire* to bring back those of them that the MacBrayne's mailboat couldn't carry. More than two hundred and eighty as I recall.' She shook her head. 'Hopelessly inadequate it was. The men were in full uniform, and wearing heavy boots. Many of them didn't have life jackets, and most couldn't even find a seat.' She took a sip from her glass. 'A rough crossing it was, too. But they were within sight of home. They could see the lights of the harbour. It was claimed by some that the crew had been drinking whisky to celebrate the New Year. Whether or not that's true we'll never know, but the captain set the wrong course for the harbour and the *Iolaire* struck the reef at the Beasts.'

She stood up, taking her glass with her, and went to gaze from the window out over the bay below. She could see her own reflection in the glass, and adopted a pose that perhaps she thought conveyed the tragedy she described.

'In fact, they were only a few yards from shore. That was the irony, after surviving all those years at war. The sea was wild, and many of them were simply dashed against the rocks. Others couldn't swim. Didn't know how.' She glanced at Fin. 'You know how it is with islanders.' She returned her gaze to the window, raising her glass to her lips. 'Some were middle-aged, others just teenagers. More than two hundred men died, nearly a hundred and eighty of them from the island. Some villages lost all their menfolk that night, Finlay. All of them.'

She turned back into the room. I couldn't see her face properly against the last of the light from the window, just flickering features highlighted by her candles. It seemed hollow, like a skull, her hair a thin, wispy halo around her head.

'I once heard the old men of the village talk about it. When I was a girl. The only time I can ever recall anyone speak of it. The bodies arriving back in Ness en masse. On horse-drawn carts that pulled four or six coffins apiece all the way up that long west coast road.' She laid down her glass and lit a cigarette, and the smoke billowed around her head like breath on a frosty morning.

'Did we lose someone? Our family, I mean?'

She shook her head slowly. 'No. The Macleods of Crobost were one of the lucky ones. Your grandfather was a boy of nineteen, returning after just a year away. God knows how, but he survived.' She looked at me, tipping her head at an oddly curious angle. 'Your father's father. You wouldn't have been here today if he'd drowned like the rest.' And I shivered, just as I had when the bus passed the shieling earlier in the evening.

'Who was John Macleod?' My own voice sounded very small. 'Was he related?'

'John Finlay Macleod, you mean?' She drained her glass. 'Not that I know of. That man was a hero by all accounts. Somehow he made it ashore with a line, right below where that monument is today, and as a result forty men's lives were saved. Including your grandfather's.'

I passed the weekend in a cloud of uncertainty and depression, unable to escape the thought of all those poor men surviving the war only to die on their own doorstep. And the fact that my grandfather had survived it lingered oddly in my mind like a faintly unpleasant taste in the mouth. It took me a while to identify it.

Guilt.

They say the survivors of major disasters are often afflicted by a sense of guilt. Why had they survived when so many others had not? I suppose I was experiencing it by association. If my grandfather had died like all the others, then I wouldn't have been there. And it made me wonder why I was.

The bad weather finally arrived on the Saturday night. Storm-force winds driving in from the south-west, big dark clouds, contused and bleeding rain. I watched it run down my window on a miserable Sunday, and couldn't wait to be on the bus back to Stornoway in the morning.

The storm had passed by the Monday, but it was still overcast, dull light suffused with a grey-green, as if we were all somehow trapped inside a Tupperware box. But the wind had dried the roads and grasses already, and I tried to empty my mind on the bus ride to town by focusing on the bog cotton that danced among the peat.

There was no chance of me being able to concentrate on schoolwork, and straight off I made my way up through the town to where the library was housed in a jumble of half a dozen or so Portakabins on the corner of Keith Street. I thought they would probably keep archives of the *Stornoway Gazette* there. Yes, the woman at the issue desk told me. They kept the archives in a locked room to my right. What year would I be wanting to look at? 1919, I told her.

She raised an eyebrow. 'A very popular year this morning, it seems. Are you doing a project at the Nicolson?' And in response to my frown she said, 'There's another lad looking at microfilm of that same year in the Gaelic and Local History section down the hall.'

I found Whistler in the reference room, sitting at a table slowly spooling through the newspaper's coverage of the *Iolaire* disaster. He turned as I came in, but said nothing. I pulled up a chair and sat down beside him to watch scratched and ageing images of words written long ago about a tragedy that folk never spoke of. They passed before my eyes like history itself.

We sat a full half-hour in front of that machine, never a word between us, and finally left the library with a nod and a muttered thanks to the librarian, only to find Big Kenny standing beside the wheelie bins on the pavement outside. The wind swept through his ginger hair in waves, and he appeared to be undecided on whether to go in or not. He was startled to see us and raised his eyebrows in tentative query. 'What did you find out?'

'Nothing that you probably don't already know by now,' Whistler said.

'My dad couldn't tell me much. He said his dad would never talk about it.'

Whistler shrugged. 'Mine wasn't sober long enough to ask.'

Kenny nodded. 'I've been at the town hall,' he said. 'The registrar's office.' I don't know why we should have been so surprised, but we were.

'And?' Whistler asked.

'Apparently there are three survivors still living. One of them's at Bhaltos, down in Uig. I know his family.'

Norman Smith lived in an old white house at the foot of the village looking out towards the islands of Pabaigh Mòr, Bhàcasaigh, and the inappropriately named Siaram Mòr. If Siaram Mòr was the big island, we couldn't imagine how small Siaram Beag might be, not that any of us had ever seen or heard of a Siaram Beag.

We rode down on two bikes, me sitting pillion behind Whistler. By the time we arrived my backside was aching. The wind had dropped, and the sea was a dull, dimpled pewter.

The old navy reservist sat in an armchair by the window, where he had an unbroken view out across the water to Pabaigh Mòr. His daughter showed us in. An elderly woman herself, she said he liked to have visitors, but that we weren't to tire him out. She went off to make tea as we settled ourselves down around the old man in a room so small and cluttered there was hardly space for the four of us. The air felt damp, suffused by the smell of peat smoke from turfs still smouldering in the fire. And I remember wondering how he had survived so long. But he had already cheated death once, why shouldn't he do it again?

He was ninety-two years old, he told us proudly, his voice high-pitched and reedy, as if pared thin by the years. He had small dark eyes like black beads. They reflected the light from the window, sharp and still intelligent. I know that age can diminish men, but Norman Smith remained a giant of a man, sitting there in his chair, big-knuckled hands folded one over the top of the other on his stick. There was hardly a hair left on a broad, flat head splashed by age spots.

'Took me years,' he said in response to our question about the *Iolaire*, 'to even let the name of that damned boat pass my lips.'

'How did it happen?' Kenny asked.

'God only knows, boy! The captain made a mistake when he set course for the harbour. Just half a point off he was. We should have been a little more to the west.' We heard his breath rattle in his chest as he drew in air in silent reflection. I couldn't imagine what pictures he was pulling back to mind. 'A lot of us were sleeping, had our boots off and our heads down wherever we could find space on deck. There was a strong wind behind us, but it was strangely quiet when I heard someone shout that they could see the lights of Stornoway ahead. That's when we struck the rocks. The noise as they ripped open her hull was almost human, like a cry of pain. And then there was panic. Panic as I've never seen before or since. If only we had grounded closer to the shore then maybe most of us would have been saved. But the rocks we struck were the furthest out.' He shook his head slowly. 'There were only two of us survived from the part of the ship I was on.'

I sat listening in concentrated silence, images appearing in my mind, evoked by simple words conveying abject horror.

'The ship turned broadside and one man got ashore with a rope.'

'John Finlay Macleod,' Whistler said.

The old man nodded. 'I remember moving his rope from the stern to the side. To this day I don't know how I managed it. But that line saved me and a lot of others. We'd never have got ashore without it.' His breathing became more rapid. 'It was black as hell that night, boys, and we could all feel the presence of the devil come to take us.'

He breathed out long and deep, as if sighing, and appeared to relax again in his chair.

'I still had no boots when I got ashore and climbed up on to the machair. I was soaked to the skin and chittering with the cold, and I knew I had injured my chest and my legs, though I couldn't really feel anything. I saw a group of men huddled at the nearest house, but I decided that I would walk into town.'

We looked at each other. We knew just how long that walk was. We had ridden it often enough on our bikes.

'When I got there I headed for the Admiralty building. There were some others who had made it off the boat, too. All sitting along the wall, wrapped in blankets and smoking, and not a word spoken among them.

'Admiral Boyle came up to me and put a hand on my shoulder. I've got a car for you, Norman, he said. It'll take you and Uilleam and Malcolm back to Uig. In fact, it only took us as far as Calanais. And from there Duncan Macrae's motor launch brought us down here to the pier at Bhaltos. Morning it was by then. New Year's day. My family didn't know I was coming home. I had been hoping to surprise them.'

A single bead of clear mucus hung from his nose, and he reached up absently to wipe it away with the back of his hand.

'They were surprised all right. I met my sister Morag on the road and she took me home to where my mother was already preparing the New Year's dinner. The news about what had happened to the *Iolaire* wasn't put up in the post office at Uig until the following day, so no one knew yet.'

I saw his jaw tighten, then, and the clarity went out of his eyes, blurred by tears.

'And I couldn't tell them. My chest and legs were hurting like hell by then, but I kept it from them and made like nothing had happened.' His breathing was becoming stertorous. 'Until Mr and Mrs Macritchie and the MacLennan family came to the door, and I couldn't face them. Because I knew their boys were all dead, and they had no idea of it. I ran to my room and shut the door and no one could understand what was wrong with me.' Big silent tears fell now from red-rimmed eyes.

The old man's daughter came in with a tray of tea, and her face creased with concern when she saw her father's tears. 'Oh, boys, what have you done to upset him?' She laid the tray on the table and hurried to wipe away his tears with a hanky. 'It's okay, Dad. You calm yourself now.'

He almost pushed her away. 'Nothing to be calm about. It's how it was.' He looked at Kenny, then. 'I know you,' he said. 'Or your father.'

Kenny looked startled. 'My father, I think. Kenny Dubh Maclean.'

Old Mr Smith nodded. 'Oh, aye. Knew his grandfather, too: Big Kenny, we called him.'

'Really?' Kenny was taken aback to learn that his great-grandfather had been known by the same moniker.

'He was at the back of the boat with me when it struck.' He shook his head. 'Never made it. I don't know why, but your family never brought him home. He's buried with a lot of others at the cemetery at Sanndabhaig.'

We both looked at Kenny and saw his shock, as if he were hearing of the death of a close relative for the first time.

The old man swivelled his watery gaze towards Whistler. 'Your father's that drunk over at Ardroil.'

Whistler's mouth tightened into a grim line, but he neither acknowledged nor denied it.

'Not half the man his grandfather was. Calum John. Risked his life, he did, taking another man with him when it would have been easier to grab the line and pull himself ashore on his own.'

And then I felt his gaze fall on me.

'I don't know you, I think.'

My mouth was dry, as if I were sitting in the presence of God Himself and He was pointing a finger at me. 'I'm Finlay Macleod from Crobost in Ness,' I said. 'My father was Angus.'

'Ahhh.' It was as if cataracts had been peeled away from the old man's eyes and he could see clearly for the first time. 'And his father was Donnie. That's why you boys are here.'

I glanced at Whistler, but he just shrugged. 'What do you mean?' I said.

'It was Donnie Macleod that Calum John Macaskill risked his life to pull from the wreck of the *Iolaire* that night. For sure, you wouldn't have been here today, son, if this lad's great-granddad hadn't brought your grandfather ashore.'

Outside we stood by our bikes for a long time without speaking. In the distance you could see the waves breaking all along the shore and the wind was the only voice among us. It was Kenny who broke the silence. He swung a leg over his bike. 'I'm going back to Stornoway,' he said. 'To take a look at the grave.' We nodded, and watched as he kicked his bike into life and puttered away up the hill. I looked at Whistler and said, 'I think there's something we need to do.'

Charles Morrison Ltd, the ship's chandlers, was in Bank Street in Stornoway, a wonderfully old-fashioned hardware shop with all manner of tackle behind its big dark counter. We came out, blinking in the sunlight, Whistler and me, clutching a bottle of white spirit, and walked down to the inner harbour where we had parked our bikes.

The ride out to Holm Point took less than fifteen minutes, but we stopped on the way, at Sanndabhaig Cemetery, to pick up Big Kenny. We had seen him from a long way off standing at what must have been his great-grandfather's grave. And the three of us abandoned our bikes at the road end and walked out to the monument.

I had an old rugby shirt in my saddlebag, and we spent the next hour working patiently and carefully at the stone, to clean away the decades of dirt and neglect which had almost obliterated the words of this memorial to the men who had died that dreadful night.

When we had finished we sat with our backs to the railing, and gazed out over the Beasts of Holm below. Slow-heaving slabs of green water, moving in cautious swells around the shiny black gneiss, broke white around its jagged edges, slurping and sighing almost as if it were alive.

So many had perished there on the dawn of that New Year's day so long ago. Kenny's great-grandfather among them. And all I could see as I looked out over the rocks was the image of the photograph I had seen that morning in the *Stornoway Gazette*. The mast of the *Iolaire*, poking up out of the water. The only part of the boat still visible. At first light rescuers had seen one man clinging to it for dear life. There had been others, but they had been taken by the cold during the night, and one by one dropped off to be claimed by the sea.

Kenny stood up. His scar was oddly inflamed. 'I'll see you tomorrow,' he said, and left without another word.

It wasn't until the rasp of his moped motor was finally lost in the distance that Whistler lit another cigarette and said to me, 'I suppose this means I'm going to have to look out for you now.'

I frowned, not understanding. 'What do you mean?'

'Saving a life makes you responsible for it. I see no reason why that responsibility shouldn't pass on across the generations.'

Later, when I reflected on Whistler's words, I thought that if that were the case then John Finlay Macleod must have felt responsible for an awful lot of lives. And when my mind drifts back to the first day we learned about the *Iolaire*, I often wonder who that old man was, and how he'd known exactly who we were.

# CHAPTER NINE

The sound of the wind outside barely disturbed the silence in Whistler's crofthouse.

Fin said, 'Your dad's great-grandfather saved my grand-father's life in the *Iolaire* disaster.'

Anna frowned.

'It was a ship bringing island men home at the end of the First World War. It sank on a stormy night just outside Stornoway harbour and two hundred and five men lost their lives.'

'Jesus.' Her voice was reduced to a whisper.

'Your dad figured that saving a life makes you responsible for it, and that the responsibility passes down the generations.'

Her smile verged on the incredulous. 'So he took on responsibility for you and your life?'

'He did. And saved it, too, not that long after.'

'Tell me.'

'Another time.'

'Who says there'll be another time?'

'Maybe there won't.' Fin paused. 'What are you doing here, Anna?'

And now it was her turn to avoid his eye. She looked away towards the remains of the long-spent peat fire.

'Did you come to see your dad?'

'No!' Her denial was fierce and immediate. 'I only come when I know he's out.'

'Why?'

She turned eyes like hot coals back on him. And he could see the conflict in her face. Why should she tell him? She had her own reasons. Personal ones. It was none of his damned business. And yet he had answered her questions, and told her personal things that had caused him pain. 'I spent the first half of my life in this house. With my mum and my dad. I have . . . I have happy memories. Sometimes, if I just sit here and close my eyes, I'm back there again. Just for a moment. But that can be enough, you know. When life's shit.' She sucked on the rings in her lower lip. 'I loved my mum. I miss her.'

'And your dad?'

'What about him?'

'Do you love him, too?'

'You must be joking. He's a pure fucking embarrassment. I hate him!'

'Which is just another way of saying you love him.'

Her face screwed up in disbelief. 'Crap!'

'Is it? If you feel so strongly about him that you claim to hate him, it's almost certainly only because you love him and hate to admit it.'

Scorn was etched into every crease in her face. 'Bull. Shit.' When he said nothing he saw her certainty wavering, and she fought to recover her resolution. 'Like you'd have told your parents at my age that you loved them.'

Fin said, 'My parents were killed in a car crash when I was very young. I'd have given anything in the world to be able to tell them I loved them.'

She turned wide appraising eyes in his direction. For the second time in the short period that they had been talking, he had told her things about himself at obvious personal cost. Perhaps she was wondering why. Perhaps she was thinking that talking about your inner feelings was easier with a stranger. No embarrassment in it. No judgements made. 'I'd rather be with my dad than with Kenny.' She took a moment to digest this admission herself. 'Nothing against Kenny. He's a good guy, and my mum loved him I think.' She paused. 'But he's not my dad.' She sighed deeply and shook her head in frustration. 'If only he wasn't such a total fucking shit-head!'

If a vehicle had drawn up outside, then neither of them had been aware of it, so they were both startled by the knock on the door, and the appearance silhouetted in the frame of it of a young woman in her thirties.

She was not unattractive, with shoulder-length blonde hair, blown and tangled by the wind. She wore pressed black trousers and a white blouse beneath an open grey anorak, and held a leather briefcase in her hand. Fin stood up.

'Mr Macaskill?' She blinked as her eyes grew accustomed to the light, or the lack of it.

'Who wants to know?'

'My name's Margaret Stewart.' She stepped in and leaned forward to shake his hand, and appeared a little nervous, eyes darting away towards Anna and back again. 'I'm from the social work department in Stornoway. I'm compiling a background report for the Sheriff. Macaskill versus Maclean for the custody of young Anna Macaskill.'

Fin raised an eyebrow and turned his head towards Anna. 'You've not met, then?'

Margaret frowned. 'You're Anna?'

'Is there someone else here?' Anna's truculence had returned.

The social worker seemed confused. 'I thought you and your father didn't get on.'

'Who told you that?' Fin said sharply.

Now she was embarrassed. 'I'm not at liberty to say.'

'Well why don't you ask the girl herself? Presumably you'll be interviewing her anyway.' Both he and Margaret turned their heads towards Anna, whose defiant facade was suddenly less impregnable. She stuck out her lower jaw and glared at them both. Fin caught her eye and raised his eyebrow an eighth of an inch. But still she hesitated, until the silence became almost embarrassing.

Then finally she blurted, 'I fucking love my dad. Okay? Why else would I be here?'

In the ensuing silence, with only the sound of the wind whistling around outside the house, the social worker appeared entirely discomposed. It was clearly not what she had been expecting. She recovered a little of her composure and looked at Fin. 'Perhaps, Mr Macaskill, we could make an appointment for a private interview?'

Fin said, 'I'm sure John Angus would be happy to meet with you, Mrs Stewart. But you'll have to ask him.'

Her face flushed red with embarrassment. 'Oh. I thought . . .' She paused. 'You're not Mr Macaskill?'

Fin smiled. 'Let's start over, shall we?' He offered her his hand once more, and she took it uncertainly. 'My name's Fin Macleod. Ex-CID, Lothian and Borders police. Now head of security here on the estate. I live in Ness, and I'm one of John Angus Macaskill's oldest friends. So if you're looking for a character reference, I'll be more than happy to give you one.'

# CHAPTER TEN

Evening was wearing on by the time Fin got back to Ness. Having failed to find Whistler, the worry of his disappearance was starting to gnaw at him.

The lull in the wake of the storm was over. The sunshine respite of this single day was already spent, and legions of dark clouds were assembling out on the western horizon, where the last dazzle of the dying sun spilled its gold on distant waters. A gale was getting up, blowing through the heather like wind on water.

He turned his Suzuki off the main road at the Crobost Stores, and climbed the hill towards the bend in the road. The land fell away to his left, to the cliffs that dropped to the crescent of beach below. The Crobost Free Church rose darkly against the sky to his right, stark and unadorned. As he reached the turn-off to it, he could see Marsaili's car on the road ahead, parked on the gravel above the bungalow. He had called her to let her know that he was all right, but she knew nothing of the discovery of the plane. That could wait.

He took the turn up towards the church instead, and rattled over the cattle grid into a parking area where neatly painted white lines guided the faithful into orderly rows like so many drive-in pews. There was a solitary car parked at the foot of the steps leading up to the manse, and he saw Donald's wife making her way down towards it bumping a large case from step to step.

She wore jeans and a knitted jumper, her coat hanging open, a satchel dangling from her shoulder. She reached the foot of the steps as Fin drew in beside her car. Her glance towards him was fleeting, a flick of auburn hair to get it out of her face, and she turned to open up the boot. By the time Fin got around to the back of her car she already had the suitcase inside it. Her face was flushed from the exertion, and perhaps embarrassment. She was reluctant to meet Fin's eye.

'Going somewhere, Catriona?'

She brushed past him and walked around to the driver's door. She opened it, and turned to face him with something like defiance in her stance. 'I'm moving in with my parents.' And then added, like an afterthought that might bring mitigation, 'Until all this gets sorted out.'

Fin frowned disingenuously. 'All what?'

'Oh, come on! You know perfectly well.'

'Maybe you should tell me.' He was playing quite deliberately on her guilt.

'You have no idea how humiliating this is.'

Fin said, 'You're humiliated because your husband's in trouble for saving your daughter's life?'

She gave him a look so filled with pain and anger that he almost recoiled from it. 'There is another minister preaching in our church. They let us stay in the manse, but we're like lepers. No one comes near. No one wants to be seen talking to us. There are those who want Donald gone. And those who don't are too frightened to stand up and say so.'

'All the more reason, then, for you to stand by him. For better or worse. Isn't that the vow you made when you married him?'

Her lip curled with contempt. 'You hypocrite! You stand there and judge me? A man who walked out on his wife a month after his son died in a hit-and-run. The very time she probably needed him most. What about *your* vows?'

Fin felt the colour rise on his face, just as if she had slapped him on both cheeks. He saw, perhaps, regret in her eyes at hurtful words spoken in anger. But it was too late to take them back. She slipped into the driver's seat and pulled the door shut.

The engine coughed into the fading evening light, and Catriona's car clattered away across the cattle grid. Fin watched it go, and depression descended on him like the night.

He stood for a long time, then, before climbing the steps wearily to the manse. There was no response to his knocking on the door. He opened it and called Donald's name, but the house was in darkness. He looked down across the car park and saw in the twilight that one half of the church doors stood open.

It was very nearly dark inside, but he saw Donald sitting at the end of the front pew, staring at the pulpit from which he had so often preached to the converted, exhorting them to greater faith and sacrifice. From the outside, Fin could hear how the wind was whipping up its anger, but here, in the body of the kirk, it was unnaturally still, haunted by the ghosts of guilt and despair.

He sat down beside Donald without a word, and the minister cast him a silent glance before returning to contemplate the emptiness in his heart. Finally Donald said, 'She's moving out.'

'I know.'

Donald turned towards him, surprised.

'I saw her in the car park.'

Disappointment settled on Donald like snow. Perhaps he had hoped she might have a change of heart. 'She's gone, then?'

Fin nodded. And they sat without a word passing between them for five minutes or more. Then Fin broke their silence. 'What happened to us, Donald?' He thought about his own question. 'I mean, all that hope and expectation. When we were just kids and life was nothing but potential. Everything we wanted to be, everything we could have been.' And he added quickly, before Donald could speak, 'And don't talk to me about God's grand plan. It'll only make me more pissed off with Him than I already am.'

He was aware of Donald's head dropping a little.

'Remember that beach party we had the summer before we left for university? On that wee island somewhere off the coast of Great Bearnaraigh.' It had seemed idyllic. Camp-fires and barbecues on the beach, drinking beer and smoking dope beneath a firmament filled with bright stars shining like the hopes they'd all had for themselves. 'Our whole lives ahead of us, and nothing to lose but our virginity.'

Donald turned a wry smile in his direction. 'Some of us had already lost that, Fin.'

And Fin smiled, remembering how gauche he had been that night, making love for the first time to Marsaili, only to discover that Donald had already taken her virginity. His smile faded. 'And look at us now. Trapped in this narrow corner of the world. Nursing our pain and our guilt. We look back with disappointment, and forward with fear.' He turned towards Donald. 'Does none of this test your faith, Donald?'

Donald shrugged. 'It is the nature of faith that it is constantly being tested. Complacency means taking it for granted. And if you do that, you lose touch with God.'

Fin blew contempt through pursed lips. 'Too easy.'

Donald leaned forward, his arms folded across his thighs and swung his head slowly towards him. 'Nothing easy about it, Fin. Believe me, there is nothing simple or easy about faith when your life is turning to shit.'

'So why do you bother?'

Donald thought about it for a long time. Then he said, 'Maybe it's the feeling that you're never alone.' He met Fin's eye. 'But you won't know what that's like, Fin. Being always alone with your grief and your hatred.'

And for the second time that night Fin felt a knowing mind reach into his soul to touch the rawness there. He said, 'Have you heard about the plane?'

'What plane?'

'Roddy's plane. The Piper Comanche. You remember? Call-sign G-RUAI.'

Donald sat up, then, frowning. 'It's been found?'

'It has.'

'How? Where?'

'At the bottom of a loch in Uig.'

Wrinkles creased around Donald's eyes in incredulity. 'How in the name of God did it get there?'

Fin shrugged.

'Bloody hell!' It sounded just like the old Donald. And then he smiled suddenly. 'I always thought that Roddy would come waltzing through the door one day, grinning all over his stupid face and telling us it had all been an elaborate joke.'

'It's no joke, Donald. Roddy was murdered.'

The smile vanished. Shock was writ large all over Donald's face. He sat bolt upright, staring at Fin in disbelief. 'Tell me.' Then he thought better of it, as if remembering suddenly where they were. 'No, not here.' He stood up. 'Let's get some air.'

And as they stepped out into the blustery night, Fin remembered how it was Donald who had set Sòlas on the road to success, until his spectacular fall-out with Roddy.

# CHAPTER ELEVEN

I suppose the band's real rise to fame began with a bet.

Roddy and Strings had written most of the original material that Sòlas was playing at its gigs during fifth year at school. Like Lennon and McCartney, they were a formidable creative duo. But like the visionary force behind the Beatles, they didn't much like one another.

There was an artistic jealousy, a constant competition to prove who was the more creative. And, of course, there was Mairead. Somehow she was at the centre of every conflict in the band, if not the cause of it. In this case she had engaged in a three-month fling with Strings during a period of fall-out with Roddy. The atmosphere both on and off stage had been horrendous.

But by June of that final year at the Nicolson the brief liaison with Strings was over, and Mairead was back with Roddy. Everything in the universe was in its proper place again. Except that Roddy and Strings could barely speak to one another without breaking into an argument.

The bet came about because although everyone agreed that the band needed a change of name before going to

Glasgow, it was impossible to reach unanimity on what it should be.

Sòlas was too comfortable, too soft. They wanted something more edgy, that would reflect the unique blend of Celtic folk and rock that was their hallmark.

In the end there were two front-runners. One Roddy's, the other Strings's. But no one was going to choose between them because it would have been like taking sides.

Roddy's preference was Amran, old Irish for song. He felt it would take the band out of what he called the Gaelic ghetto and into the wider Celtic world. Strings hated it. His choice was Caoran, the Gaelic for those little pieces of peat that are the hardest and blackest, and burn the hottest. Roddy ridiculed it by saying its pronunciation – *kuuran* – made it sound like Koran.

The solution to the impasse came during the first week in June. We had all sat our Highers by then and were just treading water till the end of the school term, so nobody was bothered about going to classes.

Since the revelations about the *Iolaire*, the motorbike group had stopped meeting at Holm Point, and gathered instead at the Bridge to Nowhere, an old concrete bridge above Garry beach beyond the village of Tolastadh on the east coast, about twenty-five minutes north of Stornoway. It was the beginning, and the end, of the Road to Nowhere – both so-called, unsurprisingly, because they went nowhere. The bridge was built and the road begun in 1920. They were the brainchild of the then owner of Lewis and Harris, the entrepreneur and visionary Lord Leverhulme. He had wanted to build a road that would lead all the way up the east coast linking Tolastadh to Sgiogarstaigh in Ness. But Leverhulme died before his grand plans for the islands could be realized, and the Road to Nowhere petered out very quickly into a rough track traversed ever since only by walkers.

It was one of those rare, delicious, early summer days when the wind was soft out of the south-west and the sky was broken by high white clouds that only occasionally masked the sun. Spring flowers shimmered yellow and purple and white across the moor, and the midges were kept at bay by the breeze. Of course, there was always something to spoil a perfect day, and in this case it was the cleggs. The little biting bastards were out in force among the long grasses. Horseflies the English call them, and they give you a real dirty bite, even through clothes if they're tight-fitting.

We were all gathered on the bridge. About a dozen of us, drinking beer, scraping our names in the concrete, or just lying along the parapet sunning ourselves, fearless of the drop into the gorge below. The sun washed across the golden sands of Garry beach and out over the Minch, and I remember thinking there was something almost idyllic about it. The exams were by us, and a new, exciting future lay ahead. Escape from the island, the first chance any of us had had to spread our wings and fly. At that moment, anything seemed possible.

I lay with my eyes closed, my head resting on my folded blazer, drifting away into an imagined future. Which was when angry voices crashed into my idyll.

'Okay! Okay!' I heard Strings' voice raised to an almost hysterical pitch. 'You're on. We'll do it. Tomorrow.'

I opened my eyes, annoyed by the interruption, and swung my legs down on to the bridge. The others were all gathered at the far end where the Road to Nowhere snaked off towards the cliffs. I sighed and jumped down to make my way towards the group.

'What's going on?'

A grinning Whistler turned in my direction. 'We've figured out a way to choose the new name.'

I frowned, surprised. 'How?'

Mairead said, 'Roddy and Strings are going to have a race on their bikes. To the blasted rock, and back.'

I wasn't impressed. 'That's not very far.'

Rambo said, 'It's about two miles. It's enough.'

And Skins added, 'Whoever wins gets to choose the name.'

I found all their faces turned towards me, as if somehow seeking my approval. 'Bloody stupid if you ask me,' I said. 'And dangerous.'

There were a lot of groans and faces turned away again. And Roddy said, 'Who the fuck's asking you anyway?'

Whistler and I walked the proposed course the following morning. It was another glorious day, and with the wind dropping away to almost nothing the midges were out in force. For the first part of the walk, as the road wound across the moor towards the cliffs, rising all the way, we were slapping our faces and necks and waving our hands around our heads like demented puppets.

The surface of the road here was rough. Tightly packed small stones, with moss and grass growing in between. Rocks rose away to our left, and to the right the land dropped by increments towards the shore, in turn smothered by bracken peppered by tormentil and scarred by peat banks. We rounded a bend and startled a clutch of grazing sheep, coats brightly slashed by green and purple markings, and they skittered away ahead of us.

'I'm not going to uni,' Whistler said suddenly, and I was startled.

'Jesus! Why not?'

He shrugged. 'Can't be bothered.'

I stared at him in disbelief. 'Christ, man, it wouldn't be any bother at all to you. I sweat blood trying to pass my exams. You sail through them without even opening a book.'

'So where's the challenge in that?'

I was open-mouthed. 'But what would you do?'

'Stay here.' He gazed off impassively across the sands.

'Are you mad? I don't know anyone that doesn't want to get off the island. And there's not a kid at the Nicolson who wouldn't give their right arm for half your brains and the chance to get into uni.'

He shrugged again. 'Fair enough. But none of them are me. And I want to stay.'

My mind was racing, trying to come up with arguments that would persuade him of the folly of this decision. 'What about the band?'

'What about it?'

'Well, everyone else in Sòlas is going to go to Glasgow.'

'So?'

'So you can't still be in the band if they're there and you're here.'

'So?'

'You're not serious?'

He turned his head slowly and fixed me with his big dark eyes. 'Why wouldn't I be?'

'Because you're a brilliant flute player. Because it's your life.'

He shook his head. 'Nah. I can blow a whistle okay, but what use is it? And it's not my life. Never has been. It's Roddy's band. Him and Strings. It's their lives, not mine.'

I knew he was not to be argued with when he'd made up his mind about something, and so we walked on in silence to the first big bend in the road. The breeze stiffened, blowing away the midges and carrying a smell of fish and dampness to us on its leading edge. Fulmars dipped and shrieked above our heads, and we saw shags down on the water. Looking back you could see Garry, and beyond it the curve of Tràigh Mhòr, literally the big beach. Tolastadh Head and the village itself stretched out on the rise, treeless and stark in the sunlight.

The road dipped, then, before rising to the second bend. It was sharper and closer to the sea, which seemed a long way below us now, and we saw the coastline stretch away to the north, rising sheer from the deceptively tranquil azure of the Minch. The sky was streaked with high cloud, almost luminous in the morning sun, as if brushed across it by some impatient watercolour artist.

Not much further on, a short stretch of grass at the left poured straight over the edge of the cliffs into an almost vertical chasm, or *geodha* in Gaelic, that slashed down sharply into the rock. Peering over from the top of it, you couldn't see the bottom.

I leaned over as far as I dared to look down. 'Bloody dangerous this is,' I said. 'We should post somebody here, just so the boys are aware of it.'

The plan was to station us in pairs at the bends, and at the turning point at the end, just to make sure there was no cheating.

Whistler left the road, and started making his way down the south side of the *geodha* to try to get a better view of it.

'Careful,' I shouted after him. It was steep. I could see sheep on a narrow grassy ledge about halfway down, but nothing beyond that.

He waved his arm. 'Come and see this.'

I picked my way cautiously over the grassy banks and rock until I could see what he saw. Household rubbish. Tons of it dumped over the edge, no doubt by the good folk of Tolastadh over many years. A skein of rusted metal, prams, bicycle frames, fish boxes, old nets, fencing wire. The sea had clawed out the bottom of the pile, but much of it was stranded halfway down, caught by clusters of jagged rock.

The sea was abnormally calm where it washed into the fissure, emerald green and clear as day. You could see the rocks beneath the surface, magnified, and simmering in the current. And even this high above it, you could hear the sea sucking and sighing, its breathing amplified by the acoustic effect of the *geodha*, almost as if it were alive.

We scrambled back up to the road. Whistler nodded then. 'Aye, we definitely need to mark this as a danger spot.'

The road beyond followed the line of the cliffs to where its builders had been forced to blast through a giant rock that blocked the way ahead. Part of it, twelve or fifteen feet high, had been left standing on the cliff side, all of its strata exposed, seams of red running through its broken surfaces, like a geological diary going back to the very beginnings of time.

This gateway to nowhere was to be the turning point. We stood in the gap blown through the stone more than ninety years before and saw how the spoil from it lay all across the hillside, a jumble of shattered rock nestling still where it had first settled after the explosion. And looking back, as the road curved away, we could see straight across to the distant peaks of mainland mountains so hazily familiar to generations of islanders.

'You know what?' I said. 'This is crazy. Why don't you guys just have a secret ballot? Majority vote wins.'

Whistler shook his head. 'Roddy would never agree. He'd be scared of losing.'

Word had got around, and apart from the dozen or so regular members of the bike group another twelve or fifteen kids turned up that afternoon to watch the race. Everyone was gathered at the bridge. Someone had brought a can of spray paint, and some of the kids were decorating the concrete parapets with their names. Roddy and Strings were hyped up and silently tense, focused on the race. There would be no problem distinguishing one from the other. Roddy with his bright-blue Vespa scooter, and the violent yellow of Strings' machine.

Whistler and I were stationed at the second bend. Skins was on duty at the blasted gateway, and Rambo was standing guard at the *geodha*. Mairead and another girl were at the first bend. Curiously she had expressed no opinion what-soever on either of the proposed names, which I took to mean that she probably favoured Caoran, but didn't dare say so.

We heard the shout go up from the bridge, and the roar of revving engines, but we had no sight of the bikes until they rounded the bend. Strings appeared first, crouched low over his handlebars, totally focused on the road ahead of him. Roddy was just a few feet behind, swerving to avoid the dust and stones being kicked up by Strings' rear wheel.

They passed me and Whistler and picked up speed on the straight stretch, engines screaming as they flew past Rambo. Then they vanished from sight. When they reappeared, on the return, it was Roddy who was marginally ahead, tyres skidding and spinning as they both changed gear on the bend. We retrieved our own bikes from the bracken and set off after them, Skins and Rambo not far behind us. Even before we got back to the bridge we could hear a loud cheer going up. Mairead had got back ahead of us, and everyone was gathered around the blue and yellow bikes, voices raised in excitement.

'What happened?' Whistler said as we drew up beside them.

'Dead heat,' someone shouted.

And one of the other kids said, 'They were neck and neck when they hit the bridge. No way to separate them.'

'Good,' I said. 'Honour satisfied. Now why don't we toss a coin?'

Strings wiped the sweat from a dust-stained face as he swung his leg over the saddle and tipped his bike on to its stand. 'I suppose we might as well.'

'No!' Roddy was adamant, and still sitting astride his Vespa. The voices around him fell away to a hush. 'There's another way to settle this. We do it again. Only this time we time it. One after the other. It's the only way to separate us.'

A girl called Dolina went delving into a pink knitted bag slung over her shoulder. 'I've got a stopwatch. We use it for sprint training at the athletics club.'

'We're on, then.' Roddy grinned his satisfaction, and looked to Strings for agreement.

Strings shrugged. 'Sure.'

'We'll toss for who goes first, then.' Roddy dug out a ten-pence piece and spun it into the air. 'Heads,' he shouted, and everyone gathered around to see how it landed when it came down. Heads it was. Roddy grinned. 'Me first.'

Rambo set off on his bike to the turning point to scrape a line in the track that each bike must cross, and to make sure that it did. Dolina stood with her stopwatch at the end of the parapet, and Roddy manoeuvred his front wheel on to the line that marked the end of the bridge and the beginning of the road. We waited to give Rambo sufficient time to get to the blasted rock, and then there was a countdown from three that everyone joined in. Roddy revved and was off as Dolina pressed the start button.

You could see from the way he held his body, how tense and determined he was, back wheel skidding from side to side as he accelerated to the maximum, up the slope towards the first bend. And then he vanished, and the sound of his motor faded into the distance, masked by the rise of the hill.

Strings sat on the parapet, hands clasped in front of him as if in prayer, and never said a word. The rest of us milled about, speculating about the outcome of the race in hushed tones, almost as if we were afraid of breaking Strings' concentration. I glanced at him and saw how some powerful inner tension was writing itself all over his face. For some reason this meant much more to him than it should. After all, what the hell was in a name? And, in the end, what did it really matter?

We heard Roddy's bike before we saw it. He was back very quickly. I glanced at my watch. Just over three and a half minutes. And then he appeared, leaning over at a dangerous angle as he came careening around the bend. It took him fewer than thirty seconds to reach the bridge. We all dived to either side as he accelerated hard over the finish line, then jammed on his brakes and pulled the front wheel around to skid to a stop by the far end.

His face was flushed, eyes shining. He knew he'd made a good time. 'Well?'

'Three minutes, fifty-seven,' Dolina called out, and Roddy cast triumphant eyes towards Strings.

But if Strings harboured any self-doubt he wasn't showing it. He stood up, cool as you like, and threw a leg over his bike to kick away its stand and start the motor. Everyone clamoured around the start line, and I stood up on the parapet to get a better view.

The countdown began.

Strings revved and released his clutch, back wheel spinning, screaming like a distressed gannet, until it gripped, and he was off in a spray of chippings. I watched Roddy watching him, and saw how doubt crept slowly but surely into his mind. And then Strings disappeared as he rounded the bend. Several of us checked our watches as the sound of his engine faded into the afternoon. Tension moved among us like a ghost.

Three and a half minutes passed and still there was no reprise of that shrieking 125cc motor. No yellow blur on the bend. Four minutes, and still nothing.

'Something's wrong,' I said, and for the first time that ghost among us morphed from tension, to apprehension, to fear.

'Ach, he's just fallen off,' Roddy said. 'Trying to go too bloody fast.'

But I wasn't waiting to find out. I jumped on my moped and accelerated over the stony Road to Nowhere, bumping away up the track towards the bend. I heard another bike on my shoulder and flicked a backward glance to see Whistler there. And beyond him, others setting off in pursuit.

There was no sign of Strings, and it wasn't until I passed the second bend that I saw a distressed Rambo at the side of the road above the *geodha*. Strings' yellow bike lay twisted in the grass, its front wheel upturned and still spinning, a large swathe of peat churned up where the bike had slewed off-track. Three sheep were scampering away up the road beyond it. Whistler and I reached Rambo before the others. He was in a panic, eyes wide.

'I was getting my bike when I heard the crash. Must have been those bloody sheep running on to the road. Looks like he went straight over.'

'Fuck.' The word escaped my mouth in a breath.

Whistler was already clambering down the slope on the south side. Recklessly. Arms windmilling, before he jumped down on to the lowest of the rock ledges visible from above, and steadied himself. I went chasing after him. When I reached the ledge I spotted the detritus we had seen that morning, trapped by the rocks halfway down the drop. The bottom wasn't visible from here, and there was no sign of Strings.

I glanced back up the hill and saw everyone crowded along the roadside. Roddy came running pell-mell down the slope towards us. He reached us gasping, eyes wide and filled with fear. 'Where is he?'

'No sign of him,' Whistler said.

'Oh, Jesus.' Roddy immediately began lowering himself over the drop.

Whistler tried to grab him but couldn't hold on. 'For Christ's sake, man, don't be a fool. There's no way down there. And if there is, there's no way back up.'

But nothing was going to stop Roddy. I saw his desperation as he climbed down, face towards the cliff, arms and legs stretching to either side, searching for hand and footholds. He had made it as far as the limit of our ability to see into the *geodha* when his face turned up towards us. 'I can't see him!' His voice echoed around the cliffs. And then he fell from sight with barely time for a muffled cry.

'Shit!' Whistler immediately started to go down after him, but I grabbed his arm.

'We should get help.' I glanced hopelessly up the slope to where the others were gathered along the track, and to my amazement saw a dishevelled Strings push through them to the edge of the *geodha*. He was covered in peat-black mud, and there was blood trickling from his forehead. I have never seen a face so bleached of colour. The others parted to make way for him, staring at him in silent astonishment. He glanced towards Whistler, then back at me.

'Where the hell did you come from?' I shouted.

He shook his head and his confusion was clear. 'Dunno what happened. Damn sheep came running on to the road. Next thing, I'm coming to in the ditch on the far side, and you lot are all gathered around the *geodha*.'

'We thought you went over!' I called back.

'For Christ's sake,' he said. 'Did no one think to look in the bloody ditch!' He lifted his arms then dropped them to his side again. 'Where's Roddy?'

'Fell in going after you!' Whistler bellowed. It was obvious that he had little sympathy for Strings. He turned to me. 'See if anyone up there's got a rope in their saddlebag.' And he swung himself over the edge, searching for Roddy's foot- and handholds.

As I scrambled back up to the road, I wondered at Roddy's desperation. Only fifteen minutes before he had been determined to beat and humiliate Strings in this foolish competition to decide the band's new name. And now he had gone and risked his life, maybe even lost it, trying to save him.

Three of the boys had tow ropes. But none of them was long enough. To everyone's surprise it was Mairead who knew how to tie the knots that would make them into one serviceable length. We shouldn't have been, since her dad was a fisherman, but the speed and dexterity with which she knotted those lengths of rope together took us all aback. Strings just stood watching helplessly. No one was inter- ested right then in how badly hurt or otherwise he might be. The focus was all on Roddy.

I ran down the slope with the rope and several other boys and inched carefully towards the edge of the drop to see if I could spot Whistler. There was no sign of him. I bellowed his name as loud as I could, and to my intense relief heard his voice echo back up at me.

'Did you get a rope?'

'We did.'

'Chuck it down, then, and make sure it's well anchored at the top.'

The only way to secure it was to wrap it around my waist and use me as the anchor, while ahead of me the other boys gripped it, hand over hand, like members of a tug-of-war team. I lay back, almost sitting, my heels dug hard and deep into the peat, and we threw the other end down into the *geodha*.

After a few minutes we felt a tug on it, and then what seemed like the full weight of two Whistlers testing our strength to hold it firm. It was touch and go whether we could. I shouted towards the road for more help, hoping that Mairead's knots were going to hold. Several of the others came running down, girls too, everyone set to lend a hand, until finally we saw the giant form of Whistler pulling himself up over the edge, the apparently lifeless figure of Roddy slung over his shoulder.

As soon as he reached the grass he let go of the rope and dropped Roddy on to the turf. Roddy let out a yell of sheer bloody agony, his right leg twisted at a horribly unnatural angle. Whistler was pink-faced and sweating from his exertions. 'Busted leg,' he said unnecessarily.

Roddy was breathing stertorously and unscrewed his eyes for a moment to open them and look up. Strings leaned over him, his bloodied face a mask of concern. Roddy's lips contorted into a sort of grimace, and he said, 'So. Amran it is, then.'

I didn't see Roddy again until after the start of the summer holidays. He had been rushed to hospital and undergone several hours of surgery on a shattered femur. Metal plates and screws inserted. The band's summer gigs were cancelled, and it wasn't until a meeting called to discuss their future that all the members of the band were reunited for the first time since the accident. I never knew what had passed between Strings and Roddy on the subject of the race, but the incident at the *geodha* was never referred to, not in my presence anyway. And in his own obdurate way, Roddy simply seemed happy that he had won the bet. His leg was plastered and in a brace, and he turned up in a wheelchair pushed by a private nurse paid for by his parents.

The meeting was held in the public bar at Scaliscro Lodge, which sat up on the west bank overlooking Little Loch Ròg. Roddy looked terrible. But he had been determined to convene the meeting, to map out the future of the group once they went to Glasgow.

However, it was Mairead who provided the shock. To everyone's astonishment she had cropped her hair to something not much longer than a crew-cut. Gone was the long, dark wavy hair that tumbled over angular shoulders. She looked stark and gaunt with this most macho of male cuts, although still strangely feminine. There were not many women who could wear their hair like that. But she had strong, striking features, and even the shape of her head, now fully revealed, was classically beautiful. I couldn't take my eyes off her.

Roddy was oddly animated, as if he were on something. And maybe he was. A cocktail, perhaps, of painkillers and beer. Or maybe it was just that restless, relentless ambition that so drove him. But his face was flushed and there was a strange glow in his eyes.

'Amran,' he said, and he threw a little triumphant glance in Strings' direction. 'It's got a good ring to it.' Nobody was going to argue with him. 'As soon as I'm back on my feet, Strings and I will go down to Glasgow to try to line up some gigs, and we're probably going to need a management company.'

I caught a glimpse of Whistler out of the corner of my eye as he laid his pint glass down on the bar with an odd sense of finality. I knew what was coming. 'I won't be going to Glasgow,' he said.

The thumping of the music playing over the stereo system only further emphasized the silence that followed.

Rambo said, 'What . . . you mean you've applied for Strathclyde, or Edinburgh, or somewhere?' You could hear the disbelief in his voice.

'I mean I won't be going to any university. Glasgow, Edinburgh or anywhere else. I'm staying on the island.'

I almost held my breath.

'What are you talking about?' Roddy said. All the light had gone out of his eyes. 'You can't stay here and still be in the band.'

'Congratulations. You just won a set of steak knives and a holiday for two in Torremolinos. You'd better look for another flute player when you're down in Glasgow.'

Roddy looked as if the world had just fallen in on him.

Mairead said quietly, 'When did you decide this?'

Whistler shrugged. 'A while ago.'

'And you never told us?' Roddy was angry now.

The sound of Mairead's open hand hitting the side of Whistler's face was like the crack of a rifle. She hit him so hard that he had to put a hand on the bar to steady himself. She stared at him for a long, hard moment with something akin to loathing in her gaze, before turning to walk out of the bar.

Ironically Amran, as they became, achieved their greatest success post-Whistler, and the accident on the Road to Nowhere seemed, perversely, to have brought Strings and Roddy closer together.

But prime mover in their transition from island Celtic rock band to mainstream supergroup was Donald Murray. Big Kenny had gone to agricultural college in Inverness, leaving the band without a roadie. And it was after my final break-up with Marsaili that I got a call one day from Donald.

'Hey man,' he drawled. He was affecting a mid-Atlantic accent in those days, somewhere between Ness and New York. One of the brightest boys of his year at the Nicolson, he had come down to Glasgow University, carrying with him all the despairing hopes of his parents. His father, Coinneach Murray, was one of the most feared and respected men in Ness. Minister of the Crobost Free Church, a man of fire and brimstone, a relentless advocate of a harsh and unforgiving Christianity. A Christianity that his son had rejected from an early age, becoming the archetypal rebel without a cause, and defying his father at every turn. He drank, swore, slept with more girls than you could count, and seemed hell-bent on a road to self-destruction.

He dropped out of first year at university before Christmas, and I had lost track of him until that phone call at my student lodgings.

'Donald?' He sounded different to me.

'It's me, bro.'

'Where the hell are you? I mean, what are you doing?'

I heard him chuckling on the other end of the line. 'I'm in the music business, bro.'

'Donald, I'm not your bro!'

'Hey, Fin boy, keep the heid. It's just a figure of speech.'

'What music business?' I said.

'Got a job in a music agency. We represent bands, singers, organize tours, negotiate deals with record labels.' He paused, and I heard the pride in his voice. 'I'm personal assistant to Joey Cuthbertson, impresario extraordinaire. Amazing guy, Fin. What he doesn't know about the music business isn't worth knowing. And I'm going to pick his brains until there ain't a cell left I don't possess.'

'Good for you.'

He laughed. 'Never could impress you, could I?'

'Not when you were trying to, Donald. The thing you've never understood is that you don't have to try.'

More laughter down the line. 'Fin, Joey Cuthbertson's signed Amran.' He paused. 'On my recommendation. They're going places, boy. Mark my words. I figure we'll have a record deal before Easter.'

'Good for them. What's any of this got to do with me, Donald?'

'We need a roadie, Fin. Big Kenny's gone to Inverness, and your name came up. The guys are comfortable with you.'

'Some of us are still trying to get a degree, Donald.'

'Nights and weekends, Fin. Good money in it. And, hey, you'll sail through your degree, bro, without even breaking sweat.'

Donald was wrong about a lot of things. But he was right about Amran. I roadied for them for the rest of that academic year, and we gigged all over Scotland and the north of England. The record deal that Donald predicted came in June. The band spent the summer in the studio recording their first album, which they called *Caoran*, as a sop to Strings. They were mostly songs on which Roddy and Strings had collaborated, but they were given a real professional gloss by a producer who came up from London. They never did replace Whistler. When their first single was released in September it went straight into the charts at No. 5.

Mairead was turning into a minor celebrity, her face appearing regularly in the Scottish red-tops and on the covers of several nationally distributed magazines. She had her own fashion guru now, at least that's what Mairead called her. A kind of dusty-looking lesbian art school dropout who advised her on clothes and make-up. I had to pinch myself at times to remember that Mairead was just a wee lass that I'd known and fancied at school.

Roddy's dad had bought him a second-hand, single-engined aeroplane. A red-and-white Piper Comanche. And the band had started earning enough for Roddy to pay for flying lessons out of Glasgow airport. But Roddy was flying high in more ways than one. He was destined for stardom and recognition of his very special talents. That's how he saw it, anyway. And it was that overweening ambition that brought him, finally, into conflict with Donald.

By the time I went into second year at university, Roddy and the rest of Amran had dropped out to concentrate on their careers in the band. Joey Cuthbertson had been reduced by a heart attack to little more than an invalid, and Donald had stepped into his shoes as No. 1 at the agency. It seems he had indeed sucked the old man dry.

But although Donald's dramatic rise to prominence in the Scottish music business had led to a resurgence of interest in mainly Glasgow-based bands like Amran, it also coincided with his spiralling descent into drink and drugs. He had always been, I suppose, a classic contender for that uniquely island condition known as the *cùram*, when childhood indoctrination in unrelenting Presbyterian beliefs resurfaces like a virus after years of dissolute living to reshape its victims in the image of their fathers. In this case, the Reverend Coinneach Murray. But it would be a few years before Donald would find himself following in his own father's footsteps. For the moment he was having too much fun in denial.

What he had done was taken his eye off the ball, and Amran's career was starting to stall, even before they had recorded their second album. Success can come in the blink of an eye, but vanish just as quickly, like an evaporating tear. The gigs were routine and repetitive and not serving in any way to advance the band's career. Donald was never there, never at the end of a telephone, never around to discuss the things that Roddy and Strings and the rest thought important to their future. He had already embarked on that long and treacherous slide into addiction.

For my own part, I didn't much care. I drove the van, and the money I made meant I didn't have to think too much about my own future. In truth, I didn't really want to think about it. I had no interest in my degree course, no ambition, no idea what to do with my life. The news which had greeted me on my return to the island for my aunt's funeral had robbed me of any interest in it. Artair and Marsaili were married. I had lost my oldest friend, and the only girl I had ever really loved.

The friction between Roddy and Donald finally came to a head one weekend in early November.

It was a Friday night, and Amran were giving a concert in one of those end-of-pier pavilions, a survivor from the days of seaside music hall, rescued from demolition and lovingly restored. It was somewhere on the west coast of England. I don't remember where, exactly. One of those Victorian coastal resorts that had somehow survived the town hall vandals of the fifties and sixties and retained a kind of faded charm. The original promenade which ran a mile or so along the seafront was still there, and the pier was an elaborate structure of iron struts and girders nearly five hundred feet long. The pavilion itself was a shambles of curved roofs on the T at the end of it, and housed an auditorium with a seating capacity of between four and five hundred. In the summer it hosted those seaside variety shows that still somehow attracted large audiences. But events in November were few and far between.

It was typical of the gigs that Donald had been booking for the band, and Roddy was in a mood even before we set off, determined to have it out with Donald, who had agreed to meet us there.

It was a filthy night, wet and blustery, light fading as we drove into a little town en route, tucked away among the unfamiliar folds of rolling green English countryside. I was peering through my rain-smeared windscreen searching for signposts when Rambo, who always travelled in the van with me, suddenly shouted at me to stop. I jammed on the brakes.

'What the hell—?'

The car carrying the rest of band nearly ploughed into the back of us.

'There's a guy on the bridge.' Rambo pointed across my line of vision towards the parapet of a bridge that spanned the brown waters of a river in spate. It was an old stone bridge, with lamp posts at intervals across its arch. A man stood up on the parapet wall, one hand clutching a lamp post. He was looking down at the water rushing past below. There was no mistaking his intent. A man steeling himself to jump.

Roddy, Mairead and the others leapt out of the following car and ran round to my door.

'What's wrong?' Roddy shouted.

I pointed over the bridge. 'Looks like that guy's about to do away with himself.'

Everyone looked and there was a momentary hiatus. 'Jesus,' Roddy whispered. 'What are we going to do?'

I glanced at my watch. 'We're running late already.'

Mairead threw me a look. 'A man's life is a little more important, don't you think, than a gig on a pier?'

We all looked at her in surprise.

'She's right,' Strings said. 'Come on, let's try and talk him down.'

But Mairead grabbed his arm. 'No, you'll scare him off. I'll talk to him.'

We watched as Mairead made her way cautiously towards him, and heard her call out. 'Hello, I wonder if you could help me? I think we're lost.'

The man's head snapped around, frightened rabbit's eyes drinking her in. He was a man in his fifties I would say, losing his hair. Unshaven, and wearing a shabby raincoat over charcoal-grey trousers and a thread-worn cardigan. 'Don't come near me!' He raised his voice above the roar of the water and glanced beyond her in our direction.

'What are you doing up there?' Mairead asked him.

'What do you think?'

Mairead looked down at the river and shook her head. 'Not a good idea. You'll ruin your shoes.'

He looked at her with something like disbelief, and then

she smiled, and there was something about Mairead's smile that no man I ever knew could resist. He smiled back. A timid, uncertain smile. 'They're not new,' he said. 'So it won't really matter.'

She looked at his feet. 'You're wearing odd socks.'

He seemed surprised, and took a look for himself. 'Who cares?'

'There must be someone who does.'

His lips tightened into a grim line and he shook his head. 'No one.'

'No one at all?'

'The only one who ever did is gone.'

I saw her eyes fall upon the man's left hand holding the lamp post and the band of gold on his third finger. 'Your wife?'

He nodded.

'She left you?'

'She's dead.'

'Recently?'

Again he shook his head. 'A year ago today. Cancer. It was a long time coming.' He turned to look at the water flashing below, then back at Mairead. 'I tried so very hard. But I just can't do it any more.'

Mairead moved carefully, then, turning around to pull herself up into a sitting position on the parapet at his feet, hands flat on the wall on either side of her. 'No children?'

Another shake of the head. Then, 'Well, yes. But he's in Australia. I told you, nobody cares.'

She tilted her head to look up at him. 'I care.'

He almost laughed. 'You don't even know me.'

'Yes, I do. I know you very well.'

'No, you don't!' His tone was hostile now.

'Yes I do.' And I saw a shadow cross her face, a cloud of real emotion. 'You're every man who's ever lost the woman he loves. You're my dad. I wish I'd been there for him. But I never knew, you see. He never said. And I never found out till he was gone. The young are too busy with their own lives. And it's easy to forget that your folks still have lives, too. Feelings. You never lose those, even when you get older.' She turned moist eyes towards him. 'Have you told him? Your son. Have you told him how you feel?'

'I'm not going to bother him with stuff like that.'

'And you don't think he'll be bothered when the police come knocking on his door to tell him his father killed himself? You don't think he'll wonder why you never spoke to him? Or the guilt he'll probably live with for the rest of his life, thinking there's something he could or should have done?'

The man's face crumpled, then, and tears rolled down his cheeks with the rain. 'I didn't want to be a nuisance.'

Mairead eased herself off the wall and held out a hand towards him. 'Come on,' she said. 'You're not a nuisance. Let's go and call him. Right now.'

'It's the middle of the night there,' he said.

Mairead smiled. 'He won't mind. Trust me.'

He looked at her for a long moment, and she held his eye, hand still outstretched, until finally he grasped it and jumped down on to the pavement beside her. Mairead put her arms around him and hugged him. The rain intensified then, as if crying with them, soaking them both as they stood in the middle of the bridge, darkness falling around them, the lights of cars raking past, drivers oblivious to the little life-and-death drama playing itself out by the parapet.

Then, still holding his hand, she walked him towards us.

'Come on, mate,' Roddy said, ushering him into the car. 'Let's get you home.'

The man lived in a semi-detached house in a short suburban street on the outskirts of the town. A drab, miserable place. Mairead switched on the lights and put on a kettle. A train rattled past the foot of a long, narrow garden with a dilapidated potting shed and an overgrown lawn.

Roddy went next door and came back with the neighbour, an elderly woman who fussed and flapped in the tiny kitchen where the rest of us were gathered, and said she knew a friend who would come and sit with him. And Mairead sat him down by the electric fire with the phone, and dialled the number of his son in Australia.

We left him then, with the neighbour keeping an eye till the friend arrived, the man talking hesitantly to his son ten thousand miles away. I could not really imagine what kind of a conversation it might be. But he was alive, and he was speaking about how he felt instead of bottling it up and driving himself to suicide. And that was all down to Mairead.

On the path, as we walked back to the vehicles parked in the road, I said to her, 'I didn't know your parents were dead.'

She shrugged. 'They're not.' And then she laughed at my frown. 'Oh, Fin, Fin, you're such an innocent. The situation called for a story, so I gave him one. When I sing about a broken heart, or everlasting love, folk need to believe that it's true. That my tears are real. I'm good at that.'

I thought about the emotion which had clouded her face as she lied to the man on the bridge, and how easily both he and I had been convinced. And I realized then that I could never trust her to tell me the truth about anything.

The upshot of it all was that we arrived an hour late for the gig on the pier. The manager was a skinny, uptight, bald little man called Tuckfield. He wore a blue suit with brown shoes. A combination I had never trusted. He was red-faced and close to apoplexy. And, of course, there was no sign of the smooth-talking Donald to pour salve on troubled waters.

'I have three hundred paying customers in there baying for my blood or their money back,' he spluttered at Roddy.

Me and the guys left Roddy to try and explain as we unloaded the van. I don't know how we did it, but the band was on stage and opening the show within half an hour. Myself, and a Glasgow boy called Archie, who drove the car, lay down in sleeping bags in the back of the van to try to get some sleep, and the band played for almost three hours to make up for their late arrival.

The first I knew that there was any trouble was when the back doors of the van were flung open and Roddy stood out on the pier, his face grey with anger. 'That bastard won't pay us!'

'What?' I sat bolt upright. If the band didn't get paid, I wouldn't get paid.

'We played nearly an hour longer than agreed to make up for being late, but he still says we were in breach of contract and won't pay.'

I jumped out the back. 'Let's go talk to him.'

We found him in his office at the end of a corridor behind the stage. He was wary and defensive when Roddy and I came in, and took an instinctive step back from the door. He raised a hand. 'I don't want any trouble.'

'There'll be no trouble,' I said. 'Just pay us and we're gone.'

He waggled a finger. 'No, no, no. You people left me hung out to dry tonight. That wasn't professional. You broke your contract. Get me your manager on the phone, and when we've agreed compensation, you'll get your money.'

'You've had your compensation,' Roddy almost bellowed at him. 'We played an extra fucking hour!'

'I still had people asking for their money back. People who left before you even showed up.'

I thought Roddy was going to go for him, and stepped in quickly, hand raised. 'Okay, let's get Donald on his mobile.' Not everyone had mobile phones in those days. Donald had the latest model, but there was no guarantee that he would be in any fit state to answer it. He should have been at the gig with us. But he wasn't. God only knew what had become of him.

I borrowed Tuckfield's phone and listened as the number rang unanswered at the other end, until Donald's messaging service kicked in. There didn't seem any point in leaving a message. When I hung up I saw murder in Roddy's eyes.

I tried to be the voice of reason. 'Now look, Mr Tuckfield, you know why we were late. We saved a man's life tonight. And we gave you an extra hour of our time to make up for it. Now, we're not unreasonable people. And I'm sure you're not an unreasonable man. So we'll just go and pack up the van, and wait out front. And when you decide you're going to pay us, we'll shake hands, and say no more, and be on our way.' I paused. 'And if you don't . . .' I could feel Roddy's eyes on me, wondering what was coming next. 'Well, you can stay in here and rot. I've driven two hundred and fifty fucking miles to get here, and I've another two hundred and fifty fucking miles to get home, and I'm not fucking leaving till I get my fucking money.'

I wasn't one to swear much, although Mr Tuckfield wasn't to know that, but Roddy did. And as I strode back out to the van, with Roddy almost running to keep up, he said, 'Maybe you should be our manager, Fin.' I just gave him a look.

We were packed up and ready to go shortly after midnight. Mairead and the other members of the band who travelled in the car wanted to go, leaving me and Roddy to deal with Tuckfield.

But I was adamant. 'No. We all stay, or we all go. And if

I go without being paid, this is the last gig I drive for you people.' And they knew I meant it.

So we stood around outside at the end of the pier, smoking, wrapped up in coats and scarves, listening to the sea washing up against the stanchions below us. The streetlights of the town, rising up across the hill beyond the promenade, twinkled in the dark. But the good people of this once popular holiday resort had long since gone to bed, and the houses that lined the hillside stood in darkness. The rain had stopped, but everything was still wet, reflecting street lamps and stars.

I didn't know how long Tuckfield was prepared to stay in there, but I was ready to sit it out till the following morning, if necessary. By one o'clock the others were getting restless.

'Come on,' Strings said. 'This is pointless. Let's go.'

Roddy was shaking his head slowly, almost like a man in a trance. He muttered, very nearly inaudibly, 'This is the end for Donald fucking Murray. He's finished. Finished!'

All the lights around the pavilion went out, plunging the end of the pier into darkness. Everyone was suddenly alert. Almost at the same time, the distant wailing of a police siren drifted to us across the night, and I turned to see the blue light of a police patrol car heading down the hill towards the front. It was no surprise when it bumped across the promenade and headed straight up the pier towards us.

'Jesus!' Rambo said. 'He's called the cops.'

I felt indignation welling in my chest. 'So? We haven't done anything wrong.'

But as it turned out, the cops weren't interested in us. The patrol car drove straight past, swerving into a sideways skid on a handbrake half-turn, and coming to a stop right outside the main door. A white-faced Tuckfield emerged, quickly locking the door behind him, and jumped into the back seat of the police car. The car revved and spun its back wheels, and sped off along the pier.

For a moment we all stood watching in disbelief.

Mairead sat in the front seat of the car, face pale and angry, like a full moon reflected on the windscreen. Roddy and Strings were in the back, Roddy sitting side-on, with his legs out of the open door. I don't really know what possessed me, but anger rose in me like overheated milk and I jumped behind the wheel of the car and started the engine.

'What are you doing?' Roddy shouted.

'Just shut the door!'

He barely had time to get his legs in and pull the door closed before I had spun the car around to accelerate hard along the pier in pursuit of the police car. 'For Christ's sake, Fin, you can't go chasing the cops!'

I saw Strings' frightened-rabbit face ballooning into my rearview mirror. 'Jesus, Fin, you'll get us all arrested.'

I said nothing, and as I pressed my foot to the floor in an attempt to close the gap on the blue flashing light ahead of us, I was aware of Mairead turning to look at me. But she never said a word.

The police car slewed across the promenade and turned south towards a collection of fairground attractions shut-tered up for the night. The driver ran a red light, and turned up the hill. I could feel the tension in my own hands as I spun the wheel and followed. There were no other vehicles around this early in the morning.

At the top of the hill the police car turned right then dog-legged to the left, and I felt my tyres sliding on the wet surface of the road as I followed, losing control for just a moment before finding grip again and picking up speed. I was almost hypnotized by the blue flashing light dead ahead, without a single thought of what on earth it was I might do if and when I caught up with it. But we were gaining on it, and the tension being generated by the others in the car was almost tangible.

Suddenly the brake-lights of the car in front filled our windscreen, blurred and dragged across it by the wipers. I stood on my brakes, feeling the car drifting beneath me, swinging left, and then right as I pumped the brake for grip and swung the wheel one way then the other to right the skid. We stopped, I think, within six inches of the rear bumper of the police car.

There was an almost collective exhalation of relief from Roddy, Strings and Mairead, and I sat clutching the wheel, breathing hard. For what felt like an inordinate length of time nothing happened. Both cars sat there, one behind the other, engines idling.

I could see Tuckfield's frightened face, half turned to peer back at us through the dark. Nobody moved. Nobody spoke.

Then the driver's door of the police car swung slowly open. A goliath of a uniformed police sergeant stepped out on to the street, pulling on his cap and tugging its shiny peak down over his eyes. He stood for a moment glaring at us, then walked slowly towards my side of the car, one hand on his hip, the other touching the handle of the baton that hung from his belt.

I wound down the window as he leaned in to peer at me. His face was impassive, and his dark eyes flickered first towards Mairead, and then Roddy and Strings in the back, before returning to me. I could see a shaving of ginger hair around his head beneath his cap. 'Are you in the band?'

'I'm the roadie.'

He nodded and took a black notebook and pen from his breast pocket. He reached past me and handed it to Mairead. 'My daughter's got your CD. I figure she'd love to have your autograph.'

Mairead gave him one of her smiles. 'Of course.' She took his notebook, found a blank page and signed it. She glanced over her shoulder. 'Do you want the others?'

'Are they in the group?'

'They are.'

He nodded, and Mairead handed his notebook back for Roddy and Strings to sign. Roddy reached over my shoulder to give it to me, and I handed it back. He returned it to his breast pocket, then focused his glare on me once more. To my surprise he thrust his big hand through my window.

'I'll shake your hand, son.' For a moment I couldn't bring my arm to move, before suddenly it reached up, almost involuntarily, for my hand to be gripped by his. A warm, firm handshake, that he held for what seemed like an eternity. When finally he returned it to me he said, 'You've got some fucking nerve, boy, I'll give you that.' He paused to draw a long breath. 'Your story had better be good.'

So I told him. He stood and listened in silence, his slow, stertorous breathing pulsing out clouds of misted breath to swirl around his head. When I had finished he nodded and drew in his lips. 'Well, I'll tell you, son. And here's the thing.' He nodded towards his car. 'Mr Tuckfield there has friends in high places. And I'm just doing what I'm told, no questions asked. So whatever the rights or wrongs of what's gone down here tonight, you'll be going home without your money, and damned lucky not to be spending the night in a police cell.' I could have sworn then that there was a smile in his eyes that he was doing his best to conceal. 'In all my years in the force,' he said, 'I have *never* been chased in a police car. And I'm damned sure it'll never happen again.' He flicked his head back down the hill towards the seafront. 'On your way.' He leaned down, then, smiling past me at Mairead, and tapped his breast pocket. 'Thanks for the autographs.'

We sat in silence and watched as he got back behind the wheel of his car and drove off into the night. I could see Tuckfield's smug face grinning back at us. I wound up the window and Roddy said, 'Donald's fucking dead!'

I never was party to exactly what transpired between Roddy and Donald, but within the week the band had fired him and signed up with an established London agency. And while Donald's career and life then went into free fall, Amran's fortunes soared. They made several television appearances, and Roddy and Strings were commissioned to write a song for a Hollywood movie being shot in Scotland. The producers liked it so much they asked the band to write and record all the incidental music, which then became the basis of their next album. The subsequent success of the film led to even greater success for Amran. The song was released as a single and shot straight into the charts at No. 1, where it stayed for almost five weeks. By the time their next CD was in the music stores, they were riding high on what appeared to be an unstoppable track to the top.

Except that Roddy, for all his talent and all his ambition, never lived to see it.

I remember that it was the following summer, June or July, when I heard. I had got drunk the previous night, on the rebound from a relationship of several months, and ended up in the bed of a girl I'd met at a party. She was a student, living in a bedsit in Partick, on the downmarket edge of Glasgow's west end. I didn't wake up till ten or eleven, pretty hungover and with very little recollection of what had passed between us the previous night. She didn't even seem familiar to me as she leaned over the bed and shook me gently awake.

'You told me last night you roadied for Amran,' she said.

I could hardly open my mouth, it was so dry. 'So?'

'Roddy Mackenzie's the keyboard player, right?'

'Jesus Christ, what about it?' I screwed up my eyes against the light.

'It's all over the morning news. Apparently his plane went missing somewhere up the west coast yesterday evening. Search and rescue have been out all night. They've given up hope of finding him alive. They're just looking for wreckage out at sea now.'

# CHAPTER TWELVE

The wind buffeted and bullied Donald and Fin as they walked down through the dying light towards Port of Ness, and Fin told Donald about the discovery that he and Whistler had made that morning. The street lamps were already on, all the way along to the big white house at the end of the road. They turned off before then, opposite Ocean Villa, and followed the winding band of tarmac down to the harbour. Lobster creels were piled up against the inner wall of the jetty. There had been some repair work done where the weather had wreaked its damage. But the far wall, standing against the furious assaults of the north-easterlies, was smashed beyond any redemption. Fin had seen waves fifty feet high breaking over it when he was a boy, white spume rising twice that height, to be whipped away by force-ten gales and carried off across the cliffs.

Tonight, with the wind blowing from the south-west, the harbour was relatively sheltered, although the few crabbers tied up within its walls were rising and falling on the swell, and tugging determinedly at their ropes. When they reached the end of the jetty wall, Donald cupped his hands around a cigarette and made several attempts to light it.

When finally he did so, the smoke was whipped away from his mouth. 'I still find it hard to believe that he's dead. Even after all these years.' He shook his head. 'Everything about Roddy was larger than life. His talent, his ego, his ambition. Talk about blind ambition! That was Roddy. It consumed him to the point where nothing else mattered. Where he couldn't see the hurt he was inflicting on the people around him.'

'People like you?'

Donald flicked him a look. 'I didn't kill him, if that's what you're thinking.'

Fin laughed out loud. 'Donald, I never thought for a minute that you did. Whoever killed him could fly an aeroplane and land it on water. Even if you could fly, in those days you were in no state to ride as much as a bicycle.'

Donald looked away, clenching his jaw. It was not something in which he took pleasure of being reminded. 'He cut me loose without a word, Fin. There was no contract with the band, then. Just trust. And he betrayed that trust. The first I knew about it was when I read in the *NME* that Amran had signed with the Copeland Agency in London. They had some tie-in with CAA in Los Angeles, and that's what brought Amran the film deal.'

'Maybe you hadn't been doing a whole hell of a lot to earn their trust, Donald. Or advance their career.'

Donald pulled on his cigarette and shook his head sadly. 'Oh, I know. I was an ass, Fin. In almost every possible way. I did things, said things in those days that . . . well, that I still can't forgive myself for. It fills me with shame every time I look back on how I was.'

'I'm sure God knows it was just a passing phase.'

Donald's head snapped around, anger blazing in his eyes. But all he said was, 'Don't be so cynical, Fin. It's ugly.'

Fin said, 'So you never actually had it out with him face to face?'

Donald sucked more smoke into his lungs. 'Never. I probably deserved his anger, though he never had the guts to face me with it. But it was me who got them that first recording deal, Fin. They would just have been another university band otherwise, all going their separate ways when they got their degrees.' He flicked his cigarette away into the wind. 'When they signed for Copeland it was the beginning of the end for me. I got the boot from the Joey Cuthbertson Agency not long after that. Went down to London. But that was just tipping myself out of the wee frying pan into the big fire.' He snorted his self-contempt. 'Addictive personality, you see. Never could resist a temptation.' The same addictive personality, Fin thought, which made him cling now to his religion. And then Fin heard the irony in his chuckle. 'Strange that it was Catriona who proved to be my salvation. Or, at least, a drunken night of unbridled passion and unprotected sex that got her pregnant. There's nothing like having responsibility for another life to make you start caring about your own.'

Fin wondered if feeling responsibility for Fin's life had made Whistler care any more about his. Somehow he didn't think so. But he didn't share the thought with Donald.

'Pure chance, too, that I met her down there,' Donald said. 'You must remember her from school. She was a couple of years behind us at the Nicolson.'

Fin nodded.

'I used to think that God had sent her to rescue me.' He paused. 'But maybe I was wrong about that.'

'Did you ever go flying with Roddy, Donald?'

'Hell, no! I've got no head for heights, Fin. I hate flying at the best of times.' He scratched his chin thoughtfully. 'As I recall, after he and Mairead split up he had his own circle of friends. Whether he went flying with them or not, I wouldn't know. I remember he got involved with some Glasgow girl. No idea what her name was. But she was quite classy. A real looker. And not short of a few quid.'

'Yes, I remember her.' Fin had a picture of her in his mind's eye at a party in a large sandstone villa on the south side of Glasgow. A beautiful, willowy, blonde girl.

'That was just before I left for London.' Donald smiled. 'Roddy never did have any trouble finding himself a woman.'

'Neither did you, Donald.'

There was a flicker of his old self in Donald's eyes before he forced the focus back on Roddy. 'It's strange, though.'

'What is?'

'How the band went from strength to strength without Roddy. Just goes to show that for all his high opinion of himself, it was Strings who was the bigger musical influence.' He shook his head. 'I haven't listened to them once in all these years. God teaches us to forgive, but it's very hard to forget. And I know that just the sound of Mairead's voice would bring it all back. And I don't need that pain as well.'

He tried to light another cigarette, but the wind was too ferocious now and he gave up. They felt the first spots of rain whipping into their faces.

'Roddy wasn't universally popular, Fin. I know that. God knows, I had reason enough to hate him myself. But who would have wanted to murder him? And why?'

Fin shook his head. 'I haven't the first idea, Donald.'

The rain turned into a deluge then, and the two men ran from the jetty towards the boat shed at the end of the beach. Donald slid one of the doors open and they slipped inside, soaked already. It smelled of diesel and fish in here, and the shadows of small boats were canted at odd angles between windows that gave out on to the beach and the sound of the sea. There was almost no light left before Donald's lighter suddenly illuminated his face, painting it orange by its flickering light, then red in the glow of the lit tobacco, before fading back into darkness.

Neither spoke for a moment, gripped unexpectedly by a sense of being in the presence of the dead. For it was here that Angel Macritchie had met his death. The murder that had brought Fin back to the island of his birth after an absence of eighteen years. In the dark, with their memories, the ghost of Macritchie made its presence felt, the chill wind whipping through ill-fitting doors and open windows, wrapping itself around them.

Fin stamped his feet, more to exorcize the ghost than to warm himself. His voice sounded abnormally loud. 'I don't suppose the Presbytery have fixed a date for your hearing yet?'

'It'll be within the fortnight. In the Free Church hall in Kenneth Street in Stornoway.' As Donald pulled on his cigarette his face again reflected its glow. 'They've engaged legal counsel, I'm told. I've read up on the Acts of Assembly that set out the conditions for establishing a judicial commission. It seems that the hearing will pretty much follow the same course it would in a court of law.'

'Then presumably you can appoint counsel yourself?'

Donald's laugh came like a gunshot out of the dark. 'Aye. If I could afford it.'

'They'll be calling Fionnlagh and Donna to give evidence, too, I suppose.'

'I've asked them not to.'

Fin was astonished. 'Why not? There's nobody closer to what happened that day than the two of them.'

'They've suffered enough,' Donald said. 'I'll not put them through it all again.'

Fin thought about raising an argument, but realized even before he opened his mouth that there would be no point. Donald had sacrificed everything to save them once. Why would he subject them to a repeat performance? He would rather they threw him out of the Church.

'Anyway, hopefully George Gunn will testify. He took statements from them both, and has to be seen as a reliable and unbiased witness.'

'He is, Donald. But that very lack of bias could work against you.'

Donald nodded solemnly. 'I know.'

More silence in the dark. Fin could smell Donald's cigarette smoke. He said, 'How do you think it will go?'

'I think,' said Donald, 'that before the month is over I'll be out of a job, and out of my house.'

'And Catriona?'

Donald's face gave away nothing in the light of his cigarette. 'You'd have to ask her that, Fin.'

# CHAPTER THIRTEEN

It never failed to affect him, seeing his aunt's house lying derelict and forgotten. Peeling whitewash, broken slates, windows smashed or boarded up, like missing teeth in a neglected mouth.

Oddly, he never thought of it as anything other than his aunt's house. Never his home. And yet he had spent the greater part of his childhood here, in a cold, damp bedroom with its rusty-framed dormer window looking out over the rocky bay below. He remembered the first time she had brought him here to live. Just days after the death of his parents. A handful of possessions in a small brown case that she had placed on the bed, telling him to pack them away while she went and made something for their tea. And he had sat on his own, feeling the cold damp of the mattress beneath him seeping into his very soul, and wept.

He stood now on the pitted tarmac in front of the house, looking up at the window of that room, a window that gave on to a past he had no wish to revisit. And yet somehow it was always there. In good memories and bad. Of a life long gone, populated by people long dead. And there was no escaping it.

As he frequently did, he wondered what point there was in it all. Were we really just here to procreate and pass on, leaving our seed upon the earth to do as we had done, as our fathers had done before us, and theirs before them? A meaningless cycle of birth, life, death?

He walked to the edge of the path that led down to the shore, a shingle beach in a boulder-strewn cove where he had often played among the ruins of the old salting house. He almost expected to see himself down there: a lonely boy seeking solace in the world of his imagination.

It was a long, sleepless night which had sparked his mood. Images of Roddy's broken, decayed body in the plane. The look on Whistler's face. The big man walking away, climbing back up to the ridge only to disappear. And Fin had woken from shallow dreams in a sweat, with the certainty in his heart that Whistler knew something he wasn't telling. And yet his shock at the discovery of the body had been as great, if not greater, than Fin's.

He had risen early, leaving Marsaili sleeping, and set off along the cliffs above Crobost, until he reached the sheltered inlet where generations earlier his ancestors had built the small harbour. A steep ramp down to a short jetty and a deep pool among the rocks where they kept live crabs in cages until they could be shipped out to foreign markets. It seemed that everything good about this island left it. Its resources. Its people. And all their ambitions.

The wind blew strong in the sunshine, cumulus bubbling up and tracking across a vast, ever-changing sky. And still it was not cold, even though October was just an exhalation away. Fin sat himself down among the dry grasses, pulling his knees up to his chest to hug them, gazing out over choppy green water that rose and fell in gently coruscating swells across the bay.

And he remembered the day that Whistler had first come to spend the night here with him and his aunt.

# CHAPTER FOURTEEN

It's strange that history should have affected us the way it did. But the discovery that our antecedents had survived the *Iolaire* together, one because of the other, formed a bond between me and Whistler that no one else could really understand. We were very different animals, he and I. I was quite a self-contained boy as a teenager, I think. I didn't make friends easily. And perhaps that's the only thing that Whistler and I really had in common. I was a cool, even-tempered lad, not much prone to depression, although there was plenty I could have got depressed about when I think back on it. Whistler, on the other hand, could fall into a black funk in the blink of an eye if things didn't go just the way he planned. Other times he would be irresistibly funny, the life and soul of any party.

He never appeared to know, though, when he had crossed the line between what was funny and what was offensive. I saw him get away with murder. Putting his hands on a girl's breasts and somehow managing to make a joke of it. And then another time getting his face slapped for making some wildly inappropriate remark. Which would send him off into one of his moods. He had meant no offence. Why hadn't anyone seen the funny side?

He was brilliant and mercurial, talented and unpredictable. To be his friend you had to work at it. But you also had to be accepted by him. And I had been granted exclusive access to that club, a club with a membership of one.

I didn't often stay over at Whistler's house. His father was seldom sober, and when he was drunk he was unpredictable, liked to throw things around the place and bellow at the top of his voice. He never did us any physical harm, but I was scared of him, and so was Whistler.

Although already growing into the giant of a man he would become, Whistler was still no match for his dad, who was two sizes bigger. Derek Macaskill had spent half his life at sea, first in the merchant navy and later on the trawlers. But he was a man hopelessly addicted to the drink, and had become not only unemployed but unemployable. He was a liability aboard a boat. He had lost an eye in an accident on a trawler and was still, apparently, on some kind of disability benefit all these years later.

The glass eye they had replaced it with never moved, and no matter where you were in the room, or where his other eye was pointing, it always appeared to be looking at you. Occasionally he would take it out and polish it in some filthy handkerchief, with a big malicious grin on his face. He only did it because he knew it gave us the willies.

I've never seen such big hands on a man, fists you wouldn't want to be on the wrong end of. His hair was cropped close to his scalp, dark once but rapidly turning grey. A long scar ran through it from his forehead to a point behind his left ear. Whether he had acquired it in the same accident that lost him his eye I never knew.

Following the death of his mother, when he was just nine, Whistler had spent a couple of years living with relatives of hers at Miabhaig, until big Derek Macaskill, fresh from being banned from the boats, came one day to claim him and take him back to live with him at Ardroil.

I'd always wondered where he got the money to buy his drink. He was, after all, an unemployed man on benefit. But I would find out soon enough.

Sòlas were really beginning to make their name then, playing gigs all over the island, at ceilidhs and school dances, in pubs and village halls. It was how I spent most of my Friday and Saturday nights, and sometimes week nights, too. Humphing gear. Me and Big Kenny. Kenny had turned seventeen before me, and was the first to get his driving licence. So it was only natural that he would become the roadie.

None of us knew it then, but Whistler had already taken his decision not to go to Glasgow, and his interest in the band had begun to wane. There were nights when he simply didn't turn up. He never told anyone, not even me, and the band would frequently find themselves having to perform without their flute player.

Not that it made a radical difference to the quality of their performance. They were always great. At least, I thought so. But the haunting wail of that Celtic flute, particularly in tandem with Mairead's violin, was the grace note that made them better than great. It made them magical. And it made Roddy mad when Whistler didn't show up.

It all came to a head one night after a gig at the Cross Inn at Ness. After three straight gigs without showing, Whistler turned up as if nothing were amiss. He was in one of his manic good moods, and oblivious to the ill will festering towards him among the other members of the band. There had clearly been meetings to discuss his absences, discussions to which I had not been privy. But I knew that something was brewing.

Kenny and I had gone into the bar behind the hotel for a pint while the band was playing. When we came out at the end of the show, night was leaching the last light out of the sky. We went to take the van around to the front. Kenny had parked it beside the big tree that grew in the car park then, the only real tree on the whole of the west coast. A giant of a tree. God knows how it had survived the winds that drove in off the Atlantic all these years, but it must have seen a few generations come and go.

Roddy and Whistler were standing in its shadow almost screaming at each other. We heard them before we saw them. The crowds streaming out of the lounge bar in the hotel, to cars and minibuses, turned heads in their direction.

'For Christ's sake keep it down, boys.' Kenny was self-conscious. But neither of them took any notice.

'It's just not fair on the rest of us,' Roddy shouted. 'All our arrangements, all our rehearsals, are based around us being a six-piece band. A lot of it built around your fucking flute. There's a big bloody hole in our sound when you're not there. It's embarrassing.'

Whistler stood his ground, unfazed apparently by their embarrassment. 'Maybe you should have thought of that before you started trying to ease me out.'

Which came with the unexpected force of a slap in the face to Roddy. 'Ease you out? What are you talking about, man? No one's trying to ease you out.'

'You blew into Uig with your mainland money in your pocket and just took over. Everything. The band, the girls, the limelight. A real fucking star.'

Roddy shook his head in exasperation. 'There *was* no band!'

'Aye there was. Me and Strings and Mairead were playing together long before you showed up.'

Roddy was scathing now. 'That wasn't a band. That was just kids playing about in someone's front room.'

Whistler took a dangerous step towards him. 'What would you know? You were an incomer. You knew nothing about us, or the way we were. You just took over. Took it all. Mairead, too.'

Which was the first time I became aware of any tension between them over Mairead.

'Mairead?' Roddy gasped. 'Don't make me laugh. Mairead wouldn't be seen dead with a loser like you.'

And that tipped Whistler over the edge. He leapt at Roddy, big hands grabbing handfuls of shirt and face, and the two of them went tumbling backwards to roll over several times in the dusty gravel of the car park, feet and fists flying. Roddy was an altogether more delicately built boy, and stood no chance against the monster that Whistler was becoming. I heard him cry out in pain, and saw blood on his face, and Kenny and I were on to them in a flash, dragging the flailing Whistler off him, ducking and diving ourselves to avoid the flying fists.

The crowd which had gathered around scattered backwards like displaced water. I heard girls screaming and some of the boys shouting encouragement. Kenny and I pushed Whistler up against the tree and pinned him there, the three of us breathing hard, almost growling, like animals. Roddy scrambled to his feet, bloodied about the lips. But his biggest injury was the one inflicted on his pride.

'You fucking idiot!' he screamed. 'This is the end. You're finished. You're fucking finished!' Strings and Skins and Rambo pushed through the group of fascinated spectators, and pulled him away, casting hostile backward glances at Whistler. And the crowd, sensing that it was over, started to dissipate.

Me and Kenny let Whistler go then, and he snarled, 'I'll kill him.'

'No you won't.' The solitary voice came out of the dark, a lone figure left standing as the crowd melted away. It was Mairead. She was looking at him with an extraordinary intensity. 'We've worked too bloody hard to get this far, Whistler. We're not going to throw it all away now. Not because of you.'

To my amazement he was almost cowed by her. He looked at the ground, unable to meet her eye.

'We've got rehearsal Wednesday night. You'll be there, right?' And when he didn't respond, 'Right?' More forcefully this time.

He nodded. Still without looking at her.

'I'll speak to Roddy. We'll just put this behind us and move on, okay?' There was such authority in her tone, such complete confidence in her ability to manage these boys who brawled over her. It was something to see, the power that she possessed. And I think, too, it was the first time I saw in her that naked ambition. *We're not going to throw it all away now.* Mairead was going places. She knew it even then. And nothing was going to get in her way. Certainly not Whistler.

Someone with a car gave the rest of the group a lift back to Uig, and Whistler wandered off in the dark, to sit brooding on a wall at the south end of the car park. Kenny and I packed up and carried everything to the van in silence. It wasn't until we had finished that I said, 'So what's the story with Whistler, Roddy and Mairead, then?'

Big Kenny just shrugged. 'You knew that Whistler and Mairead were an item before Roddy showed up?'

Of course, I'd heard about Whistler and Mairead being childhood sweethearts, but not about how it ended. I nodded.

'Ever since primary three. Inseparable, they were.'

'So what happened?'

'Roddy happened.'

'I didn't know he wasn't from Uig originally.'

Kenny lit up a cigarette and offered me one, and we

leaned against the van and smoked them. 'His grandparents were. But his folks were born on the mainland somewhere. His dad made a fortune in something or other, I've never been quite sure what. And they came back and built that beautiful big house on the road up to Baile na Cille that looks out over the sands. He still goes back to the mainland from time to time, doing whatever it is he does, and Roddy's never been short of a bob or two. That's how he could afford the synth, and the Marshall stack. And who do you think's paying up the PA, and coughed up for the deposit on the van?'

I have to confess, I had never really thought too much about where the money came from. The band was paid, of course, for the gigs, but when I thought about it then, I realized their earnings would never have been enough to cover the costs.

Kenny said, 'Whistler was right. Roddy was like a star that fell from the sky. Exotic, rich, talented. And Mairead was attracted to him like a moth to the light.' He flicked his cigarette into the night sending a shower of sparks skittering across the car park. 'End of Mairead and Whistler.'

It didn't take much to persuade Whistler to stay over at Crobost that night. I knew that he was hurting inside, in his own self-destructive way, and I couldn't bear the thought of him going back to the blackhouse in Uig, with his drunken father sitting polishing his eye in front of the fire. It was a Friday night and the band wasn't playing on the Saturday, so we had the whole weekend ahead of us. I knew my aunt wouldn't mind. There was a spare room at the end of the upstairs hall. No one ever came to stay, but there was always a bed made up in it.

Kenny dropped us off, and we went into the house to find my aunt sitting on her own in the front room, in her favourite armchair by the fire. She seemed a million miles away. The room was a nod to the sixties. Orange and turquoise curtains, boldly patterned wallpaper, big brightly coloured china pots that she bought from Eachan the potter at the bottom of the hill. She was listening to what I recognized as *Sgt. Pepper's Lonely Hearts Club Band* on her old stereo system. Vinyl! It was so dated now. Everyone had cassette players in those days, or CD players, the new big thing if you could afford it. And she was smoking. She appeared to be pleased by the thought that we would have a visitor for the weekend and told Whistler he could use our phone to let his folks know that he wouldn't be home.

Whistler was embarrassed. 'It's just my dad. He won't notice.' She gave him an odd look.

Afterwards, when we left the house to wander down the track to the shore for a smoke in the dark, he said to me, 'She smokes dope, your aunt.'

I looked at him in amazement. 'What makes you think that?'

'Don't you smell it?'

'That's incense,' I said.

He laughed. 'That's what she burns to cover the smell of the dope, you idiot. Maybe she thinks you'd disapprove.'

I was stunned. Kids my age smoked dope. Adults didn't.

Or so I thought. And my aunt seemed ancient to me. Later, I realized that Whistler was probably right, and that she almost certainly acquired her marijuana from Eachan, who sold her his pottery and was a well-known dopehead. It wasn't until much later, when I found out that she was suffering from terminal cancer, that I wondered if perhaps she had been taking it for the pain. But then I figured that more likely she'd been smoking it since the sixties, or earlier. Those heady days of youth and optimism when she must have felt that her whole life stretched endlessly ahead of her. A habit she never kicked, until those endless days finally came to the close that none of us ever quite believes in.

It was not April yet, and so it was not warm. We sat down among the rocks, huddled in our coats, and smoked a couple of cigarettes, watching periodic moonlight flit across the swell in the bay. It was more sheltered here, facing north-east, and protected from the prevailing wind. The collar of orange crustaceans on the rocks along the high-tide mark glowed in the dark.

At length I said to him, 'Is this all about Mairead? You not turning up for gigs, getting into fights with Roddy?'

He gave me one of his looks.

'It is, isn't it? She's got you and Roddy and every other boy in the school running around after her. Fighting over her now.'

'That's not what we were fighting about.'

'Isn't it?'

'No!' He almost bared his teeth. 'Anyway, it's none of your business.' He flicked his cigarette end out over the water and stood up, signalling the end of our conversation. He walked away into the dark, and I sat there for a while wondering why I bothered. There didn't seem to be much reward in a one-way friendship.

I thought about Mairead, and those dark-blue flashing eyes, and the effect she had on every male around her. And I wondered if she realized the heartache she caused, and if she did, whether she did it on purpose, maybe even enjoyed it. I decided there and then that I didn't really like her very much, even though I knew that she could reduce me to incoherence with just a look.

Which is when I heard Whistler's shout in the dark, and the sound of splashing, even above the wind and the wash of the incoming tide. I was on my feet in an instant, and running over the rocks towards the sound of his cry. I clambered up over razor-sharp shells crusted around the giant boulders supporting the harbour wall, and up on to the slipway that ran down to the jetty. Even in the dark, I could see white water frothing in the still of the sheltered pool where they kept the crabs. I ran down to the quay, and saw Whistler thrashing about, treading water and gasping from the cold.

'Jesus!' he shouted. 'Some idiot left a bloody boobytrap on the quayside. I could have killed myself!'

I knelt down and flipped a big rusted metal boat ring over on its axis. It had been cemented into the stone long before either of us was born. And I couldn't help laughing.

'It's not funny!'

'It's bloody hilarious, Whistler. You want to watch where

you're putting your big feet.' I uncoiled a length of rope lying among the creels and threw him an end. He grabbed it and pulled himself up on to the ramp. Some of the cages had burst open, and there were crabs clinging to his coat. He stood chittering in the cold and cursing as I pulled them off him and threw them back into the water, laughing the whole time. Which only made him worse. 'Come on,' I said, pushing him up the slipway ahead of me. 'Let's get you out of these clothes before you catch your death.'

It must have been midnight before we got him out of his wet things and into a bath. My aunt fussed and faffed in a way she never did over me, making sure he had big soft clean towels, and taking his clothes away to put through the wash.

He was still in the bath, and I was in my pyjamas and ready for bed, when my aunt came to my bedroom door. She had a strange expression on her face.

'I want you to come downstairs, Finlay.'

I knew immediately that something was wrong. 'What is it?'

'There's something I want you to look at.'

I followed her down the steep narrow staircase, on uneven stairs that creaked like wet snow, and into the little hall at the front door. She turned into the laundry room. It was little more than a scullery, with a washing machine and a tumble dryer. A short pulley, usually laden with drying clothes, hung from the ceiling. Whistler's wet clothes were spread out over the worktop above the machines.

She turned to me. 'Look at this.'

I glanced at them, full of incomprehension. 'What about them?'

'Look!' She lifted his socks. 'They're full of holes.' And as she held them up I saw that they were. Worn to holes at the heel and the ball of the foot, and wafer-thin along the line of the toes, almost at the point of disintegration. 'And these.' She held up his underpants, stretched out between fastidious thumbs and forefingers. It took a great effort of will for her even to touch them, and there was a look of extreme disgust on her face. 'The elastic's perished.' She dropped them. 'And his trousers. Look how he keeps them up.' She showed me the safety pin at the waistband where a button had once been. The zipper was broken. 'And here.' She turned them over and I saw where the seam between the legs had burst open, the stitching rotted and broken.

Then she held up his coat and turned it inside out. 'And this isn't much better. The lining's all torn and worn thin. And look at his trainers for God's sake.' She stooped to lift them on to the counter. 'You can't see it at a glance, but the soles have come away from the uppers, and it looks like he's used duct tape to stick them back together.' She glared at me with accusation in her eyes. 'How could you not notice?'

'Notice what?'

'Oh, for heaven's sake, Finlay. *This*!' And she waved her hand over the assembled garments. 'They're only fit for the bin.'

I shrugged. 'I don't know. I thought it was just his look.'

'Holes in your socks aren't a *look*, Finlay.' She took me by the arm and steered me through to the living room and lowered her voice. 'He lives with his father, he said. Where's his mother?'

'She's dead.'

'You've met his father?' I nodded. 'And been to the house?'

'Yes.'

She closed the door and said, 'Sit down. I want you to tell me everything.'

I said nothing to Whistler when he came out of the bathroom. I gave him a pair of baggy old pyjama bottoms that just about fitted him, and an XXL T-shirt that he stretched over his chest. He wrapped my old dressing gown gratefully around himself and went off to the spare room at the end of the hall muttering about bloody idiots who left dangerous objects lying about on jetties. We slept until almost twelve the next day.

It was the sound of my aunt's car pulling up at the front door that woke me. I screwed up my eyes against the midday sunshine and from my window saw her take several carrier bags from the back seat. There was a fresh blustery wind chasing random clouds across a broken sky, sunlight spilling from it in occasional pools and splashes. But it was dry and my spirits lifted.

By the time Whistler and I got ourselves downstairs, she had a late breakfast sizzling for us in the kitchen. Porridge, followed by bacon, egg, sausage, black pudding and fried bread, all washed down with big tumblers of fresh orange juice. Whistler wolfed into it, and barely looked up until he had finished. Then the three of us sat around the table drinking tea, and Whistler told a tall story about two men trying to take a bull on a raft across to an island in Uig. He swore it was true. They were very nervous, he said, that the raft would tip over and the bull would drown. Then the thing did capsize, halfway across, and tipped all three into the sea. The men thought they were going to drown because neither of them could swim. But then it turned out that the bull could, and so they clung on to him, and he swam to the island and got them ashore. The way he told it, Whistler had us all in stitches.

I watched my aunt as he spoke. There was more life in her eyes, I think, than I had ever seen in them before. And she laughed in a way I'd never heard her laugh. A laugh like running water, that flowed from smiling lips. I don't know what it was about Whistler that attracted her. It was certainly more than feeling sorry for him. But I've often thought that she'd probably rather have had Whistler to raise than me. And although I had never loved her, I felt a disconcerting pang of jealousy.

When we had finished eating, Whistler said, 'I'd better get dressed.' And he looked around for his clothes. My aunt flicked me a look.

'I've put them in the bin, John Angus,' she said.

There was an odd silence in the kitchen as his jaw dropped and he stared at her in disbelief. I felt like someone watching a movie. Involved in the action, but with no influence over the way it was unravelling.

'I've been to Stornoway to buy you some new. Nothing fancy mind. I went to the Crofters. They'll do you for now.' And she lifted the carrier bags she had brought from the car on to the table.

Whistler still hadn't spoken. He looked in the bags, one after the other. There was a sturdy pair of leather boots. Jeans. A chequered shirt. A waterproof jacket with a hood. And seven pairs of socks and underpants.

'I wasn't sure about sizes, so I just got the biggest I could.'

Whistler's mouth was still hanging open. He looked at her and shook his head. 'I can't afford this.'

'I can,' is all she said, and in a way that brooked no argument. 'Now go and get dressed. I'd like to be on the road in fifteen.'

'Where are we going?' I asked her.

'To Uig.'

I glanced at Whistler. His face had flushed pink, his big dark eyes filled with confusion. I could see an objection playing around his lips, but it never quite found voice. My aunt was not someone to be argued with.

We drove down to Uig in silence. Me in the front with my aunt, Whistler filling most of the back seat and unusually subdued. It was a typical day in late March, the wind blowing in strongly off the Atlantic all the way down the west coast, rain never far from its leading edge. But we could see the sky almost clear to the east, and sunshine falling in shifting patches somewhere across the dead, deserted interior. Far to the south we could see where the rain fell intermittently, rainbows fleetingly crayon-colouring the sky then vanishing again as the sunlight was swallowed by more cloud. And as we left Garynahine behind us, and followed the tortuous route down to the south-west, storm clouds gathered ominously among the mountains that rose up beyond Uig, a portent of coming conflict.

A sense of dread was already growing in me. God knows what Whistler was feeling. I glanced in the mirror and saw him sitting uncomfortably in his new clothes, but his face gave nothing away.

To my enormous relief, there was no sign of Whistler's dad when we arrived at the croft. My aunt banged her car door shut and confidently pushed open the door of the blackhouse.

'Hello?' she called out, to be greeted by silence.

Whistler and I followed her in and stood wordlessly watching as she cast an appraising eye about the place. Her nose wrinkled with disgust.

'Show me where you sleep,' she said, and Whistler led her into the tiny room at the back that was his bedroom. It smelled rank in here, his bed unmade, sheets sweat-stained and dirty. She went through the wardrobe, and a chest of drawers, finding little more than a pair of jeans with the knees out of them, and a couple of ragged old jumpers. There was a pair of mud-caked wellies, and a drawer with two or three pairs of threadbare socks and some underpants. Like the ones she had thrown away, the elastic was rotten. 'Where are the rest of your clothes?' she demanded.

He shrugged. 'In the laundry.'

'And who does your laundry?'

'I take it with me to Stornoway during the week.' It was the first time I had realized the importance of the student lodgings to Whistler. It was the one place he could keep himself clean, where he could shower and do his laundry. I glanced at my aunt and saw a look that I knew well. A contained rage. She turned and marched back out to the living room. There was an old refrigerator next to a sink filled with unwashed dishes. She threw it open and stood looking inside. The interior bulb was long gone. 'Turn on the lights,' she instructed, and Whistler obeyed without a word. She peered into the dark interior of the fridge. 'There's nothing but beer in here. Where's the food?'

Whistler shrugged and opened a wall cupboard on the other side of the sink. There was some chipped and broken crockery, a half-empty bag of sugar gone solid from the damp. Teabags. A jar of instant coffee. A jar of jam which she opened to find mould growing inside. On a worktop below it, there was a bread tin with half a loaf of stale bread inside it. I could see the horror on my aunt's face.

'What do you eat?'

Whistler blew air through loosely pursed lips. 'Fish, mostly. At the weekends. Whatever I can catch.' He glanced at me, and I felt his embarrassment for him. 'But I do most of my eating during the week.' And I remembered how he had devoured my aunt's late breakfast that morning as if he hadn't eaten in a week, and maybe he hadn't. It had never occurred to me that the only place he got a square meal was at school. It was a miracle he was growing at the rate he was.

'What the fuck's going on here?'

We all turned at the roar of Whistler's dad's voice. Mr Macaskill's big frame seemed to fill the room, casting its shadow across us.

'You will not use language like that in the presence of the children!' My aunt's voice scythed through the fetid air of the Macaskill blackhouse and reduced the big man by several inches. He looked confused. It was the first time in a long time that either of us had been called children, and I doubted if any woman had ever spoken to Mr Macaskill like that in his life.

'Who the hell are you?'

She took several steps towards him, and Whistler and I moved aside to let her past. The difference between them was almost comical. This tiny lady confronting a giant of almost biblical proportions. David and Goliath. But there was no question of who was the more dominant. 'You filthy brute of a man!' Her voice was shrill and intense and filled with fury. 'You send your child out into the world hungry and dressed in rags, while you drink your life away. Maybe it's a worthless life anyway. And maybe you don't care about it.' She flung out a clenched fist, finger pointed at Whistler. 'But here's a young life that's worth something. A young life that needs nurtured and fed. Not neglected and abused.'

She spun around and returned to the fridge, throwing open the door and reaching inside to scoop all those cans of beer into the crook of her arm and sweep them out and on to the floor. The noise of it was startling, and we all three of us looked at her in amazement.

'Next time I come, I want to see this fridge filled with food, not alcohol. And I want to see clothes in the drawers of that boy's room, and clean sheets on his bed. And if you are not capable of doing that, Mr Macaskill, then I will make it my personal crusade to have this young man removed from your care, and whatever benefits you scrounge from the state taken from you as well.' Her face was flushed now, and she was breathing hard. 'Is that clear?' And when the dumbstruck Mr Macaskill failed to respond she raised her voice in pitch. 'Is that clear?'

The big man blinked, cowed and subdued, in just the way I had seen Mairead dominate Whistler. 'Aye.'

'Call yourself a father? You should be ashamed of yourself.'

Whistler's dad glanced at his son, and I was astonished to see that there was, in fact, shame in his face, as if perhaps he had always known what a lousy father he was. But it had taken my aunt to make him see it.

'Come on,' she said suddenly. 'Coats off, all of you.' and she took off her own. 'We're going to make this place habitable.'

We spent the rest of that Saturday afternoon cleaning the house from top to bottom. There was no washing machine, but once the big Belfast sink had been cleaned, my aunt stripped the beds and hand-washed the sheets. They dried in no time on the line she got Mr Macaskill to put up outside.

Mountains of rubbish accumulated against the exterior wall as she went ruthlessly around the house selecting stuff for the bin. Boxes of full and empty cans of beer, piles of bottles. Filthy clothes and sheets. Broken and cracked crockery. The detritus of lives neglected and in decline. And as Mr Macaskill washed the floorboards with an old brush, like scrubbing the deck of a boat, Whistler and I set about cleaning years of grime from the windows. My aunt sat at the table and wrote out a shopping list.

When she had finished she thrust it at Whistler's dad. 'Priority stuff,' she said. 'Food, clothes, bed linen. You don't look after that lad of yours, trust me, your life won't be worth the living of. And I'll be back to make sure of it.'

He took it from her and nodded.

When we left that day, I was full of trepidation for my friend, and I could see, too, that he was afraid of being alone with his father. He never talked in detail to me about what happened when we'd gone, except to say that they had sat for a long time in silence that night, his father sober for the first time he could remember. And that finally, unbidden, Mr Macaskill had looked at his boy and said, 'I'm sorry, son.'

After that weekend my aunt encouraged me to spend as much time there as possible. I don't think she needed me to be her eyes and ears, because I am almost certain she made frequent trips down to Uig herself during the week when we were at school, but I guess she wanted me to be around as a constant reminder to Mr Macaskill that an eye was being kept on him. And that is how I came to be there the weekend we decided to go fishing up at Loch Tathabhal.

It was early in April that year, and there had been an uncommon amount of rain, even for the west coast of Lewis. A slow-moving front which had been picking up moisture over three thousand miles of Atlantic Ocean had settled itself over the island and was shedding its accumulated cargo in copious amounts. It was mild, though, with soft warm winds blowing up from the south-west. Excellent early-season fishing weather. There were lots of young brown trout up in the lochs, that would be delicious slow-roasted in tinfoil over the glowing embers of a peat fire, and Whistler and I were determined to bag a few.

Of course, we'd have been in trouble if the water-bailiff had caught us, though they weren't so bothered in those days. Poaching wasn't the problem it became, and the rivers and lochs were teeming with trout. The worst that might have happened would have been a kick up the backside and getting our fish confiscated. But if they'd caught us with salmon that would have been another story. So we contented ourselves with the trout, and kept our eyes skinned for the water-bailiff or the gamekeeper.

It had taken us nearly two hours to walk up to the loch. The peaks of Mealaisbhal and Cracabhal and Tathabhal above us were lost in the clouds. Water was cascading down the track in gushing rivulets, exposing the bed of big sea pebbles that were its foundation, swirling in frantic eddies and churning up potholes that could break an axle. Deep drainage channels dug in the peat were overflowing with the thousands of gallons of brown rainwater running off the mountains.

Although we wore waxed jackets with hoods, and wellies, and waterproof leggings, we were both soaked by the time we got there. I could see Whistler's big plump cheeks, pink and shining with the rain, grinning at me through the circle of hood that left his face exposed, black hair smeared across his forehead. But I also saw caution in his eyes, and he nodded towards the gate at the foot of the track leading up to Loch Tathabhal.

There was a Land Rover parked there. We scanned every horizon, then, but saw no one, and approached the vehicle in silence. Whistler put his hand on the bonnet. 'Cold. It's been here a while.' I wiped the rain away from the side window and peered inside. The keys were dangling in the ignition. On the passenger seat there was a copy of that day's newspaper, and a fisherman's woollen cap with home-made flies pinned all along its skip. Useless as protection in these conditions. But I recognized it immediately.

'It's big Jock Macrae's,' I said. The water-bailiff.

Whistler nodded. 'Better be careful, then.'

We made our way up the track towards the loch, following the line of a stream that in summer was not much more than a trickle. Now, though, it was a thunderous flow of water, breaking and splashing over the rocks and boulders that tumbled down the slope in a series of dramatic drops towards Loch Raonasgail below. The stream had burst its banks where the land levelled out towards Loch Tathabhal, swelling to a width of ten or twelve feet where it left the loch, sweeping in full spate towards the falls.

By the time we reached the loch itself, we saw that the level had risen to the point where the water was passing just inches below the old wooden bridge. Normally it had a clearance of four or five feet. If it got any higher, it would sweep the flimsy structure away, leaving just the drystone stanchions at either side. But even those were in danger, water flowing around them with a power that filled the air with its fury. Whistler raised his voice to shout above it. 'Let's cast from the bridge. Loch side. The currents are bound to draw the fish this way.' We were rank amateurs in those days.

I nodded, and we clambered up over the stones and on to the bridge itself. There was a wooden rail that ran along the loch side of it that we could lean on and cast. We dropped our bags and assembled our rods, the water rushing beneath our feet in a torrent. Scary in its power and proximity. I didn't dare look at it, or it made me giddy.

Whistler grinned. 'This is the life, eh?'

I grinned back, and for some extraordinary reason took a step backwards before casting. I was gone in a second. A momentary sense of flying through thin air, before hitting the water and feeling the power of it sweep me away. The cold took my breath with it and I couldn't even cry out. And then I was under, and knew with absolute certainty that I was going to die.

I have heard people say that in the seconds before a crash, or a life-threatening accident, time seems to stand still and you have all that you need of it to rewind your life, spooling back through those moments that exist only in your memory and are about to be lost for ever. I didn't experience it like that.

The first thing I felt was pain as I was dashed against a rock dividing the flow of water. The force of the impact and the current of the water itself lifted me out of it for a few vital seconds. I could see how the stream dropped away below me, white water breaking over boulders and cascading in spumes and spray through the rain that continued to fall. And I found myself almost beached on the slab of rock which had broken my downward momentum, sliding over its slippery black surface, face down, feet first, knowing that unless I could hold on to it I would certainly be smashed and broken by the succession of drops that lay ahead.

As I slid inexorably across the angle of its face, water breaking all around me, I tried desperately to find a hand-hold, fingers seeking anything they could grab. I felt myself going, and the conviction of death returned before, at the very last, my fingertips found a seam that broke across its smooth surface, and they locked into the two inches of ledge it provided.

For those few vital seconds, I felt my body washing about below me in the flow, as if hands were trying to grab me and pull me down. But my tenuous grasp on the rock stopped that downward drag. At least long enough for me to swing my right arm across the rock and find a crack in the gneiss that gave me something more substantial to hold on to.

It seemed somehow incredible to me, that only seconds

before I had been about to cast a line to fish for trout, without a care in the world. And here I was now, fighting for my life, against what felt like impossible odds.

In the speed with which it had all happened, I hadn't given Whistler a single thought. Now, above the roar of the water, I heard him shouting. 'Hang on, Fin! For Christ's sake, hang on!' I inclined my head to my right, water breaking over it and almost obscuring my vision. I saw him on the bank, no more than six or eight feet away. He had one foot forward in the flow of the water, an arm outstretched. But it was a long way from reaching me, and I knew that if he tried to wade into it, the force of the water would sweep him away. I could see the desperation in his face. It would be suicide to try to reach me, but there was a limit to how long I could hold on, a limit that was not far away now.

His thought processes were almost visible in his eyes. There had to be something he could do.

Suddenly he bellowed, 'I'll be right back. I promise. Just don't let go.' And he was gone. Out of my field of vision. And in that moment I felt as lonely as I have ever felt in my life. The sight and sound of the water filled my eyes, my ears, my mind, and I focused very hard on maintaining my hold on the rock. I trusted absolutely that Whistler would be back with some way of getting me out of this, but I doubted my ability to hold on for long enough. I could feel the cold numbing my body, the strength ebbing from my arms. I had almost no sensation in my hands now at all.

I let my head rest against the rock and closed my eyes, total concentration on not letting go. In a strange way, I could almost have slept and just released my hold, like drifting off in a dream from which there would be no waking. And there was something oddly comforting in that thought. Until I was startled to consciousness by the revving of a motor that felt very close.

A Land Rover was backing up to the very edge of the water, wheels spinning and sliding, and then locked suddenly in place with the ratcheting sound of a handbrake. I heard a door slam, and Whistler came running around to the back. He had a coil of rope in his hands. He quickly tied one end around his waist, and knelt down to loop the other around the tow bar to secure it. He stood up, then, and without a moment's hesitation came wading through the water towards me. Almost immediately he was swept off his feet by the force of the flow. As he went down, I saw his outstretched arm, and the rope looped around his hand and wrist, preventing him from being carried off.

Amazingly he found footholds, something beneath him to anchor his feet, and his upper body lifted up out of the flow like Neptune rising out of the sea. And suddenly there he was, right next to me, the veins on his forehead standing out like ropes, a big lad straining every sinew, pitting himself against all the forces of nature to try to save his friend. The water crashed all around him in a fury, white and frothing, as he literally scooped me up in his arms. In an enormous leap of faith I relinquished my hold on the rock and grabbed the rope, feeling his arms lock themselves around my waist. And in the same moment he lost his foothold, and we were both carried off in the surging water. Lost for just a second to a power so much greater than we could ever have imagined. Until the rope held, and we swung crazily to the side, smashing up against the near bank. Whistler somehow found the strength to reel us in on the end of the rope until we reached the Land Rover and fell gasping and wordless in the reeds and rain-sodden peat beneath the rear wheels. The water passed just inches from our faces, hissing and spitting and cursing. Cheated somehow. And it occurred to me that Whistler's great-grandfather must have used John Finlay Macleod's line from the *Iolaire* in much the same way to save my grandfather's life.

Whistler rolled over on to his back and started laughing at the sky. I fought to find my breath, and heard my trembling voice demand to know what was so damned funny. He turned his big grinning face towards me. 'You, daft bastard. Biggest bloody fish I ever pulled out of the river, and totally inedible!'

On the drive back down the valley, pitching and bumping through the potholes that the rain had scoured out of the hard core, hot air belted out of the heater and slowly brought life back to my frozen bones. I sat shivering next to Whistler, who handled the Land Rover as if he'd been driving it all his life. But I wasn't sure he even had a licence.

'What the hell's Jock Macrae going to say when he finds his Land Rover's gone?' I said.

Whistler just laughed again. 'I'd love to know. I can see the air turning blue. And he's going to have to walk back home.'

'We're going to be in trouble.'

'Nah.' Whistler shook his big head, like a dog shaking water from its fur. His grin was almost maniacal. 'He'll never know it was us. And who's going to tell him? Not me, not you. Just be grateful the old bugger was up there, and keeps a tow rope in the back.'

At the house, we got out of our wet clothes, and Whistler set them drying on a clothes horse in front of a roaring peat fire and put the kettle on. He got dressed, and I recognized the shirt my aunt had bought him. 'Back in a few,' he said, and when he went outside I heard the Land Rover start up and drive off. In fact it was half an hour before he was back, on foot, to find me huddled at the fire, hands cupped around my second mug of hot tea. 'I've got something that'll warm you up better than that.' He vanished into a back room and returned with a half-empty bottle of whisky and poured a good measure of it into my mug. He grinned. 'Central heating. My old man thinks I don't know where he hides it.' He disappeared to return it to its place of concealment, and then sat down next to me.

I looked at him. 'Are you not having any?'

But he just shook his head. 'Who knows what's in the genes. Don't want to end up like him.'

I sat staring into my mug for a long time before taking a stiff draught and turning my head towards him. 'You saved my life, Whistler.'

But he just shrugged. 'That's my job, Fin.'

I learned later that Jock Macrae had been apoplectic when he returned to find his Land Rover gone. At the end of a long walk back in the rain, he had gone into the first croft he came to and phoned the police to report it stolen. To his, and their, consternation, it was found a short time later parked outside his house. No one ever did find out who took it, or why.

# CHAPTER FIFTEEN

'Marsaili said I might find you up here.'

Fin was startled by the voice behind him, and looked up to see George Gunn looking down at him. Beyond him he saw the policeman's car pulled up at the roadside, a hundred yards or so beyond the house where Fin had grown up. He had not heard Gunn approach over the noise of the wind. He got to his feet and shook the other man's hand.

Gunn wore a white shirt, dark tie fluttering in the wind beneath a quilted black anorak that hung open. Trousers a little too long for him gathered around highly polished black brogues. His appearance here, crashing into Fin's reflections, felt ominous.

'How did the autopsy go?'

Gunn shrugged and pulled a face. 'It was pretty unpleasant, Mr Macleod. And didn't really throw any further illumination on the circumstances or cause of death.' He sucked in a breath. 'But the brass have arrived from Inverness. And they're treating it as murder.'

Fin nodded.

'The advance guard of the fourth estate has arrived, too. On the first flight this morning. God knows how the press gets hold of these things, but given Roddy Mackenzie's status in the music world, and the manner of his disappearance, we can probably expect a flood of them over the next few days. And I imagine most of them will be wanting a word with you, as the man who found him.'

Fin smiled grimly. 'Then I'll make sure to stay out of their way, George.'

'Aye, that would be a good idea.' Gunn rubbed his jaw thoughtfully. 'Did you ever manage to have that word with your friend, Mr Macleod?' The question seemed almost casual, but Fin knew that it wasn't.

'Whistler?'

'John Angus Macaskill,' Gunn confirmed.

'No, I didn't.' He hesitated. 'Is there a problem?'

'The Detective Inspector would like a word with him.'

'Why?'

'As I told you yesterday, we need his statement. About the finding of the plane.' He paused. 'Also, he knew the deceased.'

'So did I.'

'Yes, sir. But you haven't disappeared.'

Fin frowned. 'And Whistler has?'

'Well, it seems he's not to be found, or doesn't want to be. I'm assuming you went looking for him yesterday?'

Fin nodded his affirmation.

'And we sent the local bobby to go fetch him first thing this morning. But he's not at his croft, and appears not to have spent the night at the house. You wouldn't know where he might be?'

'No idea, George. Whistler's a free spirit. Goes where the fancy takes him. He probably spent the night in a shieling somewhere, in shock about Roddy.'

Gunn pushed out a thoughtful lower lip. 'Local intelligence would have us believe that Whistler Macaskill and Roddy Mackenzie were known to have had their differences.'

Fin almost laughed. 'If anyone thinks that Whistler had anything to do with Roddy's murder, they'd be barking up the wrong bloody tree, George. And anyway, he was as upset by finding the body in the plane as I was.'

'That's as may be, Mr Macleod. But it seems more than a little odd that he should just vanish off the face of the earth, don't you think?' He hesitated. 'At the risk of repeating myself, I'll ask again. Is there something you're not telling me?'

Fin felt the first spits of rain in his face as the wind freshened from the west. And he wondered again what it was that Whistler hadn't told him. 'No, George. There isn't.'

# CHAPTER SIXTEEN

Whistler's blackhouse had a deserted look about it, even from the road. Fin could not have said quite why, but he knew that he wasn't going to find Whistler there. It wasn't until he had climbed the hill that he realized the door was not closed, but lying several inches ajar, swinging back and forth in the wind, as if the house were breathing.

Carefully, he pushed it open wide, scraping it over the flags, and letting his eyes accustom themselves to the gloom before stepping inside. He half expected that he might find wee Anna there, as he had done the day before. But the house was empty. He walked in and felt the chill of the place, a smell of damp in the air. The remains of a days-old peat fire in the hearth were as cold as death. The house felt oddly abandoned, as if there had been nobody here for days. And for the first time Fin began to fear for his old friend. The Lewis chessmen stood lined up along the wall, silent witnesses lurking in the dark. But witnesses to what?

It was with a creeping sense of foreboding that Fin stepped back out into the wind. The tide was in, emerald water a foot deep over acres of golden sand, splinters of distant sunlight stabbing through breaks in the cloud, firing light in fast-moving flashes across the far machair.

A Range Rover pulled up on the road below, and two men stepped out. Fin had to squint to see their faces against the glare of sea and sun behind them, but he knew from the vehicle that the driver was Jamie. It was only as they began the climb up to the blackhouse that Fin recognized the set of the other. Solid and square, with his cap pulled low over his brow. Big Kenny.

Jamie came to a stop in front of Fin, breathing a little heavily from the climb. Kenny remained a couple of paces behind him, catching Fin's eye briefly, then averting his gaze almost as if ashamed.

'Is he there?' Jamie said.

'Who?'

Jamie tutted his irritation. 'Macaskill, of course.'

'No.'

'Where is he, then?'

'I haven't the first idea.'

Jamie tilted his head and cast a sceptical eye over Fin. 'You were with him when you found that plane.'

'Can't keep a secret around here.'

If Jamie suspected insolence, there was nothing in Fin's tone to betray it. 'So you took the bait, went up to Tathabhal after him that night?'

'Yes.'

'And?'

'And nothing.'

'He wasn't poaching?'

'No.'

Jamie sighed, barely able to conceal his annoyance. 'So what happened?'

And Fin wondered just how much, or how little, he should tell him. His own stupidity was an embarrassment. The only other witness to events up at the loch the night before the storm was James Minto. And Minto, Fin was sure, was unlikely to say anything. Although he regretted now that he had ever involved the man.

# CHAPTER SEVENTEEN

In the time it had taken Fin to drive down to Uig the day after his confrontation in the bar with Whistler, the wind had whipped itself up to a force-six or seven. But it was still unnaturally warm, and even stronger stratospheric winds had combed the incoming clouds thin across the sky in odd quiffs and streaks, like folds of gauze veiling the sun.

The tall reedy grass all around James Minto's cottage, tucked away amongst the dunes overlooking Uig sands, moved in waves and eddies like water in the wind. There was a Land Rover parked in front of a dilapidated outbuilding that hadn't seen paint for many a year. Fin turned his Suzuki off the metalled road and pulled up at the end of a sandy track that petered out at the front of the house. Beyond the dunes the mountains rose up in dark masses like waves of rock washing against the sky.

There was no sign of life behind either of the small windows set in thick whitewashed stone, and the sound of Fin's knuckles rapping on the old wooden door had an empty ring to it. He was about to give up and drive on to Ardroil, when the door opened and the dishevelled figure of James Minto stood in his dressing gown blinking in the bright morning light. He squinted at Fin, one hand raised to shield his eyes.

'Jesus Christ, mate! What kind of bloody time's this to come calling? Don't you know I work nights?'

Fin recalled the soft-voiced, flat-toned cockney accent from the first time they had met, and the latent threat that lay behind it. Minto was ex-special forces, brought in by the estate a couple of years before to deter poachers. Which he had done very successfully, by dubious means. He was feared and hated in almost equal measure by almost everyone in Uig. But no one man was equipped to deal with the poaching that was now taking place on an industrial scale, and Minto did not possess Fin's skill as an investigator. He was a Rottweiler, not a hound.

Fin regarded him thoughtfully, unremorseful for dragging the man from his bed. 'You don't remember me, do you?'

Minto glared at him for a moment, before realization washed over him. 'You're that rozzer. Came calling a year or so ago to accuse me of murdering some poacher up in Ness.'

'There were no accusations involved. We were simply eliminating you from our inquiry.'

'Yeh, well that's not how it seemed to me, mate.'

'Anyway, that's history. I'm no longer a . . . rozzer. I'm head of security on the Red River Estate. My name's Fin Macleod. And effectively I'm now your boss.'

'Oh, well, fuck me if I ain't trembling in me slippers, Mr Macleod.'

Fin looked into the palest of green eyes in a lean, tanned face. Minto's dark crew-cut hair was liberally peppered with silver now, but he was not a man to mess with. Trained to kill, and still fit and honed beneath a dressing gown that hung open to reveal only boxer shorts and a pair of flip-flops. Fin said, 'Well that's probably because you're so underdressed and feeling the cold. Why don't you ask me in and you can slip into something more comfortable?'

Minto hesitated for a moment, as if not quite sure how to take this. But the twinkle in Fin's eye brought a reluctant smile to his face. He stood back and held the door open. 'On you go then. Into the living room. I'll be with you in a minute.'

As soon as he entered the cramped little space that was the cottage living room, Fin remembered the impression he had taken away from his last visit, a sense of a manic and unmasculine tidiness. Every piece of furniture was placed for maximum efficiency and accessibility, clean white antimacassars draped over the arms and backs of a three-piece suite. Dust-free shelves were lined with carefully arranged books and ornaments. A range of fire irons hung neatly in the fireplace, tiles swept clean and polished to a shine. The open door to the kitchen gave on to tidy worktops, mugs hanging in regular rows from hooks fixed to the walls, washed dishes drying on a rack by the sink.

There was a faintly antiseptic smell in the air.

Fin turned towards the window and saw the chessboard on its small square table below the sill. There was no room for chairs at either side, but there was a game in progress.

Resin reproductions of the Lewis chessmen in crimson and ivory. Fin wandered over to take a look, and lifted the Berserker from its square to look at the bristling beard and snarling mouth, teeth sunk into the shield. The original made Fin think much more of Whistler than of Kenny. He carefully replaced it and turned as Minto came into the room pulling a khaki woollen jumper over a white singlet. He wore jeans and sneakers now, and Fin saw how puffy his eyes were and still full of sleep.

Fin nodded towards the chessboard. 'Still playing your old commanding officer by phone?'

'By email now. Times move on.' He headed for the kitchen. 'Cup of tea, mate?'

'Thanks.' Fin sank into the settee and found himself looking at a wall lined with framed photographs of Minto with various groups of men, sometimes in uniform, sometimes casual. On parade, or in jungle camouflage in some lush tropical forest on the other side of the world. And he wondered at the solitary existence the man led now after years of comradeship and teamwork. But whatever he had lost in fellowship he had retained in the fastidious attention to detail and organization that the army had dinned into him. Everything had a place and had to be in it. A reason for going to bed at night and getting up in the morning. Except that with Minto, it was the other way around.

Fin glanced from the window across the acres of beach exposed by the outgoing tide, Baile na Cille on the far shore, the church, the burial ground, the wild, untamed beauty of this place. Did Minto have any real sense of it, or was this just somewhere to hide away from a life in civvies he had found hard to cope with? A misfit living on the fringes.

Unlike his last visit, Fin was served his tea in a mug, but the tray it came on contained a little china dish of sugar lumps and milk in a porcelain jug. Minto lifted the mug carefully on to one of half a dozen neatly placed coasters on the coffee table. He chose to drink his own tea standing in front of the fireplace, as if warming himself from the glow of non-existent peats. 'You'll be after these poachers, I suppose.'

Fin nodded and sipped at his mug. 'Do you know Whistler Macaskill?'

'Who doesn't?' Minto nodded towards a two-foot carving of a Lewis chessman on a small wooden table in the far corner of the room. Fin turned to look at it. 'That's one of his. Beautiful piece of work it is, too.'

'Where did you get it?'

'Bought it off him. In fact, it was seeing that what gave old Sir John the idea for the gala day.'

Fin cocked his head and looked at him closely. 'What idea was that?'

'To have a full set of them made and placed on a giant chessboard on the beach. You know, for when they bring the originals here in October. They'll be up in the old church over there in glass cases.' He nodded towards the window. 'Interesting, it is. The geezer what found them way back didn't know what to do with them. So he took them to the

minister of the church at Baile na Cille. One Reverend
Macleod. So it's a nice touch, the chessmen going back to
that church. It's in private hands now, right enough, but
seems the new owners are happy to let them use it for the
day.' He took a thoughtful gulp of his tea. 'Apparently they're
going to have a couple of real chess masters playing a game
with the originals. And each move's going to be relayed to
a guy with a walkie-talkie down there on the beach. Then
they'll move the men on the big board to mirror the game
in the church. That was Sir John's idea anyway.'

'How do you know all this?'

Minto seemed surprised. 'Well, the old boy told me, didn't
he? It's no big secret.'

'His son doesn't seem to know.'

'Prat!' Minto muttered it almost under his breath, as if
uncertain how Fin might react to his disrespect.

'It might be an idea if you mentioned it to him.'

'Why?'

'Because Sir John is still in recovery from his stroke somewhere in England, and Jamie's claiming no knowledge of
it. So Whistler hasn't been paid.'

Minto grunted. 'Typical!'

'You know he's been poaching?'

Minto frowned. 'Who? Whistler?' Fin nodded. 'Course I
do. But it's one for the pot every once in a while. Don't do
no one no harm. So I leave him alone.'

'Jamie wants me to put a stop to it.'

Minto's mug paused halfway to his mouth. He regarded
Fin speculatively. 'Why?'

'They don't see eye to eye.'

'Well, that's hardly a surprise.' He paused. 'So what are you planning to do about it?'

Fin sighed. 'I think there's bigger fish to fry than Whistler, Minto. But there's real enmity between those two, and if we can't persuade Whistler to back off, Wooldridge junior might just bring in some heavies. And that would be bad news for Whistler, and maybe do you out of a job.'

Minto was thoughtful for a moment. Then, 'We?' he asked.

'I can't do it on my own. He's a big guy. Well, you know that. He'd probably be a handful even for you.'

'Oh, I could bring him down, Mr Macleod. No problem. But I'd have to hurt him.'

Fin shook his head. 'I don't want that. I don't want to hurt him. Just stop him. Just so he gets the message.'

Minto looked doubtful. 'How?'

'He's going to be up at Loch Tathabhal tonight.'

'How d'you know that?'

Almost subconsciously Fin ran a hand over his jaw. It still hurt. 'Because he wanted me to know. A stupid challenge.'

Minto shook his head. 'Don't like the sound of it, Mr Macleod.'

Fin set his mug down on its coaster and stood up. 'I'm going to go up to his place now, to try and talk some sense into him. But if I can't, I'll meet you up there tonight, at the old bridge, where the river runs out of the loch.'

'Okay, mate.' Minto shrugged. 'But I'll still have to hurt him to bring him down.'

*

The summer sun had been turning slowly, irrevocably towards the equator, drawing a veil of darkness over the Hebrides a little earlier each night. Those long daylight nights, when it was possible on occasion to see the sun both rise and set at the same time, were gone. Official sunset was now 20.45, but although it was after 21.30 there was still light in the sky. An unusually clear sky, even over the mountains that loomed darkly to the south. And the wind of earlier in the day had dropped to an almost eerie stillness. Fin had been unable to find Whistler, and so he was going to keep the rendezvous which had been issued as a challenge the night before.

He saw pale swathes cut into the dark hills ahead as he came over the hilltop at Ardroil, scars left on the landscape by excavations at the gravel pits below, and early moonlight shimmered silver on the road that wound up above the Abhainn Dearg distillery towards Mangurstadh.

A couple of giant red chessmen carved in wood stood guard at the entrance to the island's first and only distillery in nearly one hundred and seventy years. Abhainn Dearg was Gaelic for Red River, the same name as the estate, and the distillery was so called because it was sited close to where the Red River itself debouched into the Atlantic. The river, according to legend, had got its name following a bloody clan battle which had turned its waters red.

The last distillery on the Isle of Lewis had been closed down in 1844, when the abstainer and prohibitionist Sir James Matheson purchased the island. The irony, perhaps not apparent to the islanders at the time, was that

Matheson had made the fortune that allowed him to buy the island by selling opium to the Chinese. But it was an irony not lost on Fin, and it brought the briefest flicker of a smile to his face as the shallow-pitched red and green roofs of the disparate collection of tin and breeze-block buildings that made up Abhainn Dearg passed below him on the road.

But the smile faded as he remembered why he was here. If Whistler had been trying to avoid him all day, then he had succeeded. And Fin was heading up to Loch Tathabhal for a rendezvous he'd rather not have kept.

Half a mile further on he left the road, and his progress up into the mountains slowed to little more than walking speed on a rough, potholed track that twisted its way labor-iously up through wide, boulder-strewn valleys. Moonlight lay in silver ribbons on tiny streams, and reflected light from every scrap of water that lay in the dips and hollows of this primeval landscape.

But the moon was still low in the sky, and as the moun-tains rose up on either side, the track fell into shadow and all light was concentrated in the sky overhead. It skirted the black waters of Loch Raonasgail, the dark peaks of Mealaisbhal and Tathabhal looming ominously over opposite banks. By the time he got to the head of the loch and climbed several hundred feet more, he could see straight down the line of the valley ahead of him to the distant glittering waters of Loch Tamnabhaigh, and the twinkling lights of Cracabhal Lodge on its northern shore.

Here he turned east, tyres kicking up peat and stone in his wake as he left the track and followed the faintest outline of an ancient pathway. It rose steeply, taking him up to the still waters of Loch Tathabhal, tucked away in the shadows of sharply rising slopes of scree. Tongues of water in the river that ran out of it flickered and licked over an almost dry stone bed, tumbling in a succession of tiny falls to Loch Raonasgail below.

At the head of the loch, where the river left it, a wooden bridge straddled its banks, raised on drystone columns, a single shoogly handrail on the loch side. Here, an area of ground had been levelled to allow fishermen to park their vehicles. Minto's Land Rover was drawn in close to the water's edge, and when Fin parked up and stepped out of his Suzuki he heard the engine of Minto's vehicle ticking in the dark as it cooled down. So he had not been here long. But there was no sign of him. And no sign, either, of John Angus Whistler Macaskill. Fin was aware immediately of the clouds of midges that clustered around him in the dark, and hoped that the repellent he had smeared liberally on his face and neck would afford him some protection.

Looking west from his elevated position, Fin had a view straight through the valley between the peaks of Mealaisbhal and Cracabhal, and although he couldn't see it, he knew that the sea lay somewhere in the distance beyond them. What he could see were the clouds gathering there, black and ominous on the horizon. And the far-off crackle of lightning still too distant to be heard. He felt the first chill draught of the coming storm, the break in the weather so long anticipated, and turned to see Whistler's full moon rising in a clear sky to the east. He hoped that this would not take long, and that he would be back home in his bed before the storm broke.

A sound, like a pebble landing in the water, drew his attention, and he could see silvered rings emanating from a point not far from the opposite bank. A fish, perhaps, jumping to catch insects. There was no sign of life. No further sound.

Fin stepped up on to the wooden bridge and scanned the loch. He felt the wind rising now, clouds that had been so distant starting to gather overhead, the advance guard of the coming storm. Even as he stood on the bridge, looking back down the length of the stream which had so nearly taken his life all those years before, he felt the temperature falling. The midges were gone already, and Whistler's moon appeared and disappeared with increasing frequency, a bizarre, flitting, colourless light show.

As Fin turned back towards the loch he saw a movement on the far shore. A shadow drifting against the rise of the scree slope behind it.

'Minto!' he called out into the dark, feeling his voice whipped away from his mouth on the edge of the wind.

All that came back to him was a laugh that he knew only too well. And in a sudden blink of moonlight he saw Whistler standing there looking at him across the water. He raised his right arm, and Fin saw a huge wild salmon dangling from his hand, strong thick fingers hooked through the gills. 'We could just go back to the croft, Fin. Roast her in tinfoil over the peat. Share a glass and a memory or two. What do you say?'

Fin was very nearly tempted. 'Oh, come on, Whistler, cut it out. We need to chat, you and me.'

'Is that what you brought your muscle man for? A chat? I'm disappointed in you, Fin. Thought better of you than that.' And Fin realized then the mistake he had made by involving Minto.

Almost in the same moment, the moon vanished behind a cloud and Whistler was swallowed again by the dark. Fin heard a loud banging coming from the direction of Minto's Land Rover. He jumped down off the bridge and ran across the parking area to throw open the back door.

Minto was lying curled up on the floor, securely bound by his own tow rope, trussed up like a chicken, an oily rag shoved into his mouth. He had manoeuvred himself on to his back so that he could kick the side of the vehicle with the flat of his feet.

'Jesus, Minto!' Fin climbed in the back and untied him, pulling the rag from his mouth. Minto gasped for several seconds until he had caught his breath, saliva foaming around his lips.

'I'll kill him. I'll fucking kill him!'

Fin gazed at him in disbelief. 'What the hell happened?'

'He jumped me, that's what fucking happened.'

Fin almost found himself laughing. '*He* jumped *you*?'

'Strong as a bloody ox that geezer is, Macleod.'

'I thought you were going to take him down, Minto?'

Minto glowered at him, his pride seriously dented. No one man should have been capable of doing something like this to him. 'I would've. Given half a chance.' He sat up and winced, his left hand crossing to his right shoulder. 'I think he's dislocated my bloody shoulder.'

Fin sat cross-legged on the floor and looked at him. 'Well, you're not going to be much damn use to me now, are you?'

Minto cast him a surly look. 'You'll never take him on your own, mate. A skinny little runt like you.'

Fin got to his knees, and crouching made his way to the back. He jumped down. 'Go home, Minto.'

He stood and watched as Minto struggled into the driver's seat and started the motor. His headlights were devoured by the dark, making almost no impression on it as the vehicle turned and bumped back down the track to the loch below. Fin felt the first drops of rain in his face.

Now it was just him and Whistler.

He turned and scanned Loch Tathabhal, the surface of it dimpled and ridged by the rising wind, floods of fleeting moonlight caught in brief spangled moments of illumination. And there was the shadow of his friend moving along the far shore, his laughter lifting itself above the wind. 'Come on, Fin, catch me if you can.' The voice distant, somehow, and carried off into the night.

To Whistler it was all a game. Not to be taken seriously. And yet to cross Jamie the way he had was to court disaster. If he lost his home it was likely he would lose the court case for custody of his daughter. And if he lost both, God only knew what might become of him.

For several long moments Fin contemplated getting back into his Suzuki and going home. What good would it do to play Whistler's game? And yet to walk away would be like turning his back on the man who had saved his life. Whistler would never have done that to Fin. At the very least he needed to make him understand the trouble he was in.

'Whistler, wait!' But his voice was consumed by the night, and he saw Whistler outlined against the sky in the moment before he began slithering down the scree to the lower valley.

Fin sighed and hesitated briefly before opening up the back of his four-by-four and taking out his waterproof jacket and a small rucksack. He slipped into the jacket, slung the rucksack across his shoulders and grasped the non-slip grip of his telescopic walker's stick firmly in his right hand.

Coming, ready or not.

At first it was easy to keep Whistler in his sights. Amazingly there was still some daylight in the sky, and plenty of moonlight washing across the slopes between clouds. He saw Whistler's shadow moving nimbly among the rocks as he scrambled down the incline. The wind was increasing in strength, temperature falling further as the black storm clouds began to roll in. But the rain, as yet, was still only a spit in his face.

Loch Raonasgail was no more than a big black hole scoured out between Tathabhal and Mealaisbhal by shifting glaciers in some long-ago ice age, filled now with the millions of gallons of rainwater which the mountains that heaved up around it shed from their slopes. Fin saw Whistler circumvent its south-west shoreline, crossing the track, and heading off through the boulder-strewn valley in the shadow of Cracabhal.

The lightning came before the rain. Great jagged flashes of it that lit up the mountains and plunged their valleys into deeper darkness. His glimpses of Whistler now were few and far between as blackness settled over them like dust.

The heather and bracken beneath his feet were dry, and crackled in the dark. Normally sodden peat was hard and unyielding underfoot. Fin gritted his teeth and forced himself on. For forty minutes or more he followed the phantom that was Whistler. He found his leg muscles aching, joints hammered by the hardness of the ground, breath sucked with increasing rapidity into lungs that heaved and strained to pump sufficient oxygen to already tiring muscles.

No matter how hard he went at it, he never seemed to get any closer to him. And it became apparent that if Whistler wanted to, he could lose Fin in a heartbeat. But still he kept appearing, just when Fin thought he'd lost him. A glimpse here, leaping from one rock to another like a mountain goat. A glimpse there, as he turned to gaze back through the darkness. He was playing with Fin. Having fun. Making absolutely certain that he didn't lose him, showing himself in tantalizing moments, like the lure of a fly drawing a fish on to the hook.

Lightning crashed so close to him that Fin instinctively ducked, and dropped to his knees, an image of the valley ahead of him left burned on his retinas. A bizarre and brutal landscape littered with the spoil of ice explosions millions of years old. For a moment he could barely hear, and his nostrils were filled with the ozone that suffused the air in the aftermath of the storm's electrical discharges.

Whistler was there, too, in that image burned into his consciousness by the lightning, about three or four hundred yards ahead of him. Clambering over giant clusters of rocks. Then consumed again by darkness.

Absurdly, Fin found thoughts creeping into his mind of the bogeyman who had haunted the childhood imaginations of generations of island children. The outlaw Mac an t-Stronaich. A man credited with more brutal murders and assaults than any living soul might be capable of committing. And yet he had existed in reality, in some more minor incarnation no doubt, and on the run had escaped into these very mountains to avoid capture. Before being brought to justice, finally, and hanged in 1836. Whistler moved among the rocks like his ghost.

Sheet lightning lit up the sky once more, and Fin saw the black underside of the clouds that rumbled in low over the peaks, laden with moisture and threatening deluge. And in that moment he decided on the folly of this fruitless chase. Let Whistler go scampering off into the mountains. To hell with him! Fin would go back up to Tathabhal and pick up his Suzuki. He would drive to Whistler's place and wait for him there. He was bound to return sooner or later, and he would have it out with him then.

Another flash saw Whistler silhouetted on the shoulder of the mountain, standing still and looking back down the slope towards him. His hair was blowing all around his head, and he stood proud, like an ancient Viking warrior, his face leached of all colour by the lightning. The thunder that followed immediately was so directly overhead that it felt like a physical blow. And then the rain came. Out of nowhere. Sweeping suddenly down the valley in a blinding mist, the first exhalation of the storm. Hail was whipped into Fin's face by a wind whose sudden increase in force very nearly knocked him off his feet. He turned and began to blunder back the way he had come.

Within minutes he had totally lost his sense of direction. Visibility was zero. He could see only in those brief moments when the lightning came. And then he stumbled forward with a memory of the next few yards held briefly in his mind, until his confidence wavered and he stopped, waiting for the next explosion of light.

Very quickly he realized that he was going up rather than down. But when he turned towards the descent he had no belief that it was taking him in the right direction.

The rain whipped relentlessly into his face, finding its way beneath his jacket at the cuffs and neck. He wasn't wearing waterproof overtrousers, so his jeans were quickly sodden and heavy. His feet, in their well-worn hiking boots, were wet and already starting to grow cold.

He crouched down and took off his rucksack, delving

inside it to find his flashlight and a compass on the end of a loop of ribbon that he could hang around his neck. He clutched the torch, but before his fingers had closed around the compass, his rucksack filled with air from a blast of wind that nearly knocked him over and was torn from his grasp. He lunged at it as it flew off into the night, a hopeless leap in the dark that netted him only fresh air. And the rucksack was gone, leaving him sprawled among the grass and heather, water running like a river over the hard, impervious surface of the peat beneath him.

In desperation, he searched around for his stick, the thin beam of light from his torch making little impression on the dark. He was certain he had laid it down beside him when he crouched to open his rucksack. But there was no sign of it, and now it began to dawn on Fin that he was in trouble. He had no compass or map, no stick to help him keep his feet. He was soaked through and starting to feel the cold seep into his soul. He had no idea where he was or what direction to go in. And by now, for sure, in these conditions, Whistler must have lost him, too.

He crouched down on his hunkers, his back to the wind, and tried to make a rational assessment of his situation. But all the rational thought in the world could not displace the one that filled his mind. Men died in these conditions. Experienced walkers and climbers caught in a storm among the mountains, fully equipped and often in broad daylight, could perish in a matter of hours. Fin was inexperienced, ill-equipped and lost in the dark. One false step could lead to a twisted ankle or a broken leg, a fall that would leave him lying hopelessly exposed to the elements. The cold would steal his consciousness. Sleep would come quickly, and there would be no waking from it. He knew beyond any doubt that he had to find shelter, and find it fast.

He closed his eyes and tried to focus on where he thought he was. Whistler had led him up through the valley between Mealaisbhal, and Cracabhal to the south of it. The last time he had seen him, he had been standing on the shoulder of the rising shadow of what he took to be Mealaisbhal on his right.

Fin had covered almost no ground since then, and if he was climbing, then the rise would take him up over that same shoulder. He had never been in the valley to the north of the mountain. But he remembered from his schooldays the stories of the Cailleach of Mealaisbhal. Cailleach was Gaelic for an old woman, and this one had killed her son and lived wild in the caves of Carnaichean Tealasdale beneath the cliffs at the north end of Mealaisbhal. Or so the story went. But there were supposed to be numerous caves there, among the cliffs and rocks. Caves that would provide a man with life-saving shelter.

He decided to keep climbing.

With the beam from his torch trained on the ground immediately ahead of him, he forced himself up the slope, taking the shortest route over boulders and rocks lying in jumbles and clusters all across the slope of the shoulder. They were slippery and treacherous, and with the hail stinging his face, and the rain in his eyes, he could barely see.

But he could tell immediately when the ground beneath his feet began to level off, and at the same time he found himself even more exposed to the weather. He staggered forward through the rain, the wind hitting him with such force that he fell over several times. But still he kept going, even though every muscle and sinew in his body was crying out for rest.

The shadow of a massive rock rose up ahead of him, and he felt his way around it to the leeward side where he was briefly out of the wind. He pressed himself back against the sheer face of this giant slab and stood there gasping for breath. He had never in his life felt so small, or so vulnerable. The scale and scope of the land, and the power of the elements, dwarfed him into insignificance.

He found himself shivering now with the cold, teeth chattering. To stop would be fatal. He had to find shelter. As he turned again to face the black uncertainty that lay ahead of him, the sky lit up in a series of lightning flashes that cast their ghostly effulgence across the valley that fell away beneath him. It was startling and bleak in this unforgiving light, a landscape so alien and primordial that it would not have been out of place on the moon. Cliffs rose sheer at his right hand, pitch-black and shining wet, reflecting the flickering lightning from overhead. Then the ground fell away in shelves and inclines into a wide valley littered with boulders the size of tower blocks, massive chunks of gneiss and granite cast upon the land by long-ago ice bursts. Sometimes in clusters, sometimes in single, solitary chunks that stood at impossible angles, balanced on corners and edges, casting their shadows like elongated fists, before vanishing again into darkness. It was like nothing Fin had ever seen.

Further down the gully, a large body of water reflected the storm in long and short flashes, as if in response to some heavenly signal lamp pulsing Morse into the night. A hidden loch in the basin of the valley.

Fin began the descent, slowly at first, each step made with care. He slipped for the first time, sliding several yards before managing to bring himself to a stop. Then back to his feet, and on, faster now, as his body weight propelled him on down the slope, pushed by the wind like a hand at his back. His torchlight flashed back and forth across the tangle of bracken and heather ahead of him, before picking out the shambles of smashed stone that formed a steep scree declivity that plunged towards the dark shapes of jagged rocks distantly below. Rainwater ran off the hill in streams and rivulets, snaking its way through the stones at his feet as he stepped on to them. He had covered only a few slithering yards before the scree shifted to the left and right of him, gathering momentum. Then like an avalanche it took his feet and swept him away, to fall helplessly down into darkness, his ears filled with the rush of falling stones. Until he struck something so hard it took his breath away. For one brief, terrifying moment, his head was filled with light, before he was taken by a darkness from which he knew there would be no return.

\*

A flickering yellow light filtered slowly through the gauze that fogged his consciousness. It brought pain, fear, an uncontrollable shivering. Whistler's big pale face, with its smears of black and silver whiskers, flickered too, like a light bulb at the end of its life. The gauze was smoke. A thick, choking, hot smoke that filled the air. Fin coughed as he breathed it in, a painful racking cough, and he tried to sit up. But he couldn't. He was wrapped, as if in a cocoon, unable to move.

Three feet above him, an irregular stone roof curved away into darkness. A complex tracery of spiders' webs hung from it in broken veils, reflecting the light of the flames that licked up through the darkness no more than eighteen inches from his face.

'Bloody idiot!' He heard Whistler's voice strained through the gauze. 'If you're going to follow a man up into the mountains on a night when they're forecasting a storm, you should at least come prepared.'

Fin managed to unpeel a dry tongue from the roof of his mouth. 'You knew there would be a storm?'

Whistler showed his teeth. 'Of course I did. I thought you would have checked that.'

Fin saw his and Whistler's wet clothes stretched over dry stones, steam rising from them on the far side of the fire, and realized for the first time that he was naked inside his cocoon. 'What have you wrapped me in?'

'A couple of woollen wraps and an aluminium blanket. And keep shivering, boy. That'll generate about two degrees centigrade an hour. The blankets'll keep it in and you'll reheat yourself. With a bit of luck your clothes will be just about dry by the morning.' He leaned over and put his fingers on Fin's forehead, his touch as light as chiffon. 'You've a nasty bang on the head, though. I've disinfected it and dressed it, but you'd better see a professional.'

Fin could see now that Whistler was sitting cross-legged on the far side of the circle of stones which contained the burning peats that were generating both the heat and the smoke. His long black hair was still wet, and swept back in a tangle from his forehead. The jumper he had worn beneath his jacket was dry, as were jeans protected by waterproof leggings. 'What is this place, Whistler?'

'We're in a wee beehive dwelling at the north end of a pretty inaccessible valley somewhere between Mealaisbhal and Brinneabhal. There's a few of them clustered here. Not real beehives, of course. That's just what the archaeologists call them. God knows who built them, or why. Maybe shepherds at some point for when they brought the sheep up to the high grazing. Anyway, most of them are in ruins. Just circles of stone and turf. This one I remade myself, and keep it stocked with dry peats. Just as well, eh?'

'What the hell do you come up here for?'

'Deer. Mountain hare.' He laughed, then. 'And I've spent quite a long time in these parts searching for the cave of swords.'

Fin frowned. 'What swords?'

A grin of something close to embarrassment split Whistler's face. 'Ach, it'll be a bloody wild goose chase, I'm sure. But I was always fascinated by the story I heard once about a man who knew these valleys like the back of his hand. Got lost one time in a fog, and fell into a hidden cave among the boulders. There were steps down into it. And inside it he found a stash of rusted old swords. Dozens of the things. He couldn't carry them himself, but he was sure he would find his way back with friends to bring them down to the village.' Whistler shook his head. 'He never did. No matter how many times he looked, he couldn't find that cave again. No one ever doubted him, though, and there was a lot of speculation about where the swords had come from and who put them there.'

'And?'

Whistler shrugged. 'And nothing. I never found them either. My favourite theory was that they belonged to the men of Uig who hid them from the English after the defeat of the Jacobite army at Culloden. Everything "Highland" was forbidden, including the wearing of the kilt and the bearing of arms. So if the locals hid their weapons up here, there was no way anyone would ever find them, but they'd be quickly accessible if they were ever needed.' He laughed. 'I'd have loved to feel the weight of those Jacobite swords in my hand, Fin. Not least because they'd have been worth a bloody fortune.' He tipped his head to one side, casting Fin an appraising look. 'How are you feeling?'

'Bloody awful.'

'Good. As long as you're feeling something you'll be okay.'

He took a stout stick and tipped several blackened stones out from the embers of the fire on to the beaten earth floor.

'When these have cooled enough for me to handle, we'll wrap them into your blankets to help generate a bit more heat. Under your oxters, and at the back of your neck. God knows, you've no brain to speak of, but what little you have has a wee bit at its stem that regulates your internal temperature, along with your breathing and circulation. The hypothalamus. We want to keep that warm and in good working order.' It was typical of Whistler that knowledge like that could trip off his tongue almost without thought.

Fin let his head fall to one side, still shivering, and heard the sound of the wind thundering all around the outside of this tiny stone dwelling. 'I guess you've done it again,' he said.

'Done what, boy?'

'Saved my life.'

Whistler roared. 'Well,' he said, when he was finally able to stop laughing. 'It's a family tradition.' He grinned. 'And given that I exploited that stupid pride of yours to lure you up here in the first place, there was no way I could let you die. No matter how hard you were trying to kill yourself.' His smile slowly faded to be replaced by something like guilt. He hesitated for a moment, then: 'I'm sorry I hit you the other night.'

'So am I.' Fin managed a rueful smile.

'I shouldn't have done that.'

'No, you shouldn't.'

Whistler's smile returned, burgeoning into a grin that

made light in his eyes. 'No. I should have fucking killed that bastard Jamie Wooldridge. Next time, I will.'

Fin closed his eyes, and for the first time since consciousness had returned, felt his shivering start to subside just a little. He was aware, then, of Whistler tucking the hot stones into the folds of his blankets, and he could feel the warmth of them bringing life back to his frozen body.

Whistler was right. He was a bloody idiot.

He woke to a sound like the end of the world, and felt the earth moving beneath him, as if the whole mountain was shaking. The fire was blazing, and he could see the fear and confusion in Whistler's face on the far side of it. Fin sat up and almost cracked his skull on the roof of the beehive. 'What the hell's that?'

The noise roared, even above the blast of the storm, filling the air, the ground fibrillating all around them. Whistler placed a hand flat on the roof above his head as if afraid that it might fall in on them. 'I've no idea.' His voice sounded very small, and Fin could barely hear it.

'Feels like an earthquake,' Fin shouted above the noise.

'Aye, it does. But it can't be. Not on this scale, anyway.' If anything the shaking was getting more violent. Whistler put both hands on the roof now, like Samson in reverse trying to hold the temple up. 'Jesus Christ!'

Fin had no idea how long it lasted. It felt like a lifetime. A lifetime in which the end seemed just a breath away. Though neither of them voiced it, each feared that they were going to die, without any clear idea of why. And then almost as suddenly as it had wakened them the shaking stopped and the noise subsided, and the sound of the storm took precedence once more.

They sat in breathless silence for several minutes hardly daring to believe that it was over, whatever it was, and fearing that it would start again at any moment.

Then Whistler tipped forward on to his knees and crawled towards the entrance. 'I'm going to take a look.' He pulled aside the big flat stone that sealed them in, and Fin felt a rush of cold air that threw sparks from the fire and fanned the peats to fill the dwelling with their strange, incandescent light. Whistler wriggled out into the night, and Fin sat wrapped in his blankets full of uncertainty and apprehension.

Whistler was back in less than a minute, soaked even in that short space of time. His hair was wild and smeared across a face that was unusually pale.

'Well?' Fin searched it for enlightenment.

But Whistler just settled himself again on the far side of the fire and shrugged. 'Can't see a thing. It's pitch out there. We'll need to wait till dawn.'

'What time is it now?'

'Just after two. Another four hours or so.'

Fin lay down and rolled on to his back, still tense, waiting for the noise and the shaking to start again. But only the storm disturbed the night, rain and wind assaulting their tiny shelter with the fury of thwarted attackers. The long summer of drought was well and truly over.

*

The next time he awoke it was daybreak, which is when he had found Whistler out on the ridge in that strange, pink dawn light, looking down into the vanished loch where Roddy's plane lay canted among the rocks.

# CHAPTER EIGHTEEN

Jamie pushed his hands deep into the pockets of his Barbour jacket and shoved out his jaw. 'Well?'

'Nothing happened,' Fin said. He glanced beyond Jamie and saw Kenny's scepticism.

'Nothing?'

'Nothing much. Whistler was waiting for me up at the loch. He apologized for the other night. We talked about old times, and took shelter from the storm.'

Jamie's disbelief was patent now. 'The plane was found a long way from Tathabhal.'

Fin just shrugged. 'Why are you looking for him?'

'If it's any of your business, Macleod, I'm serving Macaskill with notice of eviction. Thought I would do it myself, rather than send in the bailiffs.'

Fin felt his hackles rise and he glanced at Kenny. 'And brought backup in case he kicked your arse again?'

'I'm not sure I like your tone.'

'And I'm not sure I want to work for someone who would throw a man out of his own home.'

Jamie bristled. 'It's not his. Neither the land nor the building. His father sold the feu of the blackhouse to my father years ago for ready drinking money. I've checked back through the books. There's not been a penny paid in rent on the house or the croft since last century.'

Fin blew air through pursed lips. 'A peppercorn rent. I'd be willing to bet we're not looking at anything more than a few hundred quid. Not a fraction of the value of those chessmen in there.' He jerked his thumb back towards the house. 'Whistler was right. You're not half the man your father is. He and Whistler had an understanding. You're just a vindictive bastard.'

Anger simmered dangerously in Jamie's unblinking gaze. 'And you're fired!' His voice was tight and soft, barely audible above the wind.

'Too late,' Fin said. 'I already quit.'

Jamie stood for a moment in seething silence, but whatever thoughts flashed through his mind wouldn't form words on his lips. He turned and strode back down the hill to his Range Rover.

Kenny remained, staring at the ground in embarrassment. As the car door slammed shut below he looked up at Fin. 'None of this is my doing, Fin.'

Fin stared at him for a long, hard moment, then nodded. 'I know.' He paused. 'Where is he Kenny? He just seems to have vanished.'

Kenny shrugged his shoulders. 'Who knows?' He glanced up beyond the blackhouse towards the mountains. 'He could be anywhere.' His eyes flickered back towards Fin. 'But I know where he'll be tomorrow morning.'

Fin frowned. 'How?'

'There's a hearing at the Sheriff Court. The custody case for wee Anna. If he doesn't show up for it, the case'll fall. So I expect him to be there.'

Fin looked at him, eyes filled with consternation. 'How's it possible, Kenny, that you can take a man's wife, and his daughter, and still remain his friend?'

'You've been away from the island too long, Fin. You can't afford for things to get personal in a place like this. I wouldn't call Whistler my friend these days, but there's more in our history that binds us than any argument over the love of a woman, or the care of a child.'

Fin watched as Kenny strode back down the hill to where a fuming Jamie awaited him in the Range Rover. In keeping with his mood, the sky had become closed, the light gone, and the land lay brooding in semi-obscurity.

# CHAPTER NINETEEN

It was a grey, miserable morning, low cloud moving at speed over the town, dropping a fine wetting rain that made every-thing shiny and stole colour from streets that looked like old black-and-white prints. The Sheriff Court, in Lewis Street, was a blonde sandstone Victorian edifice with rain-streaked gables and tall stone chimneys. It sat two doors away from the Church of Scotland. One dispensing earthly justice, the other promising judgement in the afterlife.

There was a crowd of people hanging about on the pave-ment at the railings, huddled in shelter from the rain and the wind under a cluster of shining black umbrellas. Guilty and innocent, witnesses and relatives, all equal under the dismal sky and sharing their addiction for tobacco. Most wore sombre suits with white shirts and dark ties. Sunday best trotted out to impress the Sheriff. There was an old joke which had been circulating in the town for many years about what it was you called a Stornoway man wearing a suit. The response, appropriately enough, was *the accused*.

Fin had arrived late, held up on the road from Ness by a lorry which had shed its load. So he had no idea if Whistler had turned up for the private hearing or not. He had debated long and hard about whether or not he should tell George Gunn, but decided in the end that he would rather speak to Whistler himself first.

He stood alone on the other side of the street, his back to the closed gates of a builder's yard with its cluster of concrete buildings and red tin roofs. He wore boots and jeans, a baseball cap and a waterproof jacket, and stood with his hands thrust deep in his pockets, hunched against the cold. He had been waiting for half an hour before he recognized the social worker he had met at Whistler's blackhouse. She emerged from the arched doorway of the courthouse to raise a pink umbrella towards the sky and hurry away through the waiting crowd. A couple of solicitors in black gowns came out to stand on the steps and light cigarettes, before Whistler pushed his way between them and strode down the path to the gates. It was the first time Fin had set eyes on him since the discovery of the plane, and his immediate reaction was one of relief.

But he was taken aback by the change in Whistler's appearance. He had shaved, his hair washed and shiny and pulled back in a neat ponytail at the nape of his neck. He wore his funeral suit – for Fin was certain that he never went to church – and a collar and tie. His black shoes were polished to a shine. He could almost have passed for respectable. But he had no coat or umbrella. He turned, surprised, as Fin called his name. Fin hurried across the street to catch him.

'I've been looking for you for days, Whistler.'

Whistler did not look pleased to see him, and avoided his eye, staring off into the distance as if having spotted something of much greater interest. 'I've been busy.'

Fin smiled. 'So I see. How did it go?'

Whistler's eyes flickered towards him then away again. 'The Sheriff's called another hearing in two weeks to give him time to read the social work reports.'

Fin nodded. 'Have you had a chance to talk to Anna?'

'No.' He turned a dark, resentful gaze on Fin.

Fin said, 'I spoke to her.'

Whistler's eyes blackened. 'Why would you do that?'

'I went looking for you at the croft and found her sitting in the house.' Fin saw consternation now in his eyes.

'What was she doing there?'

'Remembering how it was, Whistler. With you and her mum. Wishing she could have that time back again.'

'Well, she can't. Seonag's dead.'

'But you're not.'

'The lassie's not interested in me. She thinks I'm a . . . well, she thinks I'm weird.'

Fin couldn't contain the laugh that forced itself through his lips. 'Whistler, you *are*!' He paused to take in the dangerous tilt of the other man's head, and the brief flare of anger in his eyes. 'But that doesn't mean she doesn't love you.'

'Don't talk shite, man!'

'She told me you were a pure fucking embarrassment. *Her* words. But she also said she loved you. In her own inimitable way.'

Whistler looked at Fin for a long, unseeing moment. 'She's never told me that. Ever.' He spoke in barely a whisper, as if afraid that he might not have control of his voice.

'Have you told *her*, Whistler?'

'Told her what?'

'That *you* love *her*.'

Whistler was unable to hold eye contact and turned his head away again.

But Fin wouldn't let it rest. 'You do, don't you?'

'Of course I fucking do.'

Like father like daughter, Fin thought. The two of them were so alike. 'Then maybe you should let her know it.'

'I'm her father. It goes without saying.'

'Nothing goes without saying, Whistler.' Fin paused. 'Like what it is you've been keeping to yourself since we found Roddy in that plane.'

Whistler was wary now. 'What are you talking about?'

'You didn't want me to open up the cockpit, did you? I think you knew what I was going to find. At least, you thought you did.' Fin tried to read him, but a cloud of obfuscation had come down over his eyes. 'But you were as stunned as I was by what was inside, weren't you?'

'Why don't you mind your own fucking business?' Whistler lowered his voice to little more than a growl, but the menace in it was unmistakable.

'Is that why you've been avoiding me, Whistler? In case I asked?'

His big hand came out of nowhere. Not in a fist, but palm first, like the flat of a shovel, and it slammed into Fin's chest.

Fin was unprepared for it and stepped back, his foot dropping down from the kerb to the road, sending him sprawling to the tarmac. His baseball cap spun away across the street. Whistler loomed over him, a thick finger stabbing down through the rain. 'Stay away from me, Fin. Just stay away. All right?' And he turned and strode off through the crowd.

The hubbub outside the gates of the courthouse had faded to silence, and all eyes were turned towards Fin lying in the road. The solicitors, still smoking in the doorway, cast curious eyes in his direction.

Fin barely had time to recover his breath before a large hand hooked itself around his upper arm and almost lifted him to his feet. Big Kenny handed him his cap and looked searchingly into his face. 'What's going on, Fin?'

Fin saw the concern in the big man's eyes. 'I don't know, Kenny. I wish to hell I did.'

He spotted Anna Bheag standing outside the gate with a group of her schoolfriends. There was consternation and hostility in her face, the metal that adorned it glistening in the rain. And he saw that whatever rapport he had struck with her that day at Whistler's place was long gone. For a moment it looked as if she were going to say something, then she turned towards her friends. 'Come on,' she said, and the group of teenage girls hurried off towards Francis Street. Fin doubted that they were heading back to school.

Fin brooded darkly on Whistler's inexplicable behaviour through all the long drive back up the west coast.

October was a breath away, and the approaching winter was making its presence felt for the first time. The Indian summer had bypassed autumn, and it looked as if they would plunge straight from summer into winter. The temperature had fallen, and the wind was swinging around to the north-west. It had an edge to it as sharp as a razor, and the rain carried the promise of hail, stinging and cold.

Village after village drifted past Fin's windows in the rain. Wet and dark, and stretched out along the road like so many little boxes strung on a thread, treeless and naked, exposed to the elements. Only a few hardy shrubs grew in the peaty soil where hopeful souls had made vain attempts to hack gardens and lawns out of unyielding moorland. Barabhas, Siadar, Dail, Cros. Each marked by its prayer hall or church, the occasional village store, or filling station. Tiny primary schools. And potteries established by incomers to sell to the tourists, as if the island itself and the people who lived there were incidental.

As he reached Ness, he could see waves breaking white all along the north-west coastline, and the stubble of grave-stones rising across the machair above the cliffs where the people of Crobost had been burying their dead for hundreds of years. The thought of another winter here closed around his heart like icy fingers. Work on restoring his parents' crofthouse would grind to a halt, and without a job he would be left to dwell upon a life without purpose or direction. Through all the wrong turnings he had taken at all the crossroads of his life, it seemed that he had finally lost his way.

He thought about Donald, and his admonition that Fin was always alone with his grief and his hatred. Grief for his dead son, hatred for the man who had killed him and escaped the consequences. But Donald had left out despair. Despair of a life wasted, and a love squandered. Mona, the woman who had borne his son, but whom he had never loved. Marsaili whose love he had so carelessly discarded. He might share her bed once again, but something precious had been lost all those years before, and somehow they had never quite recovered it. Just like all those souls lost in middle age, searching for the past on social networking sites, only to find that present reality can never live up to rose-tinted memory.

He almost envied Donald his faith. *It's the feeling that you're never alone*, he had said, and Fin wondered how that must be.

As he drove up past the Crobost Free Church, he saw a strange car parked beside Marsaili's on the patch of gravel above the bungalow. When he drew up alongside it, he saw that it was a local registration, but not one that he recognized. On the island you knew your friends on the road by the registration number of their car. Windscreens were usually too wet, or occasionally reflected too much sunshine, for the recognition of faces behind wheels. He peered in through the driver's window as he got out of his jeep, and saw a car rental agreement lying on the passenger seat.

Curiosity drew him down the path and up the steps to the kitchen door. He heard women's voices raised in laughter as he pushed the door open, then silence as he stepped out of the wind into the warmth. Marsaili was standing, leaning back against the far worktop, cradling a mug of tea in her hands. A woman with cropped dark hair and a long black coat sat at the kitchen table, a mug on the coaster in front of her. She looked expectantly towards Fin, with a hint of sad amusement in her eyes.

It was Mairead.

# CHAPTER TWENTY

I suppose my obsession with Mairead began the first day I set eyes on her in the rehearsal room at the Nicolson Institute.

I had fallen out with Marsaili some time before and arrived in Stornoway aged fifteen, fancy free and awash with testosterone. Mairead came like a bright shining star out of Uig as this Crobost boy from Ness, fresh-faced and unsophisticated, began his first year at the Nicolson still dripping wet behind the ears. She was a goddess with a voice that sent chills down my back.

There were other good-looking girls at school, of course, but Mairead was a cut above. She held herself beautifully, with poise and confidence, and oozed the kind of latent sexuality that seemed solely designed to inflame a teenage boy's passions.

She had beautiful hands, I remember, delicate, with long fingers and perfectly manicured nails. Her face was fine-featured, but still strong. She was tall, and walked with a certain swing of the hips, breasts always tantalizingly suggested by the way they strained at her school blouse. Her hair was a dark auburn and had a natural wave in it, and in those days she wore it long over her shoulders, or drawn back in a ponytail that was wrapped into a knot at the back of her head and held by clasps.

But her eyes were what bewitched me. A dark, dark blue they were, with a slightly darker circle around the iris, and there was always something like amusement in them, quizzical and superior. I can remember the first time she looked directly at me. My stomach flipped over, and I literally went weak at the knees.

Naturally, I wasn't the only boy who was hopelessly in love with her. In fact, I doubt if there was a single boy at the school who wasn't. Except for a rather soft boy from Carloway called Anndra, who turned out to be gay.

Of course, Mairead herself was only too aware of the effect that she had, and she wouldn't have been human, I suppose, if it hadn't turned her head. She teased and tormented and toyed with us as if we were children. And, in truth, mentally, she was probably several years our senior, in the way that there is always a gap between teenage boys and girls of the same age. She made me think of a Beatles song that my aunt used to play, called 'Girl'. All about a girl who would put you down because it amused her, who would take your adulation for granted, and hurt you because it gave her pleasure. Such poignant observations from the pen of a still-young John Lennon, so clearly born of experience. Another Mairead, no doubt.

Singing and playing with Sòlas set Mairead apart from the rest, placed her on a kind of pedestal. And she was afflicted by the star syndrome, even in those days. But none of that

affected my ardour. The fact that she was so impossibly un-
attainable somehow made her all the more desirable.

It wasn't until the following year that I had my first close
encounter with her.

It was early summer, before the holidays, and the bike
group had already upped sticks and moved away from Holm
Point after discovering the history of the *Iolaire*. We were
all out at Garry Beach with the bikes. By that time I had
been humphing gear for Sòlas for about eighteen months,
and had long ago accepted that a relationship with Mairead
was not in my stars. It didn't stop me from admiring her
from a distance, though, and I still blushed like an idiot
when she spoke to me. But as far as the opposite sex was
concerned I had started to focus my attentions on the attainable. Although not with any great success, it has to be
said.

Mairead's on–off relationship with Roddy was in one of
its frequent off periods, and she had ridden pillion out to
Tolastadh that day with Whistler, I think to make both Roddy
and Strings jealous.

What had started with the promise of a lazy afternoon
in the summer sunshine quickly faded. Dark clouds rolled
over the moor from the west, bringing with them a chill
edge to the wind and a hint of rain somewhere in the not
too distant future. There were a dozen or so of us, just
fooling around, smoking, dipping our feet in the icy waters
of the Minch and running shrieking up the beach as the
waves broke over our calves.

We hung on as long as possible, not really wanting it to end. Then, with the first drops of rain, made the belated decision to head back to Stornoway.

Try as he might, Whistler couldn't get his moped started. Some of the others had already gone, and those of us who were left didn't relish hanging about in the rain.

I called to Whistler, grinning, 'Enjoy the walk back.' I had no doubt he would get her going in the end, but it was fun to annoy him.

He came back at me with his usual wit. 'Get stuffed, Macleod.'

I gunned my motor and was about to head off when a voice called, 'Fin, wait!'

I looked around and saw Mairead running across the sand. She had a magazine opened over her head, but it wasn't going to keep her very dry. Her face was flushed and her eyes shining.

'I need a lift.'

My heart was thumping. 'Aren't you going to wait with Whistler?'

She pulled a face. 'I would like to get home *sometime* this week.'

I laughed, a little nervously, and glanced around. There were several others that she could have asked for a lift, but she had chosen me. By now my mouth was dry. 'Sure,' I said. And I was about to tell her to hop on, but she had already swung a leg over the rear wheel to sit astride the luggage rack and slip her arms around my waist.

'Come on then,' she shouted above the racket of my little 50cc motor. 'I'm getting wet.'

I revved and let out the clutch, and accelerated across the stony car park towards the road, back wheel spinning and skidding from side to side, trying to impress her. And I felt her arms tighten around me. A thrill went through my whole body, ending in a deep ache of desire in my loins. I glanced back and saw Whistler standing by his bike, glaring after us. The rain began in earnest then.

Usually it would take about twenty-five minutes to get back to Stornoway. It took me well over half an hour that day. You could say that I went more slowly because of the rain. But the truth was I didn't ever want it to end. Even although we were both soaked to the skin within minutes. The feel of Mairead's arms around me was intoxicating, her open palms spread across my chest, the softness of her body against mine, the hardness of her breasts pressed into my back. I could feel the warmth passing between our two bodies, and I was more aroused I think than I had ever been in my life.

At one point, I could feel her resting her head against my shoulder. I wanted so much to turn and look at her face, to find her eyes with mine, and her lips, and kiss her softly. But I daren't take my eyes off the road.

My mind was seething with conflicting emotions. Desire, fear, and a thousand imagined possibilities. What was I going to say to her when we got back to town? How was I going to make the moment last? Was there even the slightest chance that she had asked me for a ride back because she had always secretly fancied me? I rehearsed a dozen lines in my head. 'What are you doing tonight?' 'Fancy going for a coffee?' Each of them utterly banal and lacking in wit or inspiration.

When we finally came over the top of Matheson Road and turned into Springfield Road, I pulled in at the pavement by the school gate. Most of the others had got there ahead of us. All soaked. But the rain had gone off by now, and they stood around in groups animated by conversation and laughter. Mairead swung her leg over my back wheel and smiled at me. Her hair was wet and smeared all over her face. She removed it from her eyes with elegant fingers, and I thought I had never seen her look more lovely.

My eyes were immediately drawn to the flash of white blouse below her blazer. Soaked and made see-through by the rain, I was shocked to see the outline of her breasts, and the darker circles of her areolae visible through the flimsiest of bras. She looked down to see what I was looking at, but just smiled and buttoned her blazer shut. Slowly, without haste or embarrassment, her eyes fixed on mine, only too aware of the effect she was having. I think I must have blushed like a girl. And all the lines I had been repeating in my head disappeared in a sea of hormones. I couldn't find a single thing to say.

She said, 'Thanks, Fin. See you later.' And she hurried off to join her friends. It was one of those moments in my life that I have replayed many times. And each time I returned her smile, unblushing, and said something clever that won her over. How smart we can be after the event, how suave and sophisticated in our imaginations. Donald would have known what to say and do, and would no doubt have ended up sleeping with her. Not that night, perhaps, but sometime. And, who knows? Knowing Donald, maybe he did.

My close encounter of the second kind came not long after that. I was down at Uig the following weekend. The band wasn't playing, and Whistler and I had decided to take the tent up into the mountains to do a little illicit fishing for brown trout. We pitched it on the shores of one of the myriad lochs west of Brinneabhal. The land there opened up below the mountains, with views across the moor and the machair towards the cliffs, the Atlantic breaking creamy white all along the shattered coastline.

The cloud was down so low you couldn't see the tops of the mountains, and the rain drifted across the loch like a mist. We sat in our waterproofs and wellies among the rocks along the shore, rods raised, lines cast out across the dark, rippling water. Neither of us was in any great hurry to land a fish. That would come, we knew. The loch was teeming with them. As long as we had a couple of trout to roast on the fire by the time we were hungry we would be happy. Those are days in my life that I look back on with great nostalgia. Moments long gone, that I wish could be recaptured and lived again. Impossible, of course.

We hadn't spoken for some time. But it was a comfortable silence. The best friendships are the ones that don't need words to fill the silences.

Suddenly Whistler said, 'How come you turn into such a bumbling idiot every time Mairead so much as looks at you?'

I was so shocked I swung my head around to look at him and couldn't think of a single thing to say. Eventually I muttered, 'Do I?'

Whistler gave me one of his looks. 'Aye, you do.'

Which gave me time enough to recover my wits and issue a hot denial. 'I do not!'

Now he laughed. 'You fancy her, don't you?'

I could hardly deny it. 'Who doesn't?'

He gazed out across the water. 'She's not like you think she is, you know.'

'Isn't she?'

He gave a little shrug of his shoulders. 'Everyone thinks she's super-cool, super-confident, arrogant even. Self-obsessed and full of herself.'

I didn't say anything. I could hardly have summed her up better myself.

But Whistler shook his head. 'Truth is, that underneath it all she's really very insecure.'

'How would you know?'

He kept his eyes on the point where his line entered the water and its reflection made an oblique angle with it. 'Me and Mairead were together through most of primary school. I even took her to the qually dance in primary seven.'

That was the first time I had heard about their past relationship and I looked at him with jealous awe. 'Wow. What happened? I mean, why aren't you still together?'

He pushed out his lower jaw and cocked his head to one side. 'All good things come to an end.'

Of course, Kenny told me later that it was Roddy coming between them that brought about the end. But Whistler wasn't about to confess that then.

'The thing is, I know her. Grew up with her. She's not really like that. She's confused and mixed up, and . . . well, trying to be something she's not.' He glanced at Fin. 'That's why she and Roddy are off and on like a hot-water tap. Roddy's girl is who she'd like to be. The image, I mean. But it's not really her.' He grinned then. 'I think maybe she's got a wee bit of a fancy for you.'

I felt myself blushing to the roots of my hair. 'Crap!'

'Is it? She could have picked anyone for the ride back to Stornoway the other day. But she chose you, Fin. And I've seen the way she looks at you.'

'Aw, give it a break!' I stopped being embarrassed and figured he was just winding me up now.

He shrugged. 'Suit yourself.' And he turned his eyes back to the loch. 'Just thought you should be aware of it, so you don't miss your big chance next Friday.'

I frowned. 'What's happening next Friday?'

'Big Donald Ruadh and Ceit "Cat" Mackinnon are getting married over at Mangurstadh. You've been invited, haven't you?'

'Oh. Yes.' I'd forgotten all about it. Donald Ruadh was from Ness, a second cousin or something. I never quite knew. It was not uncommon to be related to folk without knowing it. He was ten years older than all of us, of course, and a bit of a Jack the Lad. The last thing anyone expected was that he would get married. Least of all to a lassie from Uig that he hadn't even got pregnant. The marriage was to be conducted at the church at Baile na Cille, and the celebrations held afterwards at Ceit's house at Mangurstadh. One of those weddings that would go on all through the night and end up with breakfast the following morning. Which is why it was on the Friday, and not the Saturday. Because then the party would have had to end at midnight with the coming of the Sabbath.

Whistler said, 'Well, me and Roddy and Mairead are invited, too. And no doubt Roddy'll be taking Cairistiona.' Cairistiona was Roddy's latest flame. A flame that would flicker and die the moment Mairead wanted him back again. But for the moment Mairead was unattached, and Whistler added, 'Which means that Mairead'll be available to whichever of us is the first to ask her to dance.' His eyes were gleaming now, his smile mischievous. 'Are you up to the challenge, boy?'

'Challenge?'

'Aye. To the victor the spoils. Or maybe you don't have the balls to ask her.'

It was easy, sitting up there, to enter into the spirit of the dare, imagining myself walking up to Mairead and asking for a dance. And, even better, the thought of her saying yes, and me holding her close and feeling the heat of her body against mine and the softness of her breasts pressing into my chest as I held her in my arms. Easy to dream when you are a million miles from the reality. But the memory of her sitting behind me on the bike, her arms around me, was still fresh in my mind, and for a moment I believed that anything was possible.

I grinned back at Whistler. He'd had her and lost her. Maybe it was my turn.

The little church at Baile na Cille sat up on the hill above the machair and had panoramic views out over Uig sands. It was packed for the ceremony. Standing room only. It was late on the Friday afternoon, and by the time everyone got back to the house at Mangurstadh it was almost seven. Broad daylight, of course, since midsummer was only just by, and it would be hours before the sun dipped into the ocean beyond the far horizon. And even then it would never get fully dark.

Ceit Mackinnon's parents lived in a whitehouse at the end of a rough track heading out towards Mangurstadh beach. There had been two extensions built on to it, front and back, and there was a large stone barn with a rust-red corrugated roof where the dance would be held. There were cars parked everywhere along the track, as far up as the road, and in the field next to a disused sheep fank.

You could just see the beach from here, and beyond it a tendril of headland at the south end of the bay, slabs of cliffs rising out of the ocean where they had stood firm for eons against the onslaught of the Atlantic. This was green, rolling machair land, peppered with occasional crofts and meandering drystone dykes that had long since tumbled into desuetude. To the south and east, the mountains rose up into a gathering of clouds. To the west, the sea lay shimmering in sunshine. The young couple had been lucky with the weather.

In the crowd at the church I had only caught the briefest glimpse of Mairead. I had arrived in a white minibus with a group of guests from Ness, and was tied to them for my lift to the house. By the time I got there, Mairead was with all the Uig women in the kitchen preparing the meal.

They had set out two long tables in the house. One in the sitting room, another in the dining room. But it still wasn't enough to seat all the guests at once. We knew we would be called in to eat in shifts, and so contented ourselves with hanging about outside, smoking and laughing and drinking beer from big casks that they'd brought down from Stornoway. It was a long wait.

A number of guests had arrived with chickens and rabbits for the meal. You never took a dead animal to a wedding, so they had to be killed, and plucked or skinned, then gutted and cooked. But there was no hurry, since no one would be leaving until the following morning.

I saw Whistler once or twice, but he was busy with the Uig crowd. You hung about in your own village groups, like factions at a tribal gathering. The real mixing wouldn't start till the music kicked off and the dancing began. Then the beer, and the whisky which had come in half-bottles in the back pockets of most of the men, would have loosened inhibitions, and a good time would be had by all.

By the time the Niseachs had been called in to eat it was late, and the light was fading. I'd had quite a few beers already, and was flushed and a little unsteady on my feet. A lot of the men were dressed in kilts. But I didn't have one and was wearing my good suit, which was shiny around the arse and the elbows. My conservative dark-blue tie was pulled loose at the open collar of my white shirt. I could barely eat for nerves, because I knew that sooner rather than later I was going to have to face Mairead with the big question.

Girls have no idea how hard it is for a teenage boy to pluck up the courage to ask for a date or a dance. They must always take the initiative, with the ever-attendant risk of refusal, and therefore humiliation. And so I found myself putting off the moment.

When I had finished eating, I sought out the Ness boys who were out back, and we stood talking and smoking, and watching the sea turn from dimpled copper to blood red before fading to a dark-blue haze, the smudge on the horizon that was St Kilda vanishing in the dusk. I heard the music starting up in the barn. An accordionist and a fiddler. I had kept an eye out for Whistler, but had only caught the occasional glimpse of him. It seemed like a long time since he had winked at me and given me the thumbs up across the heads of the other guests before disappearing into the barn.

Now I saw him coming out, head down, hands thrust deep into his pockets. He pushed past us and wandered off towards the old cart track that ran down to the beach. I stamped out my cigarette and hurried after him. 'What's wrong?'

He didn't even turn his head. 'Fuck off,' he said in a low growl.

I tried to grab his arm to stop him walking, but he shook it free of my grasp. 'What happened, Whistler?'

'She wouldn't dance with me.' He turned to look at me, his eyes lost below a gathering of his brows. 'Nearly six years I went with her at primary, and she just blew me off. Said she was waiting for someone else.' He looked away again. 'I suppose that would be you.'

'No way!'

'Well, who else, then? Roddy's sitting in there smooching in a corner with that Cairistiona. Strings is with some girl from third year. And Mairead would never even look at Skins or Rambo, I can guarantee you that.' He turned a contemptuous sneer in my direction. 'It can only be you. Why else would she have asked you for that ride back to Stornoway?'

I could scarcely believe it. Could Mairead Morrison really be waiting in the barn for me to ask her to dance?

'Go on, you daft bastard. Better get in there before she gets fed up and says yes to someone else.'

The barn had felt huge when I looked in earlier and it was still empty. Now it was filled to the gunwales and appeared tiny. Folk stood two or three deep around the walls, the Drops of Brandy being danced with great relish in the centre of a mud floor strewn with hay. Couples spun up and down the lines of facing men and women waiting for their turn to go birling along the aisle arm-in-arm with their partners.

There were storm lamps hanging from the rafters, and smoke rose into the roof space along with the music and laughter. I spotted Mairead standing on her own at the far end of the barn, peering anxiously over the heads of the dancers as if looking for someone. I took a deep breath and pushed my way through the crowd. She saw me coming at the last, and gave me one of her smiles. 'Hi Fin. Having a good time?'

'Sure,' I said, suddenly uncertain, and having to shout above the noise. But it was now or never. 'Would you like to dance?'

She grinned. 'I'd love to.' And for just a moment my whole world stood still. 'But I came with someone, and I don't think he'd be very happy if I did.'

It was as if she had stuck a pin in me and I had just burst, like the balloon that I was. 'Who?' I couldn't help myself.

'Whistler, of course.' And she smiled past me as Whistler appeared out of the crowd to take her hand and lead her away to the floor. I stood gaping after them in disbelief, and Whistler half turned to glance back in my direction, his face split by the widest of grins. He winked at me and slipped his arm around Mairead's waist.

The worst thing about it, I think, was that I was trapped there with my humiliation. All I wanted to do was go home. But I couldn't. I had to endure a long night of male company, cigarettes and beer, catching all too frequent glimpses of Whistler and Mairead in and out of the barn.

When finally we nursed our hangovers through breakfast the following morning and got into the minibus for the long drive home, my humiliation had been replaced by anger. I realized then that Whistler's jealousy had been aroused the day Mairead rode back to town with me, and this whole elaborate charade at the wedding had been his way of warning me off. It took me a long time to get over it. I don't think I spoke to him again until after the holidays.

It is clear to me now, though, that he must have been trying desperately to win her back. That he had always been in love with her and always would be. And that all through her on-off relationship with Roddy, he had harboured the hope that one day she would come back to him. A hope that he had recognized, finally, in fifth year, was a forlorn one. That she was embarking on a journey he couldn't make, on a road he could never follow.

Which is why he took the decision to stay at home while the rest of us left for Glasgow. He had lost her, and wasn't about to play the role of rejected lovesick puppy through all the university years. And when I look back now, with the understanding of hindsight, I feel no anger. Only sadness.

What I could never have dreamed back then was that my fantasy of a relationship with Mairead would finally be realized three years later during my second, ill-fated year at university in Glasgow.

I had been roadying for the band for nearly a year and a half by then, paying less and less attention to my studies, and growing increasingly unhappy with my life and myself. I had fallen into a sort of tailspin in the wake of my final split with Marsaili. Driving for Amran was a mindless activity that earned me much-needed cash and gave me access to a succession of groupies who would sleep with the driver if that was the closest they could get to the band. A sordid and unsatisfying succession of sexual encounters that did nothing to increase my self-esteem.

I was never one to seek escape in drink or drugs, but I did my fair share of drinking, and smoked more than my fair share of joints. My problem was one of lassitude. I just couldn't bring myself to care. About anything.

It was late winter, around February or March. We had played a gig somewhere on the south side of the city, and had been invited afterwards to a party in one of those huge, red-sandstone mansions in Pollokshields. It sat up proud at the top of a sprawling garden, surrounded by chestnut trees, black and stark in their winter nakedness. A corner site in a gushet that must have occupied a couple of acres.

An enormous conservatory with elaborate curving roofs had been built on to the back of the house to contain an indoor swimming pool. The house itself was tastefully furnished. Thick-piled woollen carpets, signed prints on the walls, antique furniture. Hugely expensive crystal and china ornaments lined shelves and were displayed in cabinets. It was not the ideal playground for fifty or sixty young people high on dope and drink, and intent on having a good time.

Mairead and Roddy, it appeared, had finally broken up for good, and Roddy was there with his new girlfriend, a beautiful blonde-haired girl called Caitlin. This was her parents' house, and they were away on holiday. Self-appointed guardian in their place was Caitlin's brother,

Jimbo, an unpleasant young man with a designer haircut and a single ring in his ear. He appeared to have several girls on hand, and was strutting about the house in his Gucci shoes and Armani suit as if he owned the place.

A great deal of alcohol was being consumed, and by one or two in the morning almost everyone was skinny-dipping in the pool, spilling champagne and shrieking to be heard above the brain-splitting blast of the sound system.

I was tired and fed up and couldn't be bothered with any of it. I sat in the main lounge, sprawled on the settee, a can of beer in my hand, watching a video on the biggest TV screen I had ever seen. I say watching, but I don't think I was, really. I have no recollection now of what was playing. A movie maybe, or music videos. Bubblegum for the eyes. And the brain.

At first I was barely aware of someone sitting down beside me. Until I felt the warmth of a thigh pressed against mine, and a scent so familiar it was almost comforting. I turned my head to find Mairead smiling at me, a smile that might once have quickened my pulse. But I was used to it by now, and didn't trust it.

'What you doing in here on your own?' she said.

I shrugged. 'Wishing I was somewhere else.' But it felt good to be speaking just Gaelic again.

'Snap.'

I raised an eyebrow. 'You don't have to be here. You can get a taxi home any time you like. I've got people relying on me for a lift back.'

Even although I had got over her by this time, I think

I was still in awe of her beauty. Her dark hair was cropped, as it had been since the accident on the Road to Nowhere, and she had developed into a striking-looking woman. The soft features of the teenage girl were hardening into something more adult, but no less beautiful. She had lost weight and her eyes seemed larger, even more compelling.

She was still in her stage gear, a full-length black dress that hugged a pencil-thin figure and plunged from shoulder straps into a deep V between her breasts, an extraordinary contrast with her porcelain-white Celtic skin. It would be fair to say that she looked stunning.

'What if I asked you to take me home?'

I eyed her suspiciously. 'Why would you do that?'

'Maybe because I don't want to go home alone.'

When I said nothing her smile widened.

'Remember that time you gave me a lift back to Stornoway on your crappy old moped?'

I was surprised she even remembered it. 'Yeh, we got soaked.'

'And my bum was bruised for days after in the shape of your luggage rack.'

I laughed out loud. 'You're kidding!'

'I'd have shown you, only you might have got the wrong idea. Roddy always kept a blanket folded on his. Yours was raw metal tubing. It was bloody agony. All the way back.'

'And here was me thinking it was passion that made you hold on to me that tight.'

There was mischief in her eyes. 'Maybe it was.'

'Yeh, right.'

Her arm was draped over the top of the settee behind me now, and her fingers were playing absently with my curls. It made me uncomfortable. She said, 'You used to fancy me Fin, didn't you?'

'Used to.'

'But not any more?'

I just shrugged.

'What happened?'

I turned to meet her gaze. 'I got to know you, Mairead.'

It was like a light went out in her eyes, and all the animation left her face. She took her arm away from the back of the settee and sat forward on the edge of the seat, hands clasped in her lap. I couldn't see her face now. 'I think that's just about the most hurtful thing anyone's ever said to me.' There was the slightest tremor in her voice.

I had a sick, hollow feeling inside me. I hadn't meant to hurt her, and yet it was a kind of payback for all those years of frustrated teenage fantasy when she had taken pleasure, or so I thought, in exploiting my weakness. And I wondered suddenly if it had all simply been a figment of my own imagination.

'No one knows me,' she said. 'Not really.'

'Whistler thought he did. He told me once you were really insecure. And trying to be something you weren't.'

She turned surprised eyes on me, then. And I saw the tracks of silent tears shining on her cheeks. But I still didn't know whether to trust them. 'Whistler said that?'

'He was in love with you, Mairead. Probably still is. I

always figured that's why he never came to Glasgow. Removing himself from the source of the pain.'

A distant look washed momentarily across her face, then she focused on me again. 'Take me home, Fin. Please.'

I don't think anyone noticed us leaving. But I saw Mairead's backward glance through open French windows into the conservatory, where Roddy was frolicking naked in the pool with Caitlin. I didn't much care about how the others got home. They could all afford to get taxis by now. And I was feeling bad about what I'd said to Mairead. It's one thing to think it, quite another to say it out loud and carelessly inflict pain.

We drove in silence through the dark, overhead lights reflecting in wet streets, passing in an endless succession through tenemental south-side suburbia and on to Paisley Road West. Mairead had bought a penthouse flat in a restored Victorian drapery warehouse built into the triangle of a junction between two roads. On the apex of the triangle, at its most easterly point, stood the sculpture of a golden angel that looked back towards the city. The apartment block was called the Angel Building, and I had always thought that Mairead could not have lived anywhere more apposite.

She didn't bother turning on any lights in the flat. Windows all along each side of it let in the city nightlight, casting deep shadows around the sitting room. At the opposite end from an open-plan kitchen a door led through to her bedroom.

'I'll just get changed,' she said. 'Help yourself to something to drink.' Her heels clicked across polished wood floors, and she pushed the door open. Beyond the bed, from a large, arched window facing east, I could see the city spread out below. But I didn't move. Wasn't interested in a drink. She turned back, silhouetted against the city behind her, and stood looking at me in the dark for what felt like an inordinate length of time. Then she raised her hand to slip the straps from each of her shoulders, and her black dress fell to the floor in a whisper of silk. She was completely naked.

I felt a constriction in my throat, and all the pent-up desires of my teenage years returned to flood my senses. Here she was, the object of all those fantasies, standing naked in front of me, offering herself in a way that no woman has offered herself to me before or since. By the time I reached her I had already stripped off my T-shirt. I was out of my jeans in seconds, and sharing her nakedness just moments later. We stood, inches apart, looking at each other, both listening to the other breathing in the dark. I knew that the moment I touched her there would be no going back. It would be like opening a floodgate, and I was destined to drown in her.

I cupped my hand around the back of her head and felt the soft bristle of her hair, the shape of her skull, and drew her towards me. From the first touch of our lips I was lost. Our bodies came together, and I felt my passion press hard against her belly as we fell backwards in slow motion on to the bed. Her body so white, framed against the black satin sheets stretched tightly across the mattress. At long last she was mine. But, as always, it was on her terms.

It lasted for more than three months. A relationship based on sex. There were no candlelit dinners or romantic moments. No holding hands or declarations of undying love. Just lust.

We made love at her place, in my bedsit, in the back of the van. In countless hotel rooms. And I never lost my appetite for her. I never stopped wanting her. Nor she me, apparently.

I understood that, really, we were just using each other. She as a means of getting back at Roddy, of flaunting me in his face, hoping to make him jealous. Although, in truth, I think she enjoyed our sexual dalliance as much as I did. For my part, I was only interested in the sex. I never really liked her, but in a strange way became addicted to her. When I wasn't with her, I found myself missing her. We never spoke much, but in a sense I think that's what I liked the most. She made no emotional demands on me. There were no moods or fits of jealousy, no requirement to say things I didn't mean. It was, perhaps, the most sexually fulfilling but un-demanding relationship I have ever had.

And so I took it badly when she ended us one night, suddenly and without warning.

We were supposed to be going to a party and had agreed to meet in the bar of the Cul de Sac in Ashton Lane, in Glasgow's west end. Mairead had said she would meet me at seven. By 8.30 I was still waiting and was on my third pint. The place was crowded, and I could see people milling about in the lane below. There were several restaurants, bars and a cinema in the old cobbled street, and one of the restaurants on the far side had put out tables so that its patrons could enjoy the fine midsummer weather and take advantage of the light nights.

At first I wasn't worried. Mairead was prone to bouts of lateness, when she decided five minutes before going out that she really had to have a shower. At least she didn't have to spend hours on her hair, but the make-up could take half an hour. She was very conscious of her appearance or, as she liked to say, her image. Mairead had a mobile phone, and I would have called her. But I couldn't afford one myself, so that wasn't an option. I was about to leave and drive over to the Angel Building when I saw her pushing her way through the drinkers towards me. As usual she was turning heads.

'Hey,' I said, 'what happened?' I went to kiss her cheek but she averted her head in a strangely abrupt movement. I knew at once what was coming.

She moved closer, lowering her voice, and her eyes. 'Fin, I'm sorry. It's over.'

I waited until she looked up to meet my eye. 'Why?'

There was something like exasperation in her voice. 'You knew it wasn't for ever, Fin. We both knew that.'

I nodded. 'We did. But I'd still like to know why.'

She shook her head. 'There's no point. Explanations aren't going to make either of us feel any better about it.' She suddenly took my face in both of her hands, an intensity in her eyes that I couldn't remember ever seeing there before, and she kissed me so softly, and with such tenderness, that I might almost have believed she really did feel something for me. 'I'm so sorry, Fin.'

And she was gone. In those few moments everything I had been and known these last months came to an end. The dream was over. There was no hiding any more. I turned back to the bar and finished my pint.

Outside the air was cool, but soft on the skin. I walked in a daze through the west end, heading instinctively for the party that Mairead and I had been going to. It was in a block of red sandstone flats in Hyndland. I knew I didn't want to go home. It was far easier to be lonely in a crowd. I would never have believed that breaking up with Mairead could be this painful. The thought that I would never kiss her again, or touch her breasts, or feel her legs wrapped around my back was almost more than I could bear. All I wanted to do was get drunk.

The party was already jumping by the time I got there. I said hi to a few familiar faces, and heard someone ask where Mairead was. I didn't answer. I found myself a soft seat in a dark corner with a six-pack at my side and sprung open the first can.

The music was deafening, and people were dancing. The girl nearest me stepped back over someone's handbag and promptly sat down in my lap. A pretty girl with short black hair.

She'd been drinking. She giggled. 'Ooops. Sorry.'

Maybe there was something about her that reminded me of Mairead. I'm not sure now what it was, but I smiled. 'Be my guest,' I said.

She tipped her head and gave me a curious look. 'Are you at uni?'

'I am.'

'I thought I'd seen you somewhere. What year?'

'Second.'

'I'm in first.'

'Well,' I said. 'We intellectuals ought to stick together. My name's Fin.'

She giggled again. 'So we should. I'm Mona.'

And that is how I met the girl who would wake me up in the morning to tell me that Roddy was dead. The girl I would marry, and who would bear my son. The girl I would divorce sixteen years later when the one good thing we had made together was no more.

# CHAPTER TWENTY-ONE

## I

Mairead was still wearing her coat as if, perhaps, Marsaili had hoped she wouldn't stay and hadn't offered to take it. It was long and black, and concertinaed on the floor around her chair. Her style had not changed in all these years. Years that had treated her kindly. They had pared away some of the flesh from around her face, leaving her almost hawk-like but still beautiful, with clear white skin and only the hint of crow's feet appearing around the corners of her eyes. Her lips were full and strikingly dark in contrast with the rest of her face. There was a knowing quality in their smile, and an odd fondness in her eyes.

'Hello, Fin,' she said, and it was as if that final exchange in the Cul de Sac had happened just the night before.

Fin's eyes flickered towards Marsaili and back again. 'Hello, Mairead. I see you're still going to the same hairdresser.'

She grinned, and ran a hand back through her stubble. There was just a little silver appearing in it now, but it hadn't concerned her enough to dye it. 'It's my trademark.

They'll put me in my coffin with my hair like this. Only, I hope it'll be pure white by then.'

'You want a cup of tea, Fin?' Marsaili's voice cut in on the exchange like a child with her nose out of joint seeking attention.

'I'll have a beer,' he said, and turned to get a bottle from the fridge.

'Same old Fin.' Mairead took a sip at her mug. 'Always with a beer in his hand.'

Fin twisted the cap off the bottle. 'What are you doing here, Mairead?'

'She came looking for you,' Marsaili said.

'They told me in town that you were restoring your parents' crofthouse. I was amazed to hear that you'd come back. Last I heard you were being a cop in Edinburgh.' And she chuckled. 'I laughed out loud when I heard that. Fin Macleod. Policeman! Remember chasing the cops through the streets of that resort town in England?'

Fin grinned. 'I guess we were lucky not to end up in a police cell.'

'Who's this *we* you talk about, Kemo Sabe?'

Marsaili glanced, perplexed, from one to the other as they shared their laughter. 'Someone want to let me in on the joke?'

Fin waved his hand dismissively. 'It's a long story, Marsaili.' Then paused, as a thought occurred to him. 'I guess you two know one another from school?'

'We shared some of the same classes,' Mairead said. 'But had different friends.' She smiled at Marsaili. 'I would never have recognized you. Except I'd been told that you two were an item these days.'

'Of course, I knew you straight away.' Marsaili was smiling, but there was an edge to her voice. 'Who wouldn't?' She turned towards Fin. 'I saw her from the window. She was standing up there on the shoulder of the hill looking a bit like a lost soul.'

Fin quickly refocused the conversation. 'I suppose you're here for the funeral?'

Mairead's face clouded. 'Not just for it, Fin. To organize it. There are no relatives that we know of. So it's up to Roddy's friends to give him a proper send-off. You'll both be coming?'

'I won't.' Marsaili pushed herself away from the worktop to empty the last of her tea down the sink and rinse the mug. 'I never really knew Roddy. And I've got the baby to look after.'

Mairead raised an eyebrow in surprise. 'Baby?'

'Our granddaughter,' Fin said. And then felt compelled to explain. 'We had a son I never knew about till recently.'

Mairead took Marsaili's cue with the mug and stood up. 'Never could keep it in the breeks, Fin, could you?' Fin blushed and she smiled. 'And still blushing, I see. Always wore your heart on your sleeve, you did.' She held his gaze for a long moment. 'They were interesting times we lived in.'

Fin nodded. 'They were.' And he took a pull on the neck of his bottle to disguise his discomfort. 'You'll let me know when the funeral's to be?'

'I will, now that I know where you are. I'm at the Cabarfeidh, in town.' She paused, which made it sound almost like an invitation. And then she added, 'Strings and Skins and Rambo are there, too.'

It seemed odd to Fin to hear those teenage nicknames again, as if somehow they should have grown out of them. And yet he still called Whistler, Whistler.

Mairead turned an ersatz smile towards Marsaili. 'It was lovely to meet you again. Thanks for the tea.' Fin opened the kitchen door for her and she paused momentarily as she passed him, a strange searching look in her eyes. But all she said was, 'See you at the funeral,' and was gone.

There was a long silence in the kitchen after she had left. It was almost as if Marsaili was waiting to hear the sound of her car starting, to be certain that she was away, before she spoke. 'You two had a relationship, then?'

There was no point in denying it. 'That obvious?'

'Oh, yes.' A long pause. 'How come you never told me?'

Fin shrugged. 'Nothing to tell. It was another me, in another place and time.'

'Seems to me there are a lot of Fin Macleods I don't know anything about.' She lifted Mairead's mug from the table to rinse it in the sink, and caught her reflection in the kitchen window. Fin saw her raise a hand, almost involuntarily, to sweep the hair back from her face. 'She's still very beautiful,' she said, as if the contrast with her own reflection had prompted the thought.

'She is.' Fin drank some more of his beer. 'We had a relationship, yes, Marsaili. But I never liked her very much.'

Marsaili was surprised. 'No?'

Fin shook his head.

'Why not?'

'I knew her too well. She never cared much about anyone or anything, except herself. It was all me, me, me.'

Marsaili dried her hands on the dishtowel and there was a sadness in her smile. 'A bit like someone else, I know.' And she walked past him to the living room.


## II


Mairead's voice rang around the rafters of the church, clear and pure and unaccompanied. The doors were open so that those outside could hear her, and in the still of this sad grey morning, her voice drifted out across Loch Ròg, a plaintive lament for a lost friend and lover.

> *Even though I walk through the valley of the shadow of death,*
> *I fear no evil,*
> *for you are with me;*
> *your rod and your staff,*
> *they comfort me.*

Somehow, in the Gaelic, both the words and the melody were more powerful, more tribal, of the land and the place and the people. And Fin found the hairs rising up on the back of his neck. He had missed the original funeral, but the others were all here to bury Roddy again, just as they had done seventeen years before. Only then, the coffin they had carried was empty, save for some rocks and a few personal items from childhood. His parents had wanted it that way. To give a sense of closure. A chance to say goodbye.

Now the coffin with his body in it awaited them outside his old home overlooking Uig sands from the north shore. His parents had been returned to the earth now themselves, but the new owners of the house his father had built had given permission for the funeral procession to start from there.

As the mourners streamed out of the little church at Miabhaig, Fin reflected that it was more like a circus than a funeral. The Scottish media had descended en masse, along with stringers for most of the English press. Cameras flashed and pencils scribbled in notebooks, and digital video recorded all for posterity – and the six o'clock news. The discovery of Roddy's body had been occupying pride of place on the news schedules for days. Archive footage from seventeen years earlier had been unearthed and hastily cut together with the latest video to feed the public's voracious appetite for celebrity news. Celebrity death appealed even more to popular prurience. Throw in a little murder and mystery, and ratings were guaranteed. Sales of Amran's CD backlist had soared.

Fin had expected Whistler to show up. He had disappeared again following their encounter outside the Sheriff Court, but there was no sign of him at the church. And it wasn't until Fin stepped outside that he set eyes on Strings and Skins and Rambo for the first time.

He was shocked by how both Skins and Rambo had aged. Rambo was almost completely bald, and looked twenty years older than the others. Skins' hair was streaked steel-grey, and swept back from a face devoid of its once boyish charm. Strings, too, had slipped quietly into middle age, perhaps hoping that shoulder-length dyed hair tied in a ponytail would create the illusion of a younger man. But he was thinner, meaner somehow, the fingers that spidered over his fretboard longer and bonier now than Fin remembered. Only Mairead seemed to have the Peter Pan touch. She looked as radiant and beautiful as she had as a teenager. She had never lost that certain something which had bewitched so many boys, and no doubt so many men in later life. She was the sole identifiable image of Amran. It was always her face that featured on the covers of their CDs, on their website, on their concert posters. No one but the most ardent of fans would have recognized Skins or Rambo, or even Strings. They were background. Wallpaper. Just musicians. Mairead *was* Amran.

Many of the mourners drove straight to the cemetery at Ardroil. Those who intended to make up the procession gathered outside the former Mackenzie home on the road above the beach, along with the media circus.

Fin was astonished to see Donald there, come out of his self-imposed exile in Ness to expose himself to public scrutiny for the first time since the shooting in Eriskay. And he was as much a source of interest and curiosity to the crowd as the presence of the celebrities of Amran. He was, it transpired, to be one of the primary coffin-bearers, at

Mairead's request, along with Fin, Strings, Skins, Rambo and Big Kenny. All of them together again for the first time since fifth year at the Nicolson.

But since it was a two-mile walk to Ardroil, there were another six men standing by to provide periodic relief in relays. The coffin itself weighed much more than the remains of the man inside it, solid oak resting heavily on the broad shoulders that raised it from the chairbacks on which it had been resting in the road. A helicopter hired by one of the news networks flew overhead.

It took the procession of well over fifty people more than an hour to reach the turn-off to the cemetery. There was a hand-painted sign with a white arrow pointing past a tubular agricultural gate, and a rough track wound up over the machair to the walls of the cemetery itself beyond the rise. Shoulders were aching, hands numb, by the time they got there.

The mountains where Roddy's plane had come down all those years before loured over them, dominating the skyline to the south. The cemetery itself sloped down to the west, and the rain began as the procession made its way among the headstones to the small walled extension which had been built on to it at the bottom end. Its original planners, apparently, had not taken account of the relentless nature of death.

It was a fine rain, a smirr, little more than a mist. But it almost obliterated the view beyond the wall towards the beach, and made the last few yards treacherous underfoot. The lowering of the coffin on wet ropes by hands and arms which had all but seized up was made perilous by the rain, and it bumped and scraped the side of the grave on its way down. The grave itself had been excavated the day before, and the remains of the coffin they had placed there seventeen years earlier exhumed. Beneath the grass the soil was pure sand, without rocks or pebbles, and was already crumbling as the coffin settled at the bottom of the hole. The original headstone lay to one side, to be replaced once the grave had been refilled.

Although the tradition of men only at the graveside was still universally observed, nobody was surprised when Mairead ignored it. She stood among the men, pale and unflinching, a sombre figure dressed all in black, Roddy's intermittent sweetheart and lover.

It was then that Fin glanced up and saw, with a shock, Whistler standing at the top end of the cemetery, detached from the mourners. Gone was the suit, to be replaced by his waterproof jacket and jeans, and his hair hung loose, tumbling to his shoulders. He had stopped shaving again and had penumbrous shadows beneath his eyes. His usually healthy outdoor complexion was muted by an underlying pallor.

For a moment Fin thought that Whistler was simply gazing into space, somewhere above and beyond the little clutch of mourners, before he realized that his eyes were fixed on Mairead. Was it possible, after all these years, that he still loved her? And yet there was something in his expression that spoke more of hate than of love. Of contempt rather than affection. And Fin was startled by it.

His attention returned to the grave as Donald read a text from the Gaelic Bible. 'In the sweat of thy face shalt thou eat bread, till thou return unto the ground; for out of it wast thou taken: for dust thou art, and unto dust shalt thou return.' A handful of sand rattled across the lid of the coffin. And when Fin looked up again, Whistler was gone.

## III

It was with no little surprise, then, that Fin caught a glimpse of his old friend at the wake organized by Amran at the Cabarfeidh Hotel in Stornoway. The bar was packed full of mourners who had heard that there would be free drink, and members of the press were mixing freely among the crowd in search of an angle, a personal slant, something different for the evening bulletins and the morning papers.

Fin was standing at the bar with Strings and Skins and Rambo, sharing beer and recollections, and not a little fond laughter at stories of Roddy and their adventures during the early years. The spectre that hovered among them, however, and which no one dared address, was the fact that Roddy had not just died. He had been murdered. It was a spectre without a voice.

Fin caught sight of Whistler pushing his way out through the door. He put his pint down on the bar. 'I'll catch you guys later.' And he hurried after him.

By the time he reached the lobby there was no sign of Whistler. Fin hurried through to the lounge, but there was only a handful of people standing chatting in groups, or sitting around coffee tables. He returned to the lobby and was about to go back in to the bar when he heard the sound of raised voices from outside in the car park. A woman's voice, and a man's. Speaking Gaelic. Fin went out on to the step and saw Mairead and Whistler further down the drive. Whistler was trying to walk away. Mairead was grabbing at his arm to try to stop him. He turned suddenly and shouted at her, inches from her face. Fin was not close enough to make out what he said, but there was no concealing his anger. Mairead flinched. And then Whistler glanced beyond her and saw Fin watching. He said something and Mairead turned, too. By the time she turned back to him he was on his way, walking briskly out through the gate. This time she let him go, and Fin saw the slump of her shoulders.

He watched as she turned and walked back up the tarmac drive towards him, composing herself as she approached, concocting some lie, Fin had no doubt, about what it was that had transpired between her and Whistler. By the time she reached him her eyes were clear and smiling, and he remembered only too well her capacity for deception. She pre-empted his question with a sad smile. 'You told me once you thought that Whistler had never stopped loving me. And that's why he didn't come to Glasgow.' She paused for thought. 'Removing himself from the pain. I think that's how you put it.'

Fin nodded.

'Well, I think I just brought the pain back with me.'

But Fin knew that it wasn't love he had seen in Whistler's eyes at the cemetery. And there had been only anger in his voice when he shouted at her. If there was pain, then something else was the cause of it. She must have seen the lack of conviction in Fin's eyes, because she abruptly changed the subject.

'Anyway, I'm glad I caught you. I brought a photo album up with me. Full of pics from the old days. You're in a lot of them. I thought you'd like to see them.'

'Maybe another time.' Fin glanced at his watch. 'I should really be going.'

But there was an insistence in her voice. 'There might not be another time, Fin. I'll be gone in a couple of days, and I can't think of a single reason for ever coming back.'

Fin was surprised. 'What happened to your folks?'

'I took them down to Glasgow years ago. I've no family left on the island. And, to be honest, the reason we were here today has cast a shadow over all the good memories. It was hard enough dealing with Roddy's death at the time. But losing someone twice? Well, that's a killer, Fin. I would never have believed it, but it's a whole hell of a lot harder second time around.' She slipped an arm through his and turned him back through the door into the lobby. 'Give me just a little of your time. I think you owe me that.'

Fin stopped and she was forced to turn and face him. 'I don't think I owe you anything, Mairead. You were the one who walked away, remember?'

Her eyes were wide and moist, and impenetrably blue. 'And there's not a single day that I haven't regretted it.'

Heavy blue curtains were drawn across the windows in her room. A chequered blue-and-cream bedspread was neatly folded across a bed long since made up by room service. A large suitcase sat on the floor below the window, its lid up resting against the curtains. Mairead crouched to rummage through a mess of clothes to find the photo album, and she stood and threw it on to the bed before slipping out of her coat and draping it across a chair. Beneath it she wore a black blouse and a three-quarter-length black skirt over black boots.

'You don't mind if I get changed, do you?' She didn't wait for an answer, and Fin wondered what difference it would have made if he'd said no. She kicked off her boots. 'Nothing you haven't seen before.'

But he turned away, embarrassed, to pick up the photo album and open it at the first page. The most prominent image immediately to strike him was Roddy's official school photograph from fourth or fifth year at the Nicolson. The school blazer with its prefect's piping, the crisp white shirt and school tie. Roddy's slightly lopsided smile, blonde curls tumbling all around his head. He glanced up to see Mairead slipping into her jeans. She wore a skimpy black bra and panties, her skin like ivory, the smooth curves and lines of a body he had once known so well. And in spite of himself he felt the stirrings of remembered lust deep in his loins. He turned back to the album and flipped over a page.

There were several photographs glued across both of the next pages. One of a very young Mairead on stage. How much rounder her face had been then. The band setting up for a gig somewhere. Donald, sitting in an armchair at a party, red-eyed from the flash, and looking very drunk. And there was Fin, with Whistler and Strings, aged maybe seventeen. All with beers in their hands, arms around each other's shoulders, and making faces at the camera. He had no recollection of it being taken, and it gave him a start to see himself. He had no photographs from that period of his life. He'd had no camera, and his aunt had never been one for taking snaps. The young Fin, grinning like an idiot. But he could look at it now and see the pain behind the eyes, the denial of a truth he had been unable to face.

'They're good, aren't they?' Mairead leaned in beside him to take a look. She wore a sweatshirt several sizes too big for her and was still barefoot. 'I've got hundreds of pics. I'm so glad I kept them now. They trigger memories I'd have forgotten otherwise.' She reached across him to flick over a page, and he felt her breast brush against his arm.

There were more photographs of the band on stage at a ceilidh somewhere, and on the page opposite several taken at the Bridge to Nowhere. So many of the same faces as had been at the cemetery today, but so much younger.

Mairead took the album from him and sat on the end of the bed with it. She patted a place beside her. 'Sit down.'

But Fin knew it would be fatal. 'I've got to go, Mairead.'

She held his gaze for a long time, eyes laden with disappointment, before closing the album and standing up. She was tall. Almost as tall as Fin, and stood very close to him. He could feel her breath on his face. 'Don't go.' Her voice was barely a whisper.

He could almost hear the beat of his heart, the blood pulsing through his head. It would be so easy. He touched her face with the tips of his fingers. He would be lost in her in seconds. Again. All those primal passions she had aroused in him all those years before, reawakened, as powerful and seductive as they had ever been. And he thought of Marsaili, and the way he had treated her during those first weeks at university. And of Mona, and how he had never tried after the accident to find a way with her, even although they had both needed someone to share their pain. He thought of how he had taken the wrong turning at almost every crossroads in his life, even when he knew which was the right way. And he wondered how it was possible that Mairead could want to make love to him when she had just put the love of her life in the ground.

He said, 'I'm sorry, Mairead.' He leaned forward and softly kissed her forehead. 'Have a good life.'

And he left her standing there, alone in the middle of the room. She didn't turn as he opened the door and slipped out into the hall.

He felt an enormous sense of relief as he drove across the wide open spaces of the Barvas moor, like a weight lifted from his shoulders. A burden he had carried for years, almost without realizing it. The sky ahead reflected his mood, grey breaking to blue, flashes of sunlight falling in dazzling patches on distant tracts of peat bog scarred by generations of cutting. Colour appeared all across the moor with the change of light, gold and purple, the wind rising now to whip through the long grasses and usher in cooler, brighter weather.

In denying Mairead, he had somehow felt himself more committed to Marsaili, and he was anxious now to get home. To hold her. To tell her how he felt about her. If anyone deserved better from him it was her.

She was hanging out washing on the line when he drew his Suzuki in beside her car. He stood for a moment on the road above the bungalow looking down at her, hair streaming forward in the wind, like the sheets she was pegging to the rope. Her face, pink from the effort of fighting the breeze, was still lovely, even without make-up, and he remembered the little girl with pigtails and blue ribbons who had stood up for him on his first day at school, who had shortened his name to Fin and who had taken his heart from the first moment he set eyes on her. And he felt an ache somewhere inside him. A sense of grief for their lost innocence, for half their lives squandered and gone for ever.

He walked slowly down the path and stopped at the steps to the kitchen door. She hadn't heard him or seen him yet, and he watched as her still-slim body arched itself against the wind, arms reaching and straining to hold the rope and manage the furling and unfurling of the sheets. And then she turned and saw him. She stooped to pick up her empty laundry basket and wade wearily up through the grass towards him. Pale-blue anxious eyes searched his face. 'I didn't expect you back so soon.'

He shrugged. 'A funeral's not something you hang around at.'

'Didn't you go to the wake?'

'Briefly.'

There was the hint of a query in the tilt of her head, in the gaze with which she examined him. 'And how was it?'

'The wake?'

'The funeral.'

'As you'd expect. Donald was there, and helped carry the coffin.'

She raised an eyebrow. '*Un*expected.'

He smiled. 'It was.' Then hesitated. 'Mairead sang the twenty-third psalm in the church. Unaccompanied.'

'That must have been moving.' There was no hint of sarcasm in her tone, but Fin felt it there.

'Yes.' He wanted to tell her how it had been in Mairead's room. How he had resisted her, and turned his back on her. But he knew it would only ever be open to misconstruction. He reached out to touch her face, as he had touched Mairead's less than an hour before. But she turned away towards the steps.

'Anyway, I'm glad you're back. I was going over to my mother's. You can look after the baby now. And keep an eye on the washing. Take it in if it starts to rain.' She was swallowed up by the open door, disappearing into the house. And Fin stood for a moment longer, watching the sheets flap in the wind, whipping and snapping and pulling at the rope. He could see clouds gathering already on the far horizon, and knew that it wouldn't be long before he would have to take them in.

## IV

He woke up in a panic, sweating. The dream was still horribly vivid in his mind. It was burned on his retinas as if he had been watching a movie and the images had remained even although the light was gone. He fought to remember exactly what had happened. It was fading already, but the sense of his betrayal and Marsaili's hurt stayed with him like a stone in his heart. For a moment he thought it was Mairead she had found him with. Perhaps in the dream. But then he remembered, with a sickening sense of his own cruelty, the reality of what had actually happened nearly twenty years before. That day, in their shared student lodgings, when she had returned to find him in bed with the girl across the hall. Their bed. Snow falling on the wet-streaked tenements outside. The end, finally, of everything they might have been.

He lay in the dark, breathing heavily, staring at the ceiling. The only light in the room came from the digital bedside clock. He could hear the slow, steady beat of Marsaili's breath. She was still asleep.

But something elusive remained, just out of reach. Something in his dream that he couldn't quite recall. He had been in Mairead's room, he knew. Had he actually kissed her in the dream? Is that what he had wanted, really? Is that what had triggered the awful memory of the fold-down bed in the student flat? Partly, perhaps. But there was something else. He closed his eyes and saw the photo album lying on the bed in Mairead's hotel room, the whole gang of them standing on the Bridge to Nowhere grinning at the camera, and suddenly he knew what it was. He sat bolt upright and wondered why in God's name it had never occurred to him before.

# CHAPTER TWENTY-TWO

## I

Fin drew his Suzuki into the gravel parking area just above Garry Beach and turned off the engine. He sat listening to the tick of it as it cooled, looking out over the short stretch of machair towards the curve of the beach itself. It was the first time he had been back here since the day of the bike race. From where he was parked he could see the concrete span of the Bridge to Nowhere, and the road looping off around the line of the cliffs that pushed up out of the Minch.

He gripped the steering wheel in front of him with both hands and leaned his head forward to rest on his forearms, eyes closed. He thought about the way that Whistler had behaved when they found the plane, the way he had looked at Mairead at the cemetery, the anger in his voice at the Cabarfeidh. And he thought about Mairead, and how she had played to the gallery with her singing at the church, and at the grave by breaking with convention. Her protestations of grief, when there was nothing in her demeanour to show it. How she had wanted Fin to make love to her while the sand was still, almost literally, being shovelled over her lover's coffin. The twin demons of fear and confusion stalked his thoughts.

He heard a car on the road and looked back towards Tolastadh, across a scrap of a loch choked by reeds and lilies, and saw Gunn's car as it rounded the headland and began the gentle descent to the car park. It pulled in beside the jeep, and Gunn switched off the ignition. He glanced across towards Fin, but neither man acknowledged the other. Fin looked back towards the beach and gripped the wheel more tightly, before opening his hands to release it and reach for the door handle. He stepped down on to the chippings and slammed his door shut before opening the passenger door of Gunn's vehicle and slipping into the seat beside him. He pulled it closed and wound down the window and both men sat in silence for some minutes.

Finally Gunn said, 'You never did come to the house, sir, for that taste of wild salmon.'

'Don't call me sir, George. You make me feel like I'm back in the force.'

'Sorry, Mr Macleod. Slip of the tongue.'

'It's Fin, George.'

Gunn nodded. 'She got some in last night. A nice bit of fish.'

'Poached?'

'Definitely not, Mr Macleod. She prefers it grilled.' He grinned. 'You could bring Marsaili.'

Fin said, 'She'd probably like that.' There was more silence, then. Awkward now. Before finally Fin said, 'Did you bring it?'

Gunn's face darkened. 'I could lose my job.'

'I appreciate that, George.'

'Do you? I wonder if you do, Mr Macleod. It seems you're always calling in favours, and I'm not sure what I ever get in return.'

Fin had no answer to that.

'What do you want with the post-mortem report anyway? I mean, what could it possibly tell you that we don't already know?'

'I won't know that until I see it.'

'I can't give it to you, Mr Macleod. It would be more than my job's worth.' He clenched his jaw and looked out over the beach. 'But I suppose . . . if I left it lying on the back seat, and you were to look at it without my permission . . . well, that might provide me with, what do they call it, plausible deniability?' He flicked a glance at Fin. 'I need some air.'

He climbed out of the driver's seat with a swish of quilted nylon, and Fin watched him pick his way across the machair in his black anorak towards the sand. The wind whipped his dark hair up into a cockscomb. Over his shoulder Fin saw a buff A4 envelope lying on the back seat. He reached behind him to get it, and drew out the photocopied post-mortem report from inside.

It took only a few minutes to flip through it. The passage he was looking for was in the preamble. Professor Wilson's detailed description of the body. What he read sent a chill through him so profound that he shuddered quite involuntarily.

By the time Gunn got back to his car, the report was in its envelope on the rear seat where he had left it. But it was clear from Fin's expression that he had looked at it, and that something he had seen had caused the blood to drain from his face.

'What did you find, Mr Macleod? You look like you've just seen a ghost.'

Fin swung his head around to meet Gunn's eyes. 'I think I just have, George.' He pushed the door open to step out.

'Wait a minute, Mr Macleod. I deserve to know.'

Fin hesitated. 'You do, George. And I promise, you'll be the first. But not yet.' He slammed the door shut, and as he climbed into his jeep he heard the unusual sound of Gunn swearing inside his car.

## II

The sky over the sands of Tràigh Uige was painted on. Great fat brushstrokes of pale grey and cream. The wind was brisk and cool and blew through the last of the coastal tormentil, shrivelling its yellow petals like the first breath of winter. Fin turned off the metalled road and up the track to the level stony area in front of the blackhouse. He didn't have any real hope of finding Whistler here, but it was the obvious place to start.

When he stepped out of the jeep he smelled peat smoke in the air, like toasted oat bread left a little too long under the grill. So perhaps he was at home after all. The front door was not fully closed, and Fin pushed it into the gloom.

'Whistler, you there? Whistler? We have to talk.'

Silence. He stepped inside, and caught his breath at the sight that greeted him. It was pandemonium. Furniture overturned, shards of broken crockery strewn across the floor among the wood shavings. Whistler's line of chessmen had been breached, several lying tipped over on their backs. He took a further step in, and by the light that fell obliquely through the narrow window in the rear wall, he saw the big prostrate form of Whistler lying face down on the floor. There was blood oozing through his hair and pooling on the floorboards.

'Jesus, Whistler!' Fin crossed the room in three strides and knelt by his side to feel for a pulse in his neck. His lip was split and blood oozed from his mouth. Fin saw the bruising and blood on the knuckles of his big, outstretched hand. But he was still alive. The scrape of a footstep coming from behind startled Fin. He half-turned and a light flashed in his head. The pain of it shot through his body. And darkness followed in an instant.

## III

Padraig Post had been delivering the mail in this part of the island for almost as long as anyone could remember, and no one even thought his nickname funny anymore. He always left his van on the metalled road, and walked up the track to Whistler's place. Today he had a registered letter from the Sheriff Court that required a signature. Which is why he knocked and pushed the door open into the chaos beyond.

Fin could barely move, but was aware of the light that spilled across him as the door swung open. He shut his eyes against the pain and was blinded by the light in his head. When next he opened them, he was aware of someone kneeling beside him, a sack of Royal Mail discarded among the debris. He felt a hand on his shoulder, and a voice told him not to move. There was an ambulance on the way. It was a voice that thundered in his ears. He blinked away the blood running red in his eyes and saw Whistler lying not a foot away, his big whiskered face folded hard against the floor, bloodied lips parted, jaw slack. And the faces of the Norse warriors all around silently mocking.

It was impossible now to tell how much time had passed. He was aware of moments that came and went like blinks of sunlight from a cloud-broken sky. The rumble of wheels beneath him, the sound of a siren. Light, dark, then light again. A blue light now. And then white lights overhead, passing like a succession of large balloons. He thought he saw Marsaili's pale face, etched with concern, but couldn't be certain it was not a dream.

Until finally, emerging from darkness, the world seemed somehow solid again. The pain was still there, like a distant echo in the back of his mind, felt through gauze and cotton wool. He was in a bed. Tubular metal at the head and foot of it. Another beside him. Two opposite. All empty. Sunlight leaked from behind vertical blinds. The figure of a man leaned over him. A man in a white coat with a foreign accent. German perhaps. And he remembered, from nowhere, George Gunn once telling him that the hospital was full of foreign interns. God only knew what brought them here.

He peered into Fin's eyes, peeling back the lids, one after the other. 'He is severely concussed,' he said, and Fin wondered who he was speaking to. 'I will want to keep him here under observation for another twenty-four hours.' He straightened up and turned away from the bed. 'After that . . .' Fin could see the shrug of his shoulders. 'You can have a few moments with him now.'

He moved out of Fin's range of sight and Fin found he could not turn his head to follow. A shadow fell across him. And then another. He smelled aftershave, almost overpowering, worn like a whore wears too much perfume. That, and something of the demeanour of the man standing closest to his bed, told Fin immediately that he was a cop.

'Detective Inspector Colm Mackay.' The voice confirmed it. He half turned. 'Detective Sergeant Frank Wilson.' A pause. He moved closer, his voice a little lower. 'As soon as you are fit, Mr Macleod, I'll be arresting you on suspicion of the murder of John Angus Macaskill. In the meantime I'll be leaving an officer at the door. Just in case you decide to take a walk.'

And all that Fin could think, with a pain greater than the one that filled his head, was that Whistler was dead.

# CHAPTER TWENTY-THREE

## I

Sunlight slanted in through the barred window high in the wall. Fin sat on his bunk, hands holding on to the edge of it as if he were afraid he might fall off. His head was bowed, and he stared at the concrete floor. On the far side of this tiny space, a white-painted arrow on the floor near the door pointed east. If he had believed in God, and were of that persuasion, he might have been tempted to kneel down and pray. A prayer for a dead friend. A moment passed, and a life lost. No way to bring it back. No way to rewind the clock and do it all differently. Whistler existed now only in his memory, and in the memory of others. And when they were gone there would be no trace of him left on this earth, except for his bones in it, and his wind turbines and his chessmen. And a daughter who was now an orphan.

Fin's head still felt as if gripped in a vice. A white bandage around his forehead kept the dressing in place at the back of it where they had stitched up the wound. But there was no pain. He was still too numb to feel it. Only when the numbness had gone would the full realization of all that had happened visit its pain upon him. And he wondered if he would be able to bear it.

He closed his eyes. How many lost souls had passed through this place? Drunks and wife-beaters, frauds and fighters. But he was, he knew, one of very few ever likely to be charged with murder. For the moment he was just helping police with their inquiries. Not that he had been, or could be, of much help. He had no idea what had happened to Whistler, and they had not asked him yet. He had lost a day in the hospital, and now he had lost his freedom, locked up in a police cell, a victim of events beyond his control.

He heard the scrape of a key in the lock, and the door swung open. George Gunn slipped in and shut the door quickly behind him. He was still wearing the quilted anorak he had worn yesterday morning. He turned and looked at Fin, and Fin could see the tension in his face. 'I suppose the salmon's all gone by now,' Fin said.

But Gunn didn't smile. 'For God's sake, Mr Macleod! You know they want to charge you?'

Fin lowered his head to look at the floor again and nodded.

'He's a twenty-four-carat bastard that DI Mackay. Knew him when I was at Inverness.'

'I didn't kill him, George.'

'Jesus Christ, Mr Macleod. I never thought for one minute that you did.'

'Whistler was still alive when I got there. I felt a pulse.'

Gunn nodded. 'It looks like he crawled across the floor while you were unconscious. You can see the trail of blood where he dragged himself over it, almost as if he was trying to reach something. The pathologist said he died from an epidural haematoma, and that it wasn't uncommon for there to be a brief period of lucidity after unconsciousness. But then followed by coma and death. He'd had a helluva crack on the skull, Mr Macleod.'

'There'd been some kind of a fight, George.'

'Well that much was obvious. But what were you doing there, Mr Macleod? What did you see in that post-mortem report that made you go looking for Whistler Macaskill?' When Fin failed to respond he blew his frustration through clenched teeth. 'Well, let me tell you what I know. I know that I let you see the PM report on Roddy Mackenzie. I know that you saw something in it that you wouldn't share with me. And I know that you went straight from Tolastadh to John Angus Macaskill's croft at Uig. And the next thing the man's found dead, and you lying there beside him with your skull cracked open.' More silence. 'For Christ's sake! I've bent over backwards to help you, Mr Macleod. More than once. I think you owe me.'

Fin drew a deep breath. Mairead, and now Gunn. 'I do. But I can't tell you, George. Not yet.' He heard the other man's sigh of exasperation.

Gunn pulled the door open a fraction and craned his head to glance anxiously back along the corridor. He lowered his voice. 'I shouldn't be here. And I can't help you if you won't help yourself.' He glared at Fin. 'I only hope that you're not going to drop me in the shit.'

Fin lifted his eyes to meet Gunn's and raised one eyebrow. 'I think you know me better than that, George.'

'I hope so, Mr Macleod. I really hope I do.'

He opened the door a little wider and squeezed back out into the corridor, pulling it shut behind him. Fin heard the key turning again in the lock.

It was almost half an hour before he heard the rasp of hard leather on concrete and the rattle of a key in the lock once again. This time it was a uniformed sergeant who stood in the doorway regarding Fin with thoughtful curiosity. 'The DI's ready for you now, Mr Macleod.'

Fin nodded and got slowly to his feet.

There was a single window in the interview room, looking out on some kind of courtyard or car park. DI Mackay and DS Wilson stood behind a wooden table, two chairs behind them, a single chair on the opposite side of the table. The uniformed sergeant closed the door and positioned himself with his back to it, arms folded. Mackay waved Fin into the single seat opposite.

The DI was a tall, thin-faced weasel of a man, the remains of his hair grown too long, gelled and scraped back over a narrow skull in an attempt to disguise its baldness. Fin always had an instant distrust of anyone with such a capacity for self-deception. He was clean-shaven, with the faintly purple raised skin of someone sensitive to the blade. His long neck was punctuated by an oversized Adam's apple, and vanished into a collar a size too big. As he sat down, he used a long bony finger to press the record button on the digital recorder that sat in front of him on the table next to a beige folder.

Detective Sergeant Wilson was an altogether smaller man, reduced by the rank of his superior officer to the role of observer. He was almost invisible. Neither Fin nor Mackay paid him any attention.

Mackay spoke with a strong Invernesian accent as he voiced the date and time for the record along with the names of those present. He interlaced his skeletal fingers on the table in front of him. 'Perhaps you would like to tell us, Mr Macleod, why you murdered John Angus Macaskill?'

Fin returned Mackay's stare until the Detective Inspector started to become uncomfortable. He would have known that Fin had attained the rank of detective inspector himself before leaving the force, and so there was an element of something like rivalry between them. Almost open hostility.

Fin said, 'Let me make it clear from the outset, Detective Inspector, that I did not kill John Angus Macaskill.' Even as he spoke the words he felt again the pain of Whistler's death. Each and every time he gave it voice made it all the more real.

'I'm listening.'

'John Angus has been a good and close friend since we were at the Nicolson Institute together here in Stornoway more than twenty years ago.'

'Not so friendly according to witnesses we've spoken to.' Mackay regarded him thoughtfully. 'Apparently the two of you were involved in a brawl in the bar at Suaineabhal Lodge just over a week ago, when the deceased struck you, and threats were issued.' He opened his beige folder. 'And again, just the other day. Outside the Sheriff Court. You were seen to be arguing, and the deceased knocked you off your feet.'

'Perhaps,' Fin said, 'if you stopped looking at motive for five minutes and just examined the facts . . .' Fin saw Mackay's Adam's apple slide up and down his neck as he swallowed his anger.

'Go on.'

'I went to visit John Angus at his croft in Uig yesterday morning, and found him lying unconscious on the floor. It seemed clear to me that there had been some kind of a disturbance. Furniture was overturned, there was broken glass and crockery all over the floor. I knelt beside him to feel for a pulse in his neck, and at that point he was still alive. I was aware, then, of someone approaching me from behind, and can remember nothing further until I regained consciousness and found the postman crouching beside me on the floor.'

He paused, keeping the detective inspector steadily in his gaze.

'Whistler was bleeding from the back of his skull. There was a pool of blood on the floor beside him. His face was bruised. His lip was split and bleeding. The knuckles of his right hand were swollen and grazed. I am quite sure that these, and other injuries, will have been described in the post-mortem report by the pathologist. I am equally sure he will have concluded that the man had been in one hell of a fight.'

Mackay conceded, 'The evidence would certainly support that.'

Fin stood up. And the uniformed sergeant was suddenly alert, pushing himself away from his leaning position against the door.

'Where the hell do you think you're going?' Mackay demanded.

'I'm not going anywhere, Detective Inspector.' Fin unbuttoned his shirt and slipped it off, draping it over the back of his chair, while the two detectives looked on in amazement. 'You can get a doctor in to examine me if you like.' He held out his arms in front of him and spread his hands to display his knuckles. 'But I don't think you'll find a single bruise, cut or graze on my upper body, arms or hands that could possibly have been the result of being involved in such a fight. Whistler Macaskill was a big man. He will have inflicted a great deal of damage on whoever it was that killed him. And whoever that might have been, it clearly wasn't me.'

He watched as the interrogating officer ran his eyes over Fin's torso and hands, and he saw doubt creeping into them. He lifted his shirt from the chair to drag it back on.

'Now, I'm happy to help you in any way that I can. But I don't think you have any grounds for detaining me, even for the hours that the law allows. So I would suggest that you either charge me or let me go. And unless you want to make complete fools of yourselves I would strongly advise you to do the latter.'

Mackay glared at him. He reached across the table to turn off the recording device. 'You fucking ex-cops think you know it all.' He stood up and jabbed one of his bony fingers in Fin's direction. 'But I'm willing to bet, Macleod, that you know a damned sight more than you're telling us. And when I find out what that is, trust me, I'll have you back in here so fucking fast . . .'

'My feet won't touch the ground? Is that what you were going to say, Mr Mackay?' Fin paused. 'Very original.'

For the first time Fin's eyes wandered momentarily towards the detective sergeant, and he thought he saw just the hint of a smile playing around the junior officer's lips.


## II


The duty sergeant directed him to the parking area at the side of the police station, informing him that his jeep had been parked there after being brought back from Uig by a uniformed officer.

Fin stepped from the police station out into Church Street and the fitful sunshine of a blustery October day. What amazed him was that life went on as if nothing had happened. A young mother, her hair spiralling around her head, wheeled a toddler by in a pushchair. Two old men stood talking outside the Kingdom Hall of the Jehovah's Witnesses. Cars cruised down towards the harbour where clouds of seagulls wheeled in endless circles around incoming trawlers, their eternally plaintive cries carried on the wind along with the rumble of traffic from Bayhead.

Whistler was gone, but the world kept turning. It had felt like that, too, when Robbie died. Toys scattered on the bedroom floor where he had left them. A crayon drawing he had made of Fin, still lying on the kitchen table beside the open pack of crayons. *My Dadby*, he had scrawled underneath it. Even at eight years old he was still managing to confuse his *d*'s with his *b*'s. And every time Fin had walked along the upstairs hall, it had pained him to realize that Robbie would never again come running from his bedroom to jump up into his daddy's arms.

He had the clearest recollection of sitting on the edge of his bed the Sunday morning after the accident and hearing a neighbour mowing his lawn. So banal. Life just didn't stop, even although Robbie was no longer a part of it. It was that sense of a world that hadn't even noticed which affected him the most. Then as now.

His legs were leaden as he walked around into the semi-enclosed parking area next to the station. His key was barely in the door of the Suzuki when he heard the scrape of a shoe on gravel behind him. He turned, startled, to stagger back against the jeep under a hail of blows, fists hammering into his chest and his face, screams in his ears, hot breath on his skin. He had the fleeting impression of being under attack by a flock of demented birds, his vision filled with flailing arms, his ears with shrill shrieks of anger. Now feet kicked at his legs, well-aimed painful blows to his shins. It almost came as a surprise to realize it was all the fury of one small girl.

He fought to stop fists like pistons punching him in rapid succession. He saw her father in her eyes, in her anger, in the temper he had never been able to control himself. And after what felt like an eternity, he managed to grab and hold both her wrists, turning her around, pinning her arms across her chest and pulling her back hard against him to stop the assault.

'Stop it! Stop!' he shouted at her.

But she continued to struggle and he almost lost her again. 'You killed my dad! You killed him!'

'For Christ's sake, Anna, I didn't kill your dad. Would the police have let me go if I'd killed him?' He felt the effect of his words almost immediately, as the struggling began to subside. 'I loved that man.'

Her body went limp, and the uncontrollable sobbing that racked it shook him to the core, bringing tears to his own eyes. He had never before given voice to his feelings for Whistler. Had no reason to provide them with shape or form. Whistler was just his friend, the boy and man who had twice saved his life. Connected by history, and all the hours they had shared as teenagers, the hopes and the dreams, the fights and the friendship. Whistler had been unpredictable, bad-tempered, sometimes cruel. But he had always been there when Fin needed him, a commitment he had made that day so many years before at the *Iolaire* monument. And now he was gone, and all that remained of him was in Fin's arms.

He let go of her wrists and turned her to face him. Her black cropped hair with its slash of pink, the rings and studs that punctuated her face, seemed like a grotesque caricature in grief. Black eye make-up ran down her cheeks. Her purple-painted lips trembled like a child's. Her nose ran and she could barely breathe for sobbing.

'I . . . I never told him,' she said.

Fin frowned. 'Told him what?'

'That I loved him.'

He closed his eyes and felt the tears hot on his skin, and put his arms around her, enveloping her, drawing her close.

'And now it's too late.' Her voice came muffled from his chest. 'For everything.'

Fin took her by the shoulders then and made her take a step back, forcing her to look at him. 'Anna, listen to me.'

'What?' she glared at him defiantly, as if he were trying to force her to listen to something she wouldn't want to hear.

'Men don't often talk to one another about love.' He drew a deep, trembling breath. 'But we did, your dad and me. The other day, outside the Sheriff Court. And I told him what you told me at the house.' In spite of everything, he smiled through his tears. 'Of course, I left out the profanity. Though he wouldn't have minded that. Just don't think he died not knowing that his wee girl loved him.' It took him a moment or two to control his voice again. 'And I know the only regret he'd have right now, is that he never had the chance to tell you the same.'

She stood staring back at him with her father's eyes, her face a mess, her breathing still irregular, and he could feel her pain and confusion.

'Let me take you home.'

She raised an arm in sudden anger and broke his grip on her. 'No,' she shouted. 'Just stay away from me. You, Kenny, everyone. I hate you. I hate you all.' And she turned and ran away down Church Street, giving free vent to her tears as she ran. She was gone from view and hearing in seconds.

Fin stood for a long time, leaning back against the jeep before turning wearily and climbing up into the driver's seat. There he sat for even longer until finally he succumbed to his own grief. For Whistler and his little lost girl.

III

The drive down to Uig passed in a painful blur. Great fat raindrops spat on his windscreen like tears spilled for the dead. They fell from a sky so dark and so low, bumping and scraping across each rise of the land, that Fin felt he could almost reach up and touch it. The mountains of the south-west were lost in the mist of its all-enveloping cloud.

Fin's thoughts were focused and fixated on just one man. The only man capable of inflicting enough damage on Whistler to kill him.

Minto's Land Rover sat on the compacted hard core outside his cottage. The rain blew horizontally across the acres of sand that stretched across the bay towards Baile na Cille, flattening the tall grasses that grew like reeds around the house.

If Fin had stopped for one moment to consider his actions, he might have paused to rethink, but he was blinded by the pall of red mist which had descended on him. He pushed open the cottage door with such force that it smashed against the wall of the interior hallway, its handle gouging a deep hole in the plaster. 'Minto!' He heard his own voice roar back at him from the house. He barged into the sitting room and felt the faintest residue of heat from the embers of an almost dead peat fire. There was no one there. The door to the kitchen was half open. He blundered into it, but it was empty. Then he spun around at the sound of a creaking floorboard behind him.

Minto stood in a singlet and boxer shorts, a shotgun raised and supported by his left arm, and held fast against his left shoulder by his left hand. It was shaking slightly, but pointed directly at Fin. His right arm was strapped across his chest.

'What the fuck do you want?'

He glared at Fin with a mixture of anger and confusion. But Fin couldn't tear his gaze away from the sling that held Minto's arm tight to his chest. He raised his eyes to meet Minto's. He had forgotten that Whistler had dislocated the man's shoulder during their encounter at Tathabhal. 'Someone murdered Whistler Macaskill.'

'I know. The bastard beat me to it.' Minto kept the barrel of his shotgun trained on Fin. He managed a half-smile and a snort of contempt. 'You thought it was me?'

Fin shook his head. Not even Minto could take on Whistler with one arm. But if it wasn't Minto, then the only other possibility led him into the realms of the unthinkable.

# CHAPTER TWENTY-FOUR

## I

There were only a handful of cars in the parking area at the Cabarfeidh. As he turned his jeep nose-first into a slot in front of the main entrance, Fin cast a glance over the other vehicles. There was no sign of Mairead's rental car. He hurried into the lobby and crossed to reception. The girl behind the desk gave him a practised smile, but in spite of the Americanized greeting, there was no disguising her Stornoway accent. 'Good morning. How may I help you?' He saw her eyes flicker towards his bandaged head.

'Is Mairead Morrison in or out?'

The girl looked surprised. 'Miss Morrison checked out this morning, sir. Lewis Car Rental just picked up her car. She took a taxi to the airport.'

Fin glanced at his watch. 'What time's her flight?'

'The Glasgow flight leaves at 12.20.'

It was 11.45.

Fin reached the airport in just over ten minutes. As he drove up the road from Oliver's Brae towards the roundabout, he could see the small, prop-engined aircraft sitting out on the tarmac, the luggage trailer being towed out to the hold.

Rain still spat on his windscreen, smeared across the glass by well-worn wipers. There was no time to find a parking place, and he bypassed the car park to pull up in front of the sliding doors that opened into the tiny terminal building. He abandoned his Suzuki, engine idling, and ran inside. There was just a handful of people sitting around in the waiting area, silhouettes against panoramic windows looking out on to the airfield. The final stragglers in the queue to pass through security and into the departure lounge were patiently awaiting their turn.

He saw Mairead in her distinctive long black coat. She was showing her ticket to the security officer.

'Mairead!' His voice reverberated around the little airport, and heads turned from every direction. Mairead's was one of them. He was almost shocked by the whiteness of her face. So marked in contrast to her favourite black, and the dark auburn of her cropped hair.

The security officer stood holding her ticket, waiting to return it. But she was like a rabbit caught in the headlights, staring at Fin with saucer eyes. He started across the concourse towards her, his voice still raised. 'I need to talk to you.'

Finally she found hers. 'There's no time. My flight's just about to leave.' She turned to retrieve her ticket.

'Get the next one.'

The remaining faces in the queue glanced from Mairead to Fin and back again, fascinated by the unfolding drama.

Not only was the singer Mairead Morrison on their flight, but she was engaged in some kind of row with a wild-eyed man whose head was bandaged and bloody.

'I can't.'

'If you get on that plane I'm going straight back to the police station in Stornoway to tell the cops what I know.' He could see the anxiety and uncertainty in her eyes, not knowing what it was he knew.

'Have to hurry you, madam,' the security officer said.

Fin stopped and held her gaze for a long moment before he saw her resistance crumbling, surrendering to the inevitable. She took a deep breath and pushed back through the remaining passengers to walk boldly up to Fin, clutching her ticket, her demeanour unmistakably hostile. She lowered her voice to little more than a hiss, her face just six inches from his. 'Tell me.'

'I know it wasn't Roddy in that plane.'

Her blue eyes grew cold, and there was a moment when he could almost see the calculation behind them. She made a decision, took his arm and steered him quickly away towards the seating area in front of the windows. 'What are you talking about?'

'I'm talking about the operation Roddy had to repair his shattered femur after the accident on the Road to Nowhere. They put in plates and screws to hold it together. Strangely missing from the body we found in the cockpit.' She couldn't hold his eye, and looked away through the glass towards the plane, silent and thoughtful. Wishing perhaps that she was already on it. 'Who did we bury the other day, Mairead?'

Her eyes darted towards him and then quickly away again.

'Whistler knew that wasn't Roddy. I don't know how, but he did. He was never the same from the moment we found that plane. What did he know, Mairead?' And when she said nothing, he gripped her arm above the elbow, fingers sinking into soft flesh, and saw her wince from the pain of it. 'Come on! Someone killed Whistler to shut him up, didn't they?'

Her head whipped round, eyes filled with a strange mix of anger and hurt. 'No!' She was breathing hard. 'I have no idea who killed Whistler. Or why.'

'I don't believe you.' He glared at her. 'There was something going on between you two. You both knew that wasn't Roddy.' He was almost shocked to see her eyes fill up.

'Poor Whistler.' And tears spilled down the porcelain white of her cheeks.

Fin was unmoved. 'If I didn't know you, Mairead, I might almost believe they were real.' And he saw genuine hurt in the look she turned on him. 'Tell me about Roddy. Is he alive, is he dead? The truth, Mairead.' Hesitation was evident in her eyes, in her face, in her whole body language. 'I'm not letting this go. You can either tell me or you can tell the police. It's up to you.'

She turned away, gazing through the window again as if looking for help, or maybe divine intervention. And Fin saw passengers, heads bowed against the wind and rain, making their way hurriedly across the tarmac to the steps of the plane. Among them, staring into the light that shone out from the terminal building, the pale faces of Strings, Skins and Rambo. It was clear that they had seen Fin with Mairead. There was an exchange of words among them. But it was too late to turn back.

Mairead said suddenly, 'I need to make a phone call.' She pulled her arm free of Fin's grasp and walked off across the concourse, fishing her mobile phone from her coat pocket. She selected a number from its memory then put it to her ear.

Fin watched from a distance as she spoke rapidly to someone at the other end. For a moment he wondered if it might even be Strings, or Skins or Rambo as they boarded the plane. She seemed to be arguing. Gesturing into space with her free hand, and briefly he heard her voice raised in protest. And then she hung up. She stood for several seconds, as if replaying the conversation in her head, then turned back towards Fin and thrust her phone in her pocket as she approached.

There was something hard now in her eyes. Emotionless. She said, 'You want the truth?' She paused for what was clearly a long, painful moment. 'Meet me the day after tomorrow. In Malaga.'

## II

'I don't want you to go.' She repeated the refrain.

Fin looked up over the top of his laptop. Marsaili was framed in the open door of the study. The room which had once been Artair's dad's den, where he had tutored Fin and

Artair in maths and English, history and geography, through long winter nights. Fin could have sworn the smell of Mr Macinnes's pipe smoke still lingered in that room, even after all these years.

A desk lamp spilled its light all over his keyboard as he entered dates and times, and pulled up onscreen prices.

'I mean it, Fin. I don't want you to go.' It was the same refrain that Mona had used when they first sent him back to the island to find Angel Macritchie's killer.

'I need to know, Marsaili.'

'You need to go to the police and tell them what you know already. They think you have something to do with Whistler's murder, for God's sake. It's madness.'

'I'll go to them when I know the truth. The whole truth.'

'And you think you'll get that from Mairead?' The way she said *Mairead* positively dripped with sarcasm.

Fin looked up at her again, his hackles rising. 'That's what this is all about, really, isn't it? Me meeting Mairead in Spain.'

'I saw the way she looked at you, Fin. And I saw the look in your eyes too. It's a look I know. We were old lovers once, too, remember?'

Fin met her eyes very directly. 'I have no interest in Mairead, Marsaili. I didn't like her then, and I don't like her now.'

There was a momentary hiatus as Marsaili digested this, testing it for truth, but coming up with the uncertain results of a mind clouded by jealousy.

'I don't understand why you have to go there. Everyone knows Amran have a place in the south of Spain where they write and record. If Mairead has something to tell you, why couldn't she tell you here?'

Fin was losing patience. 'I don't know! But if I have to go to Spain and back to find out why Whistler died then I'll go. Jesus, Marsaili. He saved my life. Twice. And the one time he needed me I wasn't there.' He very nearly choked on the thought, and quickly refocused on his computer screen.

His search had come up with a return flight from Glasgow to Malaga in two days' time, departing just after 9 a.m., returning the following day. He would have to fly to Glasgow tomorrow and stay overnight. He hit the return key to purchase the flight and proceed to checkout.

When he looked up again over the top of his screen, Marsaili had gone.

# CHAPTER TWENTY-FIVE

The arrivals hall was very nearly deserted by the time Fin passed through customs and immigration. The tour groups had all vanished in the direction of waiting coaches, and only a handful of independent travellers ventured through the barriers into the big, dark, empty hall. The midday sun was high, and very little light from it fell directly through the tall glass walls that stretched all along one side. Outside it was very bright, overexposed, fierce sunlight bleaching colour out of cars and buildings.

Mairead stood, a solitary figure, in the middle of a large floor that darkly reflected overhead lights. Fin slung his bag on to one shoulder and walked across the concourse to meet her. There was no smile of greeting, no warmth in her eyes. 'I'm parked on the roof,' she said, and turned on her heels towards the door.

Outside, the heat came as something of a shock after the Hebridean autumn, and Fin quickly discarded his jacket, wishing he had brought lighter clothing.

Mairead was driving an automatic dusty-blue Nissan X-Trail. It wasn't a rental, and Fin wondered if it were hers, or whether it belonged to the band, a runaround for when they were down recording their latest set of songs.

It was a fine day. The palest of blue skies, devoid of clouds, stretched as far as the eye could see. They turned from the A7 on to the coastal toll road, and Fin saw the Mediterranean sparkling below them on their left, a simmering blue only slightly darker than the sky, lines of fast-moving cars in front of them heading south and west, windscreens reflecting sunlight in intermittent flashes.

'Where are we going?' Fin glanced across at Mairead, who sat tight-lipped behind the wheel, eyes fixed on the road ahead.

'The villa,' is all she said.

Fin contained his curiosity, and took advantage of their elevated position on the road to look across the parched Spanish coastal plain through which the six lanes of motorway cut a swathe. Away to their right, the purple slopes of the Sierra Bermeja rose up to rugged heights, sharply delineated against the sky like paper cut-outs. Clusters of white buildings nestled in valleys and hilltops, ancient villages that had survived since the time of the Moors. All in stark contrast with the thousands of unfinished apartments in high-rise developments that lined the highway on either side, long since abandoned by contractors whose money had dried up in the recession. Cranes had been removed when construction had stopped, and trees and shrubs were already starting to reclaim the building sites. Those apartments which had been finished lay empty.

Mairead glanced at him and followed his gaze. 'They can't give these away,' she said. 'No one wants to be the sole owner in an empty block. Too spooky.'

They passed under road signs for places Fin had only ever seen in holiday brochures. Marbella. Algeciras. Cadiz. Through two *garitas de peaje*, where Mairead pulled in to pay their tolls. It was nearly an hour before she turned off the motorway at Estepona, following signs for a place called Casares. The road then swept them up through a huge area of municipal parkland known as Los Pedregales, past a vast electricity-generating power station, and a sprawling recycling plant that pumped its perfume out into the fibrillating heat of the early afternoon.

They drove by small country restaurants gearing up for the late Spanish lunch – Venta Victoria, Arroyo Hondo – before turning off into a narrow, pitted roadway that began a steep ascent up into the mountains through forests of pine trees and cork oaks.

Dust billowed out behind them as they pitched and bumped their tortuous way up through the trees, passing occasional gates beyond which driveways wound off to hidden houses caught only in occasional glimpses. It was twenty minutes before the road finally levelled off and the land fell steeply away on their right, tree-lined slopes sweeping down into dry river valleys that snaked their way through the mountains. The sun shone in dazzling silver glitter on the distant ocean, the faint outline of the coast only just discernible through the haze.

White villas tucked themselves away among the foliage, each isolated in a sea of green and parched brown, forest rising all around. And Fin wondered what would become of them if ever fire were to sweep through these tinder-dry trees.

'That's our place.' Mairead pointed down into a ravine, and Fin saw a jumble of roman-tiled red roofs and white walls assembled around a terrace halfway up it, buzzards riding thermals in the sky overhead. Even from here you could tell that it must command the most extraordinary views. And almost as if she read his mind, Mairead said, 'On a clear day you can see all the way across the Strait of Gibraltar to Africa and the Atlas Mountains.' Anything further from the featureless peat bogs and storm-lashed coastline of the Isle of Lewis would have been hard to imagine. It seemed extraordinary to Fin that it was here in the heat, and the wild mountain forests of southern Spain, that the Celtic music spawned by his homeland was written and recorded, and sung in Mairead's clear, beautiful Gaelic.

At the top of a rise in the road, Mairead suddenly turned right, and the X-Trail tipped nose-first down into a steep concrete drive between high, white-painted gateposts, the name of the villa cemented on one of them in blue and white tiles. *Finca Sòlas.*

They descended into a flat, walled parking area, and Mairead turned the vehicle to point back up the drive before switching off the ignition. When he stepped down on to the concrete, Fin felt a blast of heat that was almost shocking after the chill of the air conditioning.

Below the wall to their right, beyond a screen of trees, a turquoise-blue swimming pool lay shimmering invitingly in the afternoon sun. Fin followed Mairead down steps and through a garden of prickly pear cactus and wild aloe vera. They passed beneath an archway that led to a cool, covered passageway which opened out at its far end on to a terracotta-tiled terrace of fountains and fish-ponds.

At the far end of the terrace, beneath the shade of a fleshy-leaved fig tree, a man sat at a table, his back to them, looking out over the view towards the sea. There was a tall glass of something red at his right hand, ice not yet melted, condensation gathering on the table beneath it. A MacBook laptop was open in front of him, and he was tapping at the keyboard.

He turned as he heard the gate opening on to the terrace, a man in his middle years, quite bald on the top of his head, but with hair growing in thick, luxuriant curls all around the sides and back. Once fair, perhaps, it was already turning grey. He carried more weight than was good for him, nut-brown legs in three-quarter-length shorts and open sandals, a white shirt hanging open over the bulge of a large, tanned, beer gut. His brown face cracked into an all-too-familiar smile, and he extended a still-slender hand. He looked to be in rude health for a man they had buried twice.

'Hello Fin,' Roddy said. 'It's been a long time.'

# CHAPTER TWENTY-SIX

They left Mairead sitting in the dappled shade provided by rush matting stretched across a frame above the table. She had been subdued, with clouded eyes, and said very little. Perhaps she had realized that this first crack in their seventeen-year silence could only mark the beginning of the end.

Roddy, by contrast, was larger than life, animated in the extreme. Fin followed the ghost of his one-time friend up steps to another level, and they crossed an east-facing terrace towards a large outbuilding at the back of the villa.

'We have six bedrooms in the house,' Roddy said. 'Enough to accommodate the whole band when they come to rehearse and record. Of course, Strings is here more often than the others. We still write together.' He pushed open a heavy soundproofed door and flicked a switch to flood the studio control room with light, rows of knobs and switches, faders and dials, peppering the shallow angle of an enormous mixing desk. Through a window that ran the length of one wall, shadows reached back into the studio itself, which was littered with sound baffles and hanging mikes. A drum kit was permanently mounted in its own soundproofed booth, the carpet-tiled floor around it a Sargasso Sea of twisted cables.

'We're on our twelfth CD now. Most of it's already recorded. I'm just working on the mix.' He leaned across the desk and pressed a switch. The room filled with the beautiful sound of Amran. Synthesizer, violin, the haunting swoop of a Celtic flute, all overlaying the repetitive beat of rock drums and bass, and the sad, pure voice of Mairead singing so painfully of Hebridean longing for a lost past. Roddy switched it off abruptly, and the room resounded with the resultant silence. His eyes were moist. 'It's the only way I can go home,' he said. 'In my music.' And then the moment passed and he smiled his genuine affection. 'It's great to see you again, Fin, it really is.'

But Fin was ambivalent. From the moment he had seen the post-mortem report he had suspected that Roddy might still be alive. But to be confronted with him in this way, in the flesh, after mourning him twice, and believing him dead for seventeen years, was more than faintly surreal. He said, 'I don't know how I feel, Roddy, about seeing you again. Confused, that's for sure. And right now pretty angry.'

Roddy laughed and took his arm to steer him back out into the sunshine. 'Don't be angry with me, Fin. None of this is my fault. Not really.' They crossed the terrace and looked out over the view. Fin was aware of Mairead's upturned face watching them from the terrace below. 'The band will go off on a US tour next year to promote the new CD. But, of course, I won't be with them. Even though I still write the songs with Strings, and it's me you hear on the recordings, I've never once been able to play live with Amran since that awful night seventeen years ago. You have no idea how frustrating that is.'

He turned to look Fin in the eye, and waved a hand vaguely towards the villa.

'Look around you, Fin. It's paradise, this place. Sunshine all year round. A view to die for. Africa just across the water. They come every seven years to strip the cork off the trees. They've done it twice since I've been here. You might think I'd be happy. But it feels like a fucking prison.'

He turned and gazed sightlessly towards the Strait of Gibraltar, gripping the railing in front of him. Fin saw the white-knuckled tension in his hands. 'You have no idea what I'd give to be standing right now on Tràigh Uige, looking across the mountains to Harris. Feeling the wind in my face. Aye, and the rain. I'd trade all this for just five minutes of home any day.'

He released his tension, and the railing, and relaxed again into a smile.

'But what am I thinking about? Terrible host, I am. Never even offered you a drink.'

Fin stared out over the tops of trees in the valley below. To his left, where the forest had been cut back, the shaved peaks of the Sierra Bermeja scraped the sky. Steps led down into a steeply sloped garden of gnarled trees and dusty shrubs, fig and olive, cactus and oleander. All the grasses and wild flowers, this late in the season, were parched and burned brown. He turned, leaning against the rail, to look back at the house with its roofs sloping at odd angles, a covered balcony high up behind a row of arches, bedrooms opening off it through French windows. A Buddha sat cross-legged below a covered fish-pond, and Mairead perched on the edge of a chair at the table, smoking. She had not addressed a word to Fin since their arrival.

Roddy emerged through an arched doorway from the kitchen carrying a tray of drinks, tall glasses of red, fizzing liquid and chattering ice cubes. 'Come and get it.'

Fin pushed himself off the railing and crossed the terrace to climb the two steps to the eating area. He drew up a chair and sat opposite Mairead in the shade as Roddy distributed their drinks and a wooden dish of macadamia nuts.

'I'll make us something to eat in a while,' he said. 'Paella okay?' He grinned. 'Very Spanish, but they probably ship the prawns down from Stornoway.' He raised his glass. '*Slàinte*.'

It was odd to hear Gaelic spoken in this place, so many miles from home, in a climate and culture so alien to its origins.

Roddy took a long pull at his drink. 'Refreshing, eh? *Tinto de verano*, the Spanish call it. Literally, wine of summer. Red wine mixed with a sweet fizzy lemon drink. I love it.' He took another sip. 'They tell me there's a distillery at Uig now. Abhainn Dearg. Red River whisky. Any good?'

Fin nodded. 'It's a fine whisky.' He took a small sip of his *tinto de verano* and fixed Roddy in his gaze. 'Who killed Whistler, Roddy?'

It was as if someone had thrown a switch, and a light went out somewhere behind Roddy's eyes. His face darkened. 'I don't know, Fin. But I'd like to meet him, because he wouldn't be breathing for long.'

Fin said, 'Seems to me there was never any love lost between you and Whistler.' He glanced at Mairead who sat staring sullenly into her drink. 'Over the affections of a certain young woman.' She threw him a dark glance.

But Roddy just shook his head. 'Sure. We had our differences over the years, me and Whistler.' He chuckled sadly. 'Whistler fell out with everyone at one time or another.' He raised his eyes to meet Fin's. 'But I always considered him to be one of my best and oldest friends. He was like a big fucking dog, Fin. He might bite you from time to time, but he never stopped loving you.' And Fin thought he had never heard Whistler so well summed up in so few words. Roddy laid his glass on the table and turned it around with his fingertips, gazing thoughtfully into its fizzing redness. 'I owed him more than most people will ever know.'

'In relation to . . . your "death"?' Fin said.

Roddy nodded without looking up.

'Tell me.'

Roddy glanced at Mairead, absorbing but ignoring her disapproval. He drew a long breath. 'I suppose I should start at the beginning.'

'Well, since we already know how it ends,' Fin said, 'maybe that would be a good idea.'

\*

Roddy leaned back in his chair and reached into his shirt pocket for a pack of cigars. He drew one out and lit it, and puffed on it reflectively for some moments. Blue smoke rose around his head in gently curling strands in the still heat of the afternoon. 'You probably remember a girlfriend I had during our second year in Glasgow. Caitlin. She was the one whose parents had the big fuck-off house with the swimming pool in Pollokshields.'

Fin nodded. He remembered her well. The blonde girl who had been skinny-dipping with Roddy in the swimming pool the night Fin and Mairead first got together.

'And her big fucking brother, Jimbo.' Roddy almost spat out his name. 'Smug bastard with a face you'd never get tired of kicking.'

Fin was taken aback by Roddy's ferocity. He remembered Jimbo, strutting about his parents' house as if he owned it. A spoiled little rich kid.

It was almost as if Roddy had to force himself to relax to continue his story. He tipped his head back and blew smoke towards the rush matting above them, chinks of sunlight falling through it to sprinkle light like fairy dust across the table. 'My own fault, really, I suppose. I was head over heels in love with Caitlin. Obsessed.' He glanced at Mairead, embarrassed it seemed to confess it in her presence. 'And I thought she felt the same way about me.' He smiled and shook his head. 'Though maybe I always knew there was an element of the star-fucker about her.' He added, unnecessarily, 'We were just starting to make it big, then.'

Mairead said, 'Just stick to the facts, Roddy.' Her distaste was clear.

Roddy took another draught from his glass. 'You saw yourself from her parents' house that they were pretty well off. Her father was in banking, she said. And she had expensive tastes. Clothes, shoes, good food, good wine. But the thing I could give her, Fin, that no one else could, was the thrill of flying. Learning to fly that old Piper Comanche was the best investment I ever made. She loved it. Couldn't get enough of it. Wanted to go up in the air every spare moment we had. Even expressed an interest in learning to fly herself.' He blew air through pursed lips. 'And like an idiot I even offered to pay for lessons.'

He sat for a long time, then, lost in his own thoughts, puffing gently on his cigar. Fin looked across the table at Mairead, but she was assiduously avoiding his eye.

Finally, Roddy said, 'It was Caitlin's idea to fly up to North Uist and land at Solas Beach.' His eyes flickered towards Fin. 'Ironic, isn't it? Solas. Minus the accent, of course. And the place name doesn't derive from *comfort*. Anything but that.' Fin saw him clench his jaw. 'Anyway, she'd read about it somewhere, she said. In some magazine. That it was possible to land a small aircraft on the sands at low tide. It was almost midsummer, and she thought it would be romantic if we could fly up there and land on the beach at midnight, and picnic through the summer solstice. Maybe even stay overnight. Sleep under the stars.' He shrugged and smiled his regret. 'Sounded good to me.'

He drained his glass and stood up, overcome by a sudden restlessness, and turned to the edge of the terrace where he stood leaning with his hands on the rail.

'I'd flown up to the Hebrides before. That was no big deal. But I didn't know if it would be possible to park up on the beach, so I might have to fly back. And I'd need night and IMC ratings for that. Even though it never really got dark at that time of year. But there was time enough to get my licence amended so I could fly at night, or in limited visibility, and I did that. We kept our eye on the weather forecasts, and it looked to be just about perfect for June 21st. So we made it a date.'

He turned around then, half-sitting on the rail, arms folded across his chest. Mairead had her back to him, lighting another cigarette, and it appeared to Fin that Roddy was looking straight through him, lost in a world of distant memory.

'Official sunset around the summer solstice on North Uist is 10.30 p.m., and I knew I couldn't land there in the dark. So we set off in plenty of time to arrive before sunset. It was a beautiful night, Fin. Perfect for flying. I'd never seen the sky such a deep, dark blue, and the red fire of sunset lighting up the ocean, streaking orange and yellow along the horizon. The last light of the day was catching the mountains of Harris against the sky to the north as we circled low over the beach. An almost flawless crescent of sand exposed at low tide. I made two passes over it to make sure conditions were okay for landing, then on the third turn prepared to set her down.'

Fin could see that he was back there in his mind, in the cockpit of that tiny single-engined aircraft, preparing to land her on a strange beach on a midsummer's night, breathless, excited, scared. And with a woman beside him to impress.

'I was nervous, that was for sure. And I kept the power on very slightly to make the landing as soft as possible, coming in faster than usual because there was no length restriction. And keeping the nose up as long as possible to make sure she didn't dig in to soft sand.' His face lit up in relived recollection, pride in his voice. 'And then she was down, and I brought her to a halt, and Caitlin was all over me as if I'd just turned water into wine.' He shook his head. 'It was a great feeling, Fin, landing on the beach like that. And jumping down on to hard, compacted sand with the wind in my face, and the last of the day sending shadows across the water from the dunes. I turned to help Caitlin down off the wing and held her in my arms, and kissed her . . . and never noticed how cold she was. And I don't mean to the touch.' His expression hardened. 'That was when I turned around and saw three men crossing the sand towards us. I didn't really think anything of it at first. I had no reason to be alarmed. I mean, I hadn't done anything wrong.' He drew a long, slow breath. 'Which is when I realized that the man leading them was Caitlin's brother, Jimbo.'

His breathing increased as he remembered the moment, and his face flushed behind his tan. It was as real to him now as it had been then.

'At first I was confused. He shook my hand and greeted me like a long-lost friend and congratulated me on my landing. Then he turned to Caitlin and said, "Well done, girl." And I noticed that the men that were with him were carrying brown canvas holdalls. Jimbo said, "A little extra baggage you'll be taking back with you, Roddy."' Roddy unfolded his arms, hands behind him, gripping the rail, and he refocused on Fin. 'Call me slow, Fin, but it took me a moment or two to realize that this was a drugs pickup, and that I'd been set up. I can remember turning to look at Caitlin, and how she wouldn't meet my eye. What a fucking fool I was!'

Now he pushed himself off the rail and slumped back into his chair, drawing on the tail end of his cigar.

'Turned out Caitlin's father had nothing to do with banking, and everything to do with heroin and cocaine and cannabis. A family business, it seemed, and doing very well, thank you. With plans to become the main supplier of illegal drugs into northern Europe. Ambitious. Wanted to take over from the drug barons in Liverpool and Manchester who were under pressure from the cops. And Caitlin was the honey trap they'd set for me. Me and my Comanche. They wanted someone "clean" to fly the pickups. Three thousand miles of coastline around Scotland. Impossible to monitor.' He leaned forward to carefully stub out his cigar in the ashtray. 'Of course I refused to have anything to do with it. But Jimbo made it clear to me the consequences of failing to cooperate. And having caught me in their web that first night, there was no way they were going to let me go. Not only did they threaten physical violence, but if I didn't fly for them, they said, an anonymous call to the cops, and a secret packet stashed away somewhere on my plane, would ensure half a lifetime in prison.' He breathed hard through clenched teeth. 'They had me, Fin. Hook, line and fucking sinker.'

Dusk had stolen up on them from nowhere, falling like fine coal dust across the valley, the mountains behind them sending long shadows towards the coast. A hidden sun still cast its light across a distant ocean. The warm evening air was filled with the sound of cicadas and frogs, and the last buzzards of the day circled above them, as if hoping there might be something left to scavenge after Roddy had finished picking over the past.

Roddy was a long way from being finished, but became aware suddenly that the day was slipping away from them. 'Forgive me,' he said. 'You must be starving. I'll get that paella cooking. Everything's prepared, so it shouldn't take long.' Before he left them he lit large candles on the table and around the terrace, then disappeared into the darkness of the house. A light came on in the kitchen and a quartered slab of yellow fell through the window across a terrace flickering now with a candlelight that cast strange dancing shadows all around them, like some bizarre puppet theatre.

Mairead's face was mostly in shadow. Only the line of her nose and the curve of her brow above her right eye caught the light. Her eyes themselves were lost. Darkness had followed dusk like a shutter descending on the day. They listened in silence to the sounds of Roddy preparing his paella in the kitchen. He had some music playing. Flamenco guitar and a guttural, alien voice wailing the tuneless melody of an ancient culture that owed more to Arab Africa than to Europe. Fin closed his eyes for a moment and wondered how it had been possible to keep the secret for so long. Mairead lit a cigarette and her face flared briefly in the darkness. He said, 'Did you know about all this?'

She drew on her cigarette and blew smoke into the night, shaking her head. 'Not a thing. Not until he confided in me and told me how he planned to escape.' She turned her head towards Fin, but he still couldn't see her eyes. 'All this was going on while you and I were having our . . . what would you call it? Affair? Fling?' When Fin failed to respond she said, 'Of course, I noticed the change in him. We weren't lovers at the time, but when you play in a band with people it's like living with them. Well, you know that.'

Fin nodded.

'He became morose, withdrawn. Not like the Roddy we knew at all. And you know Roddy. He was like an open book. No matter whether he was happy or depressed he had to tell you why. But that all stopped. He was secretive, spending less and less time with the guys. I noticed he was losing weight and wondered if he was ill. There was something wrong, I knew that much. But I had no idea what it was until the night he told me.'

She flicked her ash into the ashtray, and as she took another pull on her cigarette, Fin saw by its glow the introspection in her eyes. Eyes that flickered reluctantly in his direction. And he wondered if it was really regret that he saw in them.

'It was the night he intended to disappear for good. The same night I broke it off with you.' She paused. 'And why.'

All these years later, finally, Fin understood.

'Roddy was in trouble, Fin. He needed me. And there was too much history between us for me to give him anything less than a hundred per cent.' But the explanation was unnecessary.

They had no time to dwell on it, or discuss it further. Roddy emerged from the kitchen clutching a bottle and three glasses. He placed them on the table and removed the cork with a flourish. His good mood, it appeared, had returned.

'Rioja,' he said. 'Gran Reserva. Best you can get. Smooth as butter on the tongue, and slips over like vanilla silk.' He filled their glasses. 'Try it, Fin.'

Fin sipped at it and nodded. 'It's good.' But wine wasn't his thing, and Roddy seemed disappointed.

'Paella'll be ready soon.' He disappeared and returned with three plates and cutlery, then came back to the table ten minutes later with a large steaming paella pan full of rice and prawns and chicken and mussels. He placed it in the centre of the table and sat down. 'Tuck in, guys.'

They helped themselves and ate for a while in silence until Fin could contain his curiosity no longer. 'So what happened, Roddy?'

Roddy glanced at him, his enthusiasm for the food quickly waning. He sighed, pushing his half-empty plate away from him on the table and lifting his glass to his lips. He let the wine flow back across his tongue and savoured it for a moment. 'I must have flown ten, eleven pickups for them by mid-July, and Jimbo always came with me. There was just no end to it in sight, Fin. I was in way too deep by that time to go to the police, and probably wouldn't have lived long if I had. That's when I came up with my plan.' His chuckle was bitter and almost choked him. He took another mouthful of wine. 'It was foolproof, I figured. I was going to disappear. Me and the plane together. Somewhere out over the sea. If they thought I was dead they couldn't touch me.'

He refilled his glass, leaning forward on the table and cradling it in his palms. Fin could see the glassy quality of his eyes in the reflected candlelight.

'I never filed a flight plan on those flights up to Solas, so there would be no questions. And obviously I fuelled up enough to get me there and back. But on the night I planned to disappear I filed a flight plan out to Mull, the landing strip at Glenforsa. A short flight, there and back, so when I went missing they would be looking in the wrong place. I took on enough fuel to get me up to the Outer Hebrides, but not back. It was going to be a one-way trip.' He smiled sadly. 'To eternity.'

He took several mouthfuls of wine, staring reflectively off into the darkness, revisiting painful memories in his mind.

'I hugged the mountains on the flight up the west coast, to disrupt primary radar systems. Didn't want anyone watching me. I ignored repeated queries from air traffic control, then dropped off secondary radar by switching off my transponder and telling ATC it had failed. Radio silence then. Of course, as far as Jimbo knew it was just another pickup and we landed at Solas as usual.

'There was never anyone there to meet us. Just a set place to pick up the packages. There are no houses overlooking the beach, and the village of Solas is way the other side of the dunes. My plan was to wait at the plane while Jimbo went to pick up the goods and then just fly away without him.'

He breathed through his teeth in remembered frustration and shook his head.

'But I guess I must have been giving off vibes. I was nervous as hell, and that must have transmitted itself to him. He insisted that I come with him. What could I do? I couldn't refuse, so we left the engine running and hurried across the sand to where the stuff was hidden among the long grass. I was in turmoil, Fin. It was all set up. If I didn't do it now I figured I never would. I was carrying one of the bags. And there was a fair bit of weight in it. A few kilos anyway. I don't know what it was. Probably dope. Anyway, I hit him with it, from behind, swinging the bag at his head as hard as I could. He went down like a sack of potatoes, and I ran like hell for the plane.

'I thought I was home free. But just as I'm reaching the plane I hear him breathing like a bloody steam train right behind me. I tried to get up on the wing, but he pulled me back down. Must have had the constitution of a fucking ox. He had blood running down his neck, and a look on his face like he wanted to kill me.'

Roddy stared off into an abyss that spanned seventeen years, breathing hard, just as if he were still there.

'I knew I had to put him down, or I was fucked. But he was a strong bastard. He tried to hit me, and I hit him back, and then pushed him hard. He staggered backwards.' Roddy closed his eyes. 'Right into the fucking revolving propeller. Smashed in half his head and dropped him with a single blow.'

Fin knew now how the body in the plane had received its dreadful cranial injuries. He could only imagine what a bloody mess it must have been at the time.

'He was dead, Fin. Fucking dead. His brains all over the fucking beach. At first I had no idea what to do. My immediate instinct was to get on the plane and just go. But then I knew I couldn't leave him there. His family would think I'd killed him, and there's no way they'd believe I just went missing after it. No one would believe that.' He breathed out deeply, and Fin heard the tremble in his breath. 'So then I started to think more clearly. I got him into my jacket with my wallet and stuff inside, in case anyone ever found it. Then I got him into the cockpit.' He ran a hand over his face in recollection of the horror of it. 'You have no idea how hard that was, Fin. He was a dead weight. Literally. Blood everywhere. It was about twenty minutes before I got him into the passenger seat and was able to shut the cockpit door and take off again.'

He seemed suddenly to become aware of the two faces watching him in absorbed fascination as he recounted the events of that night. Mairead must have heard it all before.

Perhaps many times. But she was as transfixed as Fin by the retelling of it under the stars on this hot Spanish evening. Roddy picked up the bottle and refilled all their glasses. He took out another cigar and lit it.

'I took the drugs with me and dropped them out of the plane once we were over the ocean. The incoming tide, I knew, would erase any evidence of Jimbo's death. Then I set a course, as I'd always planned, for the mountains of south-west Lewis.

'It was the end of July. Official sunset was about 10 p.m. It was much later than that, but still light, and I knew exactly where I was going. Mealaisbhal was my marker as I flew low into the mountains. I'd already picked out a loch just to the north of it. Hidden away in a valley, miles from any habitation. So I knew nobody would see or hear me at that time of night. I just cruised right in, low and flat, wheels retracted, and landed her on her belly on the water. A scary moment. But to be honest, Fin, I was beyond scared at that point, and there was no turning back. I'd burned off virtually all my fuel, which was always the plan. Didn't want tell-tale oil slicks on the surface of the loch.'

He sucked on his cigar, and through his smoke told them how he had climbed out of the cockpit and hauled Jimbo's body across into the pilot's seat and strapped him in.

'The plane was floating, and would probably have taken a long time to go down. Too long for my purposes. But the good thing about the Comanche is that it takes on fuel from inlets on both wings, either side of the cockpit, and the wings were already just under water. So I climbed down on to the wings and opened them up. The tanks filled with water and down she went.'

Fin said, 'That water must have been freezing, even in July.'

'It was bloody cold, Fin. I can tell you that. But it was a good thing I was in it long enough to wash off Jimbo's blood. Because there was someone waiting for me on the shore with dry clothes, and I didn't want him to see blood, or know anything about the body in the plane.'

'Whistler,' Fin said.

Roddy nodded self-consciously. 'I couldn't have done it on my own. I needed clothes, transport out of the mountains. Whistler was the only one I trusted. I'd told him everything.'

'Not everything, Roddy. You didn't tell him about Jimbo. And that made him an accessory to murder, even if he didn't know it.'

'I didn't murder Jimbo!' Roddy raised his voice in protest. 'It was an accident.'

'I think you might have had difficulty convincing a jury of that.'

Roddy glared at him for a moment, then resigned himself to the interpretation that no doubt everyone would have made. His voice dropped again. 'It was an accident.'

'So Whistler met you on the shore,' Fin prompted.

'Yes. He was waiting for me as promised. I stripped off my wet clothes and we buried them in the peat. I got dressed, and we made our way down the valley in the moonlight to the track where Whistler had a four-by-four waiting for us.

We drove to Harris then, and I got on the ferry from Tarbert to Skye first thing next morning. All togged up like a hiker. A woolly hat and my hood up so no one would recognize me.'

Mairead spoke for the first time, unexpectedly, and her voice almost startled them in the dark. 'I met him off the ferry in Skye. I'd driven up there the night before, right after I left you at the Cul de Sac.'

'I told her everything,' Roddy said. 'About Jimbo, I mean. And we flew together down here to Spain, to look for a place. Somewhere I could still be a part of the band, at least as far as writing and recording were concerned, but dead to the rest of the world. Lost with my plane somewhere in the sea among the Inner Hebrides.'

Fin said, 'So obviously the rest of the band knew the full story.'

'Oh, not about Jimbo,' Roddy said. 'We never told anyone about that.'

Fin looked at Mairead. 'Must have made it awkward for you with the others when Jimbo's body turned up in the plane.'

She lowered her eyes. 'We're still dealing with that.'

Roddy fixed Fin with a very direct look, an appeal in his gaze. 'If it were ever to come out, Fin – you know, that I was alive. There are still people out there who would come looking for me.'

Fin sat staring into his wine for a long time before taking a small mouthful. 'If I say nothing, knowing what I know now, that would make me an accessory after the fact to murder and fraud.'

'I told you we shouldn't have told him,' Mairead said. Her voice was hard and edged by tension.

But Roddy's eyes never left Fin's. 'He's not going to tell anyone, are you Fin? I mean, who would benefit from it? None of us, that's for sure. There's nothing to be served by it. All it would do is put lives at risk.'

Fin returned his stare. 'Yours.'

'Yes, mine.'

Fin thought about it. There was, after all, no apparent connection between Whistler's killing and the body in the plane. And yet the coincidence was troubling. Whistler had been shocked to find that body. And he must have realized that Roddy hadn't told him the whole truth, maybe even suspected that he had duped him deliberately. And that Mairead was a part of it. Fin recalled the way Whistler had looked at her at the cemetery. His voice raised in anger outside the Cabarfeidh.

At the same time, Roddy's plea for Fin's silence was not without merit. He must have known the risks of telling him the truth, but was banking on an old friend not betraying him. Mairead, clearly, did not share his faith.

Fin sighed and pushed his plate away. He still had a sense of something missing. Something obvious that was eluding him, a connection he wasn't making. 'Who else knew?' he said. 'Not about Jimbo, but about you faking your death.'

'Apart from the band?'

Fin nodded.

Roddy shook his head. 'No one.'

'Are you sure?'

'Yes.' But then he hesitated. 'Well . . . there was one other person. But someone we all trusted implicitly. And still do. I mean, he hasn't said a word in all these years.'

Fin frowned. 'Who?'

# CHAPTER TWENTY-SEVEN

## I

It was the same sun that had burned his skin in Spain, but two and a half thousand miles further north it had been reduced to a pale disc in a hazy sky and barely took the edge off a cold wind blowing down from the north-west.

The chill blast of that wind came in strong across the moor as Fin stepped off the plane at Stornoway. He hurried towards the terminal building. The Indian summer was long gone, but it was a dry, bright day, and for once rain seemed a long way off.

The journey home had passed in preoccupied thoughts about Roddy and Whistler and the body in the plane. And no matter how hard he tried to put the thought from his mind, Fin felt a powerful sense of guilt. He had known at once from Whistler's reaction that there was more to the body they had found than first appeared. And yet he had allowed the issue to drift, failed to confront it until it was too late. If he had forced it earlier, maybe Whistler would still have been alive. And that thought, he knew, would haunt him for the rest of his life.

But when all other thoughts and emotions had been exhausted, Fin was still left with one. A single name. A name that had come from the lips of a dead man in Spain, leaving Fin troubled and uncertain of how to proceed.

His Suzuki was waiting in the car park where he had left it, still wet and glistening from the last shower. He climbed in and cleared the windscreen and drove out of the airport over the hill to Oliver's Brae. Sunlight washed across Stornoway's outer harbour in the distance, glinting off the glass of the new ferry terminal. The town itself would present him with a crossroads of choices. Which was not something he had dealt with well in his life. And it wasn't until the very last moment that he made his decision, turning south out of town at the roundabout just beyond the Co-op, and setting a course for Uig.

He had forgotten all about the gala day. The return of all seventy-eight Lewis chessmen to their last resting place for just one day. Sixty-seven of the chess pieces were permanently housed in the British Museum in London, that repository of stolen artefacts from around the world. The remaining eleven were kept in Edinburgh, but still a long way from home. He remembered Whistler's exhortation the day they had met at his croft for the first time since they were teenagers. *They should be in Uig year round. A special exhibition. Not stuck in museums in Edinburgh and London. Then maybe folk would come to see them and we could generate some income here.*

Well, they were generating some income today, Fin thought. There were hundreds of cars and a string of coaches parked up at the side of the road and along the machair, and a thousand or more people on the beach, which had been turned, at low tide, into something like a fairground.

Fin pulled up short of Uig Lodge and walked across the machair to stand and look out over the sands. The wind blew, as it always did, but God was on the side of the chessmen and had brought the sun with Him. It was the oddest thing to see this normally deserted beach, on the remotest corner of the island, populated by hundreds of tourists, locals and press, all milling amongst temporary wooden stalls and pitched tents. It was like a giant Lowry canvas. There were boat trips coming and going from the far shore, and helicopter rides taking off and landing from a level area below the church at Baile na Cille. There was a giant bouncy castle crawling with shrieking children, a Noddy train. Stalls offered tombola, a coconut shy and the chance to guess the weight of the salmon. There were sheep-milking time trials and haggis-throwing. It was an extra-ordinary feat of optimism in a climate that, nine days out of ten, would have rained on the parade.

The church itself was a focus of attention. It was where the chessmen were being displayed in glass cases under tight security, and two chess masters were engaged in a battle of wits with thirty-two of the original pieces. There were crowds around the church, a constant stream of people coming and going, and a line of them snaking up from the beach.

The centrepiece of the extravaganza on the sands was a giant chessboard, each square two feet by two. Whistler's chessmen filled the board, proud Viking warriors strutting across their black-and-white battleground in synchronization with the game being played in the church, each move relayed by walkie-talkie to volunteers who moved the pieces.

Whistler would have been proud to see his carvings animated in this way, Fin thought. The confusion over their commissioning must somehow have been settled. But if Whistler hadn't been paid before, then he never would be now.

Fin returned to his jeep and drove on round to the turn-off that led to Whistler's croft. The carefully tended rectangle of land that stretched down the hill would no doubt fall into desuetude now, Whistler's efforts quickly reclaimed by a process of nature that had no respect for the ephemeral efforts of man. He drew in on the gravel outside the blackhouse and saw that the propellers of Whistler's wind turbines were continuing to generate electricity that would never be used.

There was no evidence now of the crime-scene tape that must have been stretched across the door in the immediate aftermath of Whistler's murder. The forensics experts from Scenes of Crime would have dusted for fingerprints, taken their pictures, recovered blood and fibres from the mess on the floor, and been long gone. The door was not locked, and Fin pushed it open. The still air inside had a faintly antiseptic edge to it, stuffy and damp. Furniture had been righted, the floor swept clean. The only trace that remained of the mayhem there had once been was the faint, smudged chalk outline they had drawn roughly around the body, the stain of blood where it had pooled on the floor, and the trail of it left by Whistler as he had attempted to drag himself towards the far wall.

Fin perched on the edge of the worn and battered old settee and looked around the room. He remembered his aunt's indignation at the state of the place, and her fury at finding only beer in the fridge. He recalled sitting on this very settee, still shivering after his rescue from certain death in the Tathabhal stream, drinking tea laced with Mr Macaskill's whisky. And he remembered how Whistler had hugged him on the day they had been reunited for the first time in half a lifetime. His big, whiskered face rough against Fin's, the warmth and affection in his eyes. And he felt grief well up inside him. Followed moments later by anger, and a determination to focus.

He blinked to clear his vision and examined the chalk outline on the floor. One leg trailed straight out behind, the other pulled up, the knee on a level with the waist. One of Whistler's arms lay at his side, the other stretched out beyond his head. And Fin recalled George Gunn's words the day he had slipped into his cell at the police station. *It looks like he crawled across the floor while you were still unconscious. You could see the trail of blood where he'd dragged himself over it, almost as if he was trying to reach something.*

Fin tried to picture what he might have been trying to reach. And then suddenly it came to him, and everything dropped into place, like the counters on a slot machine. He was certain then he knew who had killed Whistler. But he was still struggling with the why.

He recovered his mobile phone from his pocket and found the number he was looking for in its memory.

He heard Gunn's voice when he answered after the third ring.

'George?'

Gunn sighed. 'No more favours, Mr Macleod.'

'No favours, George. But I need you to come down to Uig, and I think I can show you who killed Whistler.'

There was a long silence. 'Why can't you just tell me?'

'Because I need to be sure first. And I need you to bring something with you.'

'What?'

'The crime scene pics of the body. Just the wide shots.'

He heard Gunn's sharp intake of breath. 'You must be joking, Mr Macleod!'

'I know you can access them George. Even if just to take photocopies.'

'You're going to get me drummed out of the force.'

Fin couldn't resist a smile. 'Thanks, George.' He hesitated. 'And there's just one other thing.' Gunn's exasperation exploded in his ear.


## II


Fin left the claustrophobia of the blackhouse to find a place to sit on the hill, looking down over the beach, while he waited for Gunn. It could be a good hour and a half.

He had lost count of the number of times he and Whistler had sat together on the hill below the house, just talking. Sometimes for hours. There had never been a shortage of words between them, but their silences had been comfortable, too.

He saw a figure drowned in red and blue waterproofs two sizes too big, climbing up the track towards him. Only a small corner of the tattoo on her neck was visible beneath the big blue collar and the hood that piled up against the back of her head. She wore wellies below the leggings, and what looked like a wetsuit beneath the waterproofs. All the studs and earrings were gone, and her face was oddly naked without them. Her eyes were shadowed, her pale face drawn and devoid of make-up.

She stopped and looked down at him where he sat. 'I was on the beach and saw you drive up to the house.' She saw how his quizzical eyes took in her waterproofs and she almost smiled. 'I promised ages ago I'd help out with the boat rides. Wasn't going to do it at first, but then I thought it might take my mind off things.' She shrugged and stared out gloomily across the distant beach. 'But all those people having a good time . . .' She turned a sad smile back on him. 'Just makes you feel worse somehow.' She hesitated. 'Okay if I sit down beside you?'

'Sure.'

And it felt strange for Whistler's little girl to be sitting next to him where Whistler had once sat.

'Why are you here?' she said.

Fin avoided meeting her eyes and rested his forearms on his knees to look over them beyond the beach, to where the tide was still on its way out and shallow white breakers burst in long, uneven lines over wet golden sand. 'I wanted to take a look for myself at where your dad was killed. I don't remember much about it. Someone just about cracked my skull moments after I found him.'

'Why? I mean, what did you think you were going to see?'

'I was a cop for a lot of years, Anna. I thought maybe, I don't know, that I might see something that the rest had missed.'

'And did you?'

He paused for just a split second before shaking his head. 'No.' Then he turned to look at her, and was shocked again by how much of her father there was in her eyes. He was momentarily discomposed, and she stared back at him candidly, searching for something in his. 'Who gave permission to use the chessmen?' he said.

'I did. Jamie Wooldridge said they were needed for the gala day.'

And Fin remembered how Jamie had denied knowing anything about them.

'He said there had been some confusion about whether or not his father had commissioned them. But that had all been cleared up, and he apologized for not paying for them before now. Told me he would pay me after the gala.' She turned away to look seaward, her jaw setting in the same stubborn way Fin had so often seen in her dad. 'But I don't want his money. I want the chessmen. I want to keep them.'

She fought to control her voice. 'My dad made them. That makes them mine now, doesn't it?' She turned her father's fiery eyes on him.

Fin nodded. 'It does.'

'Everything about them. Every curve and line and chiselled feature was made by my dad. They came from his heart and his hand, and if there's anything of him left in this world it's in those chessmen.'

Fin was startled by her unexpected eloquence, the depth of her feelings and her ability to express them. This after all was the girl who no more than a week ago had reluctantly confessed, *I fucking love my dad*, after describing him as an *arsehole*, and *a fucking embarrassment*. A girl who could barely compose a sentence without peppering it with profanities. All a carefully constructed image, he saw now. A protective shell. One that would win her respect from her peers, but at the same time keep her safe from her vulnerabilities. Shed now, along with all the piercings. He remembered Fionnlagh's description of her. *Smart kid. But brains are wasted on her*. Her father's daughter, in almost every way.

'I want to keep them for ever,' she said. 'And that way I'll always have a part of him with me.'

Fin reached out to touch her face. 'You're the biggest and best part of him there is, Anna. Make him proud of that.'

Her eyes filled up and she got quickly to her feet. 'I'd better go. They'll be needing me down there. With this weather there's bound to be a big demand for the boat rides.'

Even as she spoke, a helicopter swooped up over the dunes and flew low overhead. 'Helicopter rides, too,' Fin shouted about the roar of its rotors. He stood up, and she hesitated a moment.

'Can I talk to you sometimes, Mr Macleod? I don't want to be a nuisance or anything. But it seems like you knew him better than anyone. I'd like to get to know him a little better myself.'

'I'd like that,' Fin said. And he had a sudden urge to hold her, as if in holding her he could be close to Whistler one last time. But he didn't.

She smiled wanly. 'Thanks.' And she hurried off down the track towards the beach.

## III

Detective Sergeant George Gunn parked his car at the foot of the track that led to Whistler's blackhouse. He looked up and saw Fin sitting among the tall grasses, knees pulled up below his chin, a soft westerly blowing through his hair. The sound of distant bagpipes floated up from the beach on the wind. He began a weary trek up the hill.

Fin watched him all the way, and heard the swish, swish of his black nylon anorak before he heard his breath coming hard and fast from the effort of the climb. He had a green folder tucked under one arm, and he stopped and glowered down at Fin. Fin noticed the shine on his shoes, and the crease in his trousers. An extra-generous application of oil was helping keep his black hair in place despite the wind.

'You've gone way above and beyond the call of friendship this time, Mr Macleod. I've had to go delving into an inquiry I'm not a part of to get the things you wanted. It has been noticed and questions are being asked.'

'But you got everything?'

Gunn glared at him. 'The social work report is redundant now as far as the courts are concerned. Mr Macaskill is dead, so the case disputing custody has fallen by default. It was, however, considered relevant to the murder inquiry, and so is still part of the evidence.'

'And you got a look at it?'

'I have a copy of it right here.' He patted the green folder.

'And?'

'The social worker was recommending that the Sheriff grant custody of his daughter to John Angus Macaskill, on the basis of the girl's own wishes.'

Fin let his head drop and closed his eyes. And he wondered if his own intervention had maybe led to all of this. He took a deep breath and raised himself to his feet. 'And the crime-scene pics?'

'I have them, too.'

Fin took Gunn by the arm. 'Come inside and show me.'

He cleared a space on Whistler's table, and Gun spread out half a dozen eight-by-ten colour prints over a surface scarred and stained by decades of use. It was shocking to see Whistler lying there among the debris. His blood was lurid and unnaturally red in the glare of the police photographer's lights, his face brutally pale by comparison, the blood around his mouth and nose almost black. Such a big man reduced to nothing. All that intelligence lost in the halt of a heart-beat. The mosaic of memories that comprised his life gone for ever, as if they had never existed. Fin found himself wishing that he had Donald's faith. That there was some purpose to all this, and that it wouldn't all be lost like so many tears in rain.

He examined all the photographs carefully before picking out the third of them. 'Look George. You can see clearly in this one. The outstretched hand is almost touching the fallen chessman.'

Gunn frowned. 'Why would he have been trying to reach a wooden chessman, Mr Macleod? He was dying for Christ's sake!'

'And probably knew it. He was trying to tell us who killed him, George.'

Gunn turned a look of consternation on the younger man. 'By pointing to a chess piece?'

Fin felt sick. 'No ordinary chess piece.' He stabbed a finger at the fallen carving. 'This one here is what they call a Berserker. The fiercest of all the Viking warriors. They whipped themselves up into a trancelike state, it seems, so they felt no fear or pain. Whistler faithfully replicated all the others, but he did his own version of the Berserker.' He paused. 'In the likeness of Kenny John Maclean. His own small revenge for Kenny stealing his wife and his daughter.'

Gunn's mouth hung half open as he absorbed this. 'Are you saying Kenny John killed Whistler Macaskill?'

Fin nodded. 'I am, George.'

'Why?'

Fin sucked in a long, slow breath and tried to make sense of it himself. 'I'm guessing, but I figure Big Kenny must have found out what was in the social work report.'

'How?'

'I don't know. Maybe Anna said something. Maybe she told him what she'd told the social worker.'

'And you think Kenny John killed Whistler to stop him getting his daughter back?'

But Fin shook his head. 'No, not as a simple as that. But I think that when we found that body in the plane it gave Kenny a leverage he never dreamed he had. Something that would ruin Whistler's chances of ever getting custody of Anna. My guess is he must have confronted Whistler with it. I can't believe he ever meant to kill him. But I know Whistler. And I can only imagine how he must have reacted.' He closed his eyes and had a picture of it in his mind. Two giant men, friends since childhood, crashing about this very room, locked in desperate conflict. Furniture flying. Plates and cups and glasses smashing around them.

Gunn's voice crashed into his imagination. 'There's no proof of any of this.'

Fin opened his eyes, almost startled. 'It's only a few days since Whistler was killed, George. There must have been a terrible bloody fight in here. Kenny's still going to bear the scars and bruises of that. And there's bound to be forensic evidence in whatever the Scenes of Crime boys pulled out of here. If only your boss would stop trying to pin it on me and start looking in the right places.'

There was a long silence, then, in the still of the blackhouse. 'What leverage, Mr Macleod?'

Fin's gaze flickered towards Gunn.

'You said the discovery of the body in the plane gave Kenny John a leverage he didn't know he had.'

And Fin knew that there was no way he could keep Roddy's secret.

## IV

The drive to Suaineabhal Lodge took less than fifteen minutes, enough time for Fin to tell Gunn the potted version of the story that Roddy had told him not twenty-four hours earlier.

When they pulled up outside the lodge, Gunn turned off his motor and sat behind the wheel staring out through the windscreen beyond the trees to the ruffled surface of the loch. 'Jesus, Mr Macleod, that's one hell of a story.' He turned his head towards the younger man. 'And Roddy Mackenzie's been living all these years in Spain when the rest of the world thought he was dead?' It wasn't so much a question as a reiteration of his disbelief. 'He's going to be in big trouble now.'

Fin nodded. He was. And Fin felt a fleeting pang of guilt. But none of it was of his doing, and all of it was out of his hands now.

They walked up the path to Kenny's house and banged on the door. When there was no response Gunn opened it and stepped into the gloom of the hallway. 'Hello? Mr Maclean?' His call was greeted by silence, and after a moment he stepped back out into a freshening, blustery wind. 'Let's try the estate office.'

Jamie Wooldridge's secretary looked up, surprised to see them. Neither Jamie nor Kenny John were at the lodge, she said. Both were at the chessmen gala day at the beach. Fin was taken aback. 'What's Kenny John doing there?'

'He's driving one of the boats for the gala day, Mr Macleod.'

# CHAPTER TWENTY-EIGHT

The boats seemed to be a long way off as Fin and Gunn walked across the sand. It was firm and dry underfoot, and only faintly ridged by the underlying currents of the out-going tide. The gala day was in full flow by now, and the crowds on the beach had swelled in number. The bouncy castle swarmed with youngsters, their shouts of excitement rising above the drone of the pipes that drifted across Tràigh Uige in the wind. There was accordion music belting out from speakers at one of the stalls, and as they passed the giant chessboard, from somewhere they heard the plaintive purity of Mairead's voice rising above the throng, the wail of a violin, the moan of a Celtic flute. A Roddy Mackenzie song playing on some stall owner's sound system. His music, finally, come home.

Fin paused for a moment by the chessboard, and Gunn had taken several more strides before he noticed and stopped to look back. He followed Fin's gaze to the three-foot carved figure of the Berserker being moved from one square to another by two volunteers on instructions from the girl with the walkie-talkie. There was no mistaking the thick-lipped features of Kenny John Maclean, and the

characteristic scar that followed the line of the cheekbone. Protruding teeth bit down hard on the top of his
shield.

The two men exchanged glances, and something about
the Berserker seemed to instil a greater sense of urgency in
them. Gunn turned and lengthened his stride towards the
distant shore. Fin hurried to catch him up.

A framework of stout wooden stakes had been hammered
into the sand to provide an anchor for pontoons which had
been lashed together to create a floating jetty for the boats.
A long ramp with rope rails fed back to the sands, rising
and falling with the jetty. A wooden hut on a low-loader
was a dispensary for life jackets and waterproofs for the
long lines of people awaiting their turn for the ride out
into the bay.

Both boats were at the jetty as Gunn and Fin approached.
The on-loan Delta Deep One rigid inflatables were orange
and black, with powerful 150-horsepower four-stroke engines.
Pairs of seats fore and aft of the Delta's open cockpit carried
up to twelve passengers. One of them had just finished dis-
embarking, and patiently waiting day-trippers were making
their way cautiously along the ramp to climb aboard the
other.

Fin scanned the faces at the jetty for some sign of Kenny
John. Then suddenly the big man stood up in the cockpit
of the inflatable which had just shed its passengers. He
turned almost at the same moment, and saw Fin and Gunn
heading purposefully in his direction. For a moment his
face was a blank, hiding a multitude of confused thoughts.

But as his thoughts cleared, so his face took on expression, and Fin saw the panic in his eyes.

He turned in an instant and gunned his idling motor, sending the Deep One surging away from the jetty, nose up. A small waterproof-clad figure who had been standing in the bow coiling a tethering rope fell backwards into the boat with a scream. Fin caught just a flash of her pale, startled face.

'Jesus, George! Anna Bheag's in that boat!' He ran along the ramp, pushing passengers aside, shouting at them to get out of his way. Those already aboard the second boat turned, alarmed by the raised voices. 'Get out! Get out of the boat!' Fin bawled at them.

Gunn was right behind him, waving his warrant card above his head. 'Police. Please evacuate the boat immediately.'

Frightened faces jostled in the crush to scramble back on to the jetty, and the inflatable rocked dangerously. The driver turned towards Fin as he jumped aboard. He was a man Fin knew. An older man, a worker on the estate known as Donnie Dubh. Fin saw the consternation in his eyes, his face drained suddenly of colour. 'What the hell's going on, Fin?'

'Donnie, we need you to go after Big Kenny. We think he killed Whistler Macaskill.'

'Jesus!'

'And he's got wee Anna on that boat with him.'

Gunn jumped down beside him. 'Just go, for Christ's sake!'

Donnie scrambled across the boat to untie the tethering ropes, then swung himself back into the cockpit to rev the

Yamaha engine and accelerate out into the bay after Kenny.

The wind threw salt spray back in their faces as the bow of the inflatable smacked up and down on the unforgiving surface of the incoming swell. Gunn crouched down behind the shelter of the tiny windscreen, one finger in his ear, as he shouted into his mobile phone. Fin couldn't make out what he was saying, but he could only be calling for help. He glanced back towards the shore, and saw the vast expanse of beach stretching away towards Uig Lodge on the rise, the excited shout of distant gala day revellers lost above the roar of the engine as they abandoned stalls and train rides and chessmen to come running towards the water's edge.

He stood beside Donnie, holding on to the black tubular superstructure above the cockpit, and tried to see through the spray and mist in the direction that Kenny had taken his boat. He caught only flashes of orange through the spume and surge of the waves. The wind whipped at his hair and his clothes, the noise of it deafening him, seawater soaking him. And he suddenly felt vulnerable without a life jacket, clutching black tubing with quickly numbing fingers as the boat pitched and rolled with increasingly violent frequency.

George Gunn still squatted on the floor, his back to the engine cowling now, his phone returned to his pocket and his face the colour of ash. He glanced up at Fin with troubled dark eyes that he quickly closed, taking long, deep gulps of air, and Fin wondered how long he was going to last without throwing up.

The shore lifted up in black jagged layers on either side as they sped out across Uig bay, the tiny islands of Tom and Tolm and Triassamol passing in a dark-grey blur. Once out of the shelter of the bay itself the swell increased, an almost translucent emerald green lifting them out of deep troughs through breaking, bubbling foam, to drop them just as suddenly into the next. It felt as if they were being swallowed whole by the sea, then spat out again. Fin wondered how much of this the Delta could take as they swung north, Kenny's boat a good five hundred yards ahead of them and barely visible.

They hugged a coastline that rose sheer out of the water now. The tide had turned and was breaking angrily over black gneiss in a frothing fury, driven in by wind increasing in strength and chill. Fin felt the cold seeping into his bones, and began to wonder if there was any point in this. If it had been Kenny on his own, perhaps not. He would have come ashore somewhere and was bound to have been picked up. But he had Anna with him, and in his present state of mind it was impossible to predict what he might do.

'We're not getting any closer,' Fin shouted above the roar of the motor.

'I can't go any faster than he is,' Donnie shouted back. It was a constant battle for him just to keep the boat from being driven against the rocks as waves slammed into them side on and threatened to tip them over. Fin cast his eyes towards the cliffs and the deep fissures that cracked them open, seawater boiling all around the reefs at each entrance, throwing spray thirty feet and more into the air.

It was fully twenty minutes before they reached the tip of the peninsula at Gallan Head where for a moment they were fully exposed to the anger of the incoming ocean. Kenny's boat had vanished two minutes ahead of them. A distraught George Gunn crawled on his hands and knees to the back of the boat, where he saw his vomit whipped away on the wind.

But once they had rounded the headland they were sheltered from the wind, and the ocean calmed to a deep, steady swell. The water was impenetrably green, and there was no sign of Kenny's boat.

Fin frowned and peered along the line of the shore ahead of them. In the very far distance he could see a stretch of empty beach, and off to their left, beyond the next headland, the islands of Pabaigh Beag and Pabaigh Mór lifting themselves in a rise of glistening blue cliffs out of the heaving waters of An Caolas.

'Where the hell are they?'

Donnie eased off on the throttle, and they reduced speed to a gentle cruise. 'There are inlets and caves all along the coastline here, Fin. He could be anywhere.'

Gunn stumbled unsteadily back to the cockpit. He was the same colour as the sea. 'The helicopter's on its way,' he said. 'They might be able to spot him.'

For the next ten minutes they cruised slowly along the ragged line of high cliffs that cast their shadow on the water. They could hear the sea sucking and growling as it snapped around the rocky openings to caves and chasms. Fin looked up as he heard the rotors of the helicopter, which just half an hour before had been taking joyriders on flights over the mountains. Gunn's phone rang and he pressed it to his ear. He nodded and his eyes flashed towards Fin.

'They can see his wake. It seems to disappear right into the cliffs. He's either gone down or he's gone into a cave.'

'How much further on?' Donnie called over his shoulder.

'About half a kilometre, they say.'

Donnie accelerated forward then, and they picked up speed over the next several hundred yards, their bow rising into the waves, sending yet more spray back in their faces. Fin was shivering almost uncontrollably now.

'There,' Donnie said, and they slowed again. Fin saw the pale wash left by the wake of Kenny John's boat, clearly visible in the deep, dark green. It turned in towards stacks of rock rising out of swirling froth, and they saw the treacherous teeth of granite and gneiss that would rip their inflatable open if they were to deviate even fractionally from the course that Kenny had taken before them. Either he knew these waters like the back of his hand, or he was being driven by God knew what emotional turbulence into taking insane risks.

Donnie slowed to one or two knots. They drifted gently forward between the rocks into a deep natural arch that curved darkly over their heads. It had been chiselled by the elements out of the oldest rock on the planet over millions of years, and daylight reflected off every salt-soaked face of it. Now, in the shelter of the cliffs, the wind dropped to a murmur and the sound of the Yamaha engine clattered back at them off the walls of the tunnel. The helicopter overhead vanished from sight and the sound of its rotors was lost. The water sighed and sloshed and echoed around them, until they emerged into a tiny bay, completely encircled by cliffs, rock white-streaked with guano. The roar of the rotors returned, reverberating off every hard surface of the confined space. Gulls turned and screamed above their heads, scattering in the downdraught.

Fin turned to Gunn. 'For God's sake, George, tell them to stand off. We can't hear a thing.'

Gunn barked into his phone and the chopper wheeled away out of sight. An eerie silence fell. Only the sea whispered to them in the gloom, beneath the dull, repetitive idle of their motor.

The pale wake of Kenny's boat crossed the short stretch of enclosed water and vanished into a deep cleft in the cliff face. Sharply cut seams of vividly coloured rock folded themselves over the entrance to what appeared to be a cave. Layers of lucent blue and yellow, orange, green and red. Foam gathered in an eddying circle at its entrance, and deep inside the darkness of the cave itself the sea moaned like some distressed sea mammal.

Donnie inched them forward, daylight fading behind them, the way ahead obscure and uncertain.

'Cut the motor,' Fin said, and in the silence that followed they could hear the idling of Kenny's engine somewhere further on, and the shrill sound of querulous voices echoing around the dark of this naturally vaulted cathedral cave.

Fin reached above his head and found one of several spot-lights bolted to the crossbar. He fumbled for a switch to turn it on, and suddenly the cave was flooded with light, the colours of the rock startling and lurid.

Kenny's Delta rose and fell on the gentle interior swell about thirty feet deeper into the cave. He and Anna were standing up in the bow of the boat arguing, her voice rising higher than his in anger and confusion. Both turned wide eyes towards the light, then screwed them up in the glare of it. Kenny raised an open palm to cast a shadow across his face, like someone caught unawares by the flash of a camera. In the darkness, it was a face burned out by the light. Mouth, nostrils and eyes black holes configured only to convey his fear.

'What the hell's going on?' It was Anna Bheag's voice that echoed around the cave.

Fin ignored her and focused everything on Kenny. He called out to him from the dark behind the light. 'This is madness, Kenny. Give it up.'

Kenny stared back like a startled deer caught in the head-lights of a car. 'I can't, Fin. I can't.'

Fin saw spittle accumulating at the corners of his mouth. 'Roddy told me what happened the night he ditched the plane, Kenny. That you stumbled on them up in the moun-tains. What were you doing up there?'

Kenny was breathing hard. He shook his head. 'I was still at agricultural college that year. I spent my summers working for the estate as a watcher.'

'You thought they were poachers?'

'I had no idea. I was coming up the valley when I heard the plane. And then saw it coming in, far too low, before it disappeared from sight, and I thought it must have crashed. By the time I got over the shoulder of the hill and into the next valley, it was in the middle of the loch and sinking fast. But still in one piece. That's when I saw Roddy and Whistler on the far shore.'

'How in God's name did you and Whistler keep that secret for all these years, Kenny?'

'It's what bound us, Fin. A bond stronger than marriage break-ups or custody battles.'

'But in the end it was a bond you broke. They swore you to secrecy, Kenny.' It came like a bullet out of the dark. An accusation of betrayal.

Kenny retaliated. 'They lied. They never told me there was a body in the plane.'

Fin shook his head. 'Whistler never knew. That was Roddy's dark secret. Whistler didn't know anything about it until he and I found the plane the other day. He was shocked, Kenny. Shocked to the core.'

Kenny appeared agitated by this. But whatever thoughts were going through his mind, no words came to his lips.

Fin said, 'What happened the morning you went to see him, Kenny? What did you do? Threaten to shop him unless he dropped his claim on Anna?'

A strange feral sound, like an animal in pain, issued from Kenny's mouth. He closed his eyes then opened them wide, raising them to the darkness above, before lowering them once more to gaze back at Fin. 'I love that girl with my life, Fin. I see her mother in her every time I look at her.' Just as Fin saw only Whistler. 'I thought if I threatened to tell the police what I knew about the plane Whistler would give up on the court case. I mean, it wasn't Roddy in that cockpit, and I knew it. So if Whistler really had been involved in the death of the guy you found he'd have lost Anna for ever.' He paused, still breathing hard. 'But I never would have told, Fin. I wouldn't. I thought the threat of it would be enough. But he went berserk.' The use of the word was not lost on Fin. If anyone fitted the role of Berserker, then it was Whistler. A man who had lived his life on a short fuse, with a temper that took him over the edge, time and again, negating any intelligent thought he had ever formed. 'He came at me like a maniac, Fin. I never expected that. Jesus Christ, I never meant to kill him. It was all I could do to stop him from killing me.'

'For God's sake, Kenny. You were threatening to take his daughter away from him. Couldn't you imagine how he would take it?' Fin felt sick. It was clear to him now that in a strange and unforgiving twist of fate, Whistler had sown the seeds of his own destruction by agreeing to help Roddy with his subterfuge seventeen years before. And it was Kenny's threat to break the bond of silence the three old friends had kept all that time which had killed him.

Kenny raised his hands helplessly and shook his head, the tears on his face glistening in the spotlight. And he said again, 'I never meant to kill him.' As if somehow by repeating it he could change what had happened.

The scream that reverberated around the cave turned Fin's blood to ice. He had no time even to open his mouth to shout 'No!', before he saw the light glinting off the curve of the boathook, as wee Anna swung it two-handed in an arc of fury, to bury it deep in Kenny John's chest.

# CHAPTER TWENTY-NINE

## I

The Free Church of Scotland in Kenneth Street in Stornoway, was a large, joyless, pink-harled edifice, its bell tower crowned by four miniature spires, each with its own weather vane. The weather as a topic on the Isle of Lewis was always high on the agenda.

A notice at the gate announced English services on the Sabbath at 11 a.m. and 6.30 p.m., with services in Gaelic being held at the same times at the seminary in Francis Street. Services in rural churches on the island would normally be held in Gaelic, but in Stornoway Gaelic speakers were in the minority.

The church hall ran along the right-hand side of the church itself, a building of recent vintage, with windows set high up in the walls to cast as much of God's light as possible into its gloomy interior.

It was here that a quorum of twelve members of the Judicial Committee appointed by the Church's general assembly gathered on a bleak wet Wednesday in October to hear the evidence against the Reverend Donald Murray. A large chestnut tree in front of the hall had shed most of its leaves on the lawn, as if announcing once and for all the end of summer. The portent was not good.

Every inch of the car park was taken up by wet, shining vehicles, and cars were parked on solid single and double yellow lines up either side of Kenneth Street, a special dispensation for the day, with traffic wardens controlling entry at each end of the street. This was theatre of a kind never before seen on the island, the playing out of a human drama that the Church itself would have frowned upon had it come from the pen of a playwright and been performed by actors.

But there was nothing pretend about these proceedings. A man's future was at stake. Despite the procurator fiscal's decision not to pursue a criminal prosecution, a private libel had been lodged with the Presbytery by a group of Donald Murray's own elders. They had accused him in a minuted and signed statement of committing an offence contrary to the Word of God and the laws of the Church. Following an investigation of the complaint, the Presbytery had passed it to the Judicial Committee for a trial of the evidence, with the recommendation that if the Reverend Murray be found guilty, he be summarily dismissed from his post as minister of the Crobost Free Church.

Fin had decided to park at South Beach and walk up, even though it was raining. He was anxious to get away as quickly as possible at the finish of proceedings, and that would be achieved faster on foot. He and Marsaili shared an umbrella on the walk up past the gallery and theatre at An Lanntair, and saw the crowds standing below a shiny

assembly of multicoloured umbrellas on the pavement
outside the church at the top of the hill. Residents leaned
on open windows above the barber's shop and the religious
bookshop opposite, to get a view of the circus. The Church
court had been receiving much coverage in both local and
national press, and the media had set up camp outside the
church, satellite vans in the car park, photographers and
camera operators and reporters milling among the crowd.

Although Marsaili held Fin's arm, there was a distance
between them. His trip to Spain and subsequent events had
opened up a fissure in their relationship, acknowledged for
the first time after months of papering it over. Neither,
perhaps, had been willing to admit that for all their shared
past, their future remained an unknown quantity in which
the possible admission of failure cast the biggest shadow.
As they walked up the street, two souls a world apart, Fin
wished he could just raise a hand and call a halt. And start
all over again. From the beginning. From that first day at
school when the little girl with the pigtails and blue ribbons
had smiled at him and told the teacher that she would
translate for the boy who could only speak Gaelic.

It was just days now since they had put Whistler in the
ground. By some miracle, Kenny John had survived the boat
hook, most of its length absorbed by his life jacket. But he
still lay gravely ill in a hospital bed. Of the three of them
who had gone out that day so many years before to the
monument at Holm Point, and discovered a common
history in the *Iolaire* disaster, one was dead, and another
charged with his murder. Anna was being held in a young

offenders' institution on the mainland while the authorities decided on how best to proceed with the case of a child who had attempted to kill her father's murderer.

And Fin wondered how such a loss of innocence and life was possible.

Amran, once Sòlas, the band which had provided the musical accompaniment to his teenage years, was riven by infighting and legal action, falling apart in the full glare of international publicity. The papers and TV news bulletins had been filled for days with the story of Roddy faking his own death, and being still alive seventeen years on. Extradition from Spain was being sought on possible murder charges. It was only a matter of time before a European warrant was issued for his arrest.

And now it was Donald's turn to face his moment of truth. Marsaili had come, not to keep Fin company, but to offer moral support to Donald and give evidence on his behalf. He was, after all, the boy who had taken her virginity when they were still teenagers. And Fin could only remember now how relieved he had been that it wasn't Artair.

The rows of seats laid out behind them in the hall were all filled. Fin, George Gunn, Donald's accusers and other witnesses sat along the front row behind tables that accommodated lawyers for the Church on the left, and the solitary figure of Donald Murray on the right.

Facing the assembled were the twelve members of the Judicial Committee, seated at a long table, like Jesus and the disciples at the last supper. Only these men wore dark suits and suitably sombre faces, come to pass judgment on one of their own, a task that clearly weighed heavy upon their shoulders. At least half of them were fellow ministers. The atmosphere was tense, the sense of expectation electric. The chairman banged his gavel to elicit silence in the hall, and a clerk, who was also in charge of recording proceedings, rose to read out the libel. He was a small man, almost completely bald, and Fin found himself transfixed by the shiny wet purple of his lips. He barely listened to the accusation that, as dusk fell over the island of Eriskay on a spring evening earlier that year, the Reverend Donald Murray had taken the life of another man by firing a single barrel of his shotgun into the man's chest. Which was in clear and unequivocal contravention of the sixth commandment given by God to Moses on Mount Sinai. Thou Shalt Not Kill. A commandment enshrined in the laws of the Church.

The chairman swivelled his head towards Donald. He was an older man, very possibly in his sixties, with abundant steel-grey hair brushed back from his forehead in crimps and waves. He had lugubrious, watery-brown eyes that seemed to convey, if not sympathy, then neutrality. 'You are entitled to make an opening statement in your defence, Reverend Murray.'

Donald rose to his feet. He wore a light-grey suit over his black cotton shirt and white clerical collar, and placed the fingertips of both hands on the desk in front of him, as if requiring to steady himself. The colour of his skin was the same as his suit, and like putty in tone and texture. His hair had lost its sandy sheen. Most of those in the hall heard his voice ring out clear and strong. But Fin knew him better than most and detected the tremor in it. 'I have nothing to say in my defence, sir. The facts are known and speak for themselves. You will arrive at whatever decision you reach here today on the basis of the evidence that is presented to you. And I will accept without question that decision. But I will not be judged except by the Lord my God.'

'And judged by the Lord you will be, Reverend Murray, as we all will. And that shall be between you and Him. We are here today to determine whether or not you have broken His laws and by doing so brought His Church into disrepute. And that, I can assure you, is a judgment we fully intend to make.'

The hearing took place over two days. Much of the evidence presented on the first day involved statements from the elders who had brought the initial libel against their minister. A string of grey men, resolute in their unforgiving faith, arguing the sanctity of the Ten Commandments, and Donald's unworthiness to lead their congregation. Long legal and doctrinaire arguments that sapped the energy of all present.

It wasn't until the second day that the facts of the case came under scrutiny. The most important witness in that context was Detective Sergeant George Gunn. Fin watched as he walked to the front of the hall and took his place behind the table reserved for witnesses. In a long career in the force he would have given evidence at countless trials on the island, and on the mainland. He was an experienced police officer. But Fin had never seen him so nervous. The clerk addressed him directly.

'State your name for the record, please.'

'George William Gunn.'

'Do you give a solemn assurance that you will speak the truth, that you have no malicious motive in giving evidence here today, and are not knowingly biased in any way?'

'I do.'

The chairman nodded towards counsel for the Church, a retired advocate from Edinburgh. 'Mr Kelso?'

Kelso stood up from behind his desk at the front of the hall. He was a small, round man in a dark suit, with the last remnants of dyed black hair dragged across a square, flat head. Fin could picture him with his wig and gown in the Edinburgh courts arguing his case with all the confidence that more than thirty years of legal experience instils. But today he had none of the accoutrements of his former profession to hide behind, and the Bible was not an Act of Parliament with an arguably definitive interpretation. It was a loose collection of stories and anecdotes which had spawned any number of religious sects, each drawing its own inferences and applying its own constructions.

'You are a Detective Sergeant in the Criminal Investigation Department of the Stornoway police, is that correct?'

'Yes, sir.'

'You were called to the scene of a shooting on the island of Eriskay in the spring of this year.'

'I was.'

'Which is some hours away from Stornoway by road. How did you get there?'

'I enlisted the help of the coastguard, sir, and myself and several uniformed officers were flown down by helicopter to assist the local police.'

'And when you got there what did you find?'

'A man was lying dead on the floor in the living room of the house. He had been shot in the chest. A second man had been detained by citizens present in the house, and later arrested by police officers from South Uist.'

'I understand, Detective Sergeant, that you took statements from everyone present, some of whom are unable or unwilling to be here today. On the basis of those statements, I would ask you to present the Judicial Committee with as clear a picture as you can of the events which led up to the shooting.'

Gunn took a deep breath. 'The situation arose from what appears to have been a case of revenge, sir, for an act or acts which may or may not have taken place more than fifty years ago. We are unable to verify that. What is clear is that a well-known gang leader from the city of Edinburgh arrived on the Isle of Lewis earlier that day, with a colleague, intent on doing harm to a Niseach called Tormod Macdonald. A Niseach . . . that's someone from Ness, sir.'

Kelso nodded.

'Mr Macdonald is an elderly man suffering from an advanced form of senile dementia. His family had taken him to the home of an old friend in Eriskay that morning. On discovering that Mr Macdonald was not at home, the gentlemen from Edinburgh kidnapped Mr Macdonald's great-granddaughter and her mother, and took them to Eriskay, where they intended to shoot them in front of Mr Macdonald.'

'With all due respect, Detective Sergeant, I don't believe you can speak for the intent of the deceased. I would be obliged if you would stick to the facts as you know them.'

Fin saw Gunn bristling. 'With equally due respect, Mr Kelso, the shooting of Mr Macdonald's great-granddaughter and her mother was the stated intent of the deceased, an intention declared in the presence of several witnesses from whom I took statements. And those are the facts as I know them.'

If Kelso was surprised by Gunn's rejoinder he gave no indication of it. But being on the wrong end of a rebuttal by what he probably regarded as a hick island policeman must have been more than a little humiliating. Fin found himself stifling a smile. Kelso consulted some papers on his desk. 'Let's turn to the statement you took from Mr Macdonald's grandson, and father of the baby. One Fionnlagh Macinnes. From all accounts, the gentlemen from Edinburgh left him tied up at his home in Ness while they drove down to Eriskay. And yet, he was with the Reverend Murray at the time of the shooting. How did that come about?'

Gunn cleared his throat. 'According to Fionnlagh Macinnes, he managed to free himself and make his way to the Reverend Murray's house to break the news to him about what had happened.'

'Why did he go to the Reverend Murray and not the police?'

'Because the baby's mother, Donna, was the Reverend Murray's daughter.'

'So the Reverend Murray went to the police?'

'No, sir.'

'What did he do?'

'He took a shotgun and a box of cartridges from their lock-safe place in the manse, and drove to Eriskay.'

'With Fionnlagh Macinnes?'

'Yes, sir.'

'Why didn't he call the police?'

'You'd have to ask him that, sir.'

Kelso sighed his irritation. 'Why do you *think* he didn't call the police?'

'With all due respect, sir, I don't believe I can speak for the accused. I would rather stick to the facts as I know them.'

Kelso contained his annoyance with difficulty. 'You took a statement from the Reverend Murray?'

'I did.'

'And why did he *say* he didn't call the police?'

Gunn hesitated. There was no way to avoid it. 'He said he didn't trust inexperienced and unarmed police officers in South Uist to deal with armed criminals intent on harming his daughter and granddaughter.'

'In other words he took the law into his own hands.'

'I'm not sure I would say that, sir.'

'He failed to report the commissioning of a crime, and undertook to deal with it himself. Was that not taking the law into his own hands?'

Gunn shifted uncomfortably. 'I suppose it was.'

Kelso acknowledged the admission with a sarcastic little smile. 'Thank you, Detective Sergeant.' He perched half-moon spectacles on the end of his nose and shuffled through more papers on his desk, then removed them with a flourish. 'It would be fair to assume, then, that having failed to inform the police, and having armed himself with a shotgun, he must have been prepared to use it.'

'You might make that assumption, Mr Kelso. It's my understanding that the Reverend Murray and Fionnlagh Macinnes made several attempts to reach Mr Macdonald's daughter, Marsaili, by mobile phone in order to warn her that the Edinburgh gang members were on their way.'

'Yes, but even had he managed to warn them, that would not have altered the fact that his daughter and granddaughter had been kidnapped by dangerous criminals. And he had armed himself and taken off in pursuit of them. It is unlikely that his intention was to read them a passage from the Bible.'

Which elicited some laughter from around the hall.

The chairman of the Judicial Committee, however, was not amused. He leaned across the table. 'I do not believe, Mr Kelso, that this is an occasion for levity.'

Kelso made a tiny bow of his head. 'My apologies, Mr Chairman.' He turned towards Gunn. 'Thank you, Detective Sergeant, that will be all.'

Gunn was shocked. 'Don't you want to hear about what happened at the house?'

'We'll hear that from those who were there. Thank you.'

Gunn glanced apologetically towards Donald Murray as he went to retake his seat, but Donald was impassive.

It was Marsaili who was called to the witness desk to give evidence about what happened at the house itself. Fin watched her as she spoke in a strong confident voice, recounting the events he had lived through himself. There was a sad, pale beauty about her still. There was only a touch of make-up on her clear-complexioned face, her hair drawn back and tied in a ponytail, but still he could see the little girl in her. The little girl he had loved with all his heart when he couldn't even have told you what love was. The little girl whose heart he broke, not once, but twice. The little girl whose love for him never wavered until his final act of betrayal. Was it any wonder they'd had such difficulty finding their way back to who they had once been?

Her story of what happened that night was compelling. The Edinburgh gangland boss raising his shotgun to unleash a blast of it at Donna and the baby. His revenge for some history between himself and Marsaili's father. But glass shattering through the room instead, as Donald fired at him through the window, sending the big man slamming back against the far window, and saving a young mother and her child from certain death. The people of Lewis crammed into the hall that day held their collective breath as she spoke.

Fin was barely aware of her reaching the conclusion of her evidence, or of his name being called out. It was only when Marsaili sat down again beside him and whispered, 'You're on,' that he realized it was his turn.

He took his place behind the witness desk and gave his solemn assurance to tell the truth without malice or prejudice.

Kelso regarded him speculatively. 'You were a police officer yourself, Mr Macleod?'

'I was.'

'For how long?'

'About fifteen years.'

'And what rank did you attain?'

'Detective Inspector.'

'So you have some considerable experience of crime and criminals.'

'I do.'

'And is there any circumstance in which you would recommend that people take the law into their own hands?'

'I think, perhaps, you have a basic misunderstanding of the law, Mr Kelso.'

'Oh, do I?' Kelso seemed amused. 'I practised the law for more than thirty years, Mr Macleod.'

'And I'm sure practice makes perfect, Mr Kelso. But it wasn't just your law. And it's not just mine. The law belongs to all of us. We elect representatives to make the law on our behalf, and we employ policemen to enforce it. And when they're not around to do that for us, sometimes we have to do it ourselves. That's why we have such a thing as a citizen's arrest. And if we arm a policeman and give him permission to shoot a criminal in our stead, that's taking the law into our own hands, too. We're just doing it by proxy.'

'So you believe that the Reverend Murray was correct in taking the action he did?'

'Not only do I believe he was right, I hope I would have had the courage to do the same thing myself.'

'You don't believe that the outcome would have been different had the Reverend Murray called the police?'

'Oh yes, sir, the outcome would have been very different. Donna Murray and her baby would be dead, as would probably everyone else in the house that night. As it is, only one man died. A man whose stated intention was to murder an innocent girl and her child.'

Kelso snorted derisively. 'How can you say that?'

'Because I was there and you were not. And with the experience of a police officer of some fifteen years' standing I can say without equivocation that the local police, unarmed and inexperienced as they were, could never have dealt with the situation.'

Kelso gave him a long, cold look, then slipped on his half-moons and lowered his eyes to the sheet of paper he held in his hand. 'Well, let's just return in detail to the events of that night.'

'No.' Fin shook his head. 'I think we've heard more than enough about that.'

Kelso's head jerked up in surprise.

Fin said, 'I sat here all day yesterday listening to a bunch of Holy Willies pour out bile in the guise of piety.' There was a shocked murmur of astonishment among the crowd as Fin ran his eyes among them, searching. Then suddenly he pointed. 'There. Torquil Morrison. Used to get drunk and beat up his wife. Until he found God. Or God found him. Now butter wouldn't melt in his mouth.' As gasps rose from the auditorium, he swung his finger across the sea of faces. 'And there. Angus Smith. I can think of at least two illegitimate kids that he won't acknowledge. I bet he wouldn't have had the courage to kill a man to save either of *their* lives. I don't know about the Reverend Murray's other accusers, but I'd say this. He among you who is without sin, let him cast the first stone.'

The chairman of the Judicial Committee banged his gavel, his face flushed with anger and embarrassment. 'That's quite enough, Mr Macleod!'

'I'm not finished,' Fin said. 'I'm here on my terms, not yours. I'm here because a good man did the only thing he could in impossible circumstances. Doing nothing wasn't an option. Doing nothing would have meant the loss of innocent lives. Doing what he did saved those lives at the expense of one that, frankly, wasn't worth a damn. And I don't buy into all this sixth commandment crap. Thou Shalt Not Kill? No. Unless you happen to be German in World Wars I and II, or Iraqi in the Gulf War. Then it's OK, because it's . . . *justified*. I didn't know there was a rider to the sixth commandment, Mr Chairman. Thou Shalt Not Kill – unless it's *justified*.'

Fin raised his head a little and sniffed the air.

'I smell something familiar.' He sniffed again. 'I know what it is. I've smelled it before. It's hypocrisy. It's a rank smell, and there should be no place for it here.' He swung around towards Donald, and was almost shocked to see his eyes filling up. Fin nearly choked on his own emotions before finally finding his voice. 'Your God will judge you, Donald. And if He's half the God you think He is, then He probably helped you pull the trigger.'

A hush fell over the crowd outside the hall as Fin exited with Marsaili on his arm. They parted silently, opening up a passage towards the gate for the departing couple. It wasn't until they were halfway down Kenneth Street that Marsaili squeezed Fin's arm and turned her cornflower-blue eyes on him, just as she had done that first day at school. 'Proud of you,' she said.

## II

The Judicial Committee delivered its verdict on the third day. It was standing room only in the hall, and there were hundreds more out in the street. Donald sat cool and dispassionate at his table, hands folded one inside the other in front of him. And only once, before the members of the Judicial Committee filed in to take their seats, did he turn around to scan the faces in the crowd behind him. It was a look not missed by Fin. He turned to Marsaili, an eyebrow raised in query. She shrugged. 'Still no sign of her.'

The one person conspicuous by her absence throughout the hearing had been Donald's wife, Catriona. Fin's heart ached for him. Whatever the verdict, his wife and mother of his child would not be there to offer comfort or share in his joy. Donald presented a lonely figure at the front of the hall.

Silence settled like down after a duck fight as the members of the Judicial Committee drew in chairs behind their long desk. It was impossible to tell from the row of grave faces they presented what decision it was they might have reached.

Proceedings opened, as they had each day, with a prayer. Then the Chairman looked towards Donald. 'Would you be upstanding, please, Reverend Murray?'

Donald stood and faced his future.

'This was an extremely difficult decision for the committee. We have been, as you were yourself, faced with a complex web of moral decision-making. And while we have had the advantage of time to make a considered decision, we appreciate that you did not. One could almost imagine that God had set a test for you, Reverend Murray, as He has done for us. Damned if you do, damned if you don't. In the end, whatever the moral and religious arguments, we could only, each of us, ask ourselves in all humanity what we would have done in the same circumstance, and measure our actions against the expectations of the Lord our God. And, in the end, truly, only He can make that judgment.'

He took a long breath, briefly examining his hands on the table in front of him. When he raised his eyes again the silence was absolute.

'However, we have been charged with reaching a decision. And so on that basis, we have decided not to uphold the libel against you. You are free to continue your ministry at Crobost for as long as your congregation wants you there.'

The roar that went up from the crowd, and the subsequent applause, was almost deafening. No doubting where the sentiments of the public lay. There was a rush to congratulate Donald, and among the many who shook his hand in the aftermath of the verdict were those who had earlier been afraid publicly to take his side. Donald himself appeared bewildered, lost among a sea of faces, a confusion of voices. The Chairman's announcement that a full and detailed written account of the verdict would be published within two weeks was lost in the melee.

Fin and Marsaili waited outside in the crowd for Donald to emerge from the hall. When he did he looked pale and shaken. He had no coat but seemed impervious to the rain that fell on him from a leaden sky. He was jostled by supporters and reporters, and TV lights cast an unreal light upon the frantic scene in the car park.

He fell before anyone heard the shot. Because of his black shirt, the blood where the bullet had entered his chest was not immediately apparent. At first the crowd thought he had simply stumbled and fallen. But Fin recognized the crack that followed immediately as the report of a rifle.

As others rushed towards Donald, he turned in the direction of the skyline opposite, and saw the silhouette of a man, and the barrel of his rifle, as he vanished from view among the rooftops.

Then screams rose into the wet morning air as Donald's blood oozed across the tarmac, and the crowd scattered in panic. Fin and Marsaili were the first to reach him, crouching down to assess the damage. His eyes were wide, staring up at them in fear and confusion. His whole body was trembling. Marsaili put her hand beneath his head to raise it from the wet. Fin bellowed, 'Get an ambulance! Fast!' He stripped off his jacket to lay it over Donald's chest and shoulders. And he remembered that day when they were just boys, and Donald had returned in the dark to drag him off to safety when bullies had left him bleeding in the road. And the time they had taken Fin's aunt for the drive of her life in an open-topped car, just months before she died. He felt Donald's hand clutch his arm. His voice was a whisper.

'I think God just delivered His own verdict, Fin. Looks like I'm going to have a lot to answer for.'

A tiny cough brought blood bubbling to his lips, and he was gone.

# EPILOGUE

Sunlight spilled across the green slopes of Salisbury Crags, sweeping up to the cliffs that swooped high above the Edinburgh skyline. Fin's taxi turned into St Leonard's Street and dropped him outside No. 14, the sand-coloured brick building that housed the city's A Division police station.

There was something more than faintly surreal about being here again. Like dropping in on a past life to discover that everything which had once been so familiar was alien now. Smaller, meaner, dirtier. Not like you remembered it at all. St Leonard's Lane felt narrower, squeezed in by the sand-blasted tenements on either side, and the Crags beyond it smaller somehow, less impressive.

It was a week since Donald's interment, the longest funeral procession in Crobost that anyone could remember. A funeral that had received coverage on the national news. Coverage which had already passed into archive, along with the police search for his killer. Fin doubted he would ever be caught. It had been a professional hit. Revenge, almost certainly, for the killing in Eriskay. The shooter had vanished without trace, the weapon never recovered. All that was left for Fin in its aftermath was a feeling of emptiness, if it could be described as a feeling at all.

Mona was standing waiting for him outside the tall glass facade of the entrance. By contrast she looked younger. Perhaps life without Fin had been good for her. She wore a long fawn coat, and a new, shorter haircut suited her. Like a return to her youth. It showed off her still strong features. Not exactly pretty, but in some ways almost beautiful. He felt a pang of regret as he greeted her, taking her gloved hand in his and kissing her cheek.

She canted her head. 'Do you know what this is about?'

'Robbie, I imagine. I can't think why else they would want us both here.'

DCI Black's call had been short and pointed. He didn't want to do this by phone or by letter, he said. Would it be possible for Fin and Mona to meet him in person?

Black's face had the pasty complexion of a man who rarely saw daylight. The curve of his nose and his small black eyes gave him the appearance of a hawk always on the hunt for prey. His desk was a mess, and Fin smelled stale cigarette smoke on his clothes, and saw that his fingers were still nicotine yellow. He was a man of little ceremony. Beyond the briefest of acknowledgements he lifted a clear plastic folder with a crumpled handwritten note pressed between its leaves. He held it out to the couple on the other side of his desk, and Fin took it from him. He turned it towards the light so that he and Mona could both read it. Scrawled words in blue ink.

*This has been on my mind for some time. I know most people will not understand why, especially those who love me, and whom I also love. All I can say is that no one knows the hell I have lived through. And these last weeks it has become, simply, unbearable. It is time for me to go. I am so sorry.*

Fin raised his eyes towards Black for elucidation.

'It took some weeks for that note to make its way to the officers investigating your son's hit-and-run. Connections were not immediately apparent. It was a collection of tormented ramblings in his diary that led officers finally to a link with Robbie.'

Mona's face was flushed. 'This is the man who killed Robbie?'

Black nodded. 'If it's any consolation, it would appear that really his life ended that day, too. And when he couldn't live with himself any longer, he fed a tube from the exhaust pipe of his car into its interior and turned on the engine.'

Fin shook his head. 'No,' he said. 'It's no consolation.' He glanced at Mona. 'But at least it's over.'

Mona's taxi stood belching fumes into the chill November air. They had parted before, but this time it was harder, because it seemed certain to be the last. And Fin thought how difficult it was to let go of such a big part of his life. He remembered the moment she had dropped into his lap at the party the night they met, and seeing her face leaning over him the next morning as she shook him awake with the news that Roddy's plane had gone missing.

'You'll go back to the island, I suppose.'

'I suppose I will.'

She held his arm as she leaned in to kiss him one last time. 'Goodbye, Fin.'

He watched as she got into the cab, and it accelerated away towards the city. Just one more part of his life consigned to memory. And he wondered if he and Marsaili really had a future. If it would ever be possible to rediscover the love they had felt that teenage summer before leaving for university.

And he wondered, too, about the life that awaited him on the island of his birth, the place from which he had tried so hard to escape but which had, in the end, drawn him back. He thought about everything that had been, and everything that lay ahead. The big, blank, unwritten chapter that was the rest of his life. And only two things were certain. He had a son who would require his guidance. And there was a fifteen-year-old girl who needed an advocate. The last living trace on this earth of the man who had been his friend and saviour. A tortured, orphaned little girl who had need of someone to stand up and speak for her and steer her towards some kind of hope for the future.

And he knew that it could only be him.

# PRONUNCIATION

The following is a rough guide to the pronunciation of Gaelic place and character names as well as the sprinkling of Gaelic words that appear in the book.

## PLACES

Abhainn Bhreanais (AVEEN VRAY-NEESH)
Abhainn Dearg (AVEEN JARG)
An Caolas (UN KUHLAS)
An Lanntair (UN LOUNTAR)
Baile na Cille (BALA NA KEE-LUH)
Barabhas (BARRA-VAS)
Bearnaraigh (BEEYAR-NARAY)
Bhàcasaigh (VACK-A-SIGH)
Brinneabhal (BREE-NA-VAL)
Cabarfeidh (hotel) (KABAR-FAY)
Calanais (KAL-A-NEESH)
Carnaichean Tealasdale (KEYAR-KNEECHUN TCHALLAS-DAL)
Cracabhal (CRACK-AVAL)
Crobost (CRAW-BOST)
Cros (CROSS)
Dail (DAHL)
Glen Bhaltos (GLEN VALTOS)
Loch Langabhat (LOCH LANG-GAVAT)
Loch nan Learga (LOCH NAN LYARGA)
Loch Rangabhat (LOCH RANG-GAVAT)
Loch Raonasgail (LOCH RUN-ASKIL)
Loch Ròg Beag (LOCH RAWG BUCK)
Loch Sanndabhan (LOCH SOUND-AVAN)
Mangurstadh (MANGUR-SHTAH)
Mealaisbhal (MAYAL-ASVAL)
Miabhaig (MEE-A-VIG)
Morsgail (MAWRSHCAL)
Pabaigh Mòr (PAH-BYE MORE)
Sanndabhaig (SOUND-AVIG)
Sgiogarstaigh (SKEE-GUR-STY)
Siadar (SHEE-A-DAR)
Siaram Beag (SHE-ARUM BUCK)
Siaram Mòr (SHE-ARUM MORE)
Solas (beach) (SAW-LAS)
Suaineabhal (SWAIN-AVAL)
Tamnabhaigh (TOWM-NA-VAY)
Tarain (TA-REEN)
Tathabhal (TAH-HA-VAL)
Tolastadh (TOLLOS-TAGH)
Tràigh Mhòr (TRY-VORE)
Tràigh Uige (TRY OO-EEG)

# CHARACTERS

Anna Bheag (ANNA VUCK)

Anndra (AOUN-DRA)

Artair (ARSH-TAR)

Cairistiona (CAH-RIH-SHTEONA)

Ceit (KATE)

Coinneach (KO-NEE-OCH)

Donald Ruadh (DONALD ROO-AAGH)

Eachan (YAH-CHUN)

Eilidh (AY-LEE)

Fionnlagh (FYOON-LAGH)

Kenny Dubh (KENNY DOO)

Kenny Mòr (KENNY MORE)

Mac an t-Stronaich (MACK AN TRO-NEECH)

Mairead (M'AYE'-RID)

Marsaili (MAHR-SHALL-EE)

Padraig (PAH-DREEG)

Ruairidh (ROO-AH-REE)

Seonag (SHAWNAG)

Uilleam (OO-LYAM)

# GENERAL

cailleach (KAH-LEOCH)

cùram (KOO-RUM)

geodha (GEE-YAW)

*Iolaire* (YEE-OH-LA-THE)

machair (MAH-CHUR)

Niseach (NEE-SHAWCH)

Sòlas (SAW-LAS)

# ACKNOWLEDGEMENTS

I would like to offer my grateful thanks to those who gave so generously of their time and expertise during my researches for *The Chessmen*. In particular, I'd like to express my gratitude to pathologist **Steven C. Campman, MD**, Medical Examiner, San Diego, California; the **US Army Central Identification Laboratory** for their detailed information on rates of body decomposition; **Stewart Angus**, Lewisman, writer and specialist adviser on coastal ecology for Scottish Natural Heritage; **Ronald Turnbull**, walker, writer and photographer, for his crucial advice on mountain walking; **Sarah Egan**, expert on all things Uig, researcher extraordinaire and my sherpa on a trek through the mountains of south-west Lewis in the worst weather imaginable; **Keith Patrick Stringer**, Lewis film-maker, for his short film *Hunter*, which inspired the character of Whistler; **Lewis Crombie** of Highland Aviation, Inverness, for his advice on small aircraft, flying to and landing at Solas Beach, as well as his aerial photographs of the location; **George Murray** of Stornoway Police, Isle of Lewis; **Robin Reid**, Ranger, North Harris Estate; **Revd. Nigel Anderson**, Free Church of Scotland; **Innes Morrison**, Estate Manager, Amhuinnsuidhe Castle Estate, Isle of Harris; and **Margaret Martin** of Stornoway Library.

Peter May's CHINA thrillers
are now available in ebook


Visit petermay.co.uk for more about the

China thrillers and to join Peter May's newsletter

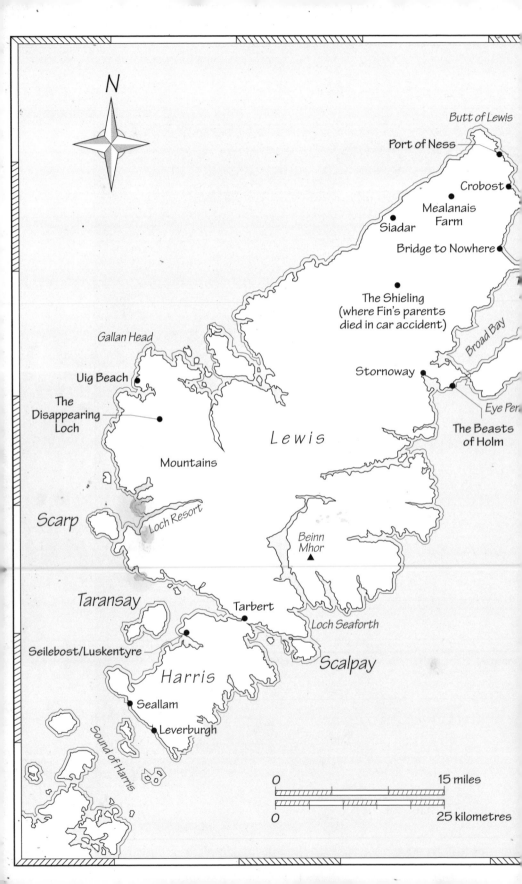